I0638746

Jude Chapman is an organisational psychologist
who has written extensively about people and their workplaces.
Recently, she has taken up the crime fiction genre and enjoys
writing short stories ending with a twist.

The Body at Bones is her first novel.

Her other passion is playing piano and telling stories
through music. Jude lives in the Southern Highlands of NSW
with her partner and two loved miniature schnauzers.

Author website
https://www.judechapmanauthor.com/

THE BODY AT BONES

ᴛʜᴇ BODY ᴀᴛ
BONES

JUDE CHAPMAN

Greyleaf
Press

This book is a work of fiction. The main action is set in the Inner West of Sydney, Australia, and the various locations may be recognised by readers. Hawthorne Park, Café Bones and Jubilee Park are, of course, actual places and are named as such. However, likenesses to real people and any resemblances to actual events are entirely coincidental. It is a different matter with the dogs that appear in this book – some are given their actual names while others are akin to dogs known to the author.
Ruff Sleepers is a charity providing services similar to those described in this book.

THE BODY AT BONES

First edition 2024
Copyright © 2024 Jude Chapman

Published by Greyleaf Press

ISBN 978-1-7636149-0-1

All rights reserved by the author and publisher.
No portion of this book may be reproduced or transmitted in any form
without prior permission in writing.

Copy editing: Susan McCreery
Layout and design: Maggie Cooper
Cover design: GetCovers.com
Typeset by Cooper Graphics

For Charlie, Jess, Hugo and all their canine friends.

PROLOGUE

BOTH DOGS INCHED towards the stillness. Crouching low, Charlie sniffed the breeze. Yes, there it was again, almost certainly from a patch by the fence that framed the park. The touch of a muzzle behind her eye and she knew that Jess had sensed it too. Odours that did not belong here.

Last time, that place by the fence had been a treasure trove of sugary syrups, buttery rolls and food wrappers, half-eaten and discarded among the bushes. Now a low platform, dull and metallic, covered the earth.

Closer, and their nostrils were flooded with the smell of out-of-place oils, chemicals and tools. And near its centre was a misshapen thing.

'Charlie! Jess!'

For a long moment after Alison had caught up, she stood silent with the dogs, their eyes drawn to the platform. Alison peered into the gloom, trying to make sense of it. Light pierced the clouds. Outlines and details emerged. She remained motionless, transfixed, a stand of casuarinas forming a whispery chorus to what she was witnessing. Alison wanted to get away, to cry out, but couldn't. A human arm rose, its fingers outstretched, the muddy shape of a shoulder, a head covered in matted hair poking out of grey slop. And a lifeless, glassy eye like a groper's.

CHAPTER 1

PACER FLICKED ON the light as he stumbled into the kitchen. Early for him to be up and about. He reached for the kettle and filled it with water. At one time he would have dashed straight out after taking the call, but not now. A cup of tea, that's what he needed. The body they had found in the park wasn't going anywhere. His shoulders lifted in the merest shrug.

Autumn was a few days old and already the days were shortening. Beyond his back porch the tips of the frangipani leaves were yellowing on the mulch. In the vegie patch the last of the tomatoes stood out against the veins of the bedraggled vines. Pacer unwrapped the newspaper, scanned the headlines and turned to the sports pages. Unlike most of his neighbours, he still had his paper delivered. Scrolling through an electronic device didn't appeal.

Sipping his tea, Pacer's mind slipped back to Janet. He remembered her final months with a deep sense of loss that struck him when he least expected it. She'd been ready to go, but he would never get used to not having her here, in this house they had restored together, gardened and shared. He treasured the little things that mattered to her, a crystal rose bowl, the tea set with its pattern of roses. Pacer cradled the teacup in his hands.

Janet had never adjusted to the irregular hours of police work but understood that it was all he had ever wanted to do. Nothing had changed, not really. He did have a rethink after being demoted on the cusp of making it to Inspector. But in the end, what other job could engage his mind like this? Where in the corporate world would his patience and bloody-minded determination be rewarded, or even tolerated?

'Just take your medicine and stick with it,' Janet had advised in her gentle but firm way. 'Don't be so hard on yourself. You made one mistake, that's all. You trusted people you shouldn't have. There are worse faults.'

'I let myself down, and the force. I saw and believed what I wanted.'

'You're wiser now. You've done so much for the community. For all those families. You'll never stop caring about them.'

Janet was right. He believed in what he did. He could recover from the stupidity that got him demoted. It was one of those tumbles you took. After that, he got into the field at every opportunity, ignored the jibes and gravitated towards officers who shared his outlook. Getting through it made him stronger. Or maybe just more stubborn.

Now that he was back as Detective Sergeant, Pacer's workload was heavy with homicide cases. The cold ones troubled him the most. The victims' loved ones never gave up hope of looking the perpetrator in the eye. It was for Pacer to provide support but not false hope. How could he tell a parent, child or partner that the criminal was unlikely ever to be brought to justice?

What had Janet said? He did care. Yes, she was right. Maybe too much for his own good. And what else? There are worse faults than trusting people you shouldn't. She must have been talking about other people. He knew better now. More than one way to stuff up on the job.

He thought of Maxine Poulos, whose daughter was taken from her.

'But, Sergeant,' she'd said during his last visit to her Federation terrace, 'I know who did this; we all do.' Her husband stood by her side, too grief-stricken to utter a word. 'People noticed him hanging around that playground. There was something not quite right about him.'

Yes, they'd noticed him all right, a man too close with no kids of his own. His presence not registering or just shrugged off? Reluctance to speak up? Or something beyond imagining. But the worst had happened. It had fallen to Pacer to bring the perpetrator to justice but he'd failed. The man was still out there, in Queensland now, leading what, for him, was a normal life – social security payments, rooms in boarding houses, an existence.

'For all I know, the mongrel has forgotten all about it.'

His voice startled him. When had he started talking to himself? Not when Janet was alive, he was sure. What would she have said about the Poulos case? Disappointed in him, probably. But not saying so.

Pacer forced his mind back to the present. The call had woken him. The details were sketchy. A body had been found at a building site in a public park. Found by a woman taking her dogs for an early morning stroll.

'Doesn't look like an industrial accident,' the police despatcher had said. A team of officers was already in attendance and the forensic crime scene people were on their way.

As he returned to the kitchen, Pacer wondered whose lives would be ruined by this crime. There would be someone close, children perhaps, a parent. What kind of person ended up dumped on a building site, discovered by dogs? Most homicides outside the home were flare-ups between friends, present or past. Had there been an argument to settle, a momentary loss of control? Or was it a planned and deliberate act?

Pacer rinsed his cup and placed it on a cloth to dry. 'Here we go again,' he said, reaching for his keys. He shut the door, his voice still echoing in the house behind him.

CHAPTER 2

IT WAS A quick drive at that time of morning. Pulling into Canal Road, Pacer felt the crunch of stones under his tyres. He left his car with police vehicles parked every which way where posts blocked further access. Dew sprinkled the windscreen of the van up front. Someone was an early bird. Might have been him, once. Pacer lifted the collar of his jacket against the chill, squared his shoulders and entered a world both familiar and unique.

Detective Constable Stuart Picone approached at a trot, eager to run through the morning's events. The officer in charge had arrived and was to be spared no detail.

'Got here an hour ago, just after the crime scene guys. They reckon it's a murder for sure, no accident. I've had a look around but they wouldn't let me into the tent. Said to wait for you.' Picone was young, a deep pink colouring his cheeks. Pacer knew the signs. He was shocked at the thought of a murder, but excited too.

With a sweep of his arm, Picone pointed out the park's features. On the right, a canal with rough banks of stone and concrete ran the length of the park. You could see the water was tidal. Small branches and plastic bottles bobbed in the flow towards the bay. A seagull swept out of the sky and into the murky water. Emerging moments later with a shrill cry, it flew south past the tennis courts and landed in trees near a pedestrian bridge.

The park was much longer than it was wide. A chain-link fence marked the perimeter along the left. The fence was serviceable but unsightly with weeds and shrubs pushing through. Inside the perimeter, Port Jackson figs hung over the footpath and slatted bench seats. The tracks of the light rail lay just beyond, the glint of metal, the hiss of a tram passing by.

Pacer shifted his gaze to an outdoor cafe that backed onto the fence. The shutter was closed but the painted brick wall announced the menu. The usual fare of pies, hamburgers, bacon and egg rolls, the coffees, teas and frappés. And some that were different – muffins for dogs, canine cookies and doggychinos. What the hell were they? Pacer took a step closer.

'That's Café Bones,' announced Picone. 'The whole place is an off-leash area. Dog-friendly. All the way to the fence at the end. You can just make it out. Runs from the bridge over the canal to the light rail entrance.'

Pacer had never been to this park, despite living quite close. Was barely aware of it. Hadn't been on the light rail, either. He liked the privacy and order of a car, his own or one from the pool, if he could get it. A big if.

The cafe stood where the park was at its narrowest. Plastic chairs and tables were dotted under casuarinas next to the canal. Others were closer to the figs on the light rail side. Next to the serving area of the cafe, a puddle had formed under a tap. Plastic water troughs for dogs lay around, one overturned and muddy, another upright. Not the most inviting cafe Pacer had come across. Grungy, unkempt.

Crime scene officers examined patches of brown earth on the north side and the pebbled areas closer to the cafe. They dropped markers, photographed and tweezered up exhibits. Picone indicated an area where a stark white tent had been erected. For the first time that morning, Pacer faced it square on. Picone had said what was inside, but it never prepared you. Pacer's pulse quickened. Another beginning. Where would this one lead?

'You'll want to have a look inside. If you'll just step over to the van, sir, I'll get you kitted out,' Picone said.

Pacer's stomach churned. It was always like this. Every new scene, the smells, the wounds, the look on the victim's face. Later, you pushed the memories away or tried to. Harder each time but it's what you had to do to stay focused on the killer. Your quarry.

An outer barrier of temporary fencing and opaque mesh shielded a white tent, partially open to the sky with an entrance of overlapping plastic flaps. Pacer pushed past and stood in front of a platform where lights on tall pedestals beamed onto the victim. The head with its cowl of grey sludge. The shoulder dipping forward. The torso and hip twisting out of the mess. And an arm raised in a salute with narrow shards of doughy cement forming stalactites.

'Nasty business.' Pacer turned as Miranda De Veen, the crime scene manager, stepped over. Her white overalls hung loosely around her small frame, blond hair tucked into a hairnet. The fabric rustled as she leaned towards him.

'The medical examiner's been?' Pacer asked.

'Left ten minutes ago,' she replied. 'Pronounced him dead. Didn't stay long, no point. Not much to see until they get him into the lab. It is a "he" though, and a big bloke from the shape of the torso and shoulder. Not young, not old. You can tell from the texture of the nose and lips.'

Pacer stepped forward for a closer look. A dead eye stared back. He pulled away.

De Veen continued, 'This appears to be the foundations for a small building, an amenities block. Over there, see, fittings for the plumbing. Four stalls, two each side with a central entry point and some basins to go in over there. They've placed the victim about a metre in and poured concrete over him.'

'They stuffed up, well and truly. Maybe the hole wasn't deep enough or something spooked them.' Pacer hesitated. 'That concrete doesn't look right. A bit sloppy? What do you think?'

De Veen reached down and rubbed some between her thumb and fore-finger. 'Yeah, a bit sloppy.'

'Do we know what happened to him? Put up a struggle, do you think?'

'No way of telling how he was killed just yet. Nothing obvious. Must have happened shortly before he was placed here. He'd have been nice and floppy when they dropped him in. With rigor setting in, the body has turned and the arm has risen. He's taken some of that concrete with him. Now he's as stiff as a board.'

Pacer had watched a program on Pompeii. This victim looked like those people caught suddenly when the lava and ash hit, their bodies moving and buckling as the soft earth cooled and set around them.

CHAPTER 3

OUTSIDE, THE SUN had risen higher. Pacer and De Veen flicked off their gloves and threw them into a waste bin. Pacer pulled at the velcro on his overalls and stepped out. The cool air was a relief after the closeness of the tent and the heat of the lights.

Stuart Picone was back by the barriers, keeping the curious at bay. A tabloid journalist Pacer recognised peered in his direction. Pacer looked away, not yet ready. Yellow police tape fluttered along the length of the canal, giving pedestrians a corridor to walk through. No point barring access. It riled people when they were stopped from doing their usual thing. Dog people most of all. In a flash they'd be on their phones to complain. There they were, sauntering along, necks craning to get an eyeful. Dogs everywhere, black, brown, brindle, white. Short, tall, fluffy, short-haired. Most off their leads, ducking under the tape then scampering back to their owners.

'Can't someone stop them getting in the way?' he snapped. Speaking aloud again: he had to get a grip on this.

But what a chaotic crime scene. Pacer had seen nothing like it. So much open space, a canal, the light rail, a cafe, and in the middle this grey slab. Most crime scenes were small spaces like a pub or domestic kitchen. Once the victim was tagged and removed, it was a simple matter of bagging the weapon, taking the photos and letting the blood-spatter guys get on with their work. Bush murder scenes were straightforward too. The lines of bored officers tramping through the scrub rarely turned up anything, but that's what the public wanted on their six o'clock news.

Pacer watched as two women, dogs milling around their feet, walked inside the taped area. What did they think they were doing? He glared, shoulders tensing. The women stopped and separated. One crossed to a bench under the trees while the taller one, with a small dog trotting beside her, headed towards them.

She drew level and addressed De Veen. 'I'm Anna Overton, Alison's friend. She's waiting over there with her schnauzers. Pretty upset.'

Pacer followed De Veen's gaze as she gave him the information. 'Alison Cassidy, sitting on the bench. She discovered the body.'

Pacer scowled at the dog by Anna Overton's side, a curious little creature, camel-coloured with a cheeky face. It sniffed around Pacer's knees then dashed across to a pile of masonry and urinated. He'd had enough. 'Get that bloody dog off my crime scene.'

'Don't yell at my dog.' Anna leaned forward, poised for a scrap. More like an attack dog than her pet itself, Pacer thought. 'You've stuck coloured tape up. So what? This is Hugo's park.' She motioned to the dog, who trotted back. Was it grinning? Pacer's jaw tightened.

'This area needs to be clear of contamination.' He stared at Anna, unblinking.

'Take it easy, Pacer,' De Veen, at his ear, murmured. 'We'll catch up later, okay?'

The woman on the bench stared straight ahead as Pacer approached. Her two dogs leaped forward, straining at their leads, barking in rapid bursts. They were an odd colour, shades of grey with thick tufts of hair around their muzzles, fluffy white eyebrows and ears that folded halfway. They didn't look dangerous, but you had to be careful. In Pacer's book, size was no indicator of what a creature was capable of, human or animal.

'Charlie, Jess, settle down!' the woman commanded. 'Sorry. They're friendly. They don't bite.' She smiled at the little dogs, ruffling their ears and reaching into a bag for treats. The dogs snapped them up, munching loudly.

Pacer introduced himself and joined Alison Cassidy on the bench. What did they say about people resembling their dogs? Alison's hair was the same salt-and-pepper shade. He tried to ignore the dogs, but the smaller one, Jess, was teasing at his pants pocket. Pacer pushed her away, firmly, but careful not to offend the owner.

'I appreciate your time,' he said. 'I understand you were the first to come upon the scene this morning. Quite a shock.' You bet. Bad enough for him, seasoned to it.

Alison adjusted her position, the memory clearly fresh and disturbing. 'I hadn't been here for a while, not since they started that building. I was walking along and there it was, right in front of me. Charlie and Jess saw it first. They knew something was wrong.' She reached into her bag for another treat, the dogs intensely focused.

Alison said she hadn't touched anything. The time? A little after six. The dogs? They'd skirted around the platform, picked up a scent and followed it to the fence. While Alison was calling triple zero they ran back and forth, highly agitated.

'There was something or someone there or had been recently,' she said. 'Next to the fence or on the other side. I'm sure of it. The killer, it might have been him, hiding. What if …?'

Pacer looked at her steadily, hoping to reassure. 'I doubt that. He'd be well away. Now, this fence – near the light rail tracks is it?'

'The light rail is on the other side, but it's not close. The track curves away. There's an industrial area in there, used for filmmaking, I think. I've never taken much notice. You should take a look. Dogs can sense things that we can't.'

Pacer snapped his notebook shut. 'This is very helpful.' He doubted it. The mutts were probably looking for a spot to do the unspeakable.

He got up to leave. The smaller dog, Jess, danced away with something in her mouth, tail wagging furiously. He felt his pocket. No handkerchief. 'Little devil!' he cried out. 'Come back here!'

At least he'd brought a smile to Alison's face. She was laughing at him. She and her irritating little dogs.

CHAPTER 4

'NOT MUCH CHANCE of getting your hankie back,' De Veen called out from the tent, wearing a grin as wide as a saucer. 'Come on over. Get back into whites and finish the job.'

An hour earlier, the cement had been the consistency of Pacer's morning porridge. Now it was firmer. He wanted the victim out before it hardened.

De Veen was thinking along the same lines. 'Just as well the public doesn't see this part.'

Two young officers stood by, tearing at plastic wrap on shovels glinting in the sunlight. With a nod from De Veen, they stepped forward. Beginning with the torso, they drove the blades deep underneath, working along to where the lower body and legs were still buried. Grunting with the effort, they pushed the blades in, levering the handles up and down to cradle and steady the body. Finally, with a sucking sound, the body lurched free from the muck. Trailing gobs of concrete, it dropped heavily onto a steel gurney.

Pacer and De Veen watched as the ambulance pulled away. They returned to the spot where the body had lain. A deep depression was visible. Concrete, like cooling lava, flowed into the gap.

'There should be steel mesh in there, not a body,' Pacer said.

'Our officers found some mesh, a couple of square metres. It's over by the fence. There was a wheelbarrow too, and a shovel. They're already in the van. The perps should have made a deeper hole before they popped him in. And done a better job with the concrete. Careless.'

Pacer had other ideas. Not careless, just plain stupid, like most killers. Concrete doesn't dry quickly, and it won't harden unless you mix it right.

Twisting about like those poor sods in Pompeii, old mate had risen to the surface. And they'd left their tools lying around. Didn't expect the body to be found, obviously.

'My guys found some vehicle tracks, two sets,' said De Veen. 'They've finished processing them. Want to take a look?'

A photographer left off packing his gear and showed Pacer the partial imprints. 'These could belong to a small cement mixer,' De Veen said. 'Some of them were smudged when they put the tent up but there's enough for us. Check out this other set. Probably from a car or small van.' She indicated an area of sandy soil. The imprints, around the edges of a puddle, were barely visible. 'It rained over the weekend, that's how we can tell these tracks are fresh. They could drive only so close. Too much metal and rubbish from the build to come right in. Someone was an untidy builder, left stuff everywhere.'

Pacer looked down at the trampled earth. They were lucky to find this much. 'You reckon they used that wheelbarrow to bring the body around?'

'Yep, could be. It's well used, rough on the bottom and sides. There's some dark stuff in there too. Looks like blood.' De Veen pulled out her phone and scrolled through photos. 'Took a few pics. See here?'

At the crime scene van they poured mugs of tea. Pacer signalled Stuart Picone to come over when the bright face turned his way. Picone was in plain clothes, the police ID on a lanyard against his chest, the suit new and fashionably grey. Despite his rush to get here, he'd managed to neatly knot his tie. Pacer was suddenly conscious of his own appearance, as tired as he himself felt. Maybe you were supposed to feel like this when you reached middle age. What was he? Forty-five last birthday. Not old, but the contrast between himself and Picone was impossible to miss. Picone had been assigned to him just weeks earlier. He was new to homicide, recently out of uniform. Open fellow, not the type to hold back, he'd spilled his life story.

Picone had never planned to join the force; it was just how it turned out. His parents had urged him to go to university and get a profession, but Picone was tired of studying and nothing on offer grabbed his interest. His contemporaries took a gap year, backpacking through Asia and Europe. That didn't interest him either. He went bushwalking, first through the Budawangs and then on to the Snowies. He met a contractor who assembled feedlots and produce storage units. The outdoor work suited him and he liked seeing the results of his labour. Then the drought hit and the contractor let him go.

Next was a job with a stock and station agent near Goulburn. Picone had planned to stay on, but a chance meeting with a police cadet got him interested in applying at the nearby police academy. The rest was history, except that Picone's history had hardly started yet. Pacer didn't want to babysit a probationary detective. Too much responsibility. He'd escaped that chore more than once, but this time the boss was adamant. Now he was stuck with him. Maybe it wasn't so bad. Picone was a likable young bloke, showing promise as a detective. Not everyone ended up washed out. You could only hope.

Picone was tall, rangy and very fit. Pacer remembered being that age. He wasn't a lot different. Built more like an outside back than a forward, maybe, but an accomplished rugby league player and keen to make his way in the force. As the years passed, the job, with its demands and irregular hours, had taken up more of his life. League was the first to go, then the mates from uni. Pacer regretted losing the friends more than the football. They anchored him to something other than the job. He could tell himself 'if only', but what was the point?

Picone was itching to get stuck in. He jiggled from one foot to the other, like a sprinter on the starting blocks. Pacer had something for him. 'I want you to do a sweep of the park, full length. Pick up anything that could be evidence. Take a uniformed officer and a photographer. Get lots of photos.' Pacer nodded to a stocky young man in a uniform a size too small. Pacer had seen him around, tried to remember his name. Tony? Yeah, that was it.

Picone hesitated. 'A lot of people walked through before we could close off access. So many people bring dogs here – how can we distinguish the evidence from the dross?'

'Don't set yourself up to miss something. Stay sharp.' Pacer growled his words and matched them with a direct stare. You had to be thorough. Useful evidence was rare, much rarer than most people imagined, but that was no excuse.

Picone nodded sheepishly. Pacer briefed him on Alison Cassidy's dogs. 'Take a look at that fence. See if there's a way in.'

As Picone went off, De Veen angled her head towards Pacer, eyebrow raised. 'Think you're a bit hard on him?'

'He drew the short straw when he got me as his boss. Can't imagine what the brass was thinking.'

'You're one of the best. He'll learn from you.'

Pacer shook his head and looked away. No words for the hollowness he felt.

An officer approached and spoke quietly to De Veen. She nodded and said to Pacer, 'A manager from the local council is coming soon. That amenities block – it's his build.'

Pacer squared his shoulders towards the white tent. 'My turn to play tour guide.'

CHAPTER 5

PACER SIZED UP the man approaching from the direction of the bay. Sharp suit, natty tie, polished shoes. Mark Baker, a director at the local council, responsible for urban planning and development. He looked irritated. A busy man, his morning interrupted.

Pacer showed Baker through the flaps of the tent.

'Whoa, so this is where it happened?' Baker asked.

'We believe they brought the victim in late last night and placed him inside the formwork.'

They looked down at the space where the body had lain.

'Mind if I take a closer look?' Baker's brow creased.

'Sure, the crime scene people have finished.'

Baker crouched and ran his fingers over the slab. He worked some material free, kneaded it with his fingers, then tossed it back with a grunt of disgust.

'This is rubbish! It's slop, not concrete. They've got the mixture wrong. Too much sand or water. Maybe both.'

'The steel mesh was tampered with. We found a section of it nearby.'

Baker walked around to where some mesh was just visible on the other side. He poked at the metal. 'None of this is pinned down. What idiot is responsible for this?'

'Hoping you can tell me, sir. The foundations for a small amenities block? Is that what this is?'

'It's been on our works schedule for some time,' Baker said. 'There are public toilets attached to Café Bones. You've seen the cafe and the dog clubroom on the end of the same building. Not hygienic. Not to council's specifications. Might have been okay thirty years ago, but not now.'

'I need everything you have on this building and the contractors,' Pacer said. 'I assume you are using contractors?'

'Of course. Farm most things out these days. We draw up a project-management plan and call for tenders.'

'And the contractor for this job?'

'I don't get involved in the details. You can talk to my people. I'm rather busy with major projects, as you might imagine.'

'I'd prefer to talk to you, sir. It will cut red tape and reduce delay if you give me the information yourself.' Pacer knew high-handed people. Too important for ordinary concerns, or ordinary people. He spoke slowly, eyes fixed on Baker. 'I want to speak to the contractor as soon as possible. I'll need his details and a full set of project plans.'

'If you insist, Sergeant. I'll put a package together as soon as I can.' Baker had backed down, but his voice was edged with annoyance.

'Thank you, sir. I'll be around later this morning, but I'm sure you can give me the name of the contractor now.'

Baker glared back, then pulled out his phone. His PA was his polar opposite, helpful and fully across the works program. The contractor's name was Arko. He was also contracted to erect picnic tables in a neighbouring suburb. Perhaps they would find him there?

Pacer signalled to the officer who'd escorted Baker in. Moments later he was in a squad car, being driven to Nield Park.

CHAPTER 6

FLYNN FINISHED HIS coffee, pushed the half-eaten breakfast aside, stretched his legs under the table and leaned back. Sandra had made one of his favourites, scrambled eggs. But he wasn't hungry after last night. Couldn't relax. He ran a hand over his hair, cut short to his liking, and reached for his joggers. A good run around the Bay, that's what he needed. The buzz of his phone startled him. Early for a call. He considered not answering.

The caller was an acquaintance who owed Flynn a favour. 'The cops have converged on the public park by the Hawthorne Canal, close to Café Bones. Word is they have discovered a body. A fresh one. Just letting you know in case you're interested.'

Interested? That didn't begin to describe it. Flynn froze, his mind spinning. Sandra came from the kitchen, saying something that didn't register. He managed to stand, waving her away, assuring her this wasn't a heart attack or stroke. In a daze, he made his way to his office, his private den. This couldn't be happening.

He had to see for himself, assess the damage. Grabbing his keys and without a word to Sandra, he drove his Lexus towards Iron Cove, left it in a layby off Canal Road and continued on foot. Police tape was visible through a small crowd. Flynn stopped. The line was too far out to allow a good look.

He could come in from the other side. Yes, much better. He went back, passed the Lexus, turned right and entered a small dead-end street of shabby workers' cottages, their backyards abutting an industrial site. The street and the people in it were right out of the 1960s: tough, watchful types who had lived there forever. There was nothing on the other side. Just an odd-shaped, weed- and rubbish-filled vacant lot that belonged to the railways.

Flynn pushed the half-open gate at the end of the street and slipped through into a weird world of rusty containers, wooden pallets, metal statues of creatures both animal and mythical, and bits of machinery with no obvious purpose. Scattered around were timber-framed sheds with corrugated sides and roofs. Through the dusty windows he could see what remained of office furniture, drafting materials and things that looked like costumes or masks. The first time he'd come here the hairs had risen on the back of his neck. He half-expected to encounter squatters or hostile gangs, but the silence told him he was alone.

Flynn made his way to the fence, constructed with corrugated iron, marking this part of the boundary with Hawthorne Park. There was a way through. You just had to push the tin sheet aside and squeeze through the weeds. There were less of those since the bulldozer had cleared land for that new amenities block, but the break was still hard to spot. He listened. People were talking, but not close. Nearby were two half-sized shipping containers, one on top of the other, tipped at a slight angle. A pile of sandbags protruded over the higher container. A ladder leaned against the side. He'd been up there plenty of times. The containers gave the height he needed for a good look and the sandbags provided useful cover.

Flynn placed his foot on the bottom rung and was about to climb when loud noises startled him. Someone was walking along the fence, banging on the metal. Flynn waited, expecting them to move away.

'Hey, Stuart, there's a break in the fence, right here.' The voice resonated off the container. Flynn pressed himself against it.

'Okay, mate,' another man replied. 'See if you can get through.'

The adrenalin rushed to Flynn's hands and feet. He had to get away. Now.

The aperture widened. As Flynn turned, he glimpsed a blue uniform and the outline of a short, bulky police officer. Heart thumping, Flynn retreated to the half-closed gate. In his haste he collided with an overflowing bin, dislodging a pizza box and scattering the contents. He kicked a bottle aside. The clatter alerted a brown labrador in the yard of the nearest cottage. It limped into the street, barking deeply. Flynn swore and kicked at it viciously.

Back in the Lexus, his breathing slowed. That was a close shave. Flynn grabbed his phone, found the number and pressed. It rang seven times. He slapped his free hand against the steering wheel. 'C'mon, c'mon.'

'Arko.' A deep voice punctured the silence.

'It's Flynn. Where are you? What are you doing?'

'Waiting for a delivery.'

'At Hawthorne Park? Are you crazy?'

'No, I'm at my other job.'

Flynn swallowed hard with relief. 'You don't know anything then? You haven't been back there?'

'No, what's up?'

'Something's gone off the rails. Just get out of there.'

'What about this delivery? He's pulling in now.'

Flynn's voice hardened. 'Just get out of there. Stay out of sight. Don't talk to anyone. You got that?'

'S'pose so.'

'Just do what I say. Go home and lay low. I'll call you later, usual time. Switch your phone off until then.' Flynn slapped his phone down, gunned the engine and put as much road as he could between himself and the dog park.

CHAPTER 7

PACER PUNCHED THE location into the car's GPS and activated the siren. The driver headed up Canal Road, then turned west, other vehicles moving aside as they sped by. The route took them around the bay, past a rowing club on the right and well-established parks on the left. In Henley Marine Drive the wind was blowing spray onto the road. Pacer peered ahead as the wipers scraped briny water and clumps of foam from the glass.

Nield Park was a spread of grass and sparsely planted gums. Pacer lowered the side window. From what Baker's PA had said, the construction work was at the far end. Pacer pointed to the orange tape and a flatbed truck alongside an area of disturbed earth. The driver veered into a pedestrian walkway just wide enough. They left the path, rode over the kerb and bumped across the grass. A man in overalls appeared from behind the truck. He stopped in his tracks, taking in the two men converging on him.

'Police officers,' Pacer announced, holding out his identification. 'Your name?'

The man hesitated. 'Phil Jones.' Pacer looked at the truck. The name was written on the side with the trade. Steel fabrication. Jones pulled out his drivers licence and handed it over.

'We're looking for the site contractor. Arko.'

'You just missed him.'

Pacer felt a stab of irritation. 'How long ago?'

'Three, maybe four minutes. He took off in a hurry. Just shot through in his ute.'

'Did he say what was up?'

'Nope, he took a call and said he had to go. Seemed like some kind of emergency. I'd just arrived with this load. He was supposed to sign for it and help me.' Jones looked perplexed.

'Did you hear what it was about?'

Jones shook his head. 'I don't know what to do now. I can't leave these materials. He didn't sign.' He turned back to his vehicle, muttering.

Had someone warned Arko? It was circumstantial, but Pacer's gut churned. Arko was involved somehow. And whoever called him.

Back in the squad car, Pacer put out an alert through the traffic and public transport division. He added caveats at the highest level. Arko was potentially a person of interest in a murder investigation. Weapon unknown. How dangerous was he? You had to assume the worst.

'Drop me at the Cooks River Council building, will you?' Pacer said to his driver. 'Not far out of your way.'

CHAPTER 8

THE ENTRANCE TO the local government offices was through an open plaza flanked by garden beds and a barista stand. Inside, a cafe rippled with conversation and the sounds of food being prepared and delivered. Pacer eyed the pastries as he walked past. A set of stairs led to the public library. He found the lifts on the other side and rode to the planning department. At reception, he waited for the clerk to notice him. He was tempted to press the bell near her bowed head but was saved by a smiling woman appearing from behind a partition.

'How can I assist you?' she asked brightly.

'Mark Baker is expecting me.'

Baker's office was generously sized. The desk was large, its surface bare, apart from the usual array of stationery and a family portrait. The chair was high-backed, reflecting, no doubt, the director's assumed status. Folders filled the shelves against the back wall and a bookcase housed the hardcover volumes people collected during their tertiary studies. There were also paperbacks on project management, the habits of successful people and other topics popular with the rising executive. Pacer had seen the same titles in Inspector Connors's office. Connors, his boss. He'd have to brief him, tomorrow morning at the latest. Pacer sighed as he dropped into a chair at a round table opposite the desk. Connors didn't have one of these, just his regulation desk. He preferred his guests to stand, or if in the right mood, invite them to occupy his sole visitor chair.

Baker swept in with the flurry of a man pulled away from more weighty matters. He looked at Pacer expectantly, as if trying to remember who he was. Pacer wasn't buying it.

THE BODY AT BONES

'Good afternoon, Mr Baker. The new amenities block at Hawthorne Park, sir. I need to see the project plans and the contract.'

'You didn't find Arko at his other contract site?' Baker remembered him all right.

'Unfortunately not. Did you contact him, sir, after we spoke at Hawthorne Park?'

Baker looked indignant. 'Of course not.' He turned to a cabinet with broad, narrow drawers. 'These are the plans for the amenities block,' he said, laying a wide sheet of paper on the table. 'We keep hard copies of our current projects on hand. The detailed specifications are in our database. As for the contract, it's in a locked cabinet in the main office. I'll be back shortly.'

Pacer bent over the plans. He didn't need to be from the building trade to see the structure was simple and spare. The fine penmanship, landscaped surrounds and drawings from three angles made it appear more impressive than it could ever be. Two toilet stalls each for male and female and a shared wash area. There was a cement floor, plumbing and fixtures, and a prefabricated metal shell bolted into the floor. Not your solid brick structure from times past.

Baker returned with the contract. 'Just four standard pages. And here are copies of the drawings and specifications.'

'Thank you, sir.' Pacer handed back the originals. 'The name is unusual. Just Arko? No other name? And the address – do you know if it's current? Have you checked it or been there yourself?'

'Why would I? If he wants to be called Arko, then Arko it is. Blokes who erect amenities blocks are not the brains trust of the building industry.'

Why the defensiveness? Pacer had met many like Baker, hiding something that might or might not have a bearing on the case. Usually some indiscretion, like undeclared income or the mistress tucked away in a harbourside unit. Nah, not that. Beyond Baker's pay grade.

'How well do you know this Arko? Is he a regular contractor?'

With a sigh, Baker sat. 'Arko works for several councils around the metropolitan area doing projects like this. Small stuff.' To someone passing his office, Baker called, 'Can you ask Craig to come in, please?'

A pale-faced younger man with a slight stoop entered. He edged towards the table and gave Pacer a weak smile. Baker introduced him as Craig Thomas. This project was in his portfolio.

'Arko started on the site ten weeks ago,' Thomas said. 'My people did the planning, laid out the site pegs and ordered the fittings and prefabricated wall and roof panels. Straightforward stuff. Good, flat site. Sewerage and water pipes already servicing the area. Just a matter of putting in the connections.' He pulled the plans closer and indicated where the connections were.

'So how do you decide which contractor gets the work?' Pacer asked.

'We publicise the job in the local paper and on our website. Interested parties are sent project specifications. We call them in for a chat and see what they have to offer. If that part goes well we start talking prices. They don't get much room to manoeuvre. Our budget is tight.' Thomas was into his spiel, looking a bit comfortable for Pacer's liking.

'And supervision? Do you keep an eye on progress?'

'We choose contractors with the right experience. They work to our specifications and deliver an outcome. We inspect when the foundations are going down and before they apply the finishing touches. We don't stand over people.'

Baker smiled at Thomas, nodding his approval.

'Is that all?' enquired Pacer. 'Nothing more … rigorous?' Modern management. Leave you to it and yank the chain hard when the boss is unhappy. An image of Connors's pinched face, eyes too close together, flashed past.

Baker leaned forward. 'I don't know what you're implying. We know these blokes, the trustworthy ones.'

Cosy. Pacer knew how it went. Another game where new players don't get a look in. You needed your contacts and insider knowledge. And trust mattered. Work done at a distance from council staff, willing to turn a blind eye to the occasional short cut, breach of safety or use of undocumented labour. In no one's interest to upset the apple cart.

Pacer gathered up the paperwork and thanked them. 'Please do not contact Arko,' he said. Baker looked at Pacer as if he had lost his mind. Pacer would have been disappointed had he done otherwise.

Pacer stopped at the cafe downstairs and chose a table out of the way. He asked for tea then added a chocolate éclair. A grating sound from the oversized coffee maker, like someone choking, caught his attention. The machine sizzled and steamed while customers fiddled with their devices. The line in front grew then shortened as the drinks were produced and carried away. When had this preoccupation with coffee in takeaway cups taken hold? Was he the only one left who found solace in a fragrant proper teacup of English Breakfast?

Pacer reflected as his drink cooled. He berated himself for missing Arko. Who made that call to him when he was in Nield Park? Was it

Baker? He called Picone. Picone had spoken to Baker for several minutes after Pacer had gone after Arko. Baker had made no calls.

Pacer lifted the pot and poured the last of the tea into his china cup. He phoned an old friend, Kurt Otway, from the surveillance and operations team. Kurt was tough and reliable. He'd stick to his target like a dog with a bone. A smart bloke, mostly two steps ahead. He and Pacer had worked plenty of cases together. The conversation got to the point. Could Otway's team cruise by Arko's depot? Nice and discreet? Unlikely Arko would be there, but you never knew. Best to check.

'And take precautions,' Pacer added. 'Assume he's dangerous.'

CHAPTER 9

PACER WAS JOSTLED by a couple of journalists and a small crowd of rubberneckers as he approached the line of police tape. They had gathered over several hours, observing the comings and goings of detectives and crime scene investigators, the arrival and departure of the ambulance, and the removal of evidence. The journalists looked towards him, impatient for news.

Pacer knew no senior officer would front up this morning to give a media statement. The brass couldn't be bothered. He'd have to do it. He hated these situations. From him, meagre facts and generalisations. From the journalists, expectant silence, cameras poised, then a torrent of questions, all absurd or impossible to answer. Who is the victim? Who do the police suspect? How was he murdered? Then frustration, derision and mutterings about police incompetence. Finally, away to their vehicles, to run stories about soaring crime rates and a state where no one is safe.

Pacer pushed past the journalists and turned around to face the mob. He cleared his throat. Get it over with. Keep it short and not so sweet. Better now than later.

Job done, he strode to the crime scene van. The proprietor of Café Bones, Joel Frazer, was waiting and clearly anxious. He had a business to run, customers to serve. When could he reopen? Pacer wanted this man onside: his observations would be more useful and his memory improved if the relationship got off to a good start.

'Well, sir,' Pacer said, 'you can open up first thing tomorrow, usual time.' Frazer looked relieved and grateful. 'I'll drop by tomorrow and take a statement. Sometime during the morning?'

Picone jogged over. Time to sign off the packages of evidence. The uniformed officer who had assisted in the sweep joined them. He was dusting off his jacket, streaked with dirt and the pocket torn.

'What happened to you, Tony?' asked Pacer. 'You got something?'

The uniformed officer looked puzzled. 'Tino,' he corrected. 'You asked us to check the fence. I found a way through.' He glanced down at the tear in his jacket. 'I glimpsed a man, but he took off. We went to where I last saw him and found a gate on the other side. An old lady, a Mrs Creed, said her dog was barking and yelping. She saw a man disappearing around the corner at the top of the road. Reckoned he was up to no good.'

'Description?'

'She didn't get much of a look. Anyway, it wasn't one of the neighbours. There are only eight houses in the row, and people have lived there a long time. The person she saw was younger. Wanted us to arrest him for kicking her dog.'

Picone chimed in. 'Mrs Creed said this wasn't the first time someone has poked around behind her place. Been there at odd times of the day and night.'

'Okay. Okay.' Pacer had heard enough. 'Stuart, get around to that street first thing tomorrow and take statements. Knock on every door. I want a list of the dates and times of any disturbances, or as close to as they can remember. And I mean first thing – old people are early risers.' Pacer chortled to himself. Picone would get used to his humour. 'Now, what about the evidence packages? You took photos and noted the location before picking each one up?'

'Yes, sir, everything by the book and properly tagged.' Picone talked him through the bits and pieces they had collected during the sweep, a potpourri of cigarette butts, sunglasses, plastic water bottles and empty food containers. There were also items from around the concrete slab, including the stub of a builder's pencil, a sock and some broken drill bits.

Looked like a load of junk to Pacer, but he didn't say so. 'Anything of particular interest?'

Picone pulled out an evidence bag and handed it to Pacer. It contained a crumpled blue and white rag. 'Found this over by the cafe. A handkerchief. Might belong to one of the perpetrators.'

Pacer recognised it as his own, prised from his pocket by the little grey schnauzer. He snatched it away, startling the young officer. 'Don't get carried away. I dropped it earlier.' Picone looked crestfallen.

'Anything else, Stuart?'

'Over there, behind the cafe. There're old boxes and other junk. Stuff from the cafe, but I think there's more to it. There were personal items, flattened cardboard and a makeshift tin roof. Could be someone using that area as a shelter. I had the guys put up temporary fencing to preserve the spot.'

'Might be the same person you saw on the other side of that fence. The light's not so good now so take a closer look tomorrow. You can ask the cafe proprietor if someone has been hanging around. But when you do, stick to this matter. I'm coming back tomorrow to interview him. I want his ideas fresh. You got that?'

Picone nodded, his shoulders sagging. Pacer, watching Picone and Tino stashing the evidence bags, felt uneasy. He could have said something, a word of encouragement maybe. Picone had done good work, Tino as well. Wouldn't hurt him to say so. Crusty old coot, that's what he was. Or had become.

Pacer's phone rang. It was Rhys Parkinson from the Coroner's Office. Pacer had encountered him many times before. Vehicle crashes, knifings, domestic homicides. You name it. Rhys did the dirty work, processing the bodies when they came in, cleaning them up and escorting relatives to the viewing, if they had any.

'Your victim is with me. I've started to syringe the muck from around the face. Your bloke said he was covered in concrete. It's a bit odd. If this is concrete, it's coming off too easily. Wanted to check with you.'

'Well, the concrete was meant to set but the perp got the mix wrong.'

'That adds up. Still, the stuff is quite sticky. It's pulling at the skin. There will be red patches from the grazing. I'll go as carefully as I can, but can't guarantee the pictures will be pretty.'

Pacer chuckled. He was used to morticians' brand of humour. 'Do what you can. Has the autopsy been scheduled?'

'I spoke to the coroner. She's interested in this case, wants to handle it herself. She does the occasional case at Glebe, not the new place in Lidcombe. It's down for two o'clock tomorrow. Prioritising it for you. Are you on for it or will someone else attend?'

'It'll be me, mate.' Pacer didn't like autopsies; no one in their right mind did. But you had to be there or risk missing something. 'Anything on the body to indicate its identity?'

'No, nothing. There was no wallet or phone. Something might show up in the external examination. They'd stripped him to his underwear. The labels weren't the usual department store brand. There were no shoes but we found one sock. He was mid-thirties, a bit on the heavy side, more

28

fat than muscle. By the look of him and the smooth hands, I'd say he worked behind a desk.'

'Could you let me know if something comes up when you take a closer look?'

'Guaranteed. Talk to you later.'

CHAPTER 10

FOR THE SECOND time that day, Flynn pushed through the gate at the end of the street. No brown dog this time: that was a relief. The light was different too. The metal statues cast long shadows across the ground and darkened the sides of the huts and containers. The air was chillier. Flynn picked his way around piles of decaying wood, empty pallets and other obstacles. He tripped over a tuft of weed sticking up from the cracks and cursed.

The double stack of containers was just ahead. Flynn grabbed the metal struts of the ladder and began to climb. His left ankle snagged against a hard metal object and a jagging pain shot up his leg. He stifled a cry. Stepping onto a wooden pallet, he assessed the damage. A raw gash was seeping blood. It looked nasty. He felt dizzy. Reaching into his pocket he located his sweatband. It tumbled out, stuck to a half-eaten protein bar. He pulled the bar free and threw it down in irritation, then tightened the sweatband around his ankle. That would do for now. The anxiety was making him careless. He got like that, didn't like it either. Worse if anyone else noticed.

Flynn grunted and edged to the fence where the cop had forced himself through. The metal sheets were back together but lower down was a gap, obscured on the other side by weeds.

With his face against the fence, Flynn had a partial view of the remaining police vehicles. Two officers in plain clothes stood by a van. They were speaking but he couldn't make out the words. A middle-aged man in a suit moved towards the bay and got into a Commodore. The other wore dark overalls and walked to the driver's side of the van. They'd finished for the day. He could get on uninterrupted.

Back at the ladder, Flynn adjusted his makeshift bandage and stepped up. From the cover of the sandbags he had a clear view of the cement slab with a white tent surrounding it, stopping passers-by from peering in.

The formwork of a few days back was covered in grey concrete. But it wasn't right. The surface was disturbed, a large depression exposing the brown earth. Two shovels stood upright, pressed into the slab. That was odd. The cement should have made that impossible. And that depression. Empty.

The anger rose in Flynn's chest. Arko, that stupid, incompetent idiot. He balled his fists and pressed them into the sandbags. A cold fear gripped him. The business did not tolerate mistakes. He had to fix it or he'd be next. Damage control, that's what was needed. Fast.

CHAPTER 11

PACER SANK INTO the driver's seat of the Commodore, feeling a mix of exhaustion, apprehension and excitement. A fresh crime scene took energy and concentration. This case was shaping up to be more than the usual: it would be a physical and mental challenge. That suited him fine. He liked a knotty puzzle, piecing together a disparate set of theories and clues before closing in on the perpetrator. Most left a wide, muddy trail. But there was the exception. You hoped it would end with the guilty party behind bars and the satisfaction that came with it. That took first-class police work and a watertight case with no loose ends for their lawyers to tamper with. But nothing came with a guarantee. He'd learned that lesson. Many times. Each one gnawed at him, none more so than the Poulos case. That little girl. Pacer bit at his lower lip, pushing the image away.

'Get back to business.' Talking aloud again.

On the surface, this was a typical gangland killing. Bump off the guy who was a thorn in the side and dump the body. Typical because the perpetrator had messed up, as they usually did. Like the getaway driver running out of petrol two streets past the jewellery store, or the would-be assassin mistaking blanks for live cartridges. The fact was, most criminals were pretty dim and got nervous on the big day. They stuffed up or left a trail as easy to follow as an Easter egg hunt.

Most gangland killings were brutal and bold. The job was done in the open, under CCTV cameras or in front of witnesses. It demonstrated power, reach and the capacity to inflict lethal force. This was different. It lacked finesse, but the victim was meant to disappear without a trace.

So no, this crime wasn't typical. Take the careful choice of the scene. Despite its proximity to the city, the place felt remote. It was bordered by a canal and a light rail line. At night it was quiet, apart from the occasional dog-owner out for a stroll. The foundations of a new building provided a perfect dumping ground. The perpetrators chose their moment. The whole thing smacked of careful planning and bad execution. Execution, he repeated to himself. Pacer enjoyed his puns.

That a well-planned crime was carried out so badly worried him. There were the brains behind it – or what passed for brains among the criminals of this world – and there were the doers. The brains walked the high street in expensive suits and kept their hands clean. The actual job was delegated to a trusted group of muscle men with few scruples and a liking for wads of untraceable dollars. In this case, the muscle men had stuffed up. The brains would not be happy, not at all. Pacer guessed there would be aftershocks.

Outdoor crime scenes were the hardest to investigate. Sifting through the evidence would take patience and persistence. There was no glamour in that. Typical of the brass to assign it to him. He had fouled up and it would never be forgotten. Rumour and hearsay, the force was full of it. He'd been demoted, but that wasn't enough for them. Pacer shrugged. He was used to the jobs other detectives wouldn't touch. He didn't mind. In fact, it gave him satisfaction. His record in clearing up difficult cases was better than most. That's how he'd regained his rank. Even better, it irked his boss. Inspector Connors wanted to bring Pacer down a peg or two, even further than he'd already been brought down, but Pacer hadn't given him the opportunity. Not yet, anyway. Connors didn't believe that people could change, that they deserved a second chance.

Right now, Arko was Pacer's only suspect. Maybe he'd settled a personal score and used the building site to hide the body. But Arko had been tipped off. There was someone else, a friend or accomplice. Most likely someone higher up the food chain. Arko was one of the muscle men. Had to be. Find Arko, and Pacer would get the brains who planned it.

Pacer needed more on this Arko. He opened his laptop and requested a comprehensive report. Criminal history, traffic infringements, photos, licences, the lot. Had he struck before? Pacer thought of this morning's victim. He desperately wanted to know the means of death and the murder weapon. Was it a gun? It would worry him until he knew. Dozens of police officers were looking for Arko and could be in danger if they got close.

Pacer's mind whirred. He'd be awake half the night, he knew that. There would be no rest until it was over. If it ever was. Images of that body, twisting and grotesque. And the families. Eyes staring at him, wondering and expectant. Searching his face for answers. Not just this crime, but others before. Not over. Not yet, if ever.

He needed to focus, keep things moving. He called Miranda De Veen. They had worked together many times, knew one another's ways. Slick and professional, she had his back every time. She knew his history, his demotion, his struggle to come back. It made a difference that she didn't hold any of it against him. One day he'd work out how to thank her.

De Veen went through the tests she'd set up with the soil samples and items logged by Picone. Nothing of interest as yet. Pacer updated her on his discussions with Mark Baker and the Coroner's Office.

'All on track then, Pacer,' she said. 'I'll send the photographs from the crime scene and the park surrounds. Be there first thing tomorrow. You know your Inspector Connors likes to see the pictures. Proves to him we're on the job.' With a laugh, she was gone.

CHAPTER 12

FLYNN CLOSED HIS living-room curtains against the stillness of the night and paced the room. It was large, comfortably furnished and spartan in its lack of paintings or ornaments. The walls were a shade of white and the carpet a blend of neutral colours, yielding a silvery effect. The room reflected Sandra's taste: elegant, like her. It suited Flynn that she was out with friends tonight. He needed space to think, sort things through before placing the call to Malcolm.

He checked that the front door and windows were locked then moved to his private den, where he poured a single malt, a nice drop from Western Australia, sank into a chair and retrieved his phone from an inside pocket.

Malcolm was very cool but didn't hide his fury at Arko's stuff-up. More to the point, Flynn's stuff-up. Malcolm made no distinction between the man who gave the instructions and the bloke who got it badly wrong.

'Cover your tracks. Don't give the cops anything else. I can trust you. We've been mates for a long while, but why did you bring that new bloke in? Bloody useless. Where is he?'

'I told him to lay low. He won't do anything until he hears from me.' Flynn tried to sound confident. Malcolm could sense weakness.

'We'll wait this out. See what the cops do over the next day or two. On a wild goose chase if their record is anything to go on.'

'By now they'll be after Arko. They'll be wondering if he acted alone.' It sounded lame, even to himself.

'The cops aren't complete fools. They'll get extra curious when they figure out who they dug out of there. But Arko is the only one who can lead them to us. Keep him under wraps until I decide. Call me tomorrow.' With that command, Malcolm ended the call.

Flynn checked the time. Arko would be waiting. Flynn had to keep it smooth, do nothing to spook him. Arko picked up quickly. He knew the worst. Flynn didn't ask how. Arko was hesitant, trying to gauge Flynn's mood, his voice betraying his fear.

'I stayed in today, real quiet. Thinking of goin' to me cousin's; he lives in Newcastle. I can stay at his place till this blows over. What do you reckon?'

Flynn forced himself to sound relaxed, even friendly.

'I'll figure something out, get you somewhere the cops won't look. Not your cousin's place, they'll be onto that.' Flynn could hear Arko breathing hard. 'Nothing to worry about, Arko. I've got it covered.'

'What'll I do now? Stayin' around here is making me nervous.'

'Are you renting that place? Is the address on your licence?'

'Been here six months. Haven't got around to changing the address.'

That bought Flynn time. He realised he'd been holding his breath.

'You'll be okay there for a few days. Turn your phone off after this and don't call anyone. Not even your cousin. There's just one thing you have to do. First thing tomorrow – really early – get over to your place in Chullora and clear out anything with a link to this. Get rid of the paper-work and pick up any gear you used. Leave the ute. Then lock the gates and get back to your flat. Stay put until you hear from me, same time tomorrow. You got that?'

'You're a real mate. I'm sorry, I really am.'

'Things will work out.' Flynn sensed Arko's relief. He might be less likely to bolt now, but Flynn didn't feel comfortable trusting him while Malcolm was breathing down his neck.

CHAPTER 13

PACER PICKED UP his morning brew of English Breakfast, stepped onto the escalator and rose towards the station exit. A young man pushed past before disappearing from view. Pacer joined the queue at the turnstiles and exited to the street. With a sigh, he moved into the stream of workers, then slipped out when he neared the police command. The sandstone and red brick had darkened with age and city grime. With the rest of this row in an unfashionable part of the city, the building was slated for redevelopment, but who knew when.

Pacer made it to the fourth floor without encountering the brass. Most were the new breed, like Connors. Everything done by the book, registered, filed and no loose ends. Pacer had no problem with that. Meticulous and systematic, his notes and records were always up to date. Any errors or omissions and slick lawyers got their scumbag clients back on the streets. All that work for nothing and you'd have to do it over the next time they offended.

No, the problem wasn't about being thorough. The brass wanted things neat and squared away, as if police work was something you did in a sterile laboratory. It wasn't that they insisted on order, it was their zero tolerance for anything else. A good detective needed both, a systematic mind and an intuition for what was outside the box. There were always loose ends – missing pieces, red herrings and witnesses who couldn't tell the same story two days in a row. Pacer had a suspicion that these anomalies would dog him throughout this investigation. He chuckled at his pun.

Pacer looked up. Inspector Connors was standing over him. 'This case is amusing you, is it, Sergeant?' His upper lip held a sneer.

Pacer hid behind an expressionless mask.

'We'll meet upstairs at ten, shall we?' Connors marched off, as stiff as a Ken doll, leaving Pacer to finish his tea and arrange his notes. He laid the crime scene photos on the desk in the order of how the incident had played out. Make it easy for the Inspector to follow. Keep the meeting short, anticipate the questions.

Pacer's phone vibrated inside his jacket pocket. It was Kurt Otway from surveillance and operations. It gave Pacer a lift to hear his voice.

'Hey, Pacer, how's it going?' Otway had news on Arko's depot. 'We had another job out that way, so me and one of the boys cruised by.'

Otway must have gone out of his way, but Pacer wouldn't embarrass him by saying so.

'Arko's depot, unit No. 38B. It's in a light industrial park, a block back from the main road. The gate was bolted but I think he'd just left. There was a half-finished coffee there by the gate, still warm. There's a site office to one side and a larger storage shed on the other. Nothing to see except empty pallets, rusted machinery and a ute that's seen better days.'

'Any sign of heavy equipment or a cement mixer?'

'Not in the yard. Can't tell you what's in the shed though. Sign out the front names the premises as "Arko's Building Services". The small print lists storage systems, asbestos removal and other services he's probably not licensed to provide. Blokes like Arko rarely own their equipment. When a job comes in, they hire what they need. He's like others on the periphery of the building trade. People who'd do anything for a quid, like dumping waste. Don't bother to cover their tracks.' Kurt reminded Pacer of the truckie caught on CCTV dumping asbestos-riddled sheeting outside a primary school. They'd talked about this story before. It had got to Kurt – he had kids in primary school. They'd caught the bloke, he knew that much. 'Court case come up yet?'

'A few weeks ago, but the charge didn't stick,' Pacer replied.

'Free to do it again, the bastard.' Pacer heard the disgust in Otway's voice.

'Got off on a technicality. The company he works for hired a top brief.'

Otway took a moment before returning to the reason for his call. 'Right, Arko. The managing agent's details for his place are listed out front. I'll text them to you,' Kurt said. 'You'll get a search warrant?'

'That's the plan. I'm doing the paperwork for Connors now. Seeing him about this case this morning.' And dreading it.

'Good. Let me know when it comes through. I'll meet you there. The chain around that gate is fairly substantial and the doors to the office and shed might have to be forced.'

'Appreciate your help,' Pacer said. So Arko had shot through, or it appeared that way. A sign he was guilty, but of what? Pacer looked at his watch. Almost ten. He completed the search warrant, gathered his notes and tapped them on the desk to straighten them. He rose slowly, pulled on his jacket and adjusted his tie.

CHAPTER 14

THE ATMOSPHERE ON Level 9 was muted. Pacer stepped onto grey industrial carpet and passed bland paintings on loan from the State Library. Stuff from a century ago, or more. In one, a family picnicked by a stream under a tepid northern hemisphere sun. In another, a tall ship floated, as if suspended, on the still waters of Sydney Cove.

The door to the Inspector's suite was ajar. Edith, Connors's PA, sat in the outer office. 'He's expecting you.'

Edith, always welcoming, was a ray of sunshine on that dreary floor. Pacer wondered how she coped with the isolation from the real human beings on the lower levels. He nodded his thanks and entered his boss's office. Connors motioned Pacer to pull up the visitor chair. A good sign, but not a green light for Pacer to relax. He leaned forward and spread the crime scene photos across the desk.

Connors sat stiff and upright, eyes boring in at Pacer. He was younger by a good ten years, held his lean body ramrod straight and never allowed a hair out of place. He was about the same height, but sitting or standing at constant attention made him look taller.

Pacer saw how the Inspector's mind worked. Connors believed his close supervision was all that kept detectives out of deep water. He knew about Pacer's demotion and watched him like a hawk, like he was waiting for that one incident to catch him out and make his unit a cleaner, safer, more orderly place.

The Inspector's pupils refocused as he picked up a black-and-white photo and stared at the corpse's fingers trailing gobs of mortar. Pacer saw him swallow hard. Connors put it aside and dug out a photo of the wheelbarrow.

'So, what have you got from this? Should be dripping with evidence.'

Pacer suppressed a laugh at the unintended pun. 'It's at the lab. There might be blood in the tray. They're checking the handles for prints.'

Connors pushed the photographs to one side. 'Looks like a gangland killing to me. They've done away with one of their own. And you have a suspect? The contractor, Arko?'

'Yes, Arko is involved, I'm sure of it. I followed a lead yesterday to his other place of work. We were too late. He left after receiving a tip-off. The vehicle he was driving was seen this morning at his depot in Chullora. I have reason to believe he has abandoned the place and gone into hiding.'

'You'll need a search warrant. I'll arrange that today.'

'I have the paperwork with me now, sir.' Pacer breathed out slowly. No need to get out the begging bowl.

Connors grunted as he looked it over and signed with a flourish. He looked up suddenly, anticipating Pacer's next request. 'And no, I can't spare detectives from the Serious Homicides Squad. You have young Stuart Picone – he's bright and keen.'

More work for Pacer, but it went both ways. He was pretty sure none of the homicide boys would want this case. The Serious Homicides Squad handled murders of prominent citizens like magistrates, business leaders and organised crime bosses. They wore sharp suits and frequented the city's smarter restaurants and watering holes. Solving a homicide brought them kudos and a step closer to promotion. This crime wasn't in their league.

Connors continued, 'And no name for the victim? Another bit of jetsam from the bikie gangs out west, I should think.'

'We don't have an identity as yet. The face was obscured and there was no other form of identification. The morticians had to take care removing the debris around the body. Big risk of ripping off skin with each patch of concrete.'

The inspector shifted uncomfortably. Half the station knew what had happened when Connors visited a crime scene during his training on the fast track: the body had been there a week. He'd left abruptly, crawled into the back seat of his car and vomited into a plastic bag.

'When can I expect to see the coroner's report?' Connors asked.

'The coroner has scheduled the autopsy for two this afternoon. I'll be there, of course.' Pacer noticed as Connors gulped twice. Had he even attended an autopsy?

Pacer turned away, smiling. He hadn't missed that delicious moment when Connors's face turned a shade of green. Got the bastard!

CHAPTER 15

DETECTIVE CONSTABLE PICONE was waiting in Pacer's office, impatient to download his conversation with Roslyn Creed. Picone's nervous energy was getting to Pacer.

'Sit down, take the weight off. So you found her at home, eager to talk.' Pacer scanned a neatly written sheet with a list of dates, times and brief notes. 'A good witness, kept a record.'

'At first she was worried about a prowler but didn't call the police.' Picone frowned. 'He seemed interested in the site behind, not her place. Besides, she had Baxter, her dog. Got a fright yesterday when that man attacked him.'

Pacer nodded for him to go on.

'She said it was odd because there was nothing in there to steal. It's part of a film production centre. That section is used to store props and other stuff they no longer use. Just rusty old junk.'

'And the other residents in the street?' Pacer asked.

Picone had spent time with the man at No. 14, next to Mrs Creed's little cottage, a friendly chap who'd worked at the local boot making factory until it closed thirty years before. Since then he had worked casually when he could. He'd bought his place in the early days when there was plenty of overtime and a bloke like him could still afford to buy.

'He showed me his garden.' Picone's frown had disappeared and he spoke more quickly. 'Gets masses of tomatoes, herbs, greens of all kinds. He keeps chickens. Lets them free-range in the lot behind his place – made a gate years ago. He even planted a lemon tree in there. Says no one notices or cares.'

'Okay, okay.' Picone was relating well to witnesses. Maybe something was rubbing off. But he could talk! 'So, by now you were enjoying a cup of tea together.'

Picone blushed. Pacer scolded himself. Was the sarcasm necessary? 'Did he see or hear anything?'

'Same story as Mrs Creed. He noticed goings-on a few months back. Something that set his chickens off. The first time, he couldn't see what the problem was. Thought it might be a fox. The next time, he was quicker and glimpsed a man near Mrs Creed's back fence. It was just a glimpse – couldn't give me a description. He went over to see if she was all right. Her Baxter was growling and pacing the fence. They figured the man had gone.'

The man from No. 14 was out the previous afternoon, but the two incidents he remembered matched the others on Mrs Creed's list.

'This confirms her observations, Stuart. Good work.' Pacer looked down before continuing. 'Look, I know I'm a bit short at times. Too used to working alone.' It was an apology of sorts. The best he could do. Picone said nothing. 'Was there anything else?' Pacer asked in a brighter tone.

'Joel Frazer at Café Bones said a homeless woman turned up a few weeks ago. She seemed harmless. Tucked herself in behind the cafe most nights. Last time he saw her was two days ago, the day before the crime. Her belongings are gone.'

'A woman. So Roslyn Creed's prowler and the person using that shelter are not the same. Come on, I've got something to show you.'

Pacer walked Picone to the end of the corridor and opened the door with a flourish.

'Our incident room.'

Pacer had used it before, a small space with ill-matched desks, cabinets and chairs. Two tables in the centre were pushed together roughly to make a flat workspace. A whiteboard, messy with the jottings of past users, stood to one side and a pinboard covered most of the far wall. It wasn't much but it was all they would get.

'We need the paperwork properly organised. It slows things down, but everything has to be squared away before we go to court.' You could do the paperwork in reverse order if no one was looking, but that wasn't for Picone to know just yet.

'The evidence records are ready, at Parramatta,' Picone said, as if to lift his game to match Pacer's effort in putting together the incident room. 'I've called the car pool, they've got one ready to go. Want to come?'

Pacer shook his head. 'There might be a witness. I'm going back to Café Bones.' He'd also ask Joel Frazer about that prowler. He was curious about the gap in the fence on Canal Road. Was this prowler the one who'd been there when Alison Cassidy chanced on the murder scene? Was he the one the little schnauzers had sensed?

CHAPTER 16

PACER STEPPED FROM the unmarked Commodore into the late morning sunshine. Taking the footpath at the south end, he entered Hawthorne Park through the railway underpass. The atmosphere was dank and heavy with the aromas of packed earth and lichen clinging to trees. Graffiti lined the rough brick walls and water dripped from the moss. The short tunnel opened to a canopy of figs.

The brown water of the canal was flowing in the opposite direction from the previous day, carrying debris. A large carp jumped then disappeared with a flick of its tail. To the right a concrete path diverged towards the light rail station. Curiously, several black laying hens were foraging in the weeds behind the perimeter fence. It occurred to Pacer that they belonged to the old chap from No. 14.

The off-leash precinct began a few steps on. Pacer pushed the gate, catching the reek of a council wheelie bin. A metal container for dog waste bags was attached to a nearby post.

A middle-aged couple sat at a picnic table while their three small dogs ran in and out of the bushes. Further along, a man was throwing a ball to a black and white collie. It hovered between intense stillness while its owner held the ball aloft and vigorous activity as it raced in pursuit. Pacer watched for a while, expecting the dog to tire of the game. It didn't. A petite, smiling woman with a spiky white chihuahua passed by. It bared its teeth and growled. Pacer imagined a piranha with fur.

The park narrowed as he approached Café Bones. Patrons sat at tables as their pets greeted each other and sniffed the legs of their new friends' owners. Seagulls pecked at scraps on a vacated table, upsetting a cup. Coffee spilled onto the grubby white gravel.

Pacer stood near the cafe counter while Joel Frazer finished serving a customer. Frazer, spotting Pacer, spoke to the other server and exited via a side door, dogs milling about his legs. He was a lean, energetic man with an open face. Smiling, he reintroduced himself and motioned to a shaded table away from the others. The dogs followed.

'They know me as the man who gives them doggychinos.' Frazer noticed Pacer's frown. 'Frothed-up dog milk with a sprinkling of liver treats. Can I get you a coffee?'

Pacer opted for a mug of English breakfast, waving away Frazer's offer of one on the house and placing coins on the table. Accepting favours, even small ones, was a bad habit. They lulled you, made you drop your guard. You lost perspective and the favours got bigger. He knew officers whose downfall was taking bribes. Pacer had gone close enough.

Frazer told him he'd followed progress on the new amenities block from the beginning, when the council had warned him about possible disruptions to the water.

'Nothing I could do other than hope it didn't happen at an inconvenient time. It did, of course. I could have complained – they provided phone numbers – but what's the point?'

Pacer was sympathetic. He'd had his own frustrations with bureaucracy. Petty, inconvenient, demanding. Connors was just the tip of the iceberg.

'Council laid out the building site, then a new bloke showed up some weeks ago. Called himself Arko. Didn't talk much. Liked my coffee and steak sandwiches.' Frazer stopped and sipped his coffee. 'He was slow, took his time. Came in a ute.'

'Any further interest from the council?'

'Yes, late last week, I think it was Thursday, a bloke came by. Seemed official. Spent about fifteen minutes looking around and talking to Arko. Before he left, he handed Arko a piece of paper. It was quiet at the cafe, so I noticed.'

Frazer's expression changed. Perplexed? Confused?

'Anything unusual?' Pacer asked.

'It was odd. I built a garage at my place once. Had to have the foundations signed off by a certifier before we could lay the concrete. I thought maybe that was happening here. That the new bloke was the certifier. Later on I had a look. The steel mesh was laid, but it wasn't pinned down. You have to pin it down before they'll sign the certificate.'

'Have you seen or heard anything unusual from the film centre behind the cafe? People going in there or coming out?'

'Nooo … I don't think so. I spend my day behind the counter facing the other direction. There's a lot of traffic, depending on the time of day. Dogs, people, prams, bikes. You get your regulars. No, nothing unusual. Sorry.'

'Would any of those regulars have information, do you think?'

'Most of them notice the dogs, not the people. It's the same with names. They know the dog's name, but not its owner's. Not me though. I like dogs but I'm in the people business.' As if reminded of a person, Frazer added, 'Your detective constable was here this morning – that young bloke, Stuart Picone. He wanted to know about the woman staying around the back.' Frazer indicated the space beyond the water troughs.

'Yes, he passed on those details. Anything to add?'

'I first noticed her sitting at one of my tables. She'd been through the wringer by the look of her – quite well turned out, but tired and jittery. Sat there and cleaned up someone's leftovers. Then she was back the next day. I asked Genie, my assistant behind the counter, to see if she needed anything. We just wanted to help, not move her on. She told Genie her name was Sofia. Said she'd fled her home. Somehow she ended up here.'

'And she just … stayed on?'

'On and off. I was stowing some cartons out the back and noticed the shelter. To be honest, that space is out of sight and I don't keep it tidy. We always have spare food at the end of each day so we left some for her. I think she felt safe there. She would disappear for a day or two but always came back.'

'When was the last time you saw her?'

'The day before yesterday.'

'If she returns, can you give me a call?' Pacer handed Frazer his card. 'And I'd like to speak with Genie, if I may.' Pacer watched as Frazer entered the cafe and had a word in Genie's ear. She looked his way, scowling, then finished what she was doing before joining him at the table. Pacer was used to witnesses making him wait.

Genie sat down and looked at Pacer with suspicion, weighing him up before deciding to talk. Pacer didn't speak; he was confident he could win any staring contest. Finally Genie gave in. 'Sofia was sleeping rough but anyone could see this was new to her. She left home in a hurry and didn't know where to go. Doesn't have friends here and her parents and sister live overseas.'

'Do you have any idea where I might find her?'

Genie looked at the queue forming in front of the counter. 'I have no clue. Where could she go? There are no women's refuges around here.'

Pacer was taken aback by her flash of anger. Genie wasn't finished. 'Even if you find her, don't expect her to say much. She didn't get help from your lot when she needed it. That bastard of a husband did what he wanted. It was worse after she called triple zero. For all she knows, you're on his side and will send her back for more of the same.' Genie rose, turned on her heel and was gone.

CHAPTER 17

THE PALE GREEN facade of the State Coroner's Court in Forest Lodge was a bland mask for the grisly goings-on inside. Pacer had been here numerous times. Autopsies carried out here for decades, but times were changing. Soon he would have to absorb the look and feel of that new place at Lidcombe. Perhaps for the last time, he mounted the steps and entered the soft-lit reception area.

Dr Mary Gibbs, the State Coroner, invited Pacer into her spacious office. Wooden wall panels and oak cabinets darkened the room. Art deco lights and voile curtains softened it. The mahogany desk with its beautifully crafted legs stood in the centre. On it, case files were piled in untidy mounds, the tallest pitched at an uncertain angle, poised to tumble at the slightest touch.

Dr Gibbs had risen to the coveted position of State Coroner because of her medical knowledge, which was extraordinary. During her tenure, she drew admiration for her efficiency in closing cases and her success in wringing resources out of the government. Medical facilities were modernised and staffing was brought to a level closer to what was needed.

Pacer was again struck by the contrast between his tidy, systematic approach and that of Dr Gibbs. All her orderliness was inside her head. Despite the clutter, she could put her hand on any file, no matter how dusty or forgotten by others. As she reached this way and that, Pacer leaned sideways, around the piles, to keep her in view.

'An interesting case, Sergeant,' she said, deftly locating a folder. 'Most unusual. I don't take many cases these days, but yours is exceptional.' She read the notes before commenting, 'The duty pathologist was Dr Wu. His initial examination was more limited than usual. Given the positioning of the body, he was unable to do more than certify that it was indeed deceased and take some readings that might help establish time of death. Rigor was well advanced, but the body was enclosed in a sticky substance that could have retarded or hastened it.'

'Did he estimate the elapsed time between death and his examination?'

'Difficult. Going on what Dr Wu has noted, the victim died about twelve hours before the examination. But please understand, this is an approximation. It can take twelve hours for rigor to set in fully. The process starts in the neck and upper limbs about four or five hours after death and then advances to other parts of the body. We will conduct tests to assess the effects of that substance … a form of concrete, was it?'

'We think the perpetrators intended to pour concrete but made an error with the mix. It should have set, but they left before realising their mistake.' It nagged at Pacer. A fundamental error. Surely Arko had mixed concrete before. If it was Arko.

'There are other things to factor in.' Dr Gibbs turned the pages in the folder. 'Your victim was quite a large man. And of course, the overnight temperature must be considered. The stomach contents will be telling. The tests we conduct here are very accurate. We will let you know when and what he last ate. Sam Wu found nothing on the victim to identify him. Do you have a name for us?'

'Not yet.' Pacer shifted uneasily. Police officers were supposed to identify victims quick smart. He was troubled by the fact that he hadn't been able to do so. No likely victim reported missing. No tip-offs from the usual underworld operatives.

'We normally combine the external and internal examinations,' Dr Gibbs continued, 'but we did the external exam immediately. We couldn't leave him in that state: there would have been unnecessary damage. Do you recognise this man? Someone known to the police, perhaps?' She removed a coloured photo from the file and turned it towards Pacer.

Pacer looked at it and shook his head. The face was clean, but red patches revealed where the concrete had attached. The dead eye stared back. For a moment he was back at the scene, inside the crime scene tent.

'I've asked Dr Wu to assist during the internal examination. He's downstairs now making the preparations. Shall we join him?' The coroner bounced out of her chair and into the corridor. Pacer followed, his legs leaden. Dr Gibbs stopped at a solid door two floors below ground level. She grasped the handle and smiled back at Pacer.

'You'll be right, Sergeant. You've done this before. Stay well back and take a break if you need it. You know where the tea things are kept.'

Sam Wu waited by the steel slab as the newcomers donned gowns and masks. The victim was on his back, a white cotton sheet covering the lower body. A block supported the upper back, raising the pale chest and exposing it to the coroner's instruments. The man was Caucasian, a little fleshy around the face and with a good head of brown hair greying at the temples.

With video- and voice-recording equipment on, Dr Wu summarised the external examination: the initial assessment at the scene, the carriage of the body and receipt into the morgue, the cleaning process, the examination of skin, nails and hair. X-rays revealed nothing recent, just boyhood breaks to the right forearm and thumb. There were no tattoos or distinguishing marks.

Pacer was distracted by the antiseptic smell and the glint of surgical instruments. Worse was to come. The deathly aromas encased you and seeped into your hair and clothing. They stayed with you for days afterwards. That was his experience. Others seemed less bothered, but perhaps they were good at bluffing. Or just plain callous.

Sam Wu's next words jolted him.

'… clean, narrow wound in the back between the third and fourth ribs … measuring 1.5 centimetres wide at the entry point, most likely due to the insertion of a sharp implement …'

Pacer reeled. Knifed in the back!

Sam Wu was still speaking. A probe indicated the wound was deep, puncturing the lung. The internal exam would show if it extended to the heart or an artery.

Pacer was confused and angry. Why hadn't Rhys Parkinson, the coroner's assistant, phoned him? He said he would when they spoke the day before. Rhys would have known yesterday, seen it when he was cleaning up the body. You pass that kind of information on. Immediately.

Dr Wu continued. 'No defensive wounds are apparent.'

These facts were critical. Pacer was looking for a professional killer. The poor sod hadn't seen it coming. This was a cold, clinical hit by a murderer who knew exactly when and how to strike. It wasn't easy to kill someone this way.

Dr Wu stood aside as the coroner stepped forward, a glint in her eye. 'Let's take a look from the other side. We'll see where that sharp implement ended up.'

The examination continued in textbook fashion, with the sawing, grinding, slicing, lifting and weighing. The coroner, engrossed in her work, spoke as much to herself as for the recording. 'Oh, yes, here we are,' she said cheerfully. 'I can see where the muscle has been cut and something sharp has nicked the bone. Come nearer, Sam. See? And here, the outer wall of the heart is penetrated. Bring that camera up close, will you, please?'

The stomach was cut free, tied off and lifted out of the abdominal cavity. Dr Gibbs continued her commentary. 'I'm palpating the stomach now. It's quite full. The victim had a good meal not long before he died. I can detect alcohol. We'll know more when we examine the contents.'

Pacer moved back a step. Dr Gibbs looked his way. 'No, we won't do that now. Sam will conduct a full examination after we finish here.'

That wound in the victim's back. Pacer couldn't get it out of his head. Rhys should have phoned. Back in the foyer, he approached the receptionist and asked for him.

'I'm sorry, sir,' she replied. 'Rhys Parkinson left work unexpectedly yesterday afternoon, an urgent family matter. He'll be off for several days. Would you like to leave a message?'

Pacer shook his head and quietly berated himself. He'd made assumptions, jumped to conclusions. Some people had it in for you. Plenty of others didn't. He turned to the exit.

Who had wielded that knife? And who was this man, dead on the coroner's slab? Pacer descended the stairs two at a time.

CHAPTER 18

FLYNN SAT IN his den, whisky in hand. He was on his second glass, a new blend from Tasmania. He barely tasted it. The wait was hard, but Malcolm was particular about when he made calls. The slit in the curtains admitted a sliver of light from the street lamp. Fully dark now. Flynn stared at the phone on the desk, willing it to ring.

Malcolm got straight to the point. 'Arko will have to go. I got a call from our friends today. They weren't happy. He was supposed to stay out of sight.'

'Are you sure? I told him to stay in the truck. Ordered him to.'

'Of course I'm sure,' Malcolm snapped. 'No mistake. He was right there. Looked straight at them. No one does that.'

Flynn was shocked. That rule could not be broken. Business at a distance. No handshakes, no contact, no trace.

'Stay where you are,' Malcolm said. 'They'll call you tonight.'

The call came twenty minutes later. From Victoria. That was the name she used with them. All Flynn knew of her was the voice. He listened to the smooth tones, intrigued by the accent, not strong, but noticeable. American with hints of Spanish? South American? Victoria's way was to talk in riddles, choosing her words carefully.

'The weather is lovely right now, isn't it? Aramis and I will take the cruiser out tomorrow evening. No sense in delaying these things. Who knows when the weather will turn? We'll pass by the boat sheds at the time you suggest. I'll watch for you and your friend by the jetty.'

'Name's Arko. He's jumpy. I'll keep him calm, but be quiet about it or he'll take off.' Flynn's voice sounded hoarse in contrast to Victoria's smooth tones. He couldn't hide it. She'd know he was anxious.

'We'll take good care of your friend Arko, and most silently, I assure you. He will be far away. In a better place, I think.' Flynn heard the amusement in her voice. She considered him weak. The accent was South-East Asian, he was sure of it now.

After the call, Flynn fell back in his chair, momentarily exhausted. He scratched at his ankle and swigged his drink. His last call of the evening was to Arko.

'How are you doing? You've done everything I told you?' Flynn mimicked concern.

Arko sounded relieved. 'Yeah, just like you said. Been to Chullora and cleared the place out. No one about. Easy.'

'Good. Do what I say and you'll be okay.'

How long do I have to stay here? Running out of stuff to eat.'

'You're moving tomorrow. We've worked out a plan. Take you away from all this.' Arko knew the jetty near the boat sheds. They'd met there before on other business. Out of sight and close enough to Flynn's home to arrive on foot.

Flynn resisted the urge to admonish Arko. He'd stuffed up mightily and landed him in this mess. Flynn reminded himself to keep his tone light. Not so easy.

'I'll bring some extra cash. Stay put, no phone calls, no pizza deliveries, no nothing. Leave your place in the afternoon peak hour when lots of people are about. And keep your head down; there's cameras everywhere.'

There was nothing more Flynn could do. His last chance. Everything hung on it. Could he trust Arko to stick to the plan and not panic?

CHAPTER 19

THE SIGN ANNOUNCING 'Arko's Building Services' hung at an angle on a heavy chain, the lettering visible through a crust of accumulated dust and grime. From the condition of the paint, the sign had been made well before Arko had rented this depot four years earlier. Anyone's guess where he had come from before this.

The morning was overcast and a chilly breeze blew from the south. Pacer blew warm air between his hands and rubbed them. The managing agent, Nigel Cooper, standing between him and Picone, was still protesting the early morning call-out. Pacer would prefer that the man wasn't there, but it was a requirement.

'It's my obligation to cooperate with you, Sergeant. I'm doing my part, but I expect to be compensated for any damage.' Cooper shivered in his light suit, more appropriate for a heated office than a depot exposed to the elements. It might have been nerves as much as the cold.

'We are grateful you could attend, Mr Cooper,' Pacer replied evenly. He indicated the search warrant for the third time. 'As I explained before, I need to examine these premises in relation to a serious crime. The main gate is bolted and the site office and shed are locked. Unless you have keys, I have no choice but to use force.'

'And as I told you, the tenant is responsible for keeping the site secure. Just make sure you don't do any more damage than you have to.'

'We will remove some items, but only those belonging to the tenant. That ute over there, can you confirm who owns it?'

'That's his – Arko's. I've seen him driving it. Parks outside my office when he comes with the rent.'

'And where does Arko stand with his lease?'

'He has a year to run. Look, I'm not happy with the police barging in when the bloke is away. Doesn't seem right. As far as I'm concerned, this is his place until the lease runs out.'

Cooper was angry, but Pacer didn't mind. Few witnesses had ever worn him down and Cooper was not in their league.

'I don't expect Arko will return. He could be in trouble. I want to locate him before matters get worse. If you know anything to help us find him, you'll be doing him a favour.'

'Don't get me wrong,' Cooper said, 'Arko is a tenant, nothing more. He keeps to himself. He does small jobs for builders and bits and pieces for local councils. Jobs requiring more in the way of experience than real skill.'

'And equipment? Does he hire it?'

'Uses the hire place at the far end of this road. Most in this block do the same.'

A police van pulled up and two officers in black uniforms jumped out. Kurt Otway and his off-sider, Jackson. Smiles all round, the men enjoying the reunion. Cooper seemed to shrink beside their towering frames.

A second car arrived. Miranda De Veen and two from her team stepped out, slamming doors behind them. 'Thought I'd join the party,' she said. 'Hope I'm not too late.'

'Glad you could make it, Miranda. Thanks for making the time.' Pacer smiled his gratitude. She had come on short notice and not for the first time.

The officers formed a huddle and discussed the operation, more for the benefit of Cooper than themselves. Kurt Otway circled to the back of his van and returned with a set of bolt cutters and a high-impact drill. 'These should do the job,' he said with a grin. 'Let's go, Jackson.'

With a snap, the chain around the main gate fell away and the group moved inside. Otway and Jackson went to the site office and the shed. The door locks clattered to the ground. Cooper looked on, dismayed.

The office contained a plain desk and chair, a bar fridge, a kettle, mugs and a battered filing cabinet with its doors hanging open. The desktop was bare of paperwork, but sheets of paper were scattered on the floor. A grubby toilet cubicle and sink were visible through an open door.

Pacer and De Veen looked at one another. 'Do you reckon someone has left in a hurry?' she asked.

'Yep, I'd say so,' Pacer replied. 'Arko got a tip-off and cleared out.'

Out in the yard the wind had dropped and the sun was peeping through high cloud. Picone peered inside the shed and located the light switch.

Three fluorescent tubes hung precariously from electricity cables high on the walls. Bags of cement and sand leaned against a pallet and empty bags were strewn about.

Kurt Otway worked on the ute with a set of keys he'd pulled from his pocket. The door was soon open. 'All yours,' he said to Pacer. Looking over at Picone, he added, 'Come around here and see what else I found.' A pile of asbestos sheeting, broken and pitted, was stacked against the shed. 'What were we saying about blokes who don't care where they dump stuff? Would you like to show Cooper, or will I? Something to add to his clean-up bill.'

Picone phoned in the plates from the ute and walked across to Cooper, who was leaning against the office wall, still looking cold. 'Is this the address he gave you?'

'Maybe, but I don't think so. Told me he lives in a flat near the railway station.' Cooper's mood had changed from indignant to sullen. 'I have to go now, open my office.'

'Just one more thing before you go, sir,' said Picone. 'There's a pile of asbestos sheeting behind the shed. Needs cleaning up. You'd like to know.'

Cooper gave him a defeated look.

'I'll check the address on his rego anyway,' said Otway, after Cooper had left. 'Just in case he's still there.' Otway and Jackson packed their gear and sped off.

Pacer looked up and down the road, then back at Picone. 'Take a walk around the perimeter fence and as far down as that parking area. See if anything shows up.'

Picone was on his way. He returned ten minutes later, grinning from ear to ear, a plastic bag in each hand. 'In the recycling bins. Down there next to the parking area. Arko's cleared out his office and tossed it in.' He spoke in rapid bursts, barely able to contain himself.

De Veen let out a whistle. 'Whoa!' In an aside to Pacer she added, 'I'll send someone around to complete the chain of evidence. Picone shouldn't have touched it, but let's not spoil his big moment.'

Pacer frowned and jammed his hands in his pockets. 'He's keen. Nothing wrong with that, but—'

'We all make mistakes, Pacer. Accept them or they'll drag you down.'

Yeah, right. Easier said than done. And what if you keep repeating them? That was Pacer's biggest fear.

Picone was filling out the evidence paperwork when Pacer joined him. Don't ball him out, he told himself. Miranda is right. Don't ball him out.

Let it go for now. He'll learn the procedure. Just another thing on the list of stuff to teach him. Bloody hell.

'Nearly finished here. What's next?' Pacer tried to keep his voice up-beat.

'How about we find that hire place at the end of the road?' Picone said with a grin.

Pacer had noticed a kiosk close by. He'd smelled the hot pies and muf-fins as he'd cruised by earlier, men and women in fluoro vests gathered around, lured by the promise of coffee and a snack.

'Good idea. Just a quick detour on the way.' Pacer could already taste a pie. Getting up early had made him hungry.

They found the hire place easily, unmissable with a red and orange sign in oversized lettering.

'It was different this time,' the manager said with a shrug. 'Arko al-ways went for the hire package that included an operator. This time it was just the mixer. He has a heavy vehicle licence so I let him have it.'

Back in the car, Picone's questions poured out. 'So we know for sure it was Arko who poured concrete over the victim? He's the one who got the burial spot ready?'

'The evidence is mounting. Nothing is certain yet, but it's going that way.'

Picone looked excited. His first real murder case. Pacer tried to re-member his. The memories were vague, incomplete. He struggled to conjure the young victim's face but couldn't. Instead, the image of his grief-stricken wife, shocked and crumpling in pain, flooded his mind. Janet was right. It was the families that stayed with him.

'Go back to the office and check for any reports or sightings of Arko,' Pacer said to Picone as they fastened their seatbelts. 'Drop me off on the way. I'm taking another look at the crime scene.'

CHAPTER 20

PACER GOT OUT near Taverners Hill Station. Take the tram or walk? Perhaps he should have resisted that pie. Picone's look had said so. The day was warming up and the open air was inviting. Pacer peeled off his jacket, slung it over his shoulder, crossed the light rail tracks and entered Hawthorne Park. The black and white collie was back, playing the same game with its owner. A young couple pushing a pram strolled by with a flat-faced pug in tow. It ignored Pacer, too busy wheezing and snuffling.

Pacer felt lighter. A tranquil place, removed from the city hustle. Ironic that a murderer was attracted to it for the same reason. At Café Bones he ordered tea and sat at a table by the canal. While deep in thought, he was startled by the press of something against his leg. Without looking, he slapped it away. A small dog jumped back. Recognition came – the mutt clambering over his crime scene. Hugo.

'Sorry, he's disturbing you. Hugo!' The owner took hold of the dog's collar. 'Oh wait, you're the detective who was here the other morning.'

'He's okay. Please call me Pacer.' He remembered Anna Overton, forthright and determined. He was pleased to see her. One witness he wouldn't have to chase down. Fair-haired and wearing the latest sportswear, she was looking at him with piercing green eyes.

'You're nervous around dogs, aren't you. Most dogs are social, same as us. Or some of us,' she corrected herself. 'They'd do anything for a pat, like Hugo here. A real charmer. Look at those big brown eyes and cute frown.' Anna reached out and scratched around the floppy ears. 'Here, you try it.'

The dog's hair was short but soft. Pacer expected it to feel like straw. 'What kind of dog is he? He looks a bit like a pug I saw earlier but he's got … well … more face.'

'Hugo is a pugalier,' replied Anna. 'Crossed with a King Charles Spaniel. The nose is longer so the dog can breathe more easily. And he's a bit taller. Rather better looking, don't you think?'

Pacer nodded, half interested. 'I hadn't been to this park before the other day. Even with these dogs running about, it's a nice place. Calm after the city.' He sank back into his chair.

'That's true, except for the odd lunatic on a bike tearing through. Some people come every day. They bring dogs or come for a dog fix.' Anna gave Pacer a long look. 'Now, what is it about you and dogs?'

Pacer was taken aback. He was the one who asked the questions, wasn't he? Wouldn't hurt to answer, he supposed.

'Not much chance to get to know them. I was raised in a semi in Enmore – not enough room for a dog. Used to encounter one on my paper round, a big brown bitzer with a nasty temper. Some days they let it out as I rode through. I kicked it away when it came too close.' He'd almost forgotten. That time he arrived home with ripped pants. His dad wanted to give him a hiding, but his mother wouldn't allow it.

'Not a great start,' Anna said. 'Dogs need to be trained and some owners are irresponsible. Ever think of getting a dog later?'

'It gets worse. My wife, Janet, and I got a terrier cross from the dog pound. We had it just a few months. We were walking near our place when a man approached with two larger dogs. They were on leads and seemed okay. Without warning they lunged for our little fellow and locked their jaws around his head. I pulled them away, but it was too late. We rushed to the vet but she couldn't do anything.'

'How horrible. I'm so sorry. No wonder you're wary. You can't be sure, can you. Not until you know them properly.'

'Yes, you're right – some owners are irresponsible. Janet was distraught. We both were.' Another incident Pacer had pushed from his mind. Janet had loved that little dog. 'I'd like to ask you about the murder if you have time?' Safer territory.

Anna hadn't seen anything unusual, or anyone who seemed out of place. Yes, she had noticed Sofia, but was unaware of a shelter behind the cafe.

'There is room between the building and the fence though. Our clubroom is on the end.' Anna indicated the doorway.

Pacer had searched it but hadn't found anything of interest among the dog leads, trolleys and play equipment.

The building contractor? Yes, she had seen a man working in that area. 'A quiet sort of a bloke. Took his time getting anything done.' Hugo nosed Anna's treat bag, distracting her. 'We don't need that new block. There are rest rooms attached to the cafe. If you ask me, the council wants to pull the cafe down and our clubroom with it. They tried to close Café Bones a few years back, but the locals got together and put up a stink. Everyone turned up at the council meeting and tore their flimsy arguments to shreds. Beautiful, it was. People power. But you can't trust that council. What do you reckon? Are they trying it on again?'

'You'd have to ask the council about that.' Pacer wasn't venturing into local politics.

'I have, and more than once. I'm on the dog-training committee. I've talked to their planning manager, Mark Baker. Slimy bugger's up to something, but he's not saying. He was here earlier, by the way. You just missed him.'

'Baker, here this morning?' Baker, self-important and busy. Why take the time to come back here?

'He tried to avoid me. He does that. Said the barriers your people put up are a trip hazard. He's going to change them.' Hugo brushed around Anna's legs. 'Wants a doggychino, but he's not getting one today. A walk is better. We'll be off if that's okay. Why not get yourself down here on Sunday morning? That's when we have dog training. Meet some responsible owners and see what properly trained dogs can do.'

CHAPTER 21

PACER FINISHED HIS tea and continued along Canal Road towards Iron Cove. On his right, the unsightly detritus from the film centre was visible above the fence. Who wanted fixed rows of plastic seats, broken and faded, or those battered containers? Like a lot of junk, he supposed – too bulky or expensive to remove.

Further along, the fence was more substantial. Well-maintained buildings of silvery sheeting rose behind it. At the end, a sign stood above an open entrance: Canal Road Film Centre. Pacer wanted to go in but was curious about the landmarks beyond and kept walking. He found an oval surrounded by shady trees and wooden buildings. They'd been there a long time, and some were rather quaint. Canal Road curved around the oval where a little street angled off. Mrs Creed and the man with the hens lived down there.

On the way back, Pacer stopped inside the entrance to the film centre. He was astonished at the size. You would never guess from the outside. The largest building was clad in corrugated iron. Pacer judged it to be four floors high. It looked unoccupied. An expanse of open space was dotted with parked trucks and a string of smaller buildings. Light spilled from the window of the nearest one. Pacer mounted the wooden steps and found two women leaning over a broad table covered in parchment and drawing materials. They looked up, surprised at their visitor.

'Manager? I don't think so,' one replied in answer to Pacer's question. 'We just share this space.'

'There's a committee,' said the other, looking at the first.

'Really? I had no idea.'

'I thought you were on it.'

'No one told me.' The first woman looked perplexed.

The second woman introduced herself as Jane. 'Sorry, you must think we're crazy. It's like she said, we are a cooperative. There is a volunteer committee. Did you want to talk to one of them? There's a list of names somewhere.'

'Yes, that would be helpful. There's a security matter I need to raise.'

'In that case, you need to talk to Barry, our security guy. I'll walk you across.'

'What do people do here?' Their words and footsteps echoed against walls of metal and plasterboard. Otherwise, the place was eerily quiet.

'Everyone is connected with film. They make them in the studio, but most of us supply the stuff they need. Props, digital recorders, costumes, rigs for the cameras, all sorts of things. I'm in set design. I supply all the bits and pieces that make it look like a real home, or whatever it is they want. We have stunts and special effects people as well. And caterers, plenty of caterers.'

Jane chatted happily until they arrived at a small booth where a man in a blue uniform was leafing through a magazine. She did the introductions before heading back.

'No, mate, nothing much happens here,' Barry said. 'But, yeah, I heard about a bloke hanging around. Seen once or twice coming up from the bottom end where they keep the leftovers from old movies. Sticking his nose here and there around the place.'

'Did you approach him?' Pacer asked.

'Didn't see him myself. The ladies who do the costumes complained. I don't think he's a threat or out to steal anything. It's just they happen to know who he is and don't like him. Don't want him anywhere near the place. Anyway, I'm onto it. If he comes back I'll see him off.'

'Do you have a name, or some way to identify him?'

'I'd know if someone was out of place. I'll show you where the costume ladies work.'

Pacer walked to the building that Barry had indicated. It was unoccupied. He wrote a note on the back of his card and left it in the mesh by the door handle.

CHAPTER 22

STILL NO SIGN of Arko. The mobile units had returned nothing, not from the streets, shopping centres or hospitals. The background report revealed little other than a date and place of birth and a grainy photo from a vehicle licence. Pacer stared at it, trying to make out the features. The man was in his forties, hair thinning on top. The beard was trimmed roughly but looked thick. There was a prominent scar through the left eyebrow, continuing across to the temple. Pacer gave it a second look. No, it wasn't from a crease in the photo. A mate got caught out that way, long time ago.

There were no criminal offences, proven or otherwise. Arko had been caught and fined twice for dumping building materials off the side of the road. Misdemeanours in the eyes of the law. Why not drive down a quiet road like most dumpers? You had to wonder. An untidy workman. Pacer already knew that. Lazy or careless, but not a trained assassin, not someone who could creep up unnoticed and slide a blade precisely between the ribs. They'd find Arko, sooner rather than later. He wouldn't keep his head down for long.

The address on the drivers licence was not current. Kurt Otway had done surveillance the previous afternoon. A man and woman with two school-aged children had bustled inside out of a drizzle that was morphing into solid rain. He'd checked the mailbox. The contents were addressed to a different name. The place was small, no room for a flat out back for Arko to rent.

There was no family on record. Arko wasn't registered as married, but that didn't mean anything. A cousin lived in Newcastle. Those on the run frequently sought out people they knew. Didn't they guess that would be the first place the police would look? The local police had checked it out. Not this time.

Pacer had accessed Arko's bank accounts through his workers compensation certificate. He used a business account, and a debit card for personal matters. There were no new transactions on either since the murder. No supermarket purchases, food deliveries or taxis. Pacer checked again for anything in the past few hours. Nothing. Probably using cash. He'd run out soon enough.

Pacer's laptop pinged. A message appeared in the top right corner. Arko was using his Opal card. Pacer called Picone, then ran for the lifts. By the time he reached the basement, Picone had the car pointed towards the exit.

Siren blaring, they took the Western Distributor and were at Ashfield Station in fifteen minutes. Pacer's laptop registered another message. Arko had switched to a bus. Pacer tapped the keyboard until the bus number came up. Picone continued in pursuit, dodging in and out of traffic until the bus appeared. He overtook and stayed ahead until the next stop, then pulled up in front, blocking further movement.

They raced to the front and rear doors as commuters started to exit. Pacer spoke to the driver and showed his ID. Moving slowly down the aisle, his eyes raked over the faces as they stared back blankly. Picone was waiting at the back. Arko was not on the bus. The driver remembered a man of that description getting on at Ashfield Station. He thought he'd alighted a few stops back.

Pacer and Picone looked at one another. 'He didn't tap off?' Pacer asked.

'Nah. Half of them don't.'

The light was fading as they located the stop indicated by the bus driver and turned into the nearest cross-street. Necks craning, they peered right and left. No one resembled Arko. Picone pulled up suddenly at the Hawthorne Park light rail station and pointed to a form in the distance.

'That man, see over there, on the other side of the rails. That could be Arko, do you reckon?' Picone didn't wait for a reply before leaping out in pursuit. Five minutes later he was back, disappointed. 'I thought maybe he had unfinished business there, something he'd left behind.'

'Worth a try. There's still some light. We'll keep looking. Go as far as the bay then swing back around in the time we have left.'

There had been nothing from Arko, now this. He was on the move, sticking his head up. Pacer opened his laptop and reissued the alerts. They'd catch him and it would be soon.

CHAPTER 23

FLYNN GLANCED AT the kitchen clock for the third time in as many minutes. Sandra had prepared his favourite pasta dish, orecchiette with pork ragu, and after stacking the plates, he donned his running gear and grabbed a wad of notes from the safe in his den.

The dew settled around Flynn's neck and shoulders as he jogged to the boat sheds. He slowed and left the main track. There was movement around the far side as someone ducked away. It was Arko, he was certain, checking that Flynn hadn't brought company. Arko had stuffed up but wasn't completely stupid.

Flynn slowed to a casual walk. Beyond the sheds a jetty protruded into the inky waters of the bay. Flynn walked its length and sat on the hard planks. The waning moon was rising over the houses on the other side and shards of light bounced off the still water. In the distance a cruiser drifted in his direction on the incoming tide. Carefully removing his joggers, Flynn placed them on the planks and dipped the ankle that hadn't been injured into the water.

Arko dropped down on his right and gazed ahead, gathering his thoughts. He was wearing a light jacket over his work gear of blue singlet and shorts. 'Look, mate, I'm really sorry. I am. I'll do anything to make it up. It wasn't s'posed to happen like that. I thought I did everything you said.'

It was a long speech for Arko. The cruiser passed on their left and started to turn. Flynn could just make out the purr of an electric motor over the splashing of his foot in the water. 'You ready to go?' he asked.

Arko nodded. 'I didn't phone anyone, just like you told me. Kept me head down till this arvo. No one saw me on the way here.'

'I've got extra cash for you.'

Arko slipped the wad of notes into the inside pocket of his jacket and mumbled his thanks.

'There's something else, Arko. That night in the park. You had the hole ready and I told you to wait in the mixer until the other mob arrived with the package. I said to stay there until they left. But you didn't, did you.' Flynn could hear the edge in his voice.

Arko looked at him uncertainly. 'But it was a woman. The package was heavy and she was struggling. So I got the wheelbarrow and took it over.'

'You should have stayed out of it. You saw their faces.'

Arko grabbed Flynn's elbow. 'There's something else I meant to tell you, about that night – '

A dark shadow rose over Arko's left shoulder. A slim figure in a black wetsuit. A finger slid down Arko's back and stopped. A flash of steel. Flynn saw Arko's look of surprise and then horror. He heard flesh tear and bone crunch, his gaze riveted on the knife, pressed to the hilt then slowly withdrawn. The body lurched forward, eyes staring lifelessly. A second figure, also slim but taller than the other, deftly flipped Arko up and together the two figures tumbled him into the cruiser.

Flynn did not dare move. He felt hot breath against his neck, then heard his name. Victoria whispered a message, that same amusement in her voice, and slid a finger down his back. Flynn was sickened. He could have met the same fate. Right now. He knew it was true. The horror immobilised him. The two figures became shadows and vanished. He watched numbly as the cruiser motored back the way it had come.

CHAPTER 24

PACER'S LAND LINE rang. 'It's Sam Wu. From the Coroner's Office. We've checked the dental records and have a name and address. Martin Sullivan.'

Pacer had seen the body wrenched from its intended grave, had pored over the exhibits and photographs from the crime scene and had stood alongside the coroner as she extracted its vital organs. The victim was no longer an anonymous corpse but a person robbed of his life. Who was this Martin Sullivan? Why had his life ended so brutally?

The mood in the car was sombre. Picone tapped the address into the GPS and cruised out of the parking lot towards Russell Lea, a well-to-do suburb nestled against Iron Cove Bay. After clearing the city streets, they took the Western Distributor and the Victoria Road exit. Picone turned left after Iron Cove Bridge and parked outside a modern apartment block.

A young woman, early thirties, tall, with a flawless complexion, answered the door, her expression bright. She was dressed stylishly, as if preparing to go out or expecting a friend to call. She introduced herself as Karla Burns. Pacer entered at her invitation, Picone trailing behind.

Pacer had made many visits like this and knew how it would go. The fact that Karla and Sullivan were only engaged, not yet married, still in the first flush of love, made the shock worse, if anything. Karla's look changed from curiosity to shock and disbelief. She stared at the floor, her face crumpling. Dabbing at her tears, she met Pacer's steady, patient gaze. She wanted details, needing to be certain. Picone returned from the kitchen with a coffee. Karla wrapped her hands around the mug.

The room was comfortable, warm and inviting. Artifacts graced the cabinet tops, elegant and artfully placed. Pacer noted the plush furnishings and quality fittings. No clumsily built Ikea lounges and bookcases here. Someone had a good eye and expensive taste. He couldn't be sure, but he doubted that Karla had put this room together.

'I suppose this is over for me,' she said, looking through the expansive windows to the view across the bay. 'I'll have to leave this place, find somewhere else.'

News of a murdered loved one was hard to absorb. People responded differently to the dreadful news. Some seemed offhand or even callous. Pacer reminded himself that it didn't mean anything, just the mask for pain and vulnerability. The full impact came later, after the police had left.

Pacer asked about Sullivan's past. Karla knew little. There had been a falling-out with his parents years earlier. She had hoped for an introduction one day. Things like that meant something. It would never happen now.

'They run a cattle property a few hours from Perth. Martin was an only child. They wanted him to take over but he had other ideas. He hated the dust and the smell.'

She stood and left the room. Minutes later she returned with a thick folder. Settling back in her chair she extracted the contact details. 'He left on a business trip last Sunday. He was supposed to come back tomorrow.' More tears. 'I just don't understand,' she repeated.

'There was nothing out of the ordinary? Were you expecting a phone call while he was away?'

'Nothing unusual. It was like every other time. Martin didn't phone, but that was normal for short trips.'

'And his destination? Do you know what kind of business he was intending to do?'

'He was going to Kuala Lumpur. He'd been before. He was meeting with some finance people. I'm sorry, I can't recall the details. Martin built apartment blocks. I expect it was to do with that.'

'Take your time. It's the shock.'

Karla dabbed at her eyes again but seemed more composed. Pacer steered the conversation to the evening Sullivan was killed. 'How did he seem – was he acting normally?'

'He was upbeat, like always when he was when flying out. Loved travelling. Business class suited his style, if you know what I mean. Nothing was wrong. It was like every other time. I just can't believe this is happening.' She looked at Pacer again, perhaps hoping that he was going to admit that he'd got it wrong, and Martin was alive. But nothing had changed. It was real.

'I prepared dinner early because Martin was on the overnight plane. We ate around six-thirty. I remember because I was clearing up just as the news started at seven. Afterwards, he relaxed in front of the television with the rest of the wine. There was time before his limo.'

'He didn't call a taxi?' Pacer asked.

'Martin doesn't – *didn't* – like taxis. Smelly and uncomfortable he says – *said*, and half the time they don't turn up.' More tears. 'He *used* a limousine service. The pick-up was eight-thirty. They texted from downstairs and he left minutes later.'

'Do you know which limo service he used?'

Karla leafed through a stack of utility invoices and household paperwork. 'These are mostly old. He does everything on his phone now, but he started with the limo service before that.' She found the item and handed it to Pacer.

'Did Mr Sullivan keep any of his business files at home?'

'Not much. It's all on his laptop or phone and he took those with him. To be honest, I don't know much about what he does. I can give you the names of his close friends. Would that help? He was good at keeping in touch.'

Pacer took down the details and closed his notebook. 'An officer from the Coroner's Office will be in touch shortly. They'll talk to you about how things will proceed from here.'

Karla needed time to herself. Pacer had felt like that too after the call from the hospital. Janet had been in many times and always picked up. But that time she had taken a sudden turn. Pacer couldn't believe it. He wasn't ready. The feelings of loss returned in waves. Sometimes gentle, other times rough, rolling you over and over.

Picone returned the empty coffee cup to the kitchen. They left Karla sitting forward on the lounge, staring across the bay.

CHAPTER 25

LILLIAN ZHANG, SULLIVAN'S accountant, was overseas on family business for ten days, but Pacer had other leads from the list Karla Burns had given him. He phoned Sullivan's old girlfriend, Bethany Hasluck, arranged an appointment, but gave no details. He met her at her office in North Sydney.

Bethany Hasluck's striking good looks were matched by her beautifully tailored suit. A top designer label, if Pacer was any judge. She'd have drawn eyes even in a crowded room. Karla Burns was just as striking in her own way. Sullivan must have had something going for him. What was it? The coroner's photos had not shown him to best effect, but even so, you could tell he was nothing out of the ordinary.

Bethany appeared calm and self-possessed as she led Pacer to a meeting room. Her composure evaporated soon after they were seated. Nothing had been released to the press and it fell to Pacer to break the news. She feared something dreadful when he had phoned earlier. Tears welled as she asked for more. 'How was he killed? Who would do such a thing?'

Pacer deflected, spoke in generalisations. She'd need time to settle.

'He was a nice guy, kind and thoughtful. He made friends easily.' Bethany dried her cheeks with a white handkerchief. 'This doesn't make sense.'

He asked how she'd met Sullivan, drawing her to earlier times when life was rosier. From his experience, that usually helped. Bethany relaxed visibly as she told her story. She and Sullivan had met at university and started a relationship soon after. Both worked in North Sydney. She liked her job, but Sullivan was dissatisfied and had moved to Singapore. That was the end of the relationship, but they'd remained friends.

'It was the opportunity he'd hoped for. In Sydney they promised him an international role but buried him in the audit division. He used to say, "A monkey could do the work. No way to shine, show what I can do."'

'Did Mr Sullivan talk about his time in Singapore?'

'The firm was in property development. They built apartments, thousands of them. A close friend of ours was already there. He arranged an introduction for Martin and he was in. He loved it at first. Then he was sent to the supply division where they managed scaffolding. Really dull stuff. Martin wasn't cut out for it.'

'So he left?'

'Not straight away. He was unhappy and said so. There's a way of doing business in Singapore; it's a hierarchy. You have to respect that. Martin was quick to give an opinion, to contradict people. Sometimes it's smarter to keep your mouth shut. He was … I'm not sure how to put it.' Bethany paused, her brow creasing.

'He had strong opinions?' Pacer was thinking, *arrogant and irritating*. Sullivan saw himself as an alpha male, hence the good-looking girlfriends.

'If he had a fault, that was it,' she replied. 'Anyway, he came home to Australia and went into business for himself. Like he always wanted. Venture capital.'

'You stayed in touch?'

'Only for the occasional drink. He was easy with me … with past girlfriends. I expect there were a few others. He preferred women's company, I think. He was very open, a good talker. Always confident, optimistic.'

'He wanted you to know he was doing well?' Pacer was getting a clearer and clearer picture of Sullivan and liked him less and less. Overconfident and brimming with self-importance. And a peacock around women.

'He had a lot of bluff about him but I didn't mind. He was rather entertaining and I was happy enough to listen. He insisted he was good at picking winners – you know, untried new ventures – but I could see he was struggling. You can keep only so many balls in the air before one of them drops.'

'Any soundings from the regulatory authorities?' Pacer asked, trying to be tactful.

'Oh, Martin wouldn't do anything illegal, if that's what you're getting at.' Bethany, shifting in her seat, was seemingly affronted. 'He closed that business in the proper way.'

That's what people like Sullivan did, as far as Pacer could tell. Create chaos and get out before the axe falls on you. Pacer stood to leave but Bethany had more to say.

'Martin fell on his feet after that. It was about six months later. He met someone at golf. He was upbeat, excited about a job offer. I couldn't believe he would work for someone else – you know, take on a regular job.'

Pacer wondered how long that had lasted before Sullivan moved on to the next big thing.

'He liked that job,' Bethany continued. 'The company was in property development. But I can't tell you much. We lost contact for a while. Next time we met, Martin was running his own company, Sullivan Constructions.'

Back on the street, Pacer was drawn to the extent of new construction in a city constantly building upwards. Jackhammers and the roar of trucks pounded in his head as he made for the relative quiet of the railway tunnel. Sullivan was drawn to construction, wanting to make his mark. He'd been offered a job, and to Bethany's surprise, he'd taken it on. What was the attraction? It must have been good. But then he didn't stick around. Why not? Another instance of Sullivan sounding off and upsetting the boss or had he got what he needed and wanted out? Off he went to form his own construction business. Maybe a bit of both then.

Back in his office, Pacer brewed a pot of tea and carried it to his desk. He thought over his meeting with Bethany as he held the cup in both hands, the decorative roses partially obscured. She was much like Karla, not just in looks, but in her regard for Sullivan. Whatever else he did, something about him engendered loyalty from these women. Pacer wondered if Sullivan's male friends liked him as much. He guessed not. He figured Sullivan as a Jekyll and Hyde character – one personality for women and an entirely different one for men. He looked through the other names Karla had given him. Among them was Jordan Alexander, a former business partner. He'd moved to Tasmania, to the Huon Valley, she'd said, and set up a farm cafe business. Karla had told Pacer that she and Sullivan had visited the previous year.

When Pacer called, Alexander was shocked by the news, but quickly became curious and willing to talk. 'He was so full of life. How could this happen to him?' He and Sullivan had remained close, despite failing together in a gourmet food venture. 'We were both naive. Rushed in where competitors had a foothold. Martin said the market wasn't ready for us. So typical of him. We weren't the problem; it was always something or somebody else.'

'Did he talk about his more recent ventures?' Pacer asked.

'Not in any detail. He flew down for a visit with Karla a few months ago. Doing well in property development. That's what he said, anyway. He reckoned it was amazing how many flats you could squeeze onto a block where two houses had stood before. Money for jam.'

'Did he say how he was funding these developments?'

'No, but it's easy enough to guess. He'd be working his magic in Singapore, Malaysia, places like that. Martin had plenty of contacts and a way with people. Very persuasive.'

'Did Mr Sullivan mention a falling-out with any of his business partners?'

Alexander laughed. A curious reaction. Pacer asked why.

'Martin wouldn't see it that way. It was hard to offend him, and he was blind to any offence he caused. He was competitive though. Went on about this deal where he got the better of another bloke. Said he was going to do something like that again. All's fair in business, he said. He'd had a few drinks so who knows if it was true? He liked to talk things up even when he was sober.'

Pacer ended the call and leaned back in his chair. A picture was forming. In their unique ways, Bethany Hasluck and Jordan Alexander had painted a similar picture. Sullivan had kept his friends close and they'd stayed loyal. On the other hand, with his cockiness and boundless ambition, he could rub his business associates up the wrong way. There were plenty like Sullivan out there, criminal and straight, always right and never responsible. They sailed on, oblivious to the people left in their wake, disappointed or seething with resentment. Had Sullivan upset one person too many? Someone who hadn't just stewed over it before moving on?

CHAPTER 26

PACER OPENED THE autopsy report, a few pages with the main findings, and references to a sheaf of supporting documents. The coroner confirmed that a blade had pierced Sullivan's heart, so death would have been instant. Other than that, the victim was in good condition, although bordering on obese.

From the stomach contents, the victim had last eaten around two hours before he died. A good meal of steak, potatoes and salad, washed down with a few glasses of red. He'd drunk enough to be over the driving limit, but not by much. There were traces of a drug commonly used in date rapes. Easily acquired, impossible to trace. And without taste. More detailed toxicology tests would come later. There was a queue, a long one.

Death had occurred between 9pm and 11pm on the Sunday night. Dr Gibbs didn't know the time of Sullivan's last meal, but Pacer did. He figured that Sullivan was knifed around 9pm, at the lower end of the coroner's estimate.

Sullivan's regular limousine service hadn't picked him up that night, Pacer had checked. 'Actually, Sergeant,' said the voice, 'Mr Sullivan did make a booking. He's a regular. We assist him with our premium service. But on that day, last Sunday, he phoned and cancelled.'

Who had made that call? Not Arko. This was above his level. Someone had known Sullivan's patterns and substituted the car. A glass of bubbly? All part of the service. Easy enough to add the drug. Sullivan was expecting nothing unusual. Not when he left home, and probably not until it was too late.

Most stabbing victims were hit from the front in a frenzied attack, their faces and torsos shredded and bloodied. Organised crime assassins favoured garrotting, or two shots to the head. The method used to kill Sullivan was unusual, the blade driven in at just the right spot with the victim off-guard. Calculated. The killer extremely cool. As silent as a murder could be.

'You've done it before, haven't you,' Pacer said aloud, as Picone stepped into the room behind him.

'Sir?'

'Not you, Stuart. Our killer. He's done it before, plenty of times, I'd say. A real pro. Might have flown in for the job. No one in our territory fits the bill. Someone with means and a serious motive is behind this.'

'So it wasn't Arko?'

'I think his job was just the burial work. You've got the evidence report from the crime scene?'

Picone indicated a thin folder on the desk. 'It's preliminary. Most of the supplementary material – photos and all that – is online.'

'Anything useful? Just the key points for now.'

Picone ticked them off. Tyre tracks, some blood, various exhibits. 'It's everything we need to prove Arko was an accessory.'

'It's circumstantial,' Pacer said. 'Blood in the wheelbarrow shows it was used in the murder. The prints tell us Arko was one of the last to touch it. He used it in his day job, so his prints mean little. A wheelbarrow? That seems opportunistic. And some of the prints were smudged, you say? What else was going on? Who else was there?'

Pacer sat back, staring at the ceiling. Clues and evidence were only half the story. Your understanding of the crime came first. It guided you through the confusion and weight of physical evidence. He knew this was true but was struggling to get the balance right. His mind snagged on a memory, that cold case. He could have spared the Poulos family some of their hurt but had lost sight of the bigger picture. Allowing himself to get sidetracked. Wasting precious time sorting the files, while Davidson got rid of the evidence. Davidson, a creep of the worst kind, with a long record of juvenile offences, mostly minor stuff, or treated as such by the magistrates. Peeping Tom, theft of children's clothing, touching up kids in pools and on buses. As an adult, Davidson had got smarter and his offending had escalated. But Davidson was too slippery to get caught for the most serious stuff. He had done time for selling photos, kiddie porn from Asia, but the cops knew he'd done a lot worse. And now he was back on the streets, a problem for the cops in Queensland.

Yes, Janet had been right. There were more serious faults than the one that had got him demoted: he had failed in his understanding of the crime and Davidson had got away with it. He got bogged down, lacked imagination, let himself be outsmarted. That was him and it hurt deeply. But Pacer knew he would never give up, not on the Poulos case, for starters. Stubborn, persistent and in it for the long haul.

Pacer pushed himself out of his chair and stood by Picone. 'Anything else from that report?'

'The sock we found at the murder site is a match for the one on the victim. Miranda De Veen is checking for DNA.'

'Every contact leaves a trace. Remember that,' Pacer said. 'You'd have to wonder why that sock was dropped or discarded. The killers might have touched it. Professionals rarely make mistakes like that.'

'Some things that night were not meant to happen.' Picone tapped his fingers on the desk, his voice animated.

'We have to step back, try to make sense of it,' Pacer said. 'Start with the victim. What was Sullivan up to and who had he offended?'

Pacer and Picone looked at each other, as if in challenge to announce the next move in the investigation.

CHAPTER 27

'I'M DUE UPSTAIRS.' Pacer rose slowly, rubbing the back of his neck. Picone looked up from his laptop, his fingers still tapping. 'Connors wants a briefing.'

Edith greeted Pacer warmly as they waited for Connors to complete a call. He was speaking to a superior. Pacer could tell from the grovelling tone. The call over, Connors stuck his head out and ushered Pacer inside, pointing to the visitor chair. Twice in a row. Pacer was on a roll.

'Well, Sergeant, we have the identity of our victim.' The Inspector spoke with the authority of a man who had made the discovery himself and was passing the information to a dim pupil. Was it his air of superiority, or the arrogant tilting of the head and the thrust of the fleshy chin that irritated Pacer more?

'Yes, sir, we do.' Pacer matched the Inspector's formality. No small talk – that was the Inspector's policy and it suited him too. Get the information across, get a bit of a lecture, and get out. 'Martin Sullivan, aged thirty-six. No obvious motive for his murder. He was on a business trip to Malaysia when he was intercepted and taken to Hawthorne Park.'

Pacer waited for the Inspector to take this in. No point guessing the cracks or eddies his mind would wander into.

'What about criminal associations, drug gangs, gun imports, that sort of thing?'

'It's early days in our investigation, sir, but nothing like that has jumped out. Sullivan was in the property development business and may have crossed a colleague or competitor. I am keeping an open mind and checking all possibilities. We have a timeline for the hours before his death. There is strong evidence of careful planning. He was administered a drug to make him drowsy and driven by the killer to a quiet place and murdered. He may have been completely unaware of what was happening.'

'That will be of some comfort to the family, I imagine.' Connors scanned the report on his desk. 'And the killer substituted a vehicle for the regular limousine service? Have you followed that up? The phone number used to cancel the limousine?'

Pacer looked at his hands. He'd hoped his boss wouldn't pick that up. 'Yes, I followed up. Unfortunately, his regular limousine service had a computer outage and they lost relevant data.'

Connors stared at him. 'Lost the data? You can't be serious? Don't they back up these things?' His look said it was Pacer's fault.

'Normally, sir, yes. But not this time.'

Pacer knew how to work Connors – when he was agitated, he got distracted, and tended to agree quickly to requests when his mind was focused on something else. He shifted the discussion to the possibility of a witness at Café Bones, the homeless woman Sofia. 'We believe this woman was sleeping rough and might have been in the vicinity at the time the murder took place. She was there the day before the murder but left that night and has not returned since. There is a good chance she saw something or was seen by the perpetrators and ran away. It is important we find and question her. Sir, an additional detective would improve our chances of locating her before the trail goes cold.'

Sure enough, Connors gave him the second detective almost as a brush-off. He'd shifted back to Arko, wanting the evidence that linked him to the crime scene. Connors liked to present himself as a man who dealt in hard facts.

Pacer updated him on the forensics. 'We are closing in on Arko and were in active pursuit yesterday evening. Unfortunately, he evaded us this time.'

'For a second time, if my memory serves me well.' Connors gave Pacer a flinty look. 'An early arrest then, I expect?' He looked at his watch as if he had spent too much time already with Pacer. 'Well, get on with it.'

Edith gave Pacer a weak smile on his way out. She was stuck here, but he could leave.

CHAPTER 28

IN THE PRE-DAWN light, a shearwater glided on stiff wings metres above the sea. With a quick movement, it shifted trajectory, lifted and dived. Moments later it emerged, beak empty, wings trailing inky droplets and minute shards of plastic. It flapped its wings mid-air, gained height and flew away.

The ocean surface was carpeted with strands of rope, bottles, black sludge and the feathers of a drowned seagull. The mess bobbed this way and that but overall it was steadily moving south. As these things go, it was small, perhaps a few hundred square kilometres. It had formed when a part of the great gyre off the east coast of Australia was torn away after a cyclone moved further south than normal. Caught in a different current and with the assistance of a northeasterly, it was making its way towards land.

The leading edge of the mess was dense with discarded nets, buoys and logs felled in storms. Skeletons of marine animals, the by-catch of large trawlers and the unintended victims of ingested plastic mixed with fishing lines and styrofoam. Further back, the mess was less concentrated, objects visible just below the surface in a confetti-like array of microscopic particles.

The crew gathered near the bow of the trawler, eager to get busy after the journey out. The sea was smooth and the breeze light. An old hand looked to the nets, neatly coiled and ready to be winched over the side. The captain sat in his cabin adjusting the sonar, alert for concentrations of fish. They were nearing the sweet spot, the place where experience told him that the catch was most bountiful. He heard his son call. Something was wrong.

The captain stepped outside the cabin and looked to where his son was pointing. A low wall of debris was just visible in the dawn light, a few hundred metres away. He returned to the cabin and turned the wheel to the right so that they motored alongside, looking for an end to it, or a way through to the fishing. His son called out again. He'd seen something human, a body spread-eagled on its back, a mat of lines and rope binding it to the remnants of a breadfruit tree.

CHAPTER 29

FRIDAY ALREADY. SUN filtered through the voile curtain. The shafts of light reached further into the office now that autumn had arrived. Pacer leaned back, not ready to start working. His thoughts were elsewhere, on that same autumn day years before, when he'd farewelled Janet. A day like this when leaves turn to gold and the garden loses its lustre. Pacer cradled the empty teacup in both hands and sighed.

Reluctantly, he dragged his mind back to the present. Connors had come through on his promise of help in the search for the witness, Sofia. Who could be so out of favour? Whoever the unlucky detective was, they were in the incident room with Picone. Pacer stood and donned his jacket. His suit was rumpled and shiny in places. It looked tired, like he felt. He hated shopping, was virtually unable to do it without Janet, but it had to be done, sooner rather than later.

The corridor was lined with the offices of the Serious Homicides Squad. Some doors were closed, others ajar. Names were mounted in metal sliders, shiny or dull with the age and tenure of the occupant. Halfway along, Pacer passed the glassed entrance to the training rooms. He glanced through to a group of detectives relaxed in plastic chairs. At the front, a uniformed officer pointed to dense text on a PowerPoint display. Two in the audience leaned inwards, talking in low voices. Others lowered their eyes as they flicked the screens of their phones.

'Must be riveting stuff,' Pacer said under his breath.

Picone was waiting in the incident room, neatly turned out as always. His face was bright, expectant. The table was piled with reports, papers and photographs. Picone had cleared the whiteboard and put up a sketch of the crime scene. Pacer resisted the impulse to mention Miss Marple or Lincoln Rhyme. He stopped inside the door and faced the man sitting next to Picone.

'This is John Wainwright, sir,' said Picone. 'On loan from Sergeant Casey's unit.'

Everyone knew Casey's as the 'occo unit'. That's where officers removed from active duty went for the weeks, months or years it took to get over whatever it was that had got under their skin – the road fatalities, the broken marriages, the grog. You did light duties under the supervision of an occupational therapist before returning to your old job. Or that was the theory. Truth was, you got out after two or three months, or were stuck for the long haul.

Wainwright nodded a greeting. He was vaguely familiar, but Pacer couldn't place him. About the same age as himself. Looked like he'd been around the block a few times.

'Thanks for coming in,' Pacer said. 'We could do with some help. Has Stuart filled you in on the missing witness – Sofia? Going on what we know, she'll be sleeping rough or in a hostel.'

Wainwright shifted uncomfortably. His eyes slid away. It struck Pacer that Wainwright knew him too. The penny dropped. Years ago, Wainwright was lead on the team investigating child victims of sexual crimes. His cases were high profile – kids snatched from front yards or missing from public playgrounds. They'd had some success, or what passed for success, when a child was brought home to the parents, abused and traumatised by some paedo who'd slunk back into the sewers. There were others who didn't come home.

Wainwright looked up at Pacer. 'We've met before. The Poulos case.'

Pacer tried not to fall into the seat across the table. He waited until his heartbeat slowed to normal. 'I remember now. During the handover when that case was reclassified as a murder.' He hadn't spoken about it for years.

'I think of it now and then.' Wainwright's eyes seemed to have sunk into their sockets.

'Doesn't do any good though, does it.' Pacer couldn't go there, not now. He shuffled through the files and pulled out a thin folder. 'Sofia is our best lead in this case. We don't know much about her. From what she told others, she was married to a man who was violent towards her. Took her chance when he was at work and ran away, perhaps as recently as a few weeks ago. Her family lives overseas so she is unlikely to have anyone to go to. Not anyone she can trust. No indication she needs money to support a habit. Any thoughts on where to start looking?'

In Pacer's peripheral vision, Wainwright settled into a new position, trying to haul himself out of the past's black hole. It must be just as big a shock for him, being confronted like that, with no warning. Strange, too, to be with another man as deeply enmeshed in that dark history as he was. Strange, and oddly comforting to share it, to feel the same.

'Do you know that cafe in Ashfield – Manna House?' Wainwright asked.

Pacer did. Manna House was an institution. Drive by around lunch-time and you'd see a steady stream of humanity heading inside or over-flowing onto the footpath.

Wainwright was joining the dots on this new case, pushing the other away. 'It's not too far from Hawthorne Park. She's sure to know it. First place to check.' He tapped a pencil against a pad and jotted down notes while relating the patterns of homeless people in the Inner West and those who fed, housed and supported them. He knew the territory, that was clear.

'Where could she stay if she's not sleeping rough?'

'There's hostels for the overnights.' Wainwright's tone was more ani-mated as he covered familiar territory. 'Not enough though. Big ones are close to the CBD, but others are around. They open and shut on a regular basis. There used to be more women's refuges but a lot of them closed when the government was looking for ways to save money. I'll get to as many as I can but it might take some time.'

Pacer was happy to leave the planning to this man. He had a look about him. He'd keep going, the weekend and beyond – that's what he said. Pacer believed him. Finding a missing person fast mattered in his past life and mattered just as much now. Old mindsets. After time in the occo unit, no matter what else they told you, you were always trying to make up for past mistakes. Sofia wasn't a missing kid, but she was a witness and on her own. That made her vulnerable for a host of reasons. Criminal gangs dealt harshly with people like her.

Wainwright left soon after. Pacer was struggling to process a mix of feelings. What boiled to the surface was anger, directed at himself. He should have acted with more haste to find Sofia. It took Wainwright to remind him of the urgency. You never knew how critical time was. He had to get to her before someone made sure she didn't talk.

CHAPTER 30

PACER'S PHONE BUZZED. Picone sat back as Pacer reached inside his jacket. The caller was Rachel McQueen, a costume designer at the Canal Road Film Centre. 'You left your business card. Sorry, I've been away from the place for a few days. It's about that man who's been hanging around.'

'Thanks for calling back. Yes, I spoke to the security officer, Barry.'

'Well, I'm amazed he called it in. Barry's pretty laid-back. But anyway, we've seen him several times. Uses the storage area down the back for his entrances and exits. Don't know what he's up to, but he's bad karma.'

'You know his man?' Pacer asked.

'Sort of. Some of us used to work out of studios in Leichhardt. They sold the building and we had to move. This guy popped up saying he'd buy our equipment. Offered prices that were insulting. I think he was in with the developers. Nice on the outside but a real vulture.'

'Can you describe him?'

'Youngish, tall, fit, smooth manners. Calls himself Flynn. And he likes nice cars. One of the guys here saw him get into a Lexus at the top of Canal Road. A week or so ago.'

Pacer thanked her, put his phone away and turned to Picone, who was following the conversation.

'An intruder at the Canal Road Film Centre. Might be the same bloke who upset your Mrs Creed. We have a name. Flynn. Drives a Lexus. Try the database for car registrations.'

Picone was onto it before Pacer finished speaking.

'Bingo,' said Picone. 'Only one result.'

'Request a report. Let's see what it turns up.' Pacer looked at his watch. 'Time to get out and stretch our legs.' They grabbed their jackets and started down the corridor.

Metres along, the doors to the training rooms burst open and groups of officers spilled out, laughing and checking their phones. Pacer and Picone stood back to let them pass. One officer stopped short, staring at Pacer, his face hardening into a nasty smile.

'Hey, Pacer, how's your weekend shaping up? Gonna put a few dollars on the gee-gees?' He spoke loudly and looked around to make sure others had heard.

The conversations stopped. Pacer registered chuckles and snorts of derision. He had endured ugly moments like this, mostly in the early days. You hoped people would forget. Or just let it go. But there was always some feral bastard who couldn't resist sticking the boot in.

Picone looked at the faces and then back at Pacer, clearly puzzled. Time to put him in the picture, Pacer thought. Should have done it before.

'We need to talk over a few things,' Pacer said softly. The corridor was now empty, apart from themselves. 'A drink after work? I know a place in Jubilee Park.' They walked together in silence, then entered the lift.

CHAPTER 31

PACER HAD NOT been to Jubilee Park for years. The line of the bay was the same but was now fringed with young saplings. Moreton Bay figs, planted long ago on reclaimed sand flats, still graced the walkways. The little canal ending in a sandy beach was still there, along with native wetlands lining its perimeter. To the west, a scrubby rise marked the park's boundary.

On the east side, sandstone cliffs framed blocks of cream and grey apartments. Those golden walls were all that remained of the natural landscape before the land in front was gouged and flattened to make way for the racetrack and, later, the light rail terminal.

The apartments had replaced the Harold Park Paceway, on that site for more than a hundred years. As the city encroached, the race club relocated out west. The land was sold to a developer. Pacer admired the architecture: plain and understated. When they were built, the designers were applauded: the units were spacious and the buildings fit the landscape. But that was ten years ago. Something had changed. Now apartment blocks were popping up all over, invading green spaces and crowding close to roads and footpaths.

A raised railway viaduct, solid and imposing, stood opposite the bay on the south side. Once, the line had transported goods in a grand circuit past Sydney's wharves but had since been converted for commuter travel. Pacer had always admired the brick arches, curving in elegant sweeps to the parklands below. The undercroft spaces were once rented for commercial use. Theatre groups were housed there too, although few would remember. Janet had delighted in a performance of *A Midsummer's Night's Dream* here – an amateur performance, but the setting was perfect.

Alongside the railway arches on the east side, the train terminal had been repurposed for retail use, mostly bars and cafes, from what Pacer had heard. The Tram Sheds, that's what it was called now. He turned to Picone.

'Have you been here before?'

Picone hadn't. 'I live near Brighton. Plenty of open space and beaches to walk my dog.'

'You've got a dog?' Pacer wondered at his own surprise.

'Golden retriever. We go for a run every morning. This looks like a nice place for dogs. It's off-leash.' Picone pointed towards the open field in front of the railway viaduct where dogs were running free. 'The light rail's an easy way to get here.'

'Used to be a goods line,' Pacer said. 'Converted twenty years ago. It's the same line that goes through Hawthorne Park.' He shifted his gaze. 'See those blocks of apartments? I want to tell you about what used to be there. Come on, let's go to the Tram Sheds and grab a table.'

Harold Park Paceway used to be a lively place. Pacer had done stints there on Friday nights, representing the law. People, mostly men straight from work, coursed this way and that between the bookies' yard, the entry paddock, and the rails when the race was underway. Afterwards they surged to the bookies if they'd had a win, or to the bar if they hadn't.

When betting was in full swing, Pacer stayed close to the bookies on their stands, heads above the crowd, calculating the odds, the pencillers beside them, scribbling chits. At first he was content to observe, soaking up the roar of the crowd as their champions passed the winning post, horses, sulkies and drivers in a thunderous pack. Then his interest intensified. He placed the occasional bet.

'As a sergeant with constables in tow, I was there to maintain the peace,' he told Picone as they settled with their drinks. 'We would walk around the place and keep an eye on things. That's it. I was supposed to keep others out of trouble, not get into it myself. There was a mix of people at those meetings. All sorts. You got the boisterous types who were there to let off steam. Didn't cause trouble most of the time. Having a uniformed officer in plain sight was enough to keep them in line. Then there were the serious punters. Picking winners was a job to them.' Pacer could see the faces in his mind's eye. 'A few of the trainers got to know me and in no time I was invited up to the members' stand.'

'Good story.' Picone's eyes were glazing over.

Pacer regarded Picone thoughtfully. 'I'm not telling you this because it's a good yarn, or a good yarn for the jokers back at the station. You need to understand how easy it is to get caught up with people you should stay clear of. They act like your friend but their motive is to get you in trouble.'

'That's what happened to you?' Picone showed more interest.

Pacer had let his guard down. It started with the Miracle Mile, the racing calendar's biggest contest. It was one of the fastest Miracle Miles on record. Courage Under Fire was tipped to win but was caught in a tussle with Shakamaker at the back of the pack and ran out of steam. Holmes DG and Atitagain were locked together in a photo finish. Holmes DG got the nod and Atitagain's connections were not happy. They bailed up the stewards and demanded to see the photo. Pacer stepped in and the mood softened. Later, Atitagain's mob were up in the stand, sharing a drink and a laugh with the winning driver. Best mates again.

After that famous race, Pacer was hooked. He rubbed shoulders with leading trainers like Donny McPherson and Vic Frost. On first-name terms with past and present members of the Harness Racing committee. Enjoyed the company of the drivers, most of whom owned the horses they jockeyed. Pacer never tired of stories about hairy rides facing the breeze on the outside of the pack. Then there were the gofers placing bets with a favoured bookie, and the minders who retrieved the boss's car at the end of the meet. Pacer was on good terms with all of them.

'There were two regulars, not connected with the club, but keen punters. They won too often and too easily. Anyway, these blokes were friendly towards me, offered me drinks. Good-natured about it when I couldn't take up their offer, being on duty, and certainly not when in uniform. But I couldn't see harm in listening to their tips. I placed bets from time to time. I didn't make much but it was more than I lost.'

Picone looked away, uncomfortable. Pacer continued. 'Yes, stupid of me, I know.'

Next time the Miracle Mile came around, Pacer's duties had changed. Harold Park was no longer on his beat but he kept going anyway. Now off-duty and out of uniform, he accepted the drinks and bet on the horses his friends recommended. Smooth Satin won the Miracle Mile that year. He wasn't the favourite but he beat Courage Under Fire in a blistering finish. Thanks to a tip, Pacer placed fifty dollars with the bookies.

'So how did it end up?' Picone asked.

'Turns out the fraud squad were watching those guys the entire time. They were importing tobacco, drugs and other stuff. Betting was part of the money laundering. I was swept up in the mix when the police closed in. At first the detectives thought I was involved, but they soon worked out I was just too close to the wrong people.'

Pacer checked himself. Finish the story, get it over with. His demotion. His stupidity exposed for all to see, and never let him forget.

'Anyway, I was busted back to Constable. I was going to leave the force, but my wife convinced me to stay. She told me to get a backbone, accept the punishment and work my way back.' Janet had certainly made her feelings plain. But beneath her angry words, Pacer knew she was as disappointed in him as he was in himself. She'd lived long enough to see him back to his old rank. He was glad about that.

'Pacers, that's what they call the horses, isn't it, sir? Is that how you got your name?'

'That's right, most of the harness racers are pacers – it's due to their gait. My problem was public, everyone knew. Someone at the station called me "Pacer" and the name stuck.' Like a stain he couldn't rub off. 'I've got used to it though. Look, you should call me Pacer too, drop the "sir" away from the station or when no one else is around. Okay?'

Pacer felt a vibration and reached into his jacket. 'Wonder who's calling this late on a Friday afternoon?' He looked from the screen to Picone. 'It's the Coroner's Office. Rhys Parkinson.'

CHAPTER 32

'A FLOATER CAME IN early today. Fished from the water by a trawler crew. About thirty kilometres out. Male, not identified as yet. Sam Wu did the triage, asked me to phone you.' Rhys Parkinson delivered his message in flat tones, not about to acknowledge his earlier failure to communicate with Pacer about Sullivan.

'I don't have jurisdiction over bodies found in the water,' Pacer said, equally deadpan. Someone had raised it. Sam Wu? Sure, Parkinson had an excuse that last time, but why not a quick phone call? He could have done that from anywhere.

'It's the condition of the body. Sam thought of you straight away. It was badly chewed in places, but he noticed a cut to the man's back. Put a probe in and found a deep wound. He thinks it penetrated the heart.'

'Just like our victim from Hawthorne Park?' Pacer's attention snapped back to the present.

'Right down to the location of the external wound between the ribs.'

'The wound was the cause of death, was it? Not inflicted after?'

'Sam thinks so. The autopsy will be done at Lidcombe. There's a backlog; could be weeks.'

'How long was he in the water?'

'Less than forty-eight hours, according to Sam.'

'Description? Any distinguishing marks?' Pacer paused, conjuring up the grainy photo from Arko's drivers licence. 'Is there a scar on his left eyebrow?' Pacer was expectant, filled with dread, while Parkinson scrolled the photos.

'You're kidding!' Surprise burst through Parkinson's wall of blankness. 'There is a facial scar, runs from the left eyebrow to the temple.

Lucky it's still visible. Something bit into his nose and ear. A small shark, maybe. How could you know about the scar?'

'My suspect for the Hawthorne Park murder has fallen off the radar. He has a scar like that. Name of Arko. You'll have his prints and DNA on file there.' Pacer's heart sank. They'd just missed him. Twice. Now it was too late.

'Prints are no use. The crabs had a good nibble.'

'Thanks for letting me know,' Pacer said, with a hint of sarcasm.

'It's Arko then?' Picone asked after Pacer completed the call.

Pacer felt sure it was. The tests would confirm it.

'Our murderer has attacked again. Must have happened just after we pursued him on that bus.' This hurt. Pacer's chest constricted. 'He was heading towards the bay, remember? I think someone picked him up and took him out to sea.'

The evening was beginning to settle over Rozelle Bay, the lights twinkling on the Anzac Bridge. Pacer imagined Arko's friendless journey. From the bay near Hawthorne Park, past the islands dotting the inner harbour, under the Sydney Harbour Bridge, around the Opera House, through Port Jackson to the tip of Watsons Bay. And the open sea beyond. Was he dead already or had they killed him out there?

A chill ran down Pacer's spine. They would stop at nothing to eliminate a threat. He turned his mind to that other person on the run. He would call Wainwright, raise the urgency. Sofia had to be found and made safe.

CHAPTER 33

FLYNN DIDN'T LIKE it when a connection was late. Anything not exactly to plan made him nervous. He told himself to get a grip. Five or ten minutes in Friday evening traffic was nothing out of the ordinary. He had chosen a cafe in an arcade away from Norton Street. Privacy mattered.

The sun had dropped behind the terraces on the other side of the street. The lights of the cafes and shops were starting to glow. It was warm, balmy even, for the time of year. Flynn winced as his injured leg brushed the table. He reached down to smooth the plaster that covered the wound. The blood was no longer seeping through.

He wondered what this meeting was for. Their earlier conversation was circumspect. Some things couldn't be discussed on the phone. He glanced at his watch again. Only two minutes had passed.

Flynn's connection slipped silently into the chair opposite, looking around nervously. The new arrival's dark hair was thinning on top, and he was not as tall or athletic as Flynn. He was neatly dressed in a suit, looked at home in it, in fact. Flynn preferred clothes you could move in.

'So why did you phone me?' Flynn asked. 'We agreed to keep our distance, so this better be good.'

'They've got a witness.' The reply was stark, shocking.

'You've got to be kidding me.' Flynn tried to keep his voice level but the constriction in his throat made this impossible. This job was turning into a nightmare. He gulped his coffee. 'Who? Who could they possibly have?'

'A vagrant hanging around the cafe. A woman by the name of Sofia. On the run from a husband who kicks her around.' He paused as a waiter approached and took his order. Flynn drained his cup and asked for another.

'Are you sure? Maybe a line from someone after the boss's attention?' Plenty like that in this business. Small fry, wanting in.

'I'm sure. It's the talk around Café Bones. I've been there, keeping an eye on things. This Sofia was there for sure; there's police tape behind the building where she stayed. And I overheard plenty.'

'Should we get over there, take a look?' Flynn knew it was pointless but he had to do something, anything, to stop this mess from escalating any further.

'Look, mate, I'm telling you this as a favour. I have a legit reason for going there, but even so, I didn't want to look too interested. From now on I'm keeping my head down.'

Flynn didn't conceal his anger. 'Don't get smart with your "favours". You're up to your neck in this, and if I need information, you're going to get it. Sure, keep your head down, but don't keep me in the dark.'

'Steady, mate, no offence. I'm just saying I don't want to draw attention to myself and you shouldn't either. I'll let you know if I hear anything else.'

'You better. The business is good to you. They don't like it when their mates go to water.' Flynn gave the other man a withering look. 'Have you told anyone else?'

'No, just you. I figured you needed to know.'

'No point upsetting anyone else. You understand that?' Flynn felt the panic rising. Malcolm couldn't know. It was already bad enough. A witness risked everything. 'Tell no one else. You with me on that?'

'Sure, of course.'

Flynn tried to clear his mind. 'So it's just one vagrant? A scared woman? I'll handle it.'

'You'll have to find her first, before the cops.'

'Easy. They don't call them "plods" for nothing.' Flynn drained his second cup as his companion stepped away. Greasy as they come, he thought, before focusing again on what to do about Sofia, this new threat.

CHAPTER 34

THE PEOPLE FROM the charity kitchen in Newtown had told Sofia about the refuge where she now stayed. They were friendly, talking to her as if she mattered, a woman new to this life. One charity worker, Peta, had said to wait, then drove her here. But late one night a man came shouting and banging on the door, demanding his wife. Sofia's fears welled. An angry husband, with fists like hammers. She hadn't seen the man's face, but pictured that of her own husband, his pleasant features morphing into hate-filled planes as hard as iron, eyes on fire. He'd hurt her, at first an open-handed slap or shove, then later, solid blows to her body and face. She'd waited in terror each time his car came to a shuddering halt outside the kitchen window, her breathing shallow, desperate to know his mood.

One night a neighbour called the police, Sofia's husband passed out from the drink. An ambulance came and took her away. 'Lay charges,' they told her. 'The only way to make him stop.' It wouldn't, didn't they know that? Sofia wanted to leave, but he said he would find her. After that, he locked her in, took her to the supermarket, watched her every move. The constant terror was too much. One day, heart beating wildly, she squeezed through a tiny window and walked away.

After the late-night disturbance, Sofia left the refuge with nothing but her small backpack, determined not to go back. For days she slept in railway sheds or inside front fences of suburban yards, always on her way by first light. Eventually she found that place behind the cafe in the park. It felt safe to start with, but that didn't work out either. Sofia shuddered at the thought of what she'd seen. There was no option but to go back to the refuge. A good place, but a compromise.

Sofia lay still as the other women gathered their belongings into bags and zippered packs. After they'd gone, she rose and started her morning rituals. In the dining area most of the overnighters were seated with their plates of cereal, toast and the day's hot breakfast. One of the staff smiled kindly at Sofia and indicated a vacant seat. The food was good; it warmed her. They had to be out by 8.30am but the people who ran the place made sure the women began the day with a solid meal. The room began to empty.

Sofia had a plan for the day and intended to make it back that night. You had to be there in good time. There was no guarantee of a bed and plenty like her were turned away. She slung her backpack over her shoulder and headed west. Her route passed by rows of narrow terraces with paved yards, green garbage bins, pots of weedy plants and bicycles chained to railings. This was the way to the university, but her destination was elsewhere. She turned left, walked down a slope and onto the railway platform.

Macdonaldtown Station. The platform was deserted. Sofia passed metal posts topped with coloured discs. You were meant to press your plastic pass against it but Sofia didn't have one. Her friends had told her not to worry. You were rarely asked, and if you looked at the railway people in a funny way they just walked on. 'Transport officers', that's what they were called. Garry and Alice had shown Sofia the expressions they bunged on when someone looked at them suspiciously. Then they burst into laughter, Sofia joining in.

Sofia had met Alice at the refuge the first day she went there. Alice was friendly, full of life and funny stories. That first morning after breakfast she looped her arm through Sofia's and led her to a nearby park where Garry was waiting. Garry was Alice's boyfriend but had stayed in the men's refuge down the road. They greeted each other and hugged warmly, as if one night apart was too much. It was for Alice, she told Sofia later. Her stepfather didn't like Garry, didn't like Alice either, then he kicked both of them out. Alice didn't say more, but Sofia could tell things at home were bad. They walked together to the train station, Alice filling Sofia's mind with tricks and ruses to get by, Garry smiling beside her.

The train slid alongside the platform. Sofia jumped into the end carriage. As usual it was nearly empty after the morning rush. She preferred to stay close to the exit and hang on tight, even though the ride was smooth. Slipping into a seat near the inner carriage doors, Sofia folded her arm around the metal pole. Trees, houses and railway pylons flew by as the train picked up speed. The day was sunny and the sky cloudless, but the sway of the trees meant a westerly breeze and colder weather was on its way. Sofia wished she'd brought warmer things but there was no time. She'd taken her chance and run.

The train was an all-stations to the city's far reaches. Sofia's destination was much closer. Summer Hill was another station where you rarely saw railway people. The woman who worked there was at the end of the platform, sweeping and keeping things tidy. She couldn't care less if you paid or not. Most people who got off didn't bother with the coloured disc, even if they had a pass.

Summer Hill was a sleepy place. There were plenty of people like Sofia who didn't have a regular home. They slept on park benches or lived in boarding houses. Garry and Alice had shown her a park at the back of the supermarket. It was a good place to hang out when you had to time to kill. The park was shady and ringed by a path. A tennis court and children's playground stood on one side and there was a community centre on the other. There were several exits, which was to Sofia's liking. Better than a house with front and back doors, both locked.

Today a man was sitting under the trees, quietly smoking. Sofia recognised him from the cafe. Waiting, like her, for the right time. Up near the road a woman moved rhythmically to a scratchy recording of Chinese music. Sofia liked the sound, with its melodic and lighthearted tones. She wondered how far that woman had travelled to get to Australia and by what method. Maybe she was homeless too, but Sofia didn't think so. She didn't have that watchful look, ready to run if her husband spotted her.

Sofia thought of her home in Sicily, a sleepy village in the hilltops far from Palermo. Her family wasn't rich, but they had land, livestock and a beautiful orchard, more than enough for their needs. Others had far less. One day a young man appeared, the son of her father's friend. He seemed nice with a kind smile and courteous manner, in need of a wife for his new homeland. Things progressed quickly and arrangements were made. Sofia's sister said not to go, but Sofia turned away, the allure of a new life too intoxicating. How she wished she had listened.

Judging the time to be right, Sofia rose, passed the dancing woman and chose the footpath in the direction of Ashfield. Alice had said, 'Don't be a target – move with a firm step, stay away from recesses and always look like you know where you're going.' And Sofia did, but always watchful, the fear never far away.

The man in the park left before she did but there he was, up ahead, going to the same place, Manna House. Sofia arrived, a little breathless from her exertions. Jostling her way through the crowded doorway, she found a seat with some others she knew. The meal was simple but hearty fare. The vegetable soup reminded her of her homeland with its rich market gardens, but the things she had loved as a young girl weren't served at Manna House. Too expensive, she supposed. Here, olives and peaches and gooseberries didn't fall off trees like they did where she came from. Sofia's musing was interrupted when her new friend, Justine, came out from the kitchen. About the same age as Sofia, Justine was holding a pastry made especially for her, warm, flaky and lemony inside. Sofia felt a surge of delight and accepted it gratefully. She closed her eyes as she bit into it, images of her mother's kitchen flooding in. She chatted for a minute or so before her friend had to go.

After the meal, the man in charge approached Sofia. The people who came here liked Chris. He understood without having to be told. He was not after something, like most men. Chris dropped his voice. 'A man called by yesterday, asking if I had seen someone like you.'

Sofia drew back in alarm.

'No, it wasn't your husband. Said he was a police detective and needed to talk.'

Chris waited until Sofia's breathing settled, before continuing. 'I am here to help. If you need me to go with you to the police station to sort something out, I will.'

'Did you tell him about me?'

'Of course not. I said I hadn't seen you.'

'No. No police,' she replied. Her voice quavered as she clutched her backpack and glanced at the exit.

CHAPTER 35

'MR FLYNN, JUSTINE here.' Flynn reached out and closed the door to his den. He registered the gravelly voice, a smoker's, and searched his memory.

'Justine. You know me from way back. I'm a chef at Manna House now.'

'Oh, yes. Justine.' Flynn remembered. A small, wiry woman, crafty and quick. They'd got on fine but had lost contact after he'd got out of the supply business. Now she was at that place in Ashfield some church bloke had set up for vagrants. 'What have you got?'

'Word got around you were looking for a woman, young, new to sleeping rough.' Justine paused, waiting for encouragement.

'If you've got something,' Flynn said, 'I'll make it right for you.'

Justine was reliable, trustworthy. He'd pay her, but at arm's length. That's how it worked. The publican at the Arms off Parramatta Road was a useful go-between.

'Saw a bloke come in yesterday afternoon, asked to see Chris, the boss here. This bloke was sniffing around, looking the customers up and down. Older bloke, looked like a copper. Didn't stay long.' Justine stopped, her breathing audible.

'So what's that to me?'

'There's more. After lunch today, Chris went over to a woman, one of the new ones, and had a little chat. I only caught a few words. She sounded scared. I reckon she was the one the copper was after.'

'This is good, Justine. What else have you got?'

Justine, badly raised and poorly educated, got by on her wits. She didn't miss much. She gave Flynn a detailed description. 'Her name's Sofia.'

Flynn didn't disguise his satisfaction. 'Okay. Keep an eye out. Soon as she comes in again, give me a call. I mean immediately she turns up. Immediately.'

'That's extra work for me, you know?'

'No problem, Justine. Go to the Arms on Parramatta Road. There'll be something for you.'

Flynn smiled to himself. He stepped over to the cabinet where he kept his drinks and poured a large dram. He rolled the peaty liquid around in his mouth, savouring the robust flavours. Something was finally going his way.

CHAPTER 36

PACER UNROLLED THE Sunday paper and spread the pages across the table on his back porch. It was a nice day, sunny and warm. A bit of summer still left. He could sit around with little to occupy him or take Anna's suggestion. The dogs at training might be amusing and the fresh air would do him good.

'Truth is, you don't like your own company,' he said aloud.

By the time he'd arrived at Hawthorne Park, the training class was underway. Play equipment was spread across the park, dog-sized jumps, a tunnel like an oversized concertina and a miniature seesaw. An onlooker said today was agility training for dogs in the advanced class. A golden-haired dog with a square, curly-haired face sat facing a row of jumps. His owner moved away and signalled with her hand. 'Archie, over.' The dog raced forward, the owner running alongside. 'Tunnel.' Archie was through and out the other side. 'Over.' Archie spotted a Aussie shepherd chasing a ball, changed direction mid-stride and tore off in pursuit. 'Archie, come back,' the owner yelled. Pacer chuckled as she took off after him.

Other dogs lined up for their turn. A black standard poodle made its way around the course in leisurely fashion, his handler gasping for air at the finish. A white poodle with an excitable nature followed. She was spooked by the tunnel but was enticed through with the offer of a treat. A pug with a serious countenance did a sterling job until the penultimate obstacle, when he dropped down for a rest.

Pacer watched as Anna Overton emerged from under the trees and lined up with Hugo. The dog was not one to be rushed. He looked around, as if to see who was noticing. Bloody little showoff, thought Pacer. Hugo

101

moved off slowly, shifted up to a saunter midway and finished at a trot. He did a little pirouette as Anna congratulated him loudly and reached into her bag for a treat. Pacer recognised the two little schnauzers. Charlie, the older one, sailed over the jumps, tore through the tunnel, attacked the seesaw and finished a perfect round. The other, Jess, looked keen and started well. A labrador, unattended by its owner, left the path and raced through the middle of the course, overturning a water bucket. Several dogs, including Jess, joined in the melee.

Pacer was still laughing when he joined Anna and Alison with the schnauzers. 'That was entertaining. I'm glad I came.' He helped them gather the equipment and return it to the clubroom.

Pacer walked over to where the white tent had stood. It was gone now. Instead, thick orange plastic covered the ruined foundations. The police perimeter had been replaced by temporary fencing with no way in. The area looked unremarkable. If you weren't in the know, you'd never guess.

The schnauzers followed Pacer and stood rigid. They seemed to pick up a scent. Then, as one, they dashed to the fence and scrambled through a gap at the bottom, followed by Hugo. Alison rushed after, calling their names. Nothing. She leaned against the corrugated iron and pushed through an aperture.

Anna frowned. 'Something has got them into that state. I'm going in – Alison might need help.' Pacer sighed, then followed. This was the fence where Tino, similar in girth to Pacer, had torn his uniform. Pacer moved carefully to avoid snagging his jacket and stepped into the yard beyond. What was this? The area was a shambles. Junk everywhere.

Anna picked Hugo up as Alison clipped a leash to Jess's collar. She pointed to a wooden pallet next to piled-up containers. 'When I came through, they were pawing at something under there. A protein bar.' She showed the wrapper, sticky and torn. 'Jess worked it free just as I caught up, then took off with it. Could have been poisoned.'

'They came in after the food?' Pacer asked Alison.

'More likely the person who put it there. The food was a bonus. From what I saw, they picked up a scent on the other side of the fence and followed it here. Smells linger for dogs, sometimes for weeks.'

Pacer looked down. A substance adhered to the pallet. It looked like blood, dried and darkened. Why hadn't Picone seen it? Easy enough to miss, Pacer supposed. Or maybe someone had been here since. A ladder stood against the containers. He grasped the metal and climbed to where a pile of sandbags concealed a small nook with a view over the Sullivan gravesite. Bloodstains on the sandbags. Yes, someone had been up here.

Back in the park, Pacer approached the cafe. The space between the wall and the fence extended the length of the building. The building site was visible from there. Was Sofia looking that night? If so, had she been observed?

Pacer's mind raced. Arko, a witness, murdered. Sofia, a witness, on the run. He had to assume the killers knew about her already, or would know, sooner rather than later. His temple throbbed. Time was running out. He phoned Wainwright. No sighting of Sofia. Wainwright had walked miles across the city, calling into hostels and talking to the people who ran them.

'Spoke to the bloke who runs Manna House, Chris Neville. Says he can't recall anyone fitting Sofia's description.'

'Was he being straight with you? From what I hear, just about everyone sleeping rough ends up there.'

'Yeah, I see where you're coming from. I'm sceptical myself. Had the feeling he was holding back. Can't blame him. He doesn't know why I'm asking questions. Most of the people he takes in have no reason to trust the authorities. Won't say, even if he knows.'

'The sooner we locate her, the better. Seriously.'

'It's okay, Pacer. I'm here to find this Sofia, and that's what I'll do. There are only so many places she can be. I'll get a lead and narrow it down.'

Pacer wanted her found. Quick smart. It wasn't just for the information she might have. 'Where are you?' he whispered.

'Come again?'

'Sorry. Got to stop thinking aloud, it's becoming a habit.'

'No need to apologise.' Wainwright's voice was thick. 'You're not the only one.'

CHAPTER 37

PACER'S SLEEP THAT night was disturbed by images of playgrounds and children on swings, hands clutching chains, eyes fear-tinged, their bodies arched away from the ground far below. And the grown people, unknowing, facing away.

He poured his first cup of the day and gazed at the mist over the garden. He would never shake the memories of those crimes, the child victims, no matter how fervently he wished he could. It would be worse for John Wainwright. His was the moment a child went missing, desperately searching against the clock, anxiety clawing at him. Most came home, relief papering over the dread. But not all. The worst of them, the Poulos child, would have burrowed deep under his skull with no way out.

It was Pacer's case too, his job to nail the bastard, get him off the streets. Bring the little girl's things home to the parents. He hadn't done any of those. Too slow, too easily distracted by leads that went nowhere, always a step behind. Not finding the critical evidence. In the end, Pacer couldn't make his case. It remained a bitter defeat.

As a detective he lacked something. His success in solving crimes was better than most. He didn't deny it. But it wasn't enough. Each failure gnawed at him, even a glimpse of it, exposing the lie of the closures and convictions. He looked down at the teacup in his hands. What would Janet say? 'You can't stop all of them, no one can.' But she wasn't here, so that was that.

Pacer arrived at his office building before the morning peak. He was alone in the foyer and had the lift to himself. A let-up after Friday's encounter. He warmed his hands around his second cup of the day and watched the beams of light flicker onto the files stacked neatly on his desk.

Pacer's call took Miranda De Veen away from her microscope. She listened as he gave her the latest from Hawthorne Park. 'The film people have noticed a fellow in a Lexus called Flynn lurking around. The energy bar, the blood, you never know. Might be nothing, but my gut tells me it's worth following up.'

'I'll be there this afternoon. Look around and take some samples. If this man, Flynn, is connected to the murder, a squirt of blood might tie him to the scene. Nice change from lifting prints.'

'Thought you'd like this job. A bit different from your usual.' Pacer dropped the landline into its cradle. Call-outs to an endless string of suburban burglaries were the stock-in-trade of crime scene detectives. It was laborious work and rarely paid off. More often than not, the same criminals were picked up, sent before a magistrate and hauled off to Silverwater for another round of failed rehabilitation. Pacer shrugged. It could wear you down if you let it. He'd come close but something deep down always clicked in. His dogged persistence? His loathing of hardened criminals? Both were there, but something else was more crucial. Janet knew. She said he wanted to rescue the families from any more pain. The thought brought his mind back to the present. Get onto it or risk another life. He opened his laptop.

The report on Flynn was in Pacer's inbox. He scanned the itemised contents. Not for the first time he was amazed at how much material was available. This was just stuff skimmed from the surface. He could get more if he wanted it – bank records, detailed tax information, census data, a full medical history from that new government health record. What a goldmine that was going to be.

What he had now was enough. Date of birth, present and past addresses, drivers licence, as well as memberships and photos. No business clubs though. Belonged to a running group that raced half-marathons and used a private Facebook page. Easy to crack. Flynn had been overseas several times for runs. Los Angeles, Singapore, Mexico City. A photo of him holding a minor place ribbon and looking cocky. More of him celebrating with his running mates. Educated at a nondescript state school followed by a couple of years at university. Didn't stay long enough to earn a degree. Married, no kids apparently. Changed his car every two or three years and currently owned a white Lexus. He'd run up speeding tickets tearing through school zones, but never accumulated enough to lose his licence.

A police report grabbed Pacer's attention. Flynn had, at one time, been under suspicion for involvement in the illegal import of cocaine. Border

Force ran surveillance when packages were detected in the hold of a cargo vessel from Guatemala. They couldn't figure out where the exchange would be made so they played it safe and raided the vessel before it docked. A few people, including Flynn, were brought in and questioned. He refused to answer, threatening legal action. The authorities had nothing solid, so they let him walk. And that's where it ended.

Flynn's place of business was the same as his home address. He gave his occupation as 'business consultant'. That could mean anything. What was this bloke really up to? Nice house, nice car and the whiff of a past. He had moved on, but to what?

With Picone behind the wheel, Pacer took in the leafy streets of Annandale and then the shabbier suburb of Leichhardt. The roads narrowed, the trees were fewer and the houses smaller. On Norton Street they slowed to dodge people stepping into the road, oblivious to the traffic and the pedestrian crossing metres away. Pacer grunted his irritation.

At the far reaches of Leichhardt the streetscape changed. Trees graced the verges and the blocks were larger. The peeling paint and lopsided gates of a few streets back gave way to modern colour finishes and modular extensions. Picone parked behind a white Lexus outside a grey and white timber-framed house. Pacer sat silent, watching. Broad windows fronted the street, curtains pulled back. Inside, a tall man paced the length of a large room, unaware of the eyes looking his way. His fair hair was cut close, the face set in a frown, a hand rubbing at the forehead.

'A worried man,' Pacer said. 'Remember what I told you. We handle this diplomatically. We have nothing on Flynn – he doesn't have to speak to us if he doesn't want to.'

CHAPTER 38

FLYNN WAS IN his living room, deep in thought, when the doorbell rang. He wasn't expecting anyone. The peephole revealed two men in suits. He slammed the door on salesmen and religious types but something told him this pair weren't of that ilk. They introduced themselves as police detectives. Flynn saw a shopworn sergeant and a constable who looked young and green.

Flynn did the smart thing and invited them inside. He stepped back. Not quick enough though. The older detective brushed his shoulder as he strode in. Flynn felt the jolt and looked into hard grey eyes. The two men settled themselves onto his wide sofa, facing the door.

Flynn dropped into a soft one-seater, a little off-balance. He tried to look relaxed but his stomach churned. He hoped it didn't show. You're supposed to be nervous when cops come around. He figured he was handling it right.

'I hope there hasn't been an accident. My wife, Sandra ...?'

'No, sir, nothing like that,' the sergeant said. 'We are investigating a crime in Hawthorne Park, a murder. Speaking to people who might have been in the area.'

'I don't understand why you want to speak with me.'

'We have reason to believe you may have visited the park recently.'

'Maybe I have, but hundreds of people use that park every day. Are you going to question all of them? And yes, I saw about the murder on the news, but I don't know anything that could be of use to you.' A voice inside told Flynn to watch himself. Sandra said he sounded prickly when nervous.

'Even a small observation, anything out of the ordinary, could be relevant.'

'I work out at a gym that's close to that park. Go for a run afterwards, sometimes. I use the track around the bay or head through Hawthorne Park.' Flynn felt better, on safer ground.

'Have you noticed a small building under construction? Near Café Bones?' the younger detective asked.

'Maybe. Buildings are going up all over the place. One more is nothing to me. But yes, I recall running past.' No harm giving them that much.

'Are you familiar with the film centre next to the park?' the older one asked, again fixing Flynn with those hard grey eyes.

'I know it's there, but that's about all.' He was speaking too quickly. Slow down, he told himself.

'Could you have visited that place, included it in your run, perhaps?'

'Not that I recall.' Where was this heading? Flynn figured they were trying to trap him. Well, that wasn't going to happen. The adrenalin coursed through his body and his ankle began to throb. He resisted the impulse to rub it. 'Is that all?'

'That film centre is on private land.'

'So that's what this is about. You want to arrest me for trespassing.' He held his wrists out to receive imaginary cuffs. 'But I wasn't there so you've got the wrong man.' Flynn's attempt to act amused hadn't come off. They just looked back at him appraisingly.

'Well, that will be all. Thank you for your time, Mr Flynn,' said the sergeant, rising slowly.

Flynn watched from the living room. They sat in a car out front, making notes. They took their time. It occurred to him they knew he was watching and were doing it for show.

CHAPTER 39

CONNORS WAS STANDING in front of his desk when Pacer walked in. No offer of a chair this time. Connors swung around, legs spread as if for a duel, his right fist clamped inside his left.

'Well, Sergeant, you've lost your man, Arko.'

Pacer stood immobile, waiting for the dressing-down. Connors shifted his hands behind his back, lifted his chin, breathed deeply and started in with a long diatribe. When he'd spent himself, he said, 'Where does that leave your investigation?'

'I admit that losing a prime suspect is a setback,' Pacer said evenly, 'but it underscores what I have considered to be the situation for some time. We are dealing with a criminal syndicate that is highly organised and cold-blooded. They have eliminated Arko because he could expose them.'

'A convenient explanation, Sergeant?'

'An accurate one, in my view. Organised, but they have made mistakes. Neither victim was intended to surface.'

'One of your little jokes?'

Pacer refused to bite. 'I have a request, sir, to aid the investigation. The discovery of Arko's body – I prefer it's kept under wraps. The perpetrators will try to cover their tracks if they find out.'

'We can hardly keep this from his family.'

'The coroner is looking for the next of kin. There appears to be no one close.'

'Very well. I'll see to it.' Connors paused to make a note. 'When a relative is located, the matter will be dealt with quietly. How do you intend to proceed?'

'In my estimation the murder of Sullivan was business-related rather than personal. I am following that angle.'

'Your reasons?'

'Sullivan was liked by his friends. They stayed loyal, despite his faults. In business he was competitive and might have betrayed the trust of his partners. I am looking for instances of that.'

'You've checked for any criminal associations, I presume?'

'He has no criminal record and he's not on the radar of the major crime squads. A cleanskin.'

'And that witness at Hawthorne Park? Do you have a statement?'

'Sergeant Wainwright is searching for her. It's just a matter of time.'

'How difficult can it be?' Connors reddened. 'Don't come back here tomorrow and tell me you've lost another one. I want her found and this case wrapped up before you cause us further embarrassment.'

Pacer grimaced at Edith on the way out. It troubled him that she was exposed to conversations like this, Connors's voice pitching higher as his agitation grew. Edith responded with a crooked smile and a slight shrug, as if she heard worse than this every day.

CHAPTER 40

JOHN WAINWRIGHT RARELY slept well. He rose early and was on his way before seven. An overnight shower had left the footpath greasy and the morning air was crisp. He pulled his jacket in closer and stepped up to the railway platform. A breeze swirled leaves around his feet.

At Central he left via the tunnels on the south side. Devonshire Street, a bustling hub at this time of day, and until recently a construction zone for the light rail. Old bits of orange webbing still fluttered about, as commuters rushed towards the station entrance. None of the commuters appeared to notice the detective as he walked in the other direction towards Crown Street.

During his previous visits, Wainwright had checked the hostels and refuges in the little streets and old warehouses beyond Crown Street. His enquiries at several had been fruitless. 'It's policy,' he was told. 'People come for shelter and safety. We don't ask for names and when they give them freely, we don't pass them on. Sorry.'

Sorry, thought Wainwright. Always sorry. If only people were willing to share what they knew. He could return to the hostels, watch people leave and hope that Sofia was among them. No point, he told himself. He'd tried that for several mornings. No sign of Sofia, but he had learned what her day might entail. Some leaving the hostels headed east towards Moore and Centennial parks. Others went in the other direction, skirting around Waterloo and the bottom end of Sydney University to Macdonaldtown Station. From there they made their way to parks dotting the Inner West. Most ended up at Manna House.

Today he'd try a different strategy. Wainwright continued down Devonshire Street until Prince Alfred Park opened on the right. It was a

111

pleasant oasis, with good shading, flowerbeds and seating. He'd been here the day before, getting to know its habitual visitors. Wainwright spotted one of his new mates on a bench over the far side, a homeless bloke named Cliff. The man's beard was scraggy and a blue beanie covered his greying hair. He was wearing the same corduroy pants and sports jacket as before but had a different plaid shirt. His riding boots were worn but substantial enough. He looked to be in his sixties but was probably twenty years younger. He'd shared his life story with Wainwright when they'd met yesterday. This man's life had fallen apart ten years ago when he lost his job and couldn't hang on to the mortgage. Or his marriage.

Wainwright patted his pockets and felt the small packages. The man on the bench looked his way and grinned broadly. This was a good sign – he had something to offer.

'Morning, Cliff. Cold enough for you?' They sat in companionable silence for a minute or two, sharing the park surrounds and the people hurrying by, necks drawn into thick jackets and hands in coat pockets.

'I did what you wanted,' Cliff said. 'Talked to people heading back to their dorms. They come and they go; you know the regulars.' Cliff licked his lips as Wainwright withdrew a small package from his inside pocket.

'Got you a packet of smokes. Want to show my appreciation.' With the exchange made, Cliff cleared his throat.

'Found out something might interest you. Friends of mine saw a woman like the one you described. At one of the women's hostels the other day. Not for the last few nights though. Got any more smokes? Want to pass them around, a little thankyou for my observant friends.' Wainwright reached into his other pocket and handed over another box.

'You're a nice bloke, John, thanks.' They shared the silence. Wainwright stayed put, waiting.

'I might have something else for you,' Cliff said. The detective nodded his interest. 'A woman I know shared a room with your Sofia. Said she's linked up with a couple of others, young like herself and new to the streets. A girl called Alice. Don't know the bloke's name because he couldn't stay there – it's only for women. Anyway, my friend heard Sofia and Alice talking at breakfast. Planning to go to a camp with a mob in Glebe. That way Alice gets to be with her boyfriend instead of splitting up every night. They asked Sofia to go with them.'

'So you think she might have done that?'

'Wouldn't be surprised if she did.'

'Did your friend say where the camp is, exactly?'

Cliff's eyes darted to Wainwright's pockets, then back to his face.

CHAPTER 41

'MR FLYNN, IT'S me again.' This time Flynn recognised the voice immediately. 'You told me to phone as soon as she came in.'

'That's right, Justine. She's been there how long?'

'Maybe ten minutes. It was a while before I could sneak out the back and get my phone.'

'Well, hang on to it now. Keep an eye on her and call me as soon as she makes a move. I'll be watching from opposite the main entrance. Identify her, then get back inside and act as if nothing's happened. You got that?' Flynn was already reaching for his keys and wallet.

He gunned his Lexus and set off with a squeal. At the first corner he slowed down, reminding himself to play it cool. It wasn't easy. He had woken that morning in a sweat after a restless night replaying his conversation with those detectives. His ankle was angrier and throbbing badly. Fortunately, Sandra had slept in the spare room after a late night out with her friends. She would have nagged him about getting it seen to. Well, he would do that soon enough. But first he'd take care of this other matter.

Flynn parked outside a dental surgery opposite Manna House. Old church buildings had been converted into this cafeteria and day centre decades earlier. Heavy pine trees towered above as men and women milled about. Singly and in pairs they filed through the heavy doors. His ankle was killing him. He swallowed some painkillers, fiddled with his radio and glanced at the time. How long did it take for vagrants to knock back a cup of barley soup and an apple?

Justine was true to her word. Flynn glimpsed her near the doorway, but his gaze was riveted on the dark-haired young woman in the green dress on the footpath. She was slightly built, an easy mark. But she wasn't alone. On one side was another young woman, tall and willowy. Wearing a bright dress and matching headscarf over her long blond hair, she chatted excitedly and smiled at Sofia. A slightly shorter man in denim jeans and bomber jacket nodded and grinned. Flynn would have to contend with all three. That was a nuisance, or was it? Sofia's attention would be on her companions. Easier to follow. He'd be patient and wait to get her on her own.

The trio set off in the direction of Summer Hill. Reluctantly, Flynn left his car and followed from a distance. They seemed to be heading towards the railway station but passed it by, continuing along the road by the tracks. Flynn stayed in the background, his quarries in and out of sight around the curves of the narrow road. He could hear their chatter. The tall girl was a livewire. At intervals she broke into song, skipped out a dance and gloried in entertaining her companions. She was beginning to piss him off.

The little group turned into the labyrinth of new apartments on the Lewisham side. No one else was about. Flynn had to be careful. They would spot him if they turned. The light rail station was ahead. The three were peering in the direction of the city-bound tram. The station monitoring screen signalled the next arrival – four minutes. He hung back until it came into view. Sofia and her friends leaped into the last carriage. Flynn entered from the front, eyes down. Sofia might have seen him that night. He had to assume she had. He'd stay out of sight and wait for his chance. No more mistakes.

CHAPTER 42

SOFIA PREFERRED THE tram to a railway carriage. Easier to hop on and off. It was good sitting alongside Alice and Garry, her first real friends in Australia. Her husband never let her out, except for shopping and English lessons, and even the lessons had stopped after the police came. She picked up English quickly and tried with people, but the others in the class were from all over and had their own lives. There were the wives of her husband's friends, but she couldn't bring herself to trust them. They were just as scared as she was. She pretended not to see their bruises and they did the same for her. Anything else would have been too complicated.

The tram slid smoothly along the tracks, staying briefly at each station. Sofia stiffened as they passed the park where she had hidden. She relaxed when they moved on, skirting roads, streets and open parkland. A large bay with a wide steel bridge came into view, the old train station with its bright red roof just beyond. The three friends left the platform quickly, on the lookout for transport officers. A few steps more and they were descending the escalator, among the shops and cafes within the old station. People called it the Tram Sheds.

Domed tents formed a protective knot on the other side of the park, their bright colours contrasting with the brick-red railway arches. The open field in front was dotted with people and dogs chasing balls, racing to their owners and demanding another go. Sofia and Alice walked arm in arm. Garry picked up a ball and tossed it to a black and white border collie. They laughed as the dog took off across the grass, jumping and rolling.

'Wedge!' Garry called as they closed in on their destination. A black and tan kelpie dashed out of a tent and tumbled into Garry's arms. He leaned into the dog for a friendly wrestle and rubbed her ears vigorously. Then Wedge broke away and ran towards the two women. She stopped in front of Sofia, whimpering softly. Sofia rubbed the dog's smooth back.

'She's really taken to you,' Alice said. 'Follows you everywhere, doesn't she.'

As the afternoon wore on, others returned from their day, slipping in and out of tents and arranging belongings. Sofia sat on a milk crate, chatting and feeding Wedge from a large bag of kibble. Garry filled a silver bowl from the tap on the green rise near the road. He greeted a man who had parked nearby. The man gathered items from a car boot, approached and offered blankets, pillows and towels. They were accepted with smiles and nods, then he was on his way.

Alice was the first of the friends to head down the narrow bush track to the public toilets. Before long she was back, singing all the way and picking up the conversation where she'd left off. Sofia stood. With a smile and a backward glance, she set off, Wedge gazing after her.

CHAPTER 43

PACER WAS STILL smarting from his conversation with Connors. The bastard had a gift for hitting a raw nerve. Nothing to do with Pacer's demotion. That wasn't the issue. He'd moved on. No, what bothered Pacer was the barb over losing a suspect.

Sofia was still out there, most likely in danger. He could feel the threat, deep in his bones. Pacer reached for his phone and was about to call when it rang. The man he wanted was on the line.

'Pacer, it's John Wainwright. I've found her. Got a tip-off, a good one. Turned up a short time ago at Jubilee Park.'

Pacer felt dizzy as relief washed over him. They had found Sofia and could make her safe. He grabbed his jacket as Wainwright filled him in.

'You mean near the Tram Sheds?'

'That's the one. She's with a mob in tents under the railway viaduct. There's about a dozen or so living there.'

'Does Sofia know you're there? Have you spoken to her?'

'No, I don't want to spook her. I'll stay out of sight until you get over. And buy some coffees on your way here. Might work better than a police badge as a calling card.'

Pacer joined Wainwright outside the pet supply business above the park, sizing up the situation. How to handle this? No one felt comfortable when a police officer approached, let alone someone on the edge. Pacer figured Wainwright looked the part. With his tired eyes and slight stoop, he wouldn't startle anyone. As for himself, he looked like any middle-aged bloke thickening around the middle. Too neat but at least he'd left his jacket and tie in the car. Those people would be more interested in the coffees.

Pacer narrowed his eyes, peering towards the campsite. 'Which one is she?'

'Can't see her now. She arrived with that young woman in the bright outfit. Probably inside a tent.'

'Okay, let's make our way over.' Pacer set off first but held back when a black and tan dog, a kelpie, ran towards them from the bushes. Unperturbed, Wainwright stepped forward and showed his hand. He spoke soothingly to the dog. 'She seems a bit agitated.'

Pacer clutched the tray of coffees and tried to look relaxed. They could sense your fear, he'd been told. The kelpie trotted over to him.

Pacer froze. The dog wagged its tail vigorously. Pacer did what Wainwright had done, holding out his hand for the kelpie to examine. He patted the dog's head and felt its soft ears. It was strangely pleasant, almost natural. He told himself this one was okay.

'Hey there. Wedge has a new friend.' A bearded man from the camp walked over, smiling broadly. 'She doesn't take to everyone.'

Pacer searched the group, trying to identify Sofia. No one was remotely like the image he had painted. He offered the coffees to people on milk crates and handed the last to a woman who popped her head through a tent flap. She wasn't Sofia either, far too old. Wainwright was chatting amiably with the man who had walked across with them. He introduced himself as Clancy.

Something didn't feel right. Pacer looked at Clancy. 'Is Sofia here?'

CHAPTER 44

I T WAS EASY to follow Sofia and her friends. From high on the escalator, Flynn observed their progress across the park. Engrossed in conversation and silly games, they were unaware of their surroundings. People stared at them but they didn't notice. Probably thought they were on drugs. They stopped at a campsite that looked nasty and squalid. Unpleasant-looking dogs slunk about. He'd come close enough.

Flynn skirted the camp and walked the service road above. Too bad he hadn't anticipated their destination. Could have brought his car here, there was plenty of parking. The road ended in a turning circle. On the park side, a small building housing male and female toilets was partly concealed by trees. A rough track ran back through the bush towards the campsite.

On the other side of the toilet block, stone steps led down to the bay. Flynn spotted an empty bench and made his way there, wincing with each downward step. A good spot for observing the campsite. It was a relief to sit down and stretch out his leg. His ankle was too painful to touch. The painkillers were wearing off so he knocked back a few more. Getting dehydrated. He wished he'd brought a bottle of water. How long would he have to wait? It was weary work, keeping tabs on a bunch of people who seemed content to do nothing. Some do-gooder delivering blankets and whatnot broke the monotony.

Flynn felt dizzy and passed out for he didn't know how long, then woke with a start, feeling queasy. It took a few seconds to remember where he was. With a sidelong glance he surveyed the camp. He couldn't have been out cold for more than a few moments. Sofia was standing. She patted the dog next to her, smiled at the woman in the colourful scarf, headed along a nearby track and disappeared into the bushes.

Flynn was already on his feet. In less than a minute he was in place. He heard footsteps through the bush as someone hurried towards him. A rough stone the size of his fist was on the ground near his feet. He bent to pick it up, ignoring the pain in his leg as he rose to his full height. The rock felt rough in his hand, heavy and reassuring. He crept forward. It occurred to him fleetingly that he had not thought this through.

CHAPTER 45

PACER'S CONVERSATION WITH Clancy was interrupted by a young man in jeans and black bomber jacket surging from the bush, gasping for breath. 'There's someone out there. Creeping around in the bush. I followed but he disappeared. He scared me … his eyes … wild, crazy.'

The woman in the bright headscarf rushed up and threw her arms around him. 'Garry! Where's Sofia?'

'Yeah,' Clancy said, concerned. 'Where is she?'

Garry pulled out of his girlfriend's embrace and looked blankly. 'I thought she'd come back here.'

'I'll take a look,' Pacer said, heading towards the bushes. The track was rough and narrow, rimmed by waist-high foliage. Pacer pushed through to a stand of wattle and bottlebrush clinging to a slope. He saw a shape leaning into a tree. Sofia, he was sure. She started to scream at his approach. He gathered her up as she stumbled past him. 'It's all right,' he said. 'I'm police.' Taking a punt he added, 'I'm not that other man.'

Clancy and the woman in the headscarf caught up. Sofia, shaking and crying hysterically, pushed away from Pacer and ran into Alice's arms. Alice held her until the sobs subsided. The two women started back towards the camp. Pacer and Clancy continued to where the sandstone steps led out of the bush.

'Something's down there,' Pacer said. It took a moment to register motionless legs, then the shape of a man lying face down. Pacer pushed through the bushes and knelt. He took the man's wrist and felt for a pulse.

'He's alive, but not conscious.' Pacer had the ambos on speed dial and identified himself. 'It's okay,' he said to Clancy, 'we're not here to make trouble.'

Clancy went up to the road to wait. Pacer shifted the man into recovery position. His complexion was ashen and the mouth hung open. Pacer recognised him immediately. 'Mr Flynn! Mr Flynn,' he repeated, more slowly. There was no response.

Sirens wailed and a trolley bumped across uneven ground. Two ambos dropped their gear and took vital signs. 'This man is in a bad way,' Pacer told them. 'He hasn't regained consciousness in the ten minutes I've been here.'

'We'll stabilise him and get him to Emergency. Do you know what happened?'

'I assume he fell down those steps. They're rough.'

'His temperature is way high – I'd say there's a serious infection. Take a look at this leg.' Pacer leaned across as they cut the trousers and peeled off a bandage coiled around the ankle. The area was angry in reds and purples. Pus oozed in several places.

'That's the source of the problem,' the ambo continued. 'This ankle has been festering for some time. Should have got it seen to before this.' Pacer's nose wrinkled with the smell.

Flynn was carrying a wallet, phone and keys. The ambos dropped them into a ziplock bag and placed it under the trolley. They set off, Pacer following. People from the campsite watched from a distance. Clancy was recounting the drama, accompanied in dance by the woman in the bright scarf.

Flynn's white Lexus was not on the road. Pacer widened the search. Nowhere. He joined Wainwright. Sofia and her friends sat close, speaking softly.

Wainwright anticipated what Pacer wanted to do. 'No, not now. She's not ready to talk, too shaken up. Thinks the man she saw was sent by her husband.'

'I doubt that. I recognised him. He's off to RPA, not going to bother anyone for a while. But I'll make sure we have eyes on him.'

Pacer didn't believe in coincidences. When someone turned up at two places connected to a crime, he or she was almost certainly involved. Flynn had his perch at Hawthorne Park and here he was at Jubilee Park. The killers knew about Sofia, he was almost certain. And not just Flynn. He had to be part of a bigger outfit. But it was worse than that. How had they found her before the police? Was it someone Wainwright had spoken to, or did the tip-off come from elsewhere? They'd found Sofia, but the danger to her was now greater than ever.

CHAPTER 46

FLYNN SLIPPED IN and out of consciousness. In moments of wakefulness he registered the barest details, unable to comprehend where he was or how he had come here. He was on his back, unable to move. A mask covered the lower part of his face. Air hissed as he sucked in the oxygen. He moved his head to shake the mask off, but it was held tight by a band pressed to his head. He opened his eyes and tried to focus. An arm, his. Tubes protruded from bands of tape then snaked upwards out of view. Something odd was where his legs were meant to be. He tried to feel them, move his toes. Everything black again.

A low hum, constant, the sound of machinery or electrical static. It came from a place to his back or side. There were voices in hushed tones, but he couldn't make out the words. Shapes moving close, touching him, blurry faces peering in. He was swaying, as if falling. Another face. Dark eyes boring into his, the teeth sharpening and growing in size. No longer human. A dog, black and tan, menacing, crouching low. Flynn felt a hard object in his hand. He lifted it and brought it down on the advancing dog. Not quick enough. He took a long step back, his foot brushing the first step, then missing. Tumbling, pain shooting up his leg as the wounded ankle banged against the rough ground. Then nothing.

Flynn jerked his eyes open. He saw his hand slapping and pulling away from another. He gasped for air, feeling the tension in his neck and back. Sandra's hand. He looked up and saw the anxiety in her face.

'Mr Flynn.' Another woman was speaking. 'Mr Flynn, you're safe here. You're in hospital, the Royal Prince Alfred.'

He looked at his wife. Heard himself muttering, trying to speak. They didn't understand. Frustrated, he pressed back against the pillows.

'Try to rest, Mr Flynn. There's no need to say anything. Doctor will be back soon.'

Flynn could see more clearly now. Sandra had withdrawn her hand. He was in a hospital, the bed narrow, grilles up to keep him in. Twisting his head, he could make out the lines from his arm sticking into pouches hanging from a tall stand. Some kind of drip. There was a throbbing sensation in the lower part of his leg. He couldn't see the end of the bed. A sheet was raised over a box shape. His legs from the thighs down disappeared into it. Someone leaned in close and gave him a jab. Moments later he felt better and drifted off.

A vibration through the frame of the bed woke him. Someone was standing at its end, a man with a stethoscope draped around his neck, clipboard in hand. He lifted the sheet at the side of the box, wrote something, and dropped the clipboard back with a clang. He whispered something to Sandra then stepped closer, introducing himself as Doctor Clarkson.

'How are you feeling, Mr Flynn? Can you hear me? Do you know where you are?'

Flynn nodded, not attempting to speak. Clarkson turned to Sandra and asked, 'Has he been told?' She looked stricken, shaking her head.

'Mr Flynn, you need to prepare for bad news.' Flynn was filled with dread. What was going on? 'You have a serious infection. It's right through your system. We've pumped antibiotics into you, as much as you can take. I've seen the latest blood test results. Fortunately, the infection is waning. You have a good immune response.'

Flynn was thinking this had to be good news. So why was the doctor frowning? Lousy bedside manner? Or something else? What wasn't he telling him?

'It's the ankle, the source of the infection.' Flynn was alert now. It was coming back. All of it. Why he had fallen and what had happened before. He stared at the boxed area over his legs. This couldn't be happening. He was a fit guy. Had to be.

'We found a serious wound and the early signs of gangrene. It's been left far too long. I'll spare you the details, Mr Flynn, but I need to operate. I'll do what I can, bore the infection out from the bone, remove the dead material, pack the wound.' Flynn trembled with relief. Serious, but it would take more than this to stop him.

'So I'll be okay?'

'I can't second-guess what I'll find in there. If the foot can't be saved I'll take it off as close to the ankle as I can. Better for your rehabilitation.'

A brief smile crossed Clarkson's face. He was sure of his craft, dealt with this every day. But his patients didn't.

'No, sorry, doctor. You've got to fix it. I have to get out of here. I've got work to do so just fix it.' Flynn grasped the railing of his bed and tipped his body sideways. He arched his back as the pain ripped through.

CHAPTER 47

FLYNN SHIFTED RESTLESSLY. They had come for him early and stuck another line in his arm. It made him drowsy. He felt the jolt of the bed as it shifted from the cubicle and tumbled through corridors into a lift with padded walls. The bed settled among drifts of curtains and people shrouded in green smocks, masks and gloves. Pre-op, one of them said. He reached out for the pen and watched as his hand was guided to a place for his signature. Someone turned towards him and smiled. Doctor Clarkson.

He woke in another room. It was quiet apart from the hum of machines and whispers from people nearby. A nurse came closer and looked at the machine by his bed. She pressed an object to his ear and saw his open eyes.

'You're awake, Mr Flynn. You're in post-op. We'll keep you here for a while to make sure everything is okay.'

'My leg.' Flynn's voice was husky. It was hard to get the words out.

'You're doing fine, try to rest. Doctor will be by later.'

He looked towards his leg, desperate to know. A raised sheet still obscured the lower part. Adrenalin coursed through his body. He shifted forward, wanting to bolt for the door. The nurse pressed her hands against his shoulders and looked into his eyes. He dropped back.

'Please try to settle,' she said in a soothing tone.

It was hard to judge but Flynn calculated that the hours were passing. Other patients were brought in unconscious and were out again after coming around. The urge to get away kept rising but he managed to control it. He needed to get a grip, think about something else. Like after his scrape with Border Force. Time out on Queensland's Gold Coast, the training and his first half-marathon. Running, now an obsession. The rush it gave him, and the hours he spent in the gym. His new life.

Flynn glanced at his leg. This couldn't be happening. A nurse told him the doctor was operating and would come by soon. He started to reach down but stopped, gripped by fear. He tried to move his toes. He thought he felt something but it didn't seem real. Maybe they'd given him a pain blocker. Or was he not feeling pain because there was nothing down there?

He wondered where Sandra was. She'd always been there for him in times of crisis, like after he got out of the drugs business. He'd bought a house in need of repair and funnelled in lumps of cash. Then he met Sandra, good-looking, stylish and easy to be around. Self-contained and independent, she didn't ask questions. That suited him fine. Best she didn't know. But where was she? Flynn beckoned a nurse.

'Waiting outside. We don't allow relatives into recovery. You'll see her soon, after the doctor has been.'

He started to protest but realised the futility. His mind drifted. Business had moved up a notch after Malcolm had bought into a run-down row of terraces. A bunch of squatters had dug in hard. Flynn watched as their meeting with Malcolm came to an unsatisfactory conclusion. Flynn moved forward and offered his hand. Told Malcolm he had ways to remove the squatters. They shook. In the end it was easy. The squatters were exhausted and ready for the sweetener. Rooms in empty terraces owned by the Anglican Church in Glebe. A few dollars for equipment they could not shift. Rail and bus tickets for those wanting to move away or return home.

'Malcolm! He can't know there's a witness,' Flynn whispered. He had nodded off but was now wide awake. His mouth felt dry. He reached for a box of juice but knocked a bowl that clattered to the floor. A nurse looked his way, concerned.

Across the room the main door flew open and Doctor Clarkson strode in, two junior attendants in his wake. He spoke to the charge nurse, glanced through the charts and looked Flynn's way.

Good news. Clarkson had saved his foot. 'So when am I out of here?' Flynn asked, his strident voice the strongest thing about him.

'Steady on, Mr Flynn. It's early days. You've a way to go.'

Flynn hated Clarkson's fake smile and the ooze of confidence. 'No way. I'm out of here today. Where's my wife? They said she's waiting outside.' He had to get out, find Sofia, and finish the job.

Lunging across the bed, Flynn slipped to the floor before medical staff had time to react. He crawled towards the lift with nurses in pursuit. He snarled at them as the needle went in.

CHAPTER 48

'IT'S A FUNNY name, Wedge. How did she get it?' Wainwright asked. He and Clancy sat on milk crates, away from the main group.

'I've got a story for you. It was early in the New Year, months back. A few of us set up this camp and were finding our way around. A good spot, it turned out. That's why we stayed on. Anyway, one evening May and me were walking along by the water, catching the cool breezes. We heard this sound, like a moan or a wheeze. At first we thought it was the wind in the trees, or the water lapping about. It was eerie and getting dark so we headed back here. The next morning I went for another look. Early. No one else about. I heard a sound again, this time like a whimper. It was coming from a drain just above the water. I looked in and there was this little creature staring out at me, covered in sludge and stuck fast between rocks.'

'So you pulled her out, brought her up here?'

'She was scared. Tried to move away but the rocks had closed around. Paws were bleeding. I talked to her in a quiet voice and moved the stones and muck away. Then I lifted her out. She grabbed on to me, wouldn't let go. Smaller than she is now. People up at the pet place cleaned her up and bandaged the paw. They had one of those machines you use to read the chip that dogs get when they're pups. That's how you know where they belong. She didn't have one. No collar, either.'

They were watching Garry and Wedge together on the grassed area. Garry stood, relaxed, feigning disinterest. Wedge crouched motionless. Between them, the ball lay in the grass in a charade they had repeated for almost an hour. Without warning, Garry grabbed the ball, lifted it high and pretended to toss it at the railway viaduct. Wedge leaped into action, her eyes following Garry's arm. She stopped abruptly, realising the ball was still in Garry's hand. She grinned at Garry. Not fooled. Then the ball was flying in the other direction and Wedge went after it. It bounced twice before she took it between her teeth and trotted back. This time she dropped the ball further away.

The clouds were rolling in. Wainwright and Clancy pulled their crates into the shelter of the viaduct as the first drops fell. Most of the group had stayed put for the day, knowing the risk of a downpour. There was a flurry of activity as people gathered up items. Garry and Wedge abandoned their game and joined Sofia and Alice.

'Not a lot to do, and plenty of time to do it in,' said Clancy, watching the small group as they settled back against the brick facing.

'They get used to the boredom?' Wainwright asked.

'Not boredom. That's a luxury for regular folks with a job and a nice house. People like us, we're on the lookout all the time, got to be. You worry about the next meal, where you'll sleep, them who'll steal from you. Or worse. It's harder for the women.' Clancy was quiet for a few minutes, then continued. 'When you're homeless long enough you find a routine to fill the time. I know one bloke goes to the same park every day. Collects the litter and puts it in the bin. Refers to it as his "job". One lady who walks her dog there thanks him for cleaning the park every time she sees him.'

Wainwright smiled. 'Days like this must throw things out. And it's no joke knowing winter is on the way.'

'I don't mind the cold weather. I'm used to it. Get the flu though, and it really brings you down. I've had to convince people to go to the hospital emergency, they've been that bad. They don't like to go – hospitals scare them. Living this life, they forget their manners, cause a scene with the nurses and next minute the police are there. But you've had enough of my stories. You're here for another reason, aren't you. Your friend from the other day said he was a detective. Pacer. I'm guessing you are too.'

Wainwright nodded. 'We're looking for someone who might have information on a case we're working on together. We've located her here, with this group.'

'Look, no one here is on the run from the police. That's not why we are homeless.' Clancy gave Wainwright a stony look.

'No, no one is in trouble. There's just a matter we need to clear up.'

'You're saying "her". You can't mean May? She wouldn't know anything.' Clancy thought for a moment. 'Do you mean one of those young women over there with Garry? Sofia and Alice? They turned up last week. Alice is a bit batty but she livens the place up.'

'I don't want to frighten anyone. Would you walk over with me, help with the introductions?'

Clancy took his time thinking it over. 'Okay. But pick up your seat and bring it along. It won't help if you're standing over them.'

As they approached the small group, Sofia stood abruptly and disappeared into a tent. Wedge watched for a moment before moving over and settling outside.

The conversation ranged across predictable topics, casual and safe. The weather was clearing after the brief shower. The water of the bay and the Anzac Bridge in the distance was a sight to admire.

'Clancy's told me about Wedge, how she came to be here,' Wainwright said. 'A kelpie, is she?'

Garry replied, 'Sure looks like it with that shape and colour. She's black across her back and on the top part of her legs, with splotches of light brown around her face and the lower part of her legs. And see her ears? Pointed and sticking up.'

'And there's more of that tan colour across her chest,' Wainwright added. 'A good-looking dog. She likes a ball game. I saw you two playing on the grass before. Plenty of energy. I'd like some of that.' Wainwright looked towards the tent as the dog stood, scratched and resumed its position. 'Your dog, now, is she?'

'Not really. She was dumped. Lucky Clancy pulled her out of that drain. Stuck fast, she was. Dogs and people. Sometimes they want you, other times they don't.' Garry looked across at Alice, who nodded and smiled.

Clancy turned to Wainwright. 'So, John, that's the answer to your question. That's why we called her Wedge.'

Alice had an unfocused look. Her head bobbed, as if in a reverie. She changed suddenly, glaring at Wainwright. 'It's Sofia you're interested in, isn't it. You keep looking over at her tent. Are you after her? Going to send her back to her husband?' Her voice was pure steel.

CHAPTER 49

CONNORS, ON THE prowl, had dropped by and was demanding results, but coming from him, it was more like a threat. Pacer was troubled and couldn't sit still. Not because of Connors, but from not knowing where the real threat might come from. He stood to take the call from Wainwright, then dropped the phone on his desk and jammed his hands into his pockets. Things seemed quiet at Jubilee Park, but that didn't mean anything. Sofia was staying put and not ready to give a statement. Worse: the killers were onto Sofia. He'd been fooling himself to hope otherwise before Flynn turned up.

He called the hospital. Flynn was still in intensive care and not yet out of the woods. What was he up to? How far would he have gone? Now he was out of action, had he been replaced by someone else? Pacer would have liked full surveillance put on both Flynn and Sofia, but Connors figured he'd given him enough resources, given all the 'mistakes' he'd been making.

The medical staff permitted no visitors apart from close relatives. 'He'll keep,' Pacer said hopefully to Picone. 'He's not going anywhere, dead or alive.'

Pacer removed a notebook from his inside pocket, copied a list of numbers onto a blank sheet and handed it to Picone. 'These are calls Flynn made or received over the past week or so. Look them up and get some names.'

Picone took the page, looking from it to Pacer and back again. 'He gave you his phone?'

'Didn't hand it to me as such – he wasn't conscious. Maybe it fell out of his pocket and I retrieved it for him. Whatever.' This was awkward, but you grabbed your chance when it came along. Luckily, Flynn used a finger tap to open his phone. Easy enough for Pacer to press the phone to Flynn's limp hand. 'Just do it,' he growled.

The first number belonged to a Justine Rawlings, who had form for a string of break and enters and minor drug crimes. Nothing recent. She'd called Flynn early afternoon on the day of his accident, from the vicinity of Manna House.

'Go there now. See if the manager knows her. They don't ask for names, so you might draw a blank. If she's around, talk to her, but take it carefully.' Pacer looked at Picone uncertainly. This required tact, but it was time to give the young detective some responsibility. He looked eager and was off before Pacer had a chance to change his mind and go himself.

They had assumed Justine Rawlings was a customer, there for the lunch or whatever else was on offer, so Picone was surprised when Chris Neville, the manager, disclosed that Rawlings worked as a kitchenhand.

'I'll call her in,' Neville said. 'You can use my office. Don't get heavy. I gave Justine this job over a year ago and she's turned out very reliable, trying to make something of her life.'

Justine entered the room looking nervous, but she fobbed off Picone's questions.

'Flynn? Maybe I knew someone by that name years ago. Maybe not.'

'Come on, Justine, you know Flynn. You've been talking to him.'

'How do you know that? You been spying on me? This is harassment. You can't do that.'

Picone watched as Justine scratched at her arm. It looked raw. 'How did you get those marks, Justine?'

'You're weird, you know that?' Justine pulled the sleeve lower.

'You're still using, aren't you. Does Chris Neville tolerate addicts? Maybe I should let him in on your secret.'

'You won't do that.' Justine looked at Picone, a flash of anger crossing her face.

'Tell me about that call. I might reconsider.'

'Maybe I phoned an old friend. Look, I don't want you telling Chris anything. I need this job.'

'You reckon just making a phone call could have such serious consequences? Must have been an interesting conversation.'

Justine didn't reply.

'How do you know Flynn?'

'I'd almost forgotten him, it's been that long. Look, I need to get back to work.'

Picone sat expressionless. 'Who's your supplier, Justine? Would you like to tell me about him instead? Or is it Flynn?'

'Maybe Flynn supplied some people. That was ages ago.'

'Still fresh in your mind, I bet. Come on, Justine.'

'I used to live in a squat in Zetland,' she said with a sigh. 'Flynn came by sometimes. He was good to have around, better than most blokes. When they started knocking down the old houses I had nowhere to go. He found me a place.'

'Really, Justine? And why would he do that?' A small smile crossed Picone's face.

'We were friends. He wanted to help.'

'You were dealing for him, weren't you.'

'Maybe once or twice. He wanted help with his customers and I needed the money.'

'Is dealing what got you in trouble with the police?'

'Nah, I got done for stealing – you know, break and enter.'

'And Flynn? Is he still in the drug trade?'

'He got out years ago. There were hard types out there, always wanting a bigger cut of the profits. You had to stare them down or pay them off. Then he got a scare from the cops.' Justine hesitated.

'We can check. Better for you if you tell me everything.' Picone could feel her starting to crack.

'Flynn used to say the cops were a minor inconvenience until Border Force got onto a shipment coming in by boat. He was pulled in. Reckoned he kept his cool and didn't say zip. But he was scared. You could feel it.'

'Did you see him after that?'

'He used to come by.'

'Why would he do that if he wasn't still dealing? You were in it together, weren't you.' Picone's tone hardened.

'No, I told you. Flynn knew people who lived in the warehouses and boarded-up places around where I lived. Most were owned by the churches or left vacant when the owners died. Good for people with nowhere to live. All gone now. Half of them ended up on the streets. I still see them around, come in here for a feed.'

'So what was Flynn after?'

'There were artists and creative types. They had equipment that was hard to shift when those places were knocked down. Flynn took their stuff and sold it on. A business opportunity, he said. No point leaving it to be crushed under ceilings and walls by the bulldozers.' Justine looked at her phone. 'Look, I've got to get back in there.'

'I've got all day.' Picone stood impassive, his arms crossed.

Justine hesitated, weighing her options. 'I heard that Flynn was on the lookout for someone, a woman who was sleeping rough. Someone like that is new here. She's nice, we get on. So I called Flynn. He told me to phone back when she came in next time.'

'And you did?'

'Why wouldn't I?' Justine shifted guiltily in her seat, perhaps regretting the conversation now.

'Name?'

'Sofia.' She looked away, eyes sullen and downcast.

'Any clue as to what Flynn wanted with her?' Picone asked.

'No idea. He has a lot of contacts. Maybe he's doing someone a favour.' Justine pretended to be bored.

Picone wasn't buying it. 'Who's Flynn doing business with these days?'

'I told you I don't know anything about Flynn. And don't say anything to Chris. Please.' Justine searched Picone's face for assurance.

'Keep what we've talked about to yourself. Don't pass it on. You know what I'm saying?'

'You don't get it. I owe Flynn. He helped me out with that place he found when I was kicked out of the squats.'

'You're not listening, Justine. Flynn is bad news. Stay clear.'

As soon as Justine left the room, Picone grabbed his phone. His voice trembled with excitement as he relayed the information to Pacer.

CHAPTER 50

PACER GATHERED HIS notes, headed upstairs for a briefing and was barely through the door before his boss started in. Connors's thin face was drawn and he'd taken on a peevish tone. Leaning over, he picked up a file and banged it on the desk. 'You do understand that cases are to be closed, not just worked. I have been patient but I expect a result.'

Edith had whispered a warning to Pacer as he waited in the outer office. Connors's performance review had come around and he was feeling the pressure.

Pacer had nodded his thanks. He knew the signs. He steeled himself for the usual claptrap, the management-speak. Instead, he endured a monologue about the successes of other squads: the arrest of an antique dealer who sold forgeries, the conviction of a politician who doled out gaming licences for a fee. None of it relevant to Pacer but a reminder that others could solve their cases expeditiously.

Connors dropped into his chair, drained. An opportunity for Pacer. 'The Sullivan case, sir. We have a new person of interest. A man by the name of Flynn. He was seen near the crime scene and has a criminal past.'

Connors opened the file and read through the latest entries. 'Is he looking good for an arrest?'

'Not as yet. I'm after a link between Flynn and the victim. If he was involved, he was an accomplice, not the actual killer.'

'How can you be sure? Perhaps he had a reason to kill Sullivan and planned it with Arko's help. Later on they had a falling-out.'

Pacer briefly weighed it up. Connors's supposition was fair, on the surface, but completely wrong.

'There is nothing to suggest Flynn has the knife skills,' Pacer said. 'Both murders took finesse. The killer handles himself well under pressure. Flynn doesn't fit the profile.'

Connors flicked through the file. 'There's no update in here on that witness, Sofia. Have you found her?'

'We have located her with a group of homeless people, but she's reluctant to make a statement. Sergeant Wainwright is working that aspect.'

'Is Wainwright doing enough?'

Pacer had searched his mind for a better way, but there was nothing. They would offer protective custody, but he knew Sofia wouldn't have a bar of it. There was no trust. It would take time to build.

Connors's attention was shifting erratically. He snatched a bundle of petty cash receipts from the folder and tossed them down. 'Look, Sergeant, I give you a free hand with expenses, but stringency is expected. What's this? Cigarettes? Coffee? You treat the department like a vending machine.'

Pacer stared into the middle distance, searching for words to quell Connors's agitation. A tense five minutes and it was done. Connors shut the Sullivan file and slapped it onto the pile in his out-tray.

Connors's hand hovered over the desk, then settled on a folder thicker than the others. 'Your cold case, the Poulos child. The suspect has left Queensland. They were tracking him as a favour, as much as they could do without a surveillance order in their state. He took a bus out of Brisbane, went over the border and caught a flight to Sydney.'

Pacer was thrown, a chill running down his spine. If Robert Davidson was back, he would make his way to the Inner West, Pacer was sure. Davidson's type preferred known territory, roamed every inch of it, waiting for their special moment. But why would he risk it?

Connors was speaking again. 'Look into it, will you? He's dangerous.'

Back in his office, Pacer wrapped his hands around the teapot. The tea was cooling and he was on his second cup. Davidson had been caught once since the murder, for spreading porn, but that was all law enforcement had on him in recent times. He'd done a stint in jail then relocated to Queensland. He was on several radars up there. Alarms would sound if he made the wrong move. In Brisbane he had started as a gofer in a manufacturing plant. That didn't last, a natural loner, disagreeable and easily riled. He roamed the suburbs, never quite close enough to a school or playground to be picked up. Should Pacer be troubled by his return to Sydney? Most certainly. Davidson must have come back for a reason. Pacer drained his cup and set to work. People in his network needed to know. John Wainwright most of all.

CHAPTER 51

PACER FOUND WAINWRIGHT walking across the park towards the Tram Sheds, stopping to pick up a ball, toss it, and watch one of the dogs take chase.

'The regulars are getting to know me,' Wainwright said, laughing. 'The dogs, I mean. They sense who's on for a game. I wouldn't be surprised if they spread the word. Look at this little fellow.' He indicated a heavy-set staffy making his way over on bowed legs, a deep chocolate colour tinged with maroon. The dog drew close and dropped.

Pacer stared. In his mouth the staffy held not one tennis ball but two. He placed the balls, grubby and chewed, in front of his paws.

'It's okay, Pacer, he doesn't fetch. You won't have to touch them. He'll gather them up in a minute and wander off.' On cue, the dog picked up one ball in his mouth, and with his paw manoeuvred the other between the incisors on the other side. Rising slowly, he trotted to a man who appeared to be his owner.

The late-afternoon sun cast shadows across the park. 'Let's take a break. Go to the same place as last time?' Pacer suggested. As they walked, Wainwright filled him in on events at the campsite.

'So you haven't actually spoken to Sofia?' Pacer asked.

'She disappears into a tent when she sees me. It would be a mistake to pursue her. I tried to convince her friends that the husband hasn't sent me. Fear is second nature to these people. It's what got most of them here. It's their default lens, their alarm system. Sofia was beaten and locked up by her husband. Lucky she got away, but she's terrified he'll come after her.'

'Is she likely to take off again?' This was one of Pacer's biggest fears.

'I don't think so. Clancy reckons she feels safe here, to the extent that she can. She stays close to the other two, although when it comes to winning her confidence, Alice is more of a hindrance than a help. Trusts no one except Garry. She gets ideas into her head and won't shift.'

'We need Sofia's statement soon. I don't know how much time we have or how safe she is.' Would giving a statement make Sofia safer? Pacer didn't know. Maybe not. She'd still have to attend the court hearing, and the killers would be keen to stop her.

'Flynn's safely out of the picture for the time being, isn't he?' Wainwright frowned.

'Still flat on his back, I'm happy to say. But after what happened to Arko, these people will stop at nothing. There will be more like Flynn to send after her. She'd be safer in protective custody.'

'You're right, but that can't happen unless she agrees.' Wainwright shrugged.

'Any way you can talk to her?'

'I'll do what I can but it'll take time. In the meantime I'll keep an eye on her.'

'You're not expected back at Sergeant Casey's unit?' Pacer asked.

'It's okay, Pacer. You can call it "occo". I'm part of the furniture there. I've let the boss know I'm needed on this case. Anyway, she's arranging things with your boss.'

They'd reached the Tram Sheds. Wainwright indicated a table and pulled out a chair. The place was empty. He sat with arms crossed, unwilling to say more about his past and why he himself had landed in occo.

Pacer was the first to speak. 'It's good to have you on the team.' He meant it. Wainwright didn't judge or question. He had a settling effect on people. Reassuring, a listener. Pacer had seen it with the group of homeless and he felt it too. Despite what Wainwright had witnessed in the child crimes unit, and his role in all that, he had an ease about himself that Pacer envied. Bruised, but not bitter or defeated.

More patrons sauntered in as they sat over their beers. Wainwright pulled receipts from his jacket and handed them over. More rounds of coffees for Sofia and her friends. Pacer told him about Connors's reaction to the last batch. It was good to see that Wainwright was still capable of a hearty laugh. Pacer's laughs, unlike his solitary thoughts, were trapped on the inside.

'Sorry about the dressing-down,' Wainwright said, still smiling. 'I owe you a beer.' When he returned, he gave Pacer a sly look. 'I've got an idea, something that might draw Sofia out. Not saying right now – I have to tee something up. I'll let you know.'

'Be good if it comes off.' Pacer looked into his glass. This would be difficult. 'There's something else we need to discuss. It's Davidson. He's back in Sydney.'

Pacer saw the shock come over Wainwright's face, the sharp intake of breath, the shoulders tensing back. It was as though something hard and heavy had slammed into him.

'No, no way,' was all Wainwright could say.

CHAPTER 52

PACER WAS ITCHING to pay Flynn a visit. He had his suspicions, strong ones, but nothing firm enough to justify charges. He judged Flynn as the flaky type, so no harm in letting him stew. Another call to the hospital confirmed Flynn's condition was now stable. And no, he was unable to get out of bed. Stuck there, then. Pacer finished the call with a grunt of satisfaction.

Picone was standing in front of the whiteboard. He pointed to Flynn on his diagram. 'He's the only suspect we've tied to the crime, the only live one, but we're missing a link with the victim.'

'According to his company and tax records,' said Pacer, 'he's connected to the building trade, but how, I don't know. I wonder who he does business with.'

'Maybe there's a phone line in his home office?' Picone hinted.

'Not possible to tap it. Requires a special order and in this instance it wouldn't get through. Privacy issues. We don't have a strong enough case to put him in the frame.'

'But you got those numbers from his mobile.' Picone's cheeks flushed. He sounded indignant.

'It's different when you're in the field,' said Pacer. 'You use your initiative.' Did he have to explain everything? He watched as Picone added boxes, names and lines to his diagram. 'I see you have a box for Justine Rawlings. Anyone else from that list of phone numbers I gave you?'

'Several were burners.'

'What does that tell you, Stuart?'

'Flynn knows people who don't want their calls traced?'

'That, or he knows a lot of tourists, which I doubt. Justine Rawlings was going straight. She kept a regular phone. They couldn't all be burners, surely.' Picone was dragging the chain on this one, pushing back against Pacer's methods.

'I haven't finished checking,' Picone said tersely.

'Well, get onto it,' Pacer snapped, pulling Flynn's file closer and turning to the financials. His income fluctuated and he didn't seem to earn enough to own a well-maintained home on a double block. And he did own it. Pacer had checked. Perhaps his wife brought home the bacon or there'd been a windfall.

Pacer dialled the number for Jack Higgins in Investigations Research. His department had the authority to delve deeper.

Higgins listened to Pacer's request and replied in clipped tones. 'Certainly, we can do that for you. There is a wait though. At this point, I'd say three to four weeks.'

Pacer didn't hide his irritation. 'This is a murder inquiry. The information I need is on a key suspect. Can't you give it some priority?' Higgins was new. Pacer hadn't spoken to him before.

'It's still three to four weeks. I'm understaffed. Sorry.'

Pacer doubted he was. Just a bureaucrat, sitting pretty. In the past, Pacer had waited his turn, letting people like Higgins dictate the terms. They didn't wear the consequences. Pacer was learning. Stay on top of the case, close in on your quarry or watch him slip away. No, Pacer would not wear it. There was a way around, someone else to call.

Pacer trudged back to his office. He preferred that Picone not overhear. He wasn't ready for the short cuts you had to take. Pacer called Lenore Watson, who investigated fraud for the Australian Taxation Office. They'd worked together when two business partners turned on one another with fatal consequences. Watson uncovered a motive when she discovered the victim was embezzling the joint account.

Watson knew Pacer's voice immediately. She sounded pleased to hear from him. Probably remembering that case they'd solved together, although they'd never met because Watson worked in Canberra. She was eager to help, perhaps with the sniff of another criminal to bring down. Flynn's business wasn't on her radar, but that wasn't a problem. With a few strokes of the keyboard, she was in.

'Oh, I see. Your Mr Flynn has his fingers in quite a few pies. He's making a bit less than I'd expect though. Suggests he's taking cash payments. Some years back, he had an export business. Ferrying factory equipment to Indonesia. I can tell it was used goods from the duties that applied.'

'Can you see who he does business with now?' Pacer asked.

'He has income from several companies. I'll trace the business names through their ABNs, if you have a few minutes. And there's something else. Mr Flynn receives a six-monthly payment from the same source each time. This one is trickier. It's through a bank on an island the press likes to describe as a tax haven. Nevis. It's quite legal; you'd be surprised how many Australians use them, mostly to minimise taxes. I'm not sure why Mr Flynn would though. Does he travel overseas for work, do you know?'

'I'm fairly sure he doesn't.'

'Well, someone chooses to pay him this way. It's often done to obscure the money trail or to cover up illegal activity. The payments to Mr Flynn are all for the same amount. I'd say he's on a retainer.'

'Can you identify the source?' Pacer asked.

'The details of the bank are in front of me, but not the identity of the payer. I can get it for you, apply a bit of leverage. It will take a day or two. Would that help?'

Pacer stood and walked around his desk. 'It certainly would. I'm grateful.'

He could hear the smile in Lenore's voice. 'Pleased to help. Oh, that other information has just popped up. The companies Mr Flynn invoiced. I'll email them to you.'

CHAPTER 53

ALL THE BUSINESSES on Lenore Watson's list dealt in reclaimed or repurposed building materials. There were flooring suppliers, buyers of copper wire, roofing tilers, and sellers of art deco lighting and the surrounds of fireplaces. Pacer recognised several from when he and Janet were renovating.

Pacer felt a stirring of excitement, a feeling he got when his gut told him he was onto something. Flynn was connected with the building trade and so was Sullivan. Sullivan built new apartments on cleared sites, while Flynn gutted the old buildings before they were torn down, selling the reusable materials to retail suppliers. Two ends of the same process. Their paths would not have crossed, necessarily, but there was a good chance they had. Pacer was counting on it. He would find out how Flynn operated and find the link with Sullivan.

Most of the business addresses were reasonably close to the CBD. Pacer phoned the car pool. A vehicle was available and the guy advised Pacer to grab it while he could. There'd be nothing else until late next week.

On top of Watson's list was a roofing company located on Parramatta Road. The sign out front said it had been operating for sixty years. A family business, solid and reliable. Pacer remembered Keith Schell, the owner. He'd fixed the roof on Pacer's place. They used Welsh tiles reclaimed from old houses. That way, you got the best quality and a match for what was already there.

From the front office, Pacer could see the old man out the back talking to a younger man and woman. Pacer introduced himself. He didn't expect Keith to remember him. A flicker of recognition, perhaps, as the conversation went on. It had been years.

'A lot of our clients own Victorian and Federation houses with tiled roofs. Original tiles, not the modern terracotta stuff. We import new tiles, the ones from Wales if we can get them, but we prefer to use salvage. It used to come from places that had seen better days, but lately good houses have been demolished to make way for the M4 extension and the new developments.' Keith was warming to his subject. Pacer steered the conversation back to the purpose of his visit.

Keith did business with Flynn and Associates, quite a bit of it. His daughter, Marie, handled that side of things. She shook Pacer's hand and took him around the back where tiles were stacked against the building. A tin roof stretched over the tiles and the door to a small office stood open. She patted the nearest stack as they walked inside.

'It's amazing how they form into neat slates when cut properly. It's in the grain. A lot of the old tiles used to be chipped, but now the places they pull down are in really good shape. We get beautiful product.'

'I'm interested in your work with Flynn.'

'Of course. I keep the records here. Flynn's a good supplier, lets me know when there's a property for demolition. It's usually a row of houses with him, sizable projects.'

'How does that work? Is he the owner of the properties?'

'Oh, no, Flynn is just a contractor who guts them. There's an official process. The local council has to approve the salvage and issue a certificate. The contractor contacts me and we agree a price. I pay the contractor's invoice, then send in my team to collect the material.'

'Do you keep the certificates?'

'Of course, but there's not much to see.' Marie Schell pulled a thick file from a shelf above the desk. She found one naming Flynn and Associates. It was brief, just one page. It gave the address of the property to be demolished and the details of the contractor, in this case, Flynn. The bottom of the page was signed off by the planning department of the Cooks River Council. Schell leafed through her file and located other salvage premises where Flynn had been the contractor.

'Did you see anyone with Flynn? Does he have staff?' Pacer asked.

'No, it was just him. There were no "associates". Never are with those types.' She laughed.

The next business on Lenore Watson's list was a flooring company at Burwood. Joe Avramidis, the manager, was taking a break and invited Pacer to join him in a cup of tea. They sat inside a large warehouse surrounded by thousands of planks. Joe showed Pacer his prized possession, a small stack in variously shaped and sized pieces.

'Feel this. Huon pine. Smooth, isn't it? Easy to work with. Polishes to a beautiful finish. It comes from Tasmania, the rainforest, the only place in the world it grows. You've probably heard of Sarah Island, that convict place? They'd float the logs down the river for the convicts to mill, poor sods. Durable too. Some of these pieces could date from those times, maybe even come from there.'

'How did you come by it?'

'Found it in an old convent. Used in their cabinetry. I get calls from boatbuilders. They love the stuff, but I don't like to let it go. Come and see the other stock, the floorboards. I've got jarrah, spotted gum, kauri and Tasmanian oak.' Joe walked towards the back of the warehouse. 'None of this stuff is farmed, all grows naturally. It's becoming harder to get, that's why reclaimed wood is such a prize. Sometimes I can't tell what it is until it's back here and the boys clean it up.'

'Salvaged from houses in this area?' Pacer asked.

'Mostly. You were saying you did up an old place in Haberfield? What kind of timber does it have?'

'Kauri, I think.' Janet had been delighted when they pulled up the ancient Axminster carpet and found the planks beautifully preserved. She'd clapped her hands together and thrown her arms around his neck. One of those special moments.

Joe Avramidis was stroking the planks. 'A lovely timber – you only find it in old houses. Honey-coloured, comes up well. Now, you wanted to know how I come by this stuff?'

'I'm interested in contractors who sell you access to houses with this wood. One in particular, Flynn and Associates.'

'Oh, I know Flynn well. Don't like the man. No respect for anything. He's just an asset stripper. It's all about the money with him.' Joe shook his head in disgust.

Back in his car, Pacer compared the addresses that Marie Schell and Joe Avramidis had given him. This was confirmation that Flynn was indeed connected to the building industry, in salvage operations. He thought about what Justine Rawlings had told Picone – that Flynn used to take equipment from the squats and sell it on. Probably had no right to the stuff, just barged in. Maybe that's where he got his start. Brash and full of himself, that was Flynn. Yep, it all made sense.

Pacer now had plenty of addresses to cross-check with Sullivan's operations. Were there enough? Pacer had always been meticulous in following leads. The old instincts kicked in. It was mid-afternoon, with plenty more businesses on the list Watson had given him. One in Summer

Hill specialised in coloured glass and leadlights. It wasn't far off the main road back to the station. He would drop in on the way back.

The proprietor, Angus Monroe, was about to close early, as he often did. Grumbling, he invited Pacer to sit. A man not used to company. Fixtures encasing leadlights and coloured glass leaned against walls, three and four deep: doors, windows and decorative features in deep reds, greens, yellows and blues, dulled by coatings of dust.

'I do my work here by the window where the light is best. It's mostly repairs to lead work and replacing glass. Painstaking, but it's my life. I get more requests than I can accept.'

Monroe watched as Pacer took in the salvaged items. 'I can do nothing more than preserve them and hope that some day they will find a home. That day may be a long way off.'

Pacer and Janet had prized the leadlight panels on their front door, and the matching patterns gracing the hall door in the centre of their home. And here were hundreds of similar panels from houses torn down.

'And how do they make their way here?' Pacer ran his hands over a particularly beautiful window in oranges and blues.

'They're from properties set for demolition. The developers bring the glass to me with an "offer", as they call it. What can I do? If I say no, the pieces will be destroyed. Those people couldn't care less.'

'Do you recall an operator by the name of Flynn?'

Monroe's look told him so. 'He's the main one.'

'Do you know where he sources it?'

'I insist on the addresses for my inventory. It's an important part of the history.'

Monroe took a notebook from a shelf behind his bench and opened it to a list of addresses and the specifics of what had been supplied. 'This page covers the last few months or so. A lot of the supply was brought here by Flynn. See here, an "F" next to this one. Here, and again here.'

'Mind if I borrow your notebook, just for a day or so? I need those addresses.'

'I'd rather not.' Monroe reached out and pressed the notebook onto the benchtop.

Pacer searched Monroe's expression for a reason he should be so protective. The man's watery eyes reflected the colours of the leadlight lying in the sunlight. 'It's history,' Monroe explained. 'I can't risk you losing it.'

Pacer was tempted to assure Monroe he would look after his records but backed off. It was true, you couldn't trust the police not to stuff up.

'Mind if I make a copy?'

Monroe consented. Pacer took out his phone and started photograph-ing the pages. Somewhere in there, he thought, I'm going to find you, Martin Sullivan, somehow you are linked with Flynn.

CHAPTER 54

THROUGH THE WINDOW, Flynn saw trees swaying and clouds scudding by. He tried to eat the muck they served for dinner but gave up in disgust. Sandra told him that food tasted different when you were pumped with antibiotics and stuff to control the pain. He always stayed away from junk, even when selling it to other people. Now there was no choice. The pain came screaming back before each dose. If he had less pride he'd beg for it. At least he was out of intensive care, not that he remembered much. After this there would be rehab. Or so they thought. Not if he had anything to do with it.

Sandra turned on the television before she left. 'Take your mind off things.' Flynn listened as her sharp heels clipped along the corridor. He reached for the remote and switched the television off. Nothing on but the news. He didn't want to see it. Not after last night, with Hawthorne Park in his face all over again. He was shaken, unnerved. He couldn't sleep after that.

He'd had a shocking day. They'd insisted he get up and walk a few steps. Putting weight on his leg nearly killed him. He'd cracked a bone above his damaged ankle when he went for that tumble. From the knee down it was encased, plaster on the underside and swathes of bandages above and around. They did it that way because of the swelling. In a few days they would put it in a full cast. He hated anyone touching it, especially that ghoul, Clarkson. He could have sawn it off at the ankle and flicked it into the hospital incinerator. Flynn had that to be thankful for, he supposed. His leg was still intact.

It was dark outside now. He switched the television back on and scrolled through the stations. *Border Security*. He laughed. Could show them a thing or two. A woman watched with a surprised look as packets of fish and plant roots tipped onto the counter. No, she hadn't known to tick the box. Oh, dear.

Flynn tried to sleep. The surrounding night fed his sense of unease. Sandra was his only visitor. He'd told her – demanded – that she keep his accident quiet. It was just to delay things. They'd find out soon enough. At least Malcolm was unaware of Sofia. Well, there was one person, but he'd keep his mouth shut. There would be consequences if he talked. For both of them.

He was going to silence this Sofia, and Malcolm would never be the wiser. The real danger was if the police found her first and the news leaked out. He had a tinge of regret about Arko, but Arko was gone.

Flynn's anxiety grew. How long before he was back on his feet? He made good money. He had to keep going. Clarkson was wrong. Flynn ran marathons, didn't he? He'd be out in no time, no need for rehab. That was for old guys.

Out in the corridor the lights dimmed. A nurse gave him a shot, recorded his temperature and checked his leg. Flynn's eyes closed and he drifted. Not asleep, but not awake either. Something troubled him, a memory. Standing in a warehouse, newly acquired. Light filtering through a hole in the roof. Malcolm wanted him there, a part of the team. Edgar, Malcolm's driver, stood by his boss's side, holding a mallet. Another man cowered against a workbench, looking at Flynn, mouth open and eyes pleading. Malcolm related the man's crimes. Building materials ordered in excess and siphoned off. Invoices paid for bogus services. Flynn knew; he'd been tasked with tracking the man down and bringing him back. On Malcolm's signal, Edgar grabbed the man's wrist, held it to the bench and smashed the mallet into his hand.

Flynn gasped. A nurse looked in, saw his eyes wide and staring. She checked his temperature. 'Just a bad dream, Mr Flynn. Everything's normal.'

CHAPTER 55

WHEN PACER ARRIVED at work, the city was shrouded in fog. He filled a teapot in the little kitchen and carried it to his office. Retrieving his teacup from a desk drawer, he held it for a moment, admiring the rose pattern, before pouring the liquid. Going to second-hand places had brought back memories of renovating with Janet. Replacing the chipped bath, retiling, pulling up old carpet, fixing the roof and pulling away the chipboard to reveal the magnificent fireplace behind. Days of frustration and disappointment followed by moments of surprise and elation. And at the start and end of every day, a shared cup of Earl Grey or something exotic Janet had brought home.

Lenore Watson called mid-morning. Platinum Living, with a registered address in Ryde, was the company that paid Flynn's half-yearly retainer. She'd looked up Platinum's profile. It built apartments. The profits looked good and it was growing.

'So Flynn was working for this company, Platinum Living.'

'It appears so. The company was founded by a Malcolm Hendry early in the new millennium, using private equity,' Lenore said. 'Several companies like Platinum Living sprang up around the same time when the development boom started. A few have been in trouble lately, large apartment blocks developing cracks. Structural faults. Platinum Living has a clean slate. So far, anyway.'

'Flynn is in the salvage business,' Pacer said. 'He strips properties for developers. One of them might be Platinum Living.'

'It's unlikely he'd be on a retainer for that. People in that line of work usually pay the developer for the stripping rights. It's the other way around. They get their money back from the second-hand dealers.'

Picone was listening to Watson on speakerphone. When the call finished, he picked up the lists Pacer had collected the day before and shook his head. 'If it's not asset stripping, what is Flynn doing for Platinum Living?'

'Flynn's into more than one line of business, that's for sure. Versatile fellow,' Pacer replied. 'We'll put Platinum Living to one side for the present and focus on his asset-stripping activities. That's most likely how he met Sullivan. We'll start with the addresses of those properties, then do a check with the local councils to see who the developers were. Sullivan has got to be among them.' Or else it would be a helluva waste of time. Try explaining that to Inspector Connors. A gamble, but a lead he couldn't ignore.

Pacer glanced at Picone, who was fiddling with his phone. Social media or something work-related? 'Put that thing down and get stuck into those lists,' he barked. Pacer heard the irritation in his own voice. 'Cool down,' he told himself. 'This isn't about Stuart.' The tension was getting to him. Sofia was still out there with only Wainwright and a few friends between her and a bunch of killers. 'See what you can do with those property addresses – try to narrow it down to something we can investigate. I've got a meeting. Be back in an hour or so.' At least Connors wouldn't be at this one.

Two hours later, Pacer found Picone sitting back and looking pleased with himself. Fiddling with his phone again. Pacer resisted commenting, if only because Picone was expecting him to.

Picone's eyes shifted to Pacer's tie. Pacer looked down. Specks of pink icing stood out against the dark green. A post-meeting respite at the downstairs cafe, tea and a finger bun. He brushed the specks away, feeling self-conscious.

'Okay, go on. What have you discovered?'

Picone smoothed his hands across a large sheet of unlined paper filled with boxes, lines and commentary.

Like a kid with a treasure map, Pacer thought. Here we go.

'I sketched a map covering parts of the city where Flynn's salvage properties were located. Here's the area west of the CBD, and over here the northwest suburbs centering on Epping. Down there, at an angle of about ninety degrees, is a cluster of suburbs going as far as Yagoona. Nearly all the properties on the lists, from Angus Monroe, Marie Schell and Jo Avramidis, fit into one of these.'

'That's a pretty wide area.' Pacer was tired just looking at it, thinking of the footwork required to check out every property.

'There's a pattern.' Picone stood back and considered his work. 'Those properties on the north side are near the new Northwest Rail Link corridor. Looks like those around the Inner West follow the light rail. It was extended a few years back when stations south of Leichhardt were added. The light rail ends at Dulwich Hill now.'

'Some addresses don't fit that pattern,' Pacer said, pointing towards the centre of the map. 'Those in Haberfield, for one thing. Where I live. Whole streets were ripped up to make way for the M4 extension. Lucky for me, my place is a bit further back.'

'You said before that development applications and the approvals for demolition and the removal of resalable materials are handled by local government.' Picone tapped a marker against his front teeth.

'Yes, that's right. The details of the developers are held by the local government councils,' Pacer replied.

Picone jiggled his leg against the table, readying himself for action.

'We need to figure out which councils did the approvals,' said Pacer.

'Already done.' There was triumph in Picone's voice. 'The properties on the north side are in Parramatta River Council's territory.'

'What about those places in the Inner West along the light rail?'

'They're in the Cooks River Council area.' Picone was grinning now.

Pacer hesitated. A little voice was telling him to dampen Picone's enthusiasm, but another, a stronger one, told him the opposite. Plenty of others out there to knock the wind from his sails.

'You're using your initiative, Stuart. Well done.' Pacer cleared his throat. 'Now, I'm overdue for another visit to Cooks River Council, so I'll handle that one. You can cover the developers in the Parramatta River Council area. You're ready to handle something on your own.'

In rapid movements, Picone sorted the papers in neat piles. 'I'll make up the two lists and print them out. Won't take long.' He'd already started tapping the keys.

'Something else first. Did you finish checking the numbers on Flynn's phone?' Pacer tensed, waiting for an answer.

'Er, yes,' Picone said. 'One came in earlier. It sounds familiar – you might recognise it. A Mark Baker.'

Pacer sat back in surprise. 'Well, now, that is a coincidence.'

Picone looked confused.

'I've an appointment with him. First thing tomorrow.'

CHAPTER 56

PACER HAD MADE the appointment several days earlier when there was only one matter to raise with Baker, the building certification at Café Bones. Now he had three. Arriving early, he settled into the same cafe he'd visited before. The teapot was set before him, the tag from the tea bag drooping from under the lid. A common supermarket variety with an insipid flavour. It came with a heavy white mug. Not the same level of service as last time.

Pacer checked the time, pushed the half-empty mug aside and brushed crumbs from his shirtfront. He started for the lift but thought of Picone and took the stairs. He had expected Baker would keep him waiting, just to show he could. Pacer was surprised when Baker greeted him personally at the front desk and led him to his office.

Baker resumed his seat at the same round table as before after showing Pacer to the chair opposite. Pacer took his time settling, sensing a wariness, an element of discomfort in the other man. Was Baker like this with all his visitors? He liked to project himself as confident, in control, his status reflected in the finely crafted woollen jacket and neat tie. A different suit from last time they met, but just as smart. No, it was Pacer himself, or what he represented, that unsettled the man.

Baker hadn't met Martin Sullivan but was aware of him as a new property developer in the council area. A respected businessman, his murder a shock for council staff. Formalities completed, Baker waited for the purpose of Pacer's visit.

'I need the complete documentation for the amenities block. I missed something when I was last here.' It was true. Joel Frazer at Café Bones had alerted him to the issue. He should have cleared this up earlier, but there were other priorities. 'The certification for the foundations. Do you have a copy?'

'I doubt there was time for those checks to be done, before ... one moment.' Despite Baker's disquiet, he seemed eager to help, relieved perhaps. Was Baker expecting a different matter? Something more ... sensitive?

Baker was back in minutes. 'Here is a copy of the certificate.' He seemed puzzled, then shrugged his shoulders.

Pacer looked at the single page Baker had retrieved from the printer. 'Not your own staff member, I see. A private contractor?'

'Yes, Phillip Downes. We rarely use internal staff for routine matters. We have a list of qualified inspectors. This chap is one of those.'

Baker sat stiffly on the other side of the table. He must be wondering too. Pacer slipped the paper into a folder. This certifier hadn't done his job properly. There was only one reason Pacer could think of, apart from gross incompetence. He needed to surprise this Phillip Downes, find out who had paid him off.

Baker was starting to look more at ease, as if their business was settled and Pacer would leave.

Pacer relaxed into his chair. 'I take it that Cooks River Council has responded to the State Government's call for medium- and high-intensity housing development?'

'More of a demand than a call. The government requires us to expand our capacity to house new arrivals and anyone else looking to settle here. They loosened the controls over zoning a few years back and gave us more autonomy. In the four years I've been here, we have bolted ahead.' Baker looked pleased with himself.

'You can't pull development sites out of the air. The suburbs around here were settled in the 1800s. There can't be that much usable space.' Pacer was content to fit Baker's profile of a dumb cop.

'You'd be surprised, Sergeant. This area has good bones. We have Parramatta Road running through the middle, good public transport and plenty of parks. People complain about too few playgrounds and dog runs. On the contrary, what we have is underutilised and there are plenty of sites where the original use is no longer appropriate.'

'So that leaves you with plenty of sites to work with?'

'Of course. Big outfits like Mirvac and Stockland build on the larger holdings. But we wouldn't fill our housing quotas without the smaller operators. They remove run-down shops and houses, improve the streetscapes along major roads. Some of the boarding houses around here were in a terrible state of repair. It's been good to see those go. Unsafe and unsanitary.'

'I guess your department has an important role in regulating this activity?'

'We have zoning regulations and a development planning process, Sergeant.' Baker spoke slowly with an air of resignation. He'd have to spell it out for this police officer.

'Railway yards spawn high-rise. Light industrial becomes apartment living. Suburban streets sprout blocks of flats. Unless there are heritage protection orders, which are harder to change. It's not impossible though.'

Baker stopped, as if ending the discussion. Pacer reached into his jacket for his notebook.

'I have a list of sites in your area that were developed over the past five years. I'd like the names of the companies that constructed them.'

'Certainly, Sergeant. I'll have my staff compile that for you.'

'Your PA mentioned on the phone that you keep a database on your computer. Perhaps you could open it for me?'

Baker mumbled, barely audibly. He reached back to the laptop on his desk, pushing a sheaf of papers aside. The page on top drifted to the floor while the rest of the pile pivoted into Pacer's view. As he waited for Baker to download the file, Pacer scanned the page now on top. Council business, mundane and unremarkable except for one small thing. Pacer's curiosity was aroused. Baker was a strategy man, a delegator, above the minutiae of council business. Or that was the impression he liked to give. This page showed that he couldn't keep his nose out, just like the rest of the management caste. Made a thing of trusting valued employees but kept a close eye all the same. And here was Baker, signing off on a job better suited to a base-grade clerk.

Baker had found the file he was looking for and asked Pacer for the first address.

'The developer for that property was Platinum Living,' Baker said. 'A well-established firm, reputable. Not in the big league – their niche is apartment living on the smaller sites, as I mentioned before.'

Pacer gave Baker a second address and then a third. He stopped after eight. All the same but one. Platinum Living. Pacer was surprised and a little disappointed. Sullivan Constructions was not among the developers. It was puzzling. The link between Sullivan and Flynn would have to be found elsewhere. Interesting though, that Flynn was stripping properties owned by Platinum Living. Lenore Watson had told him about the retainer but had not mentioned any payment to Platinum Living for the salvage rights. Pacer made a mental note to ask her about this.

Pacer stood to leave, then turned.

'You will be aware of a man by the name of Flynn?'

'Will I?' Baker replied quickly.

'He works with property developers in your area. Platinum Living, for one. He's sure to have crossed your path.'

Baker creased his brow. 'Vaguely. My staff will know him better than me. We have met socially though. My wife, Carolyn, and his wife, Sandra, are quite good friends. He's had a bad accident, did you know? He's in hospital.'

'Oh?' Pacer said, feigning surprise. 'Is it serious?'

'He had a fall and damaged his ankle, a compound fracture, I think. Sandra said it happened when he was out running.'

'Have you had any cause to contact him recently, before his accident?'

'I don't think so. No, not recently. But our wives have spoken. Sandra is very worried, as I'm sure you can imagine.'

Pacer stood outside the ground-floor cafe and dialled. Time was critical. He needed to speak to the certifier, Phillip Downes, before Baker could contact him. He left his name with the receptionist. No police title. Another short cut, but best to let them think this was regular business.

CHAPTER 57

PACER AND PICONE met in front of the converted terrace that housed Downes's business. The building was nondescript, squeezed between more imposing structures, the paint peeling and weeds sticking up from the gutters.

Pacer grabbed the doorhandle and marched in, Picone at his heels.

A middle-aged woman stood up from behind her desk, startled. 'Mr—'

Pacer cut in. 'Sergeant. We have an appointment with Mr Downes. Please show us through.'

A man in casual business attire met them halfway across the room. He exchanged a nervous glance with the woman, then stepped aside. The woman left the room and closed the door behind her.

Pacer announced they were investigating a breach of the *Local Government Act 1993* pertaining to false declarations. He had thought this up on the way over. Sounded right, or close enough to get the conversation off in the right direction.

Downes sat, rigid with guilt. Pacer spelled out the breach. Downes admitted the transgression, that he had signed off on the foundations even though the steel mesh wasn't tied down. Then the excuses flowed. It was just the once. No, actually, it had happened another time when it didn't matter. It wasn't as if flooring in contact with the ground could collapse and hurt anyone. Others did worse. Why weren't they investigating them?

'You wouldn't believe what goes on,' Downes said. 'Whole floors of apartment buildings not reinforced. They put the mesh down, the certifier signs it off, then the same mesh is moved to the next floor. Steel is expensive; concrete isn't. I do building inspections. That's how I know.

The floor dips just that little bit after a few years. I've never heard of one caving in though.'

Pacer raised his hand for Downes to stop. 'Let's get back to Hawthorne Park. You let that one slip by. Why?'

'The builders, they can choose anyone. There are plenty of certifiers around. Give them what they want and get called in for the next job.'

'You took a kickback,' Picone weighed in.

Pacer let him run with it. Downes nauseated him. A bad liar, a weasel.

'How much did they pay you, Mr Downes?' asked Picone.

Downes sank in his chair. 'The money was for the inconvenience, it wasn't a bribe. He wanted the job done on a particular day, Thursday I think it was. I was busy. I wanted to do it the following week, but he insisted.'

'The name, Mr Downes.' Pacer reminded himself to breathe. 'Who paid you?'

'I can't tell you because I don't know. Honest truth. I really don't know.'

'Then how was it arranged?' Pacer asked, leaning forward.

'Phone call. I was to head over there and fix the certificate. He said I would meet up with the builder, name of Arko.'

'And the money?'

'Arko handed over an envelope with the cash. But it wasn't from him – he was just the intermediary.'

'And where is that envelope now?'

'I stashed it at the back of that filing cabinet.' Downes indicated a standard three-drawer. 'It didn't feel right. Not after what happened there.'

'Will you give it to us voluntarily?' Pacer asked.

'Will that be the end of this if I do?' Downes said in a whispered tone.

'You'll need to make a statement. It's your best course of action, in my view.'

Picone produced an evidence bag. Downes dropped the envelope in and signed the receipt in duplicate. Pacer put one copy in the bag and handed the other to Downes.

'Get it to Melanie De Veen as quick as you can,' Pacer said as soon as they were out the door.

'Downes really didn't seem to know who the payment was coming from. Are you thinking it could be Flynn?' Picone asked.

'We know he was there. A good chance, I'd say.' Pacer called Melanie. 'I'm sending you a new exhibit. Bribe money. We think Flynn's prints might be all over the notes. His car was impounded at the depot in

Silverwater. Could still be there. Can you get over and take some prints? And collect DNA samples. Might be useful later on.'

'Consider it done, Pacer.'

Pacer turned to Picone. 'Before you go. What happened at Parramatta River Council this morning? Cooperative, were they? Didn't stand in your way?' A lot of people didn't like detectives. Picone would learn to wear the delaying tactics, the lukewarm reception, the veiled insults.

'No trouble at all. The receptionist was very helpful, called someone over from the next office. It was all on her computer. I gave her the addresses, she tagged them on her database, then did a printout.' He stopped.

'And?' asked Pacer. He was starting to wonder if Picone drew things out to needle him.

'Most of Flynn's properties were developed by the same outfit. Platinum Living.'

'None belonged to Sullivan Constructions?'

'No, I drew a blank.'

'Same for the properties from Cooks River Council,' Pacer said. 'No Sullivan. We're not looking hard enough. Come on, time to pay Flynn a visit.'

CHAPTER 58

CLARKSON'S EXAMINATION WAS over in minutes. Flynn endured the lecture, the advice to do his rehab, take better care of himself in future. The infection was gone, but the crack in the tibia would need time to heal.

Flynn guessed what Clarkson was thinking. Flynn was expected to be grateful. The great man had saved his leg.

The afternoon was wearing away, the time dragging. He was missing Sandra, who was checking on rehab places. If she found one, they would let him go tomorrow. Flynn wanted to go home, but that was vetoed. 'You'll recover more quickly if you go to rehab,' the hospital's physiotherapist had said.

A shadow fell across the bed. With a start, Flynn registered the presence of the detectives who'd been to his house. The older one regarded him coolly. Flynn sat up straighter. There was a chair for visitors but neither of them sat.

'Just a brief chat,' said the older one, the Detective Sergeant. 'Your accident, Mr Flynn. You were near Jubilee Park. Why were you there?'

'I was out for a run, like other people. I don't remember much. An ankle injury. I passed out and was brought here by ambulance.' That's what he told Sandra to say if anyone asked.

'Jubilee Park is a long way from your home. How did you get there? Do you remember that?'

'Ran, drove, took a taxi. Does it matter?'

'You didn't drive there. You left your car in Ashfield, on Liverpool Road. It was parked illegally and impounded by the local authority. It's at a depot in Silverwater, accruing fines and storage costs.'

'Look, I said before. I don't remember. It was parked outside my place. I want to report it stolen. Can you fix that?'

'Mr Flynn. The car was locked. You had your keys with you when you were found in Jubilee Park.'

'I don't believe this,' Flynn said. 'First you want to arrest me for trespassing and then it's for parking in the wrong place. Don't the police have better things to do?'

'We do, Mr Flynn. We are investigating a murder. Did you know Martin Sullivan?'

Flynn forced himself to look right back. They were waiting for a reaction. Say 'yes' and make up an unremarkable acquaintance or just stonewall?

'I don't think so.'

'You don't think so. Are you sure, Mr Flynn? Perhaps you met through business. I understand you work in the building industry. Mr Sullivan was a property developer.'

'No, I'm sure I'd remember if I'd met him. It's possible we were at an exhibition at the same time – there are several throughout the year. Give me the details of events he attended and I'll look in my diary.'

'No, nothing like that. A more personal encounter, perhaps?' Pacer waited.

'You really won't take no for an answer. I can't help you. Sorry.' Flynn reached back to adjust the pillow behind his head, wishing they would bugger off.

'But you do work in the building industry. In what capacity? Can you tell me that?'

'I assist property developers. They need their sites cleared before construction starts.' How much could they possibly know? He'd just give them stuff on the public record.

'You strip the sites of saleable assets and sell them to second-hand dealers.'

It was a statement. Flynn didn't answer. He'd given them enough.

'A cozy arrangement,' Pacer said, 'with the developer. I imagine the rights to enter and clear those sites don't come cheap.'

'A business deal like any other.' Flynn decided to keep it simple. No details.

'A competitive business,' Pacer said. 'Easier if you have a standing arrangement with one or two developers. Martin Sullivan, perhaps.'

Another statement. What were they getting at? They were way off the mark. Flynn sat impassive.

161

The two detectives made to leave. Flynn relaxed back against the pillows.

Halfway to the door, the Detective Sergeant turned.

'Just one more thing, Mr Flynn. Do you know a company by the name of Platinum Living? Do you have a business arrangement with them?'

'I've heard of them, sure.' Flynn rubbed his forehead, tried to look nonchalant. The detective was giving him one of those searching looks. Flynn expected more questions, but they didn't come. The officers left as silently as they had entered.

Sandra arrived soon after, chattering on about some rehab place she'd found. He half-listened, distracted. It was a bombshell, dropping Platinum Living like that. So what if they knew he was on Malcolm's books? Just a business arrangement. The cops were fishing.

And that thing about Sullivan, trying to get him to admit a connection. Both in the building industry? Like a million others. Come on.

How much did they know? It gnawed at him. Two locations, one opposite Manna House and the other at Jubilee Park. He was at both, they knew that. They would know about that witness, Sofia. She was there too, at both those places. They had suspicions about him, but it was circumstantial. Maybe she'd talked. But if she had, wouldn't they have what they needed? Arrested him? No. Their questions were lame. They didn't have enough.

It was like that other time with the cops. When he was in the import business. If you say nothing, you're okay. Don't incriminate yourself. But Sofia, she could be a serious threat. He couldn't be seen near her again. He'd have to find another way to get to her.

Sandra said her goodbyes. Flynn registered the familiar staccato clip of metal heels on polished floors, then silence. He reached for his phone, then put it back. They could be listening. He struggled to his feet and grasped the crutches. He made it as far as the corridor before stopping an orderly. The man wheeled Flynn to the visitors room. It was empty and it had a phone.

He made two calls. Justine Rawlings needed convincing. Sofia was her friend now. Flynn said he would help Sofia, like he'd helped Justine find a place to live, in return for a favour. Justine finally agreed to get the information he wanted.

A second call went to the man who told him about Sofia. Flynn asked a straight-out question: 'Does anyone else in the business know she's out there?'

'Nah, no one. They're sitting tight, preoccupied with bigger things. Nothing to worry about.'

Flynn wanted to believe him. 'Okay,' he said, closing the conversation. 'I'll have the information we need tomorrow afternoon. Come over here then, we'll have things to arrange.' There was still time. He could survive this.

CHAPTER 59

SOFIA STRETCHED HER legs out in front and looked at her shoes. They were once white, but the dust had dulled them to an uneven tan and the grass had left marks along the sides. The soles were worn flat in a few spots and when she wiggled her toes she could see where the holes were starting to form. A few days earlier she'd still had her black trainers, but a hand had reached into the tent and whisked them away in the middle of the night. Alice recognised the culprit as she flashed by and yelled after her. She almost lost her coloured headscarf but pulled it back.

The next morning Sofia wore a pair of scuffs meant for indoors. That's all she had. They were the worse for wear by the time she reached Manna House. Fortunately the people there found this pair. Garry showed her how he wrapped his shoes in a towel at night and used them as a pillow.

She liked it here under the railway arches in her own tent near Alice and Garry. A few of the original group had left and some new ones had arrived. Mostly men, making her nervous sliding their eyes over her, but the women were all right. Clancy kept watch over their group. When a man came down with a bag of warm socks, Clancy made them share. Sofia got two pairs. It lifted her spirits.

Sofia adjusted the cushion covering her milk crate and rubbed Wedge behind the ears. The dog looked deep into Sofia's eyes. She was sure Wedge really loved her. Dogs were the best. Most of the time. Her husband kept a nasty-looking hound on the end of a thick chain. He kicked it and fed it scraps. When Sofia asked why, he laughed and said he needed his dog to be mean. He went out pig shooting with the dog and his mates. Sofia didn't like it that he kept a gun at home.

Her husband was never far from her thoughts. She was always on guard. He said he would kill her if she tried anything like that again, after that time her neighbour phoned the police and they sent for the ambulance. They wanted her to press charges but she was too afraid. He would have killed her as soon as he got out of jail. She'd got away, but she knew he would try to find her. That man hiding in the bushes. Maybe her husband sent him. Alice thought so.

Up on the flat near the road, charity people had set up a gazebo and put chairs around. Sofia could smell the coffee they were offering. Alice and Garry were chatting to a young man and woman. They wanted to get their own apartment and had their names on a waiting list. They talked about it to anyone who looked like they were official or knew how the system worked. Sofia couldn't say so, but she hoped it wouldn't happen too soon. What would she do without them?

'The list of names is really long,' Alice had said, stretching her arms out wide to show how long that was. Then she reached her hand almost to the ground to indicate where she and Garry were in the order. 'Garry says at least a year.'

Not long after the gazebo people arrived, a van pulled up with Benny's Dog Wash emblazoned on the side. The driver leaned out the window and greeted them. Then he jumped down and reached into the cabin for a short-haired dog with white markings around one eye and black around the other. The man was stocky and balding, bustling with energy. He accepted a coffee and sat under the gazebo, wearing the expression of a man who enjoyed company. People from the camp and from nests scattered through the bush came over to look. Dogs milled about greeting one another.

Benny had parked the van so the back doors faced the gazebo. He opened them and dropped a ramp down. He called his dog and they went inside. Sofia had the side view so she couldn't see what was going on. It must have been good because the onlookers were entertained. She could hear sounds of splashing, then the high pitch of a dryer. The dog emerged, followed by Benny. He stood with hands on hips, grinning from ear to ear. The newly washed dog did the rounds, rewarded with pats, hugs and words whispered into his little ears. People fed him biscuits from the box near the water urn.

'Who's next?' Sofia heard Benny say. His eyes searched the onlookers. A man from a bush hideaway stepped forward, a mix of goldern retriever and cattle dog by his side. Benny greeted the man with a smile and felt the dog's thick, dusty matt.

'Won't come back to me when he's had a bath,' the man grumbled. Benny guided the dog up the ramp as his owner accepted a coffee and sat down.

Alice left the others and danced her way back to Sofia. 'Come on, it's fun. Bring Wedge, she could do with a wash.'

Sofia wasn't sure, but Alice insisted in that way she had. They found seats in the shade. Alice was right, it was fun. She could see into the van with its silvery tub, hoses and rows of soaps and washcloths. Benny held onto the wet dog's neck so it wouldn't shake out the water. His hand dropped for a moment and the dog took his chance. He started to quiver from the head down and was about to give his rump a good shake when Benny reached over and stopped him. The onlookers hooted with laughter. Sofia was laughing too, before realising she had joined in.

From the corner of her eye, she noticed John Wainwright slip into a chair. Alice noticed too. Alice put her hand over Sofia's and shot her a glance that said, *He can't do anything while I'm here.* Wainwright was talking to one of the charity people, a woman. Sofia recognised her from the food place near Newtown Station, the woman who had driven her to the hostel. The woman pulled her chair close and reintroduced herself as Peta. She asked if Sofia knew Wainwright. Would she talk to him about matters to do with her safety? Sofia wasn't sure what that meant, or why a police officer would care. But she trusted Peta, and Alice was there.

Wainwright's questions were unexpected. He asked her about the time she lived in that other park, behind the cafe. Had she seen anything to upset her? Sofia was fearful, wary. She tried to look blank, like she didn't know. A voice in her head was saying, *Don't tell him what you saw. They'll make it your fault.* She had seen worse where she came from, before Australia. Her parents always said to look away, tell them nothing.

Now he was asking something else. About her husband. Alice spoke for her, telling Detective Wainwright what he was like. The detective said the police would warn him to stay away, if that's what Sofia wanted. Sofia considered and in the end she said his name. Wainwright promised he would not tell where she was staying. He seemed like a good man. She wanted to believe him.

CHAPTER 60

PACER WAS INTRIGUED. Wainwright had asked him to come by but didn't say why. He noticed the small crowd around a gazebo. Was this it? He spotted Wainwright talking to Clancy. A van was parked on the grass verge. He wasn't sure, but it looked like one of those dog-wash contraptions. As he neared, Wedge emerged, ran down a ramp and was gathered up by Sofia. A stocky man wearing a dripping apron, with a crooked nose and one ear higher than the other, followed. Pacer recognised his grin, and the writing on the side of the van confirmed it. Benny, known to his mates as 'Benny the Toe'. The real name didn't matter. No one remembered.

Benny was an old foe, or friend, Pacer wasn't sure which. He'd met Benny during the Harold Park days when he was a car minder in a white coat. He opened doors for the bigwigs and cashed-up punters. He'd drive the vehicles around the back to the valet parking and keep the local kids away. Benny loved those cars with a passion. Couldn't resist taking a Porsche or Merc for a spin before tucking it away in the lot. One evening he was caught red-handed. The owner, the committee chair, hauled Benny in front of Pacer, demanding an arrest for car theft. Pacer talked the chair down. Benny, shame-faced and glum, slunk away, only to appear the following week as cheerful as ever. He got his job back. No one held a grudge against Benny.

After that, Benny had sought Pacer out every week, eager to provide any small service. Pacer provided brotherly advice, but Benny, who had a vulnerable nature, didn't listen. He got caught up with a mob that stole cars and changed the identifiers before selling them on. Benny jumped behind the wheel at service stations while the owner was paying and drove the car away. Benny, with his carefree attitude and eye for quality wheels, was a natural. He would have done it for nothing. Pacer knew of Benny's stints in and out of jail. He'd always hoped that Benny would stay out for good.

Pacer circled around the group at the gazebo and caught up with Benny as he was packing up.

'Good to see you, Benny.' Pacer looked at the van. 'What's this, your own business?'

'I've changed for good. No more cars. I'm all for dogs. Really enjoying this life.'

'Not doing this as community service, then?'

'Not that kind of community service.' Benny gave his lopsided smirk. 'Mostly I do regular jobs around the Inner West. This job is for Ruff Sleepers. They set me up where homeless people hang out and I take care of their dogs. Did five of them today, plus my own dog, Toby here.' Pacer noticed the dog sitting alongside Benny, panting with its tongue hanging out. It looked overweight, but Pacer was no judge. Benny reached into his pocket and extracted a lump of dried meat. Toby chewed it greedily.

'Where did you find Toby?'

'Came with the van. Another bloke wanted out so I got this van cheap and had the duco and artwork done. You reckon it looks good?'

'Sight for sore eyes. Really glad it's going well for you.'

Benny looked towards the apartments that had replaced the racetrack. 'Remember what used to be over there? The good old days, eh?'

'Most of the time. Hey, here's a mate of mine I'd like you to meet.' Pacer had noticed Wainwright edging closer and motioned him over. 'John Wainwright. Benny.' The men shook hands. Pacer didn't need to explain that Wainwright was a police officer, or Benny an ex-con.

'Thanks for coming,' Wainwright said to Benny.

'You organised this?' Pacer asked.

Wainwright nodded. 'Just made the call to Ruff Sleepers and they arranged it.'

Benny looked from one police officer to the other. 'You wouldn't be here on a casual visit. One of them fallen foul of the law?' He indicated the group near the gazebo.

'Nothing like that, Benny. But always interested in anyone who might be up to no good.'

'More around than most people think.' Benny thought this was a good joke. 'No one who loves a dog though. We're the good guys.'

'You've moved on, Benny? Keeping away from the bad guys, your old mates from inside?'

'This bloke I seen the other day. No mate of mine.' Benny looked down as if he'd already said too much.

'Who?' Pacer was suddenly interested.

'Know him from the slammer. Didn't like him one bit, him and his mates.'

'Go on.' Pacer remembered Benny's preambles. A storyteller needing to set the scene.

'Davidson. He was in for some porno thing, but everyone knew he'd done a lot worse. Got away with it though. Had friends who helped.'

Pacer and Wainwright exchanged a quick glance.

'How do you know that, Benny?'

'Seen him one day in the exercise yard with his mates. Boasting, he was, about outsmarting the cops. Then he clammed up.'

'You saw him the other day? Where?'

Benny furrowed his brow. 'Can't remember exactly. Around here somewhere. I was driving between jobs. Saw him standing on a corner talking to someone. One of his mates from inside.'

Pacer felt the electricity humming off Wainwright. No doubt Wainwright felt the same thing on him. It was as they had feared. Davidson in all the wrong places.

CHAPTER 61

PACER AND WAINWRIGHT dropped their empty cups in the bin and walked along the road to Pacer's car.

'The dog wash was a smart move,' Pacer said as he shifted the seat back. 'Sofia's attached to Wedge.'

'I managed to have a chat with her.'

'Did she talk about Hawthorne Park?'

'Didn't admit to seeing anything, but the look on her face gave it away. Saw something all right. Scared her half to death.'

'People who live on the edge are afraid they'll be blamed,' Pacer said. 'They play it safe, like the three monkeys.' Some lived in fear, others strutted about as if they owned the shop. You got denials from one lot and lies from the other.

Wainwright pulled out his notebook and showed Pacer what he'd written down.

'The husband's details. Brett Eyland. She's terrified of him. Wants me to help but has the idea we'll take her back to him. I said the police would warn him off. There was someone here today from a homeless charity, someone she knows and trusts. Just as well. The friend, Alice, glared at me the whole time.'

'Built a bit of goodwill then?'

'Maybe I've broken the ice.'

'Do you think she'll stay put?'

'No guarantees. A lot of homeless people are moving to warmer places up the coast. Might stay if she's not worrying about the husband. How about I check him out first thing tomorrow? The address is out Campbelltown way. I know people in the police command there.'

They watched as Benny drove past. 'How do you know that bloke?' Wainwright asked.

'We go back a long way. He used to work at Harold Park when I was the sergeant on duty at race meetings. Funny bloke, loved the place. I helped him out when he was in trouble. He followed me around like a puppy after that. Been in and out of jail a few times since. Mostly for minor stuff – you know, car theft.'

'He's Benny the Toe? Supposed to be an enforcer. Doesn't look that tough.'

'He's a bit of a softie. When you're a little bloke you make yourself very small or try to build yourself up. Less of a target for the nastier inmates.'

Pacer and Wainwright sat in silence, staring absently through opposite windows. The Sullivan murder had suddenly become a second-order emotion, and they both knew it. Pacer cleared his throat.

'Connors was right about Davidson coming back to Sydney. I wasn't certain until Benny identified him from that photo.'

'I keep a cold-case file, look at their ugly mugs sometimes.' Wainwright pulled out his phone and scrolled through the faces. Neat, ordinary, heavily bearded, mean-looking, even-featured. 'Most of these blokes you'd pass on the street and never guess what they're capable of.' Wainwright jabbed his finger against the screen and stopped the feed. A Caucasian man, fortyish, brown-haired and blue-eyed, stared open-mouthed at the camera, deep creases down both cheeks, a slight twist to the lips and a front tooth snapped off halfway.

'Come back, not just to Sydney, but here. The Inner West. Arrogant mongrel.' Wainwright almost spat the words.

'He'll have his reasons. Smarter than us, or so he thinks.' Pacer shifted uncomfortably. 'And maybe he is. He was one step ahead. I wasn't sharp enough. He concealed the evidence, who knows where. I couldn't nail him without it. Now he's out there, planning God knows what.'

'You weren't the only one. We all missed things. I should be first in line with the mea culpas. I was meant to find that girl before it was too late.'

Pacer stared at Wainwright. 'She was dead within thirty minutes of being snatched. Before you took the call. You hadn't even started.'

Wainwright's shoulders sagged. He looked away, blinking. He turned to Pacer, forcing a small grin. 'You'd think we'd be tougher in our business.'

CHAPTER 62

IT FELT LIKE a physical blow, then a sick feeling in the pit of his stomach. Pacer pushed the computer aside, rose and stared out the window. Nothing to see, just the bleak reality of office towers with their tangles of cooling units and utility boxes. He'd been so sure, but it wasn't Flynn. He flicked at the computer and looked again. No, it wasn't Flynn. As if this hadn't registered when he opened De Veen's email. She had checked the prints on the kickback money given to the certifier, Downes, against those from the Lexus, but there was no match.

He stepped around the desk and rubbed at the back of his neck. There was that movie, the man waking each morning to the same scenario in endless re-runs. So like him. Fix on a thread and go for it, blind to other possibilities. Then wake up to find that the opportunity, or the real culprit, has slipped away and you're back to square one.

De Veen was quick to answer her phone. 'I'm sorry, Pacer, I know you were counting on it. It was a good lead, worth following. But now you've ruled him out. What's wrong with that?'

'I don't like the man. Maybe that coloured my thinking.'

'I was pretty confident too, after those results from the pallet. It was definitely Flynn's blood. You got those, didn't you? I sent them through the other day.'

'Yeah, thanks. It would have made sense if the prints were his.' Pacer collapsed into his chair.

'Sometimes it just doesn't go your way. Flynn was a likely suspect, hanging around the crime scene like that. Any idea what he was up to?'

Pacer had given little thought to that question, beyond the assumption that Flynn's presence tied him to Sullivan's murder. What did he have on the man, really? He had been at Jubilee Park, but that was all. No link with the victim, no obvious motive. When the pieces didn't fit, you had to have a good think. Revisit your theories and question your assumptions. It wasn't a comfortable thing to do. He'd invested a lot of time and effort in chasing Flynn as a suspect in the murder of Martin Sullivan. Not as the one who'd wielded the knife, but, in Pacer's theorising, the man who'd arranged the disposal of the body. Now there was the prospect his energy had been misdirected, that he lacked flexibility in his thinking. Not for the first time.

Pacer went to the kitchen and filled his pot. 'Get on with it.' He spoke aloud, angry with himself. 'Work on the theory. That's what you'd tell Picone.'

What was Flynn doing on top of those containers? Peeping Tom? A nasty hobby involving a camera? Plenty of families visited the park. From his perch he could photograph kids without anyone noticing. Pacer would check with Vice. A dog fetish? Or Flynn just needing to be on his own for some other twisted reason?

There was another possibility, something Pacer hadn't properly considered. Flynn was following Sofia, he was certain. Was he using that place to spy on her? Did he have another reason to do that? Was the murder just coincidentally nearby?

Sofia was terrified her husband would find her. A natural fear, probably justified. Leaving the home heightened the danger for women like her. Pacer had focused single-mindedly on the murder and pushed that matter aside. What if Flynn was acting on her husband's behalf? Pacer could kick himself. He'd been a fool. Flynn might be out of action but the husband, Brett Eyland, was still out there. Perhaps more dangerous than Flynn. What if he tracked her down and harmed her? Pacer couldn't imagine how he would feel if that happened.

Pacer's energy ebbed as his anxiety increased. He called Wainwright.

'I've heard back from Campbelltown,' Wainwright said. 'Brett Eyland went to the station and put in a missing person's report about a week after Sofia left home. Wanted the police to look for her. They found a domestic incident on file from a few months back. An ambulance was called and she was taken to hospital. Discharged the next day. No AVO was recorded. That's often the way. The women are too scared.'

'So what did the police at Campbelltown do? They investigate?'

'They concluded there was no foul play. Eyland seemed genuinely worried. There was a bit of an investigation. A person fitting Sofia's description was identified on CCTV at Campbelltown station the day she left. Took the train towards Central. They concluded she'd left home. No bank account of her own, so too hard to trace.'

'That fits with her turning up at Hawthorne Park,' Pacer said.

'One of their detectives talked to the husband at his place this morning. A large dog, chained up, was throwing itself against the side gate. He was glad when Eyland answered the door and yelled at the dog to quieten down. Rough sort of character. Looked half-asleep. Turned out he works as a crane driver at the new airport and had just come off shift. Hadn't heard from his wife and said he wasn't looking. The detective left a clear message that any searching should be left to the police.'

'Doesn't sound like the type to be in with Flynn,' Pacer said.

'No, he doesn't. I've added his mug shot to the file on my phone. I'll recognise him if he turns up at Jubilee Park. So, is Flynn still in the frame?'

'It's looking less likely. There's no evidence, no link with the victim.'

'Hang on,' said Wainwright. 'Does he have to know the victim? These crimes are the work of a syndicate. Maybe he had a different role, picked up Sullivan in the limo?'

'Flynn was there, at Hawthorne Park. Makes sense he would have bribed the certifier. But he didn't. A syndicate, sure, but they'd keep it close.' What was Wainwright expecting? A football team? 'Nope, I'm thinking he could be linked to Sofia's husband. He's got money; he can get a good lawyer. I think my days of bowling up to Flynn and asking him questions are over.' Criminal lawyers could twist anything into reasonable doubt. Get their bloke off and call it a win. Guilty or not, they didn't care. 'I just can't find any link to Sullivan.'

The call ended abruptly. Pacer couldn't tolerate criminals going free. A stab of anger brought him back to the present. Not this time. He wouldn't be beaten. Those fingerprints. If not Flynn's, then whose? He reached for a slim folder and removed a single page. Holding it by a corner, he manoeuvred it into a plastic sleeve and filled out the chain-of-evidence paperwork. He picked up his phone.

'I didn't expect to hear back from you so soon,' De Veen said. Pacer could hear the anticipation in her voice.

'It might be nothing, but I have another set of prints for you.'

'For the money?'

'Yep, for the money.'

CHAPTER 63

LILLIAN ZHANG, SULLIVAN'S accountant, was back in Sydney. Pacer wasted no time in arranging an interview. He headed west along Victoria Road, drove across the smooth arc of the Gladesville Bridge and turned into a street alongside Ryde Park. He slowed and backed into a parking space just beyond the destination in the car's GPS.

The building housed professional services, including several accounting firms. Zhang's offices occupied a corner suite on the fifth floor. The view took in the suburbs, parkland and waterways from Cabarita in the southeast to Melrose Park and Meadowbank north of the Parramatta River. Zhang, receptive and businesslike, met Pacer in the reception area. She was tall, matching Pacer in height, and elegantly dressed in a silk skirt and matching jacket in shades of mauve. With a smooth turn of her heel she invited Pacer to sit at a round table in her office. An assistant delivered jasmine tea. Pacer nodded his appreciation.

Lillian Zhang wasn't just an accountant, she told Pacer, but a business manager and consultant. Yes, she confided, she kept a nice office, but that was to inspire clients' confidence. She had a full book and turned new business away. Pacer thought of Pat, who did his annual tax, in his dingy cubicle and tatty suit.

'Martin was a regular client. Active in business, always on the lookout for an opportunity.'

'What kind of opportunity took his interest?' Pacer asked.

'It changed over the years. I first met Martin after he'd had an unsatisfactory experience with an employer in Singapore. He wanted his own enterprise. I encouraged him. He was bright and energetic, with the work ethic and drive to succeed. But we didn't agree on all points. Martin was set on a course I thought too risky for a person starting out. Venture capital. Do you need the details, Sergeant?'

'I would like to know how it ended and if he made enemies along the way.'

'I see.' Zhang hesitated and sipped her tea. She took her time in answering. 'Martin was lucky, at least for a while. Not that he saw it like that, he believed in his own talent. He had links to Malaysian investors. There's excessive red tape in their country, not to mention the corruption. An opportunity to slip money out and invest overseas is attractive.'

'In that case, why did he close the business?'

'Martin made the usual errors. He put too much finance into setting up his office before the cash flow was secure. Bought lovely furniture and art works. After the first flush of success, he went for a business with little chance. A gourmet food venture with an old friend from school, a Jordan Alexander. Expensive to set up. Industrial kitchen, vehicles, all sorts of overheads. He couldn't be told. The investor lost badly.'

Pacer looked up from his notes. 'I have spoken to Mr Alexander. He and Sullivan remained on good terms. But the investor? Can you provide the details?'

'Certainly,' she said, checking her files. 'A Musa Bidanau. From Sarawak, one of the old Malaysian families. Martin said they originally made money from tin mining.'

'Did Mr Sullivan close his venture capital business after that?'

'Yes. The business was close to insolvency. I convinced him to shut it down and minimise losses while the opportunity was still there.'

'Did other investors lose their money?' Pacer asked.

'The payouts were quite small. It's business. These people don't expect to win every time.'

'And Musa Bidanau. He went away empty-handed, more or less, but was not unhappy or upset?'

'I don't know how he felt, but he got what he was entitled to.'

'But he might hold a grudge?'

'Perhaps. He was more vocal than the others. Disappointed, certainly. Going in with Martin was a new chapter for him, his opportunity to branch out from the family.'

Zhang excused herself to take a call. She smiled, apologetic. Pacer rose and stepped to a window, admiring the view. If this Musa Bidanau was involved in Sullivan's murder, he had bided his time. Several years had passed. Murderers rarely had the patience or control to wait it out. There had to be a trigger to awaken the original insult or affront. A chance meeting. A new transgression by the same individual. A cold, seething rage that grew with time.

Zhang completed her call and joined Pacer.

'And what was Mr Sullivan doing recently?' Pacer asked.

'Property development appealed to him. You'll want a list of his recent business associates, I'm sure. I'll have my PA send it through.'

'Thank you. Was that interest sparked during his time in Singapore?'

'Yes, I understand that was the case. He also worked with a local property developer for about eighteen months. The headquarters of the firm are close by. If you look over that way you can see the name on top of that narrow building, the one in front of the shopping mall.'

Pacer looked to where Zhang was pointing. The silver script stood out against the white background. Platinum Living.

Zhang smiled. 'A very successful business. Turnover has doubled in just three years, I'm told. Several thousand apartments are under development with more on the planning table. The CEO has quite a profile in this area. Malcolm Hendry. You might have heard of him? He heads up the local Chamber of Commerce.'

CHAPTER 64

WAS THIS THE breakthrough Pacer had been waiting for? First it was Flynn in two places linked to the crime, and now there was the Platinum Living connection. What was going on? Had Sullivan and Flynn met there? If so, did it add up to a motive for murder? Putting more time into investigating Flynn was a gamble – it was eating up a lot of his time. He could imagine what Connors would say, his irritation at screaming point. Would he try to close the investigation, replace Pacer with a detective more resolute?

Pacer's stomach churned as the old uncertainties rose to the surface. The case was going cold. The facts he had gathered felt like pieces of broken glass that didn't fit together. Failure was on the horizon, staring his way. 'C'mon, smarten up,' he rasped. 'Get a grip.'

His gut said keep going with Flynn but change tack. Pacer's breathing slowed, his mind shifting gears. Right, so do something different. Go back to Sullivan, see what he was up to and if Flynn was in the mix. After his meeting with Lillian Zhang, there were plenty of leads. Pacer pushed files aside and picked up his landline.

Zhang had suggested he contact one of Martin Sullivan's most important business associates, a man named Hassim Evans-Khan, a builder. Together, they were in construction. The voice on the other end of the phone belonged to a young man. He had been shocked by Sullivan's death and was scrambling to work through the business implications. Sullivan had organised everything to do with the business – the development sites, the finance, the architects – while he himself managed the construction side.

'He was good at that stuff,' said Evans-Khan, still processing the loss of his business partner. 'A bit of a visionary, you know?'

Pacer arranged to meet him at his work premises near the light rail. He was determined to move quick, waste no more time.

'You'll find me on the ground floor of our current build. In Leichhardt.'

Pacer boarded the light rail at Capitol Square on Hay Street. The streetscape was awash with contrasts. A colonial building, grounded and stately, was overshadowed by a Lendlease tower. Further along, Pacer could see the facade of Paddy's Market and the entrance to Chinatown. Across the road was a construction, its name, Urban Nest, emblazoned in green. Could that really be for people to live in? With its borderless windows reflecting silvery light, it looked like a beehive.

The streets disappeared as they entered a world of concrete and steel, the light rail stops located in the folds of underground car parks and delivery docks. This was the Darling Harbour precinct, the rear side. The tram was full now, with as many passengers standing as seated. A stir of excitement passed through the crowd as they pulled in to The Star, gateway to the city's casino. Most of the passengers, tourists from overseas and seniors on a day excursion, poured out. Only a dozen or so remained.

The tram entered a deep cutting with sandstone walls darkened by soot and tufts of lomandra sticking out of crevices. Pacer eyed the long staircase at John Street Square, glad that this wasn't his stop. The tram returned to ground level as it passed by the Sydney Fish Market and opened to the expansive views of Wentworth Park and Glebe. The Anzac Bridge was now visible on the right.

The tram arrived at Jubilee Park Station. This was the stop for the Tram Sheds, near where Sofia and the homeless group were camped. He saw the waters of the bay on one side and the pet supply business on the other. Before long, the tram was travelling through light-industrial areas mixed with houses and terraces on small blocks. A motorway overpass loomed and a row of mustard-coloured sheds caught his eye. So this is what Leichhardt looked like from above. An old suburb with cramped streets, rusting factories and workers' terraces. Not much open space and a sparse tree canopy.

Now they were approaching Hawthorne Station, with its mature trees and open spaces. Pacer caught sight of a black and white dog chasing a ball. Was that the same collie he had encountered before? The triangle of land housing the film centre was clearly visible. Impossible to miss the discarded props in the storage area at one end. Pacer could just make out the containers with the sandbags on top as the tram came to a halt. Flynn would have had a good view from there.

The tram was moving again. Scrubby trees on either side blocked the view for a short way. After getting off at Marion, Pacer didn't have far to walk. He spotted the residential complex, almost completed, as soon as he stepped off. Looking up, he admired the symmetry of the building and the earthy shades of the facade.

Evans-Khan came out to greet him, handing over a hard hat. 'Hope you don't mind. It's a building site.'

'A nice-looking building.' Pacer adjusted the headgear. 'Better than most of the new ones.'

'Martin had a good eye for design. He used architects, of course, but liked to work on the plans himself. Pored over the details. People deserve to live in beautiful spaces. That was his motto. Come on, I'll show you around.'

Pacer was surprised. He thought they were all the same, developers. Sullivan had his faults, got people's backs up. But he did care about his trade. He built quality.

Inside the cramped site office, Evans-Khan made coffee for himself and a loose-leaf tea for Pacer.

'This place is close to the light rail. Was that Mr Sullivan's strategy, build near public transport?'

'Yes, especially the light rail. The best opportunities are around the new stations. Plenty of builders like us are after them. It's getting harder to snare the best sites.'

'You have competitors? Like Platinum Living?'

'I've heard of that outfit,' Evans-Khan replied. 'Well established. They build medium-sized apartment blocks, same as us, but a lot more of them. I wouldn't call them a competitor. Different league.'

'Do you know a man by the name of Flynn? He clears properties of their assets before they are demolished. Mr Sullivan might have had an arrangement with him?'

'No, I don't know him. Martin didn't mention anyone by that name. If there was someone like that, the place would have been cleared before my boys moved in.'

Pacer reflected briefly. Cast the net wider, don't get stuck on Flynn. He asked Evans-Khan about possible run-ins with associates or competitors.

Evans-Khan laughed. 'Martin was easygoing on the surface but underneath he was a shrewd operator. Had a thicker skin than people realised. You can't be friends with everyone in this business, he'd say.'

'A thick skin? In what way?' Cryptic. Evans-Khan had more to say, Pacer could feel it.

'This is a competitive game. Martin stepped on a few toes to get what he wanted. Some might have taken it personally.'

'Anything you can recall?' Yes, Sullivan had made enemies. Maybe Flynn was one, but there could have been more.

'There was one time, his first project. That was before we started working together. He told me about it over drinks. Bloke threatened to kill him.'

'Did he report it to the police?' Pacer spoke quickly, reaching inside his jacket for his notebook.

'Course not. Laughed it off. That was Martin. Like I said, he had a thick skin.'

'Did Mr Sullivan give you any details? A name, perhaps?'

'He didn't say who it was, just a bloke who thought he had made a deal, only for Martin to break it. There was no deal, nothing signed off.'

'His first project, you say. Do you know where that was?'

Evans-Khan rubbed his chin. 'It was a build quite close by. In Mill Street, I think. That was it, Mill Street.'

CHAPTER 65

PACER WASN'T ABOUT to waste any time. As soon as he left Evans-Khan, he ducked into the recessed doorway of a shop long closed, mail spilling from under the door. His call was answered on the first ring. Picone was bored with reports and paperwork and was grateful for the distraction. Pacer could detect it in his voice. In the background he heard the tap-tapping of the laptop as Picone searched for news on Mill Street.

'Not much on the actual build, but there's a reference to protests around the construction. This stuff isn't digitised. The reports and other information are kept at the council library.'

'Get over there and have a dig. There are no cars today. Fancy the train and a bit of a jog?' Pacer laughed after he hung up. Picone would prefer to run the whole way. He might have run himself at one time, but that was a while ago.

The Mill Street development was a few blocks away, an easy walk. Pacer surveyed the outside of the building. The architectural lines were clean and the chocolate and cream hues pleasing to the eye. No coloured plastic detailing to mask the blandness of the design. Not like the garish street frontages he had seen in Summer Hill. No, this was a good-looking building. He wondered why the community had objected.

He walked the perimeter. Retail outlets stretched along three sides at ground level. Two sides housed an accountant, a chemist and a convenience store. On one corner a small cafe opened onto the footpath, a barista set-up next to a case filled with pastries and wraps. Pacer's eyes were drawn to a mound of chocolate brownies. No, not this time.

Further along, a door was flung open. A fit-looking man in training gear hurried away, loud music booming from the room he'd left. Pacer peered through the windows. Rows of treadmills and fitness equipment filled the cavernous space, mostly empty of patrons. Not the busiest time of day. So Sullivan had put a gym on the ground floor. Pacer recognised the brand. They were all over, not that he'd stepped inside any.

Back at Marion Station, Pacer waited for a ride to the city. The tram going in the outward direction arrived first. On a whim, he got on. I need time to think, he told himself.

The tram passed over Parramatta Road, a tired-looking streetscape with houses, shops and industrial buildings crammed in. No room for new builds unless they knocked this lot down. The tram was approaching Lewisham West. The scene here was completely different due to the recent spate of development. Apartment blocks rose on both sides of the track, the entrances to some just a few paces from the platform. A converted mill had pride of place but was overshadowed by an apartment tower at least ten floors high. And so it continued, large blocks at the tram stops and medium density in between. Pacer stared in disbelief at the structure abutting Arlington Station. Brutalist in design, the building looked dark and menacing. The side facing the tracks had recessed balconies in long rows, small and finished with vertical bars. Who could live in those prisons? A few stops more and he was at Dulwich Hill, the end of the line. Here, the landscape was in transition, the skyline bare apart from the skeletons of apartment blocks topped by cranes.

Pacer was the last passenger. He stayed on and greeted the driver as she switched to the far cabin for the return journey. What was he to make of it? Huge apartment projects had sprung up around those last five tram stops. Like that converted mill near Lewisham.

The stretch from Leichhardt to Lilyfield was of a different character. The housing was higher density and there were numerous factories and warehouses, mostly run-down. Space left for some big developments, maybe, but the real opportunities were for builders of the medium-sized apartment blocks. People like Sullivan. And Platinum Living.

Pacer checked himself. Not all of that stretch was filling with apartments. Hawthorne Park was right in the middle. Passing by the second time, the absence of development was startling. A nice place, close to the bay. A serene oasis, a place for dogs and people to walk and play. As yet untouched. But for how long? Were the developers already circling?

CHAPTER 66

PACER GOT OFF the tram at Jubilee Park, crossed the tracks, took the few steps up to Maxwell Road and entered the Tram Sheds on the high side. Built in 1904, according to the sign. The interior had been gutted, apart from the industrial-sized exhaust hoses and steel framing lining the ceilings and below, an array of cafes, bars and markets. Pacer stepped onto the escalator and took in the movement of the crowd as he rode down. Outside, he walked through the car park and over a footbridge.

Wainwright was waiting on the other side, absorbed in a game of fetch with a sable and white collie. It dawned on Pacer that he was as much at ease with dogs as he was with people, and they with him. He had the knack of losing himself in the moment, enjoying the simple things. Did the past weigh as heavily on him? Pacer felt sure it did, but Wainwright seemed to cope with it differently. More kindly, perhaps?

Pacer quickened his pace and walked over. 'What is it with border collies and balls? Do they ever get tired of chasing them?'

'Not so far,' Wainwright answered. 'There's a bench over there. Want to take the weight off?' The collie jumped at the sound of a whistle from a woman near the car park and raced to her. Wedge wandered over from a tree where she had been resting, almost invisible against the brown earth. She gave Pacer's leg a nudge, then lay between him and Wainwright.

'How come you've got Wedge?' Pacer asked, leaning down to pat the dog.

'She was following Sofia this morning and she wouldn't go back. Garry asked me to mind her. They were off to Manna House. Almost a routine.'

'I got word from Connors on the way here. The Assistant Commissioner has made it official. You're on the team.' Pacer glanced at his companion. Wainwright was pleased, too.

'Just as well. Did the rounds with Kurt Otway this morning. Showed him the places Davidson liked to hang around.'

'Tough on you, going back there, talking to Kurt about it.' Bringing it all back, it must hurt.

'Nothing much has changed. The playground. Her school.' Wainwright spoke slowly, as if he was reliving each moment.

'I'll pay the school principal a visit. It's the same person, been there a long time. Remember her? Mariam Ahmed. She should be told.'

Wainwright nodded and sighed. 'You're still in charge of the investigation.'

'Can't touch him unless he breaches the rules and goes near places for kids. We still don't know where he's staying. Probably couch surfing. Makes it hard.'

'Kurt's looking, but his team has only so much time. Plenty more like Davidson to keep an eye on.' Wainwright kicked at a tuft of grass.

'Kurt is across all the places, the playgrounds, the ovals?' Pacer knew he was.

'He's onto it.' Wainwright sighed again.

'Almost forgot. Connors wants to see you. His welcome speech. Expect to be lectured on spending the petty cash.' They both laughed, and then Pacer's expression changed. 'What about Sofia? How will you keep an eye on her and look for Davidson as well?'

'I'll be on that case when I know Sofia is safe. I advised her to stick with the group, not go off on her own. She trusts me up to a point. Had a quiet word this morning. She wanted to know if she would be sent back to her home country if she leaves her husband for good, makes it official.'

'You'll get a lot closer if Alice is out of the way,' Pacer said.

Wainwright rose and tossed the ball to Wedge. She gave chase and dropped it at Pacer's feet.

'Your turn,' Wainwright said, grinning.

Wainwright's phone buzzed. He nodded at Pacer and stepped further away, then put the phone to his ear and listened intently. His hands moved in emphasis as he replied to the message. He looked back at Pacer. It involved both of them. When the call ended, Pacer got to his feet and hurried over.

'That was Kurt. Davidson was sighted twenty minutes ago in that park along Old Canterbury Road. There's a school for little kids and a playground close by. You know the place. Kurt's bloke saw him and started to approach. Davidson spotted him and took off.'

'He lost him?'

'Easy to do. That area is a maze. Davidson could have gone anywhere, once our man lost line of sight.'

'Should we get someone over there?'

'He'll be long gone. But this tells us one thing. Davidson is not just back – he's on the prowl. That's definite.'

CHAPTER 67

BETH ROLLINS SIGHED as she went over the numbers. It was always the same this time of year. Too many dogs to house and too little money to feed them. People excited to welcome a new member in their family at Christmas were now tiring of the chewed-up shoes, stepping in dog poo and expensive visits to the vet. The mornings were colder too. Pre-breakfast walks were harder to take and the evenings were closing in. Who wanted to leave the house again after getting home from work? And didn't the kids promise to wash the dog?

Beth had heard it all during the last weeks. Dogs, once the centre of their world, dumped on her. She was a dog rescue service, wasn't she? The dog lying beside her, a three-legged beagle with a broken tail, looked up with sorrowful brown eyes. She gave it a pat and popped a liver treat in its mouth.

'Sorry, old boy. Two weeks is all we can wait.'

The door creaked open and a stout man with a round face peered around. Beth beckoned him inside, a small cavoodle drawing close to his leg. Through the half-open door, Beth glimpsed a tall man in a khaki shirt, blue jeans and trainers standing in the reception area, leaning over the array of dog leads on sale.

'Umm ... ahhh ... there's someone wants to take a dog. This one.'

'Okay, Stan, that's good. Get the paperwork done and I'll sign it off.'

Stan drew closer, his whisper accentuating the stammer. 'It ... it ... doesn't seem right. Big blokes like him, they go for the robust breeds, rottweilers, pinschers, staffies.'

'Maybe he wants it for his kids. Look at that sweet little face and big floppy ears.' She bent down to ruffle them. 'He's got the Cavalier

King Charles look, hasn't he? Snub nose and huge brown eyes. Just the thing.'

'I don't think so, not for his kids. Didn't get that impression.'

'Didn't you take him around the pens? We've got plenty of others. No pure breeds of course, but some good-looking bitzers. Or what about the Weimaraner that came in the other day? Well trained, in good nick.'

'I showed him the lot. He ignored them. Only got interested when we reached the little fellas down the far end.'

Beth stretched her neck and peered round the door. The man was reaching for a bag of kibble. His sleeve slipped up, revealing spidery tattoos on a sinewy forearm. He sensed her eyes on him and turned. The lips in the craggy face parted in a smile that revealed a broken front tooth.

Beth turned back to Stan. 'He can pay for the vaccinations? You gave him the spiel on taking care of a pet?'

Stan nodded, but looked worried.

'Look, Stan, we don't have a lot of choice. You know what happens if we can't rehome these dogs.' Beth's hand brushed the beagle beside her. 'Bring me the paperwork and see him out.'

CHAPTER 68

FLYNN PRETENDED NOT to see the man hovering outside his door, an old bloke in for rehab after a hip replacement. He occupied the room next to Flynn's and was always up for a chat. Flynn's room was at the end of the corridor, next to the outdoor staircase that led from the first floor to ground level. It was added a long time ago, a fire escape, so the door was never locked. Patients and visitors were expected to take the lift at the far end of the corridor where the nurses' station was located, but it was no good using it if you didn't want to be seen.

He was still there. Flynn turned his head and nodded. The old man winked, indicating the cigarette sticking up from the pocket of his plaid shirt. Flynn heard the man's grunts and gasps as he made his painful way down the metal steps. He was heading for the bench behind a hedge. Sometimes Flynn detected the smoke wafting upwards. He hated the smell, always had.

This place was described to Sandra as a modern facility in a quiet, restful street. That was half true. The rehab wing was new, all glass and steel with white walls and crisp finishes. A torture chamber of the most modern sort. There was a hydrotherapy pool, therapeutic devices with pulleys and straps, and cheerful staff immune to the resistance of their patients. Flynn was ensnared for two hours in the morning and again after lunch. The accommodation wing was a different matter. He had no idea when it was built but imagined it crammed with the war-wounded when his grandfather was a young man. Not that Flynn had ever met his grand-father, or his own dad for that matter. The spartan rooms were laid out in long rows on either side of the corridor and were devoid of any comfort to assuage what occurred in therapy.

Sandra had promised to come back later that evening. She was handling it better than he was, telling him to go with the flow and take the time to get better. But Sandra had no idea. He had work to do, and time mattered if Flynn was to save his skin.

Craig Thomas entered the room and pulled up the only chair. Flynn was glad to see him. He'd have news. Flynn accepted the burner and hid it in his bedside locker.

'Use it for me and anyone else in the business,' Thomas said.

'So, what's happening out there? I haven't heard a thing. There's been no calls, no visits from the cops, no nothing.' He wasn't going to admit anything.

'There's questions being asked, people watching their backs. They don't like surprises. But that's not why I'm here. The heavies want to know what's happening at your end. There's been a development.' Thomas checked that no one was in the corridor. He sat again.

'Huh?' It would be bad; Flynn could feel it.

'The cops found Arko.'

Flynn was dumbfounded. 'How the hell did that happen?' He gripped the side of the bed, under an impulse to push himself away.

'You were supposed to see to it.'

'I wasn't in on that one. Don't put it back on me.' Flynn's voice was dry, rasping.

'Keep your voice down. You sure the cops haven't paid you a visit?'

Flynn shook his head. Had Thomas heard something?

'The cops were keeping it under wraps. Contacted Arko's cousin. He wanted nothing to do with it, but they made him arrange the cremation. Private. No one there. Anyway, this cousin is a mate of Edgar's. That's how we found out.'

'All I did was make Arko lie low until they could get him away. I didn't know what was coming.' Flynn tried to keep his voice in check.

'Too late for that. What about that witness, the homeless woman? You take care of her?'

'Sofia. I know where she is but couldn't get to her before this accident.' Flynn tapped on his plaster. 'But I've got it in hand. We are sending someone. I can't do it. I'll need you to organise him for me.'

'Edgar?'

'Of course not. You haven't told him about Sofia, have you? We agreed to keep it between us.' If Edgar, Malcolm's driver, knew, he would be sure to pass it on.

Thomas shook his head. 'Why would I do that?'

Flynn's head was clearing. 'That contact I told you about – the one close to Sofia. She picked up information about the husband. Name, where he lives. I can't do any more from here. The cops could be watching.'

'What are you saying? Send the husband after her?'

'I'm told he's got a nasty streak. He'll take care of it. So here's the deal. Take these details I've written here, get a phone number and give him a call. Rile him up, but don't overdo it.'

CHAPTER 69

'I'VE GOT THE lowdown on Mill Street,' Picone said, as Pacer walked into the incident room.

'Off you go then. Just the main points.' Pacer sat down and placed his cup of tea on the table.

'That new block replaced a warehouse owned by a Marco Zanetti. He'd rented the space to a bunch of artisans – potters, jewellery makers and people like that. There was a real community feel. The council wasn't so happy though. Their inspectors went through, said the building was unsafe, insisted he make alterations.'

'Cooks River Council?' Pacer asked.

'Yes, their area covers all of Leichhardt.'

Pacer sipped his tea. It had reached the perfect temperature. 'Does the death threat against Sullivan fit anywhere in this story?'

'Yes, but the background is important. The council required more than the owner could afford, another fire exit, new sprinkler system, all sorts of stuff. They gave him an out. They'd change the zoning from public purpose to medium-density residential. That way he could sell to a developer.'

'So, what's included in public purpose?' Pacer didn't know that term. Baker hadn't mentioned it in his little lecture.

'Whole lot of stuff. Schools, community halls, cooperatives and even warehouses not covered under the business categories.' Picone spread his collection of notes, clippings, documents and diagrams across the table.

'That covers a lot of bases,' Pacer said. Anything they want it to be. Convenient.

'Anyway,' Picone continued, 'the rezoning happened and the building was sold.'

'To Martin Sullivan.'

'It seems so. It wasn't straightforward. The tenants wanted Sullivan to reserve a space on the ground floor for their cooperative. He agreed.'

Pacer finished his tea and put his cup to one side. 'But he put a gym there instead.'

'Yes, how did you know?' Picone didn't wait for a reply. Excited again. Pacer recognised the signs, the flushed cheeks, the jiggle of the knee.

'There were protests from the community. They made quite a fuss.'

'The death threat?'

'From Marco Zanetti.'

'You didn't get that from these records.' Pacer flicked through the documents Picone had collected.

'No, it was the librarian. She was there when it happened – one of the protesters.'

'Do we know anything about Zanetti?'

'Runs a cafe in Leichhardt.'

'Let's pay him a visit.' Pacer was already reaching for his jacket.

CHAPTER 70

THEY FOUND MARCO Zanetti at the back of his cafe preparing for the next morning's rush. A server showed them through, removed her apron and left via the back entrance. Zanetti was about Pacer's age, with dark hair and an olive complexion.

As he ushered them in, Pacer noticed his movements were quick and agile. Not a large man, but his physical presence conveyed strength.

'Can I get you guys a coffee? I'm about to close but I keep a machine going while I'm doing the books.'

Picone accepted but Pacer declined.

'I understand you owned a warehouse in Mill Street, which you sold about three years ago.' Pacer's tone was deadpan. Zanetti was too relaxed for Pacer's liking.

'That factory belonged to my parents.' Zanetti smiled as he spoke. 'They migrated to Australia after the war, met here and started a business. Bought that place – it was previously used by the army during the war – and got into hat making. They hoped I would carry it on, but my heart was in food.'

'So you decided to sell?'

'I had to. The local council insisted on an inspection. They gave me a list of safety upgrades that they insisted I carry out. Compulsory. Would have cost a bomb.'

'And you sold to Martin Sullivan?'

'That's how it turned out. Hey, he's the guy who was murdered in Hawthorne Park, right?'

Pacer watched the muscles in Zanetti's face tighten as he faked casualness. He'd get straight to the point, apply pressure. 'Yes, that's correct.

We understand you had a disagreement with Mr Sullivan and threatened his life.'

'Who told you that? Must be crazy.' Zanetti stood up and took a step back.

'Please take a seat, Mr Zanetti. We have a credible witness.' Pacer fixed Zanetti with an unflinching stare.

'Okay, I might have said more than I should have,' Zanetti dropped back into his seat. 'He got me stirred up. But I didn't touch him. Not that I didn't want to, the treacherous bastard.'

Zanetti was a bit of a hothead. Pacer waited for him to calm down.

'I had tenants and felt responsible. They wanted the original buyer to retain space for them on the ground floor, but he was dismissive, arrogant. I was relieved when Sullivan contacted me out of the blue and made an offer. Different approach entirely from the other mob. So I switched horses.'

'But he didn't keep his word,' Pacer said.

'I blew my stack when I found out. To make things worse, he said it was just business, that the deal with the gym franchise was too good to refuse. He just stood there smiling and making excuses. The rest is a bit of a blur, to be honest. Apparently I said I'd blow his brains out. I didn't own a gun. Haven't even held one.'

'Did you see Sullivan after that?'

'No, this happened after the sale. Look, if I was going to kill anyone it would be that bloke from the council.'

'Go on, Mr Zanetti.'

'They hit me with their inspection and called me to a meeting. Said they understood my situation was difficult and explained about the rezoning. I argued with them. Plenty of places in a worse state than mine. But you've got no comeback.'

'Who attended that meeting, do you remember?' Pacer could see Picone from the corner of his eye. The young detective was transfixed, the excitement building.

'I remember all right. Mark Baker. Mr Nice Guy – not. Smooth on the outside but a real manipulator. And his sidekick, Craig what's-his-name.'

'Why do you describe Mr Baker as manipulative?'

'Because that's what he is. There's more to the story. The original buyer contacted me right after they rezoned. Platinum Living. That was the company. Tipped off by Baker is my guess, for some kind of kickback. My uncle's friend owned a building similar to mine. He got the same treatment. Maybe it wasn't illegal, but I felt set up.'

'So you'd chosen Platinum Living before Sullivan came along?' Picone interrupted, choosing his words carefully. 'How did they take your decision to change buyers?'

'Pissed off, believe me. I never met the boss, always acted through his lawyers and agents. Tried to cajole me into changing my mind. Wouldn't accept that I was selling to Sullivan Constructions. Their agent kept coming around, sweet-talking the tenants. I didn't trust him. No one there did. The real fireworks happened just before I settled with Sullivan. We'd just started a meeting when Flynn walked in …'

'Flynn?' Pacer said. It was a jolt.

'That's what he called himself. The agent. For Platinum Living. Anyway, Sullivan and Flynn caught sight of each other. It was pure hate. They shoved each other around the side of the building and had some kind of reckoning. Then Sullivan came back inside. He looked pale and shaken. Flynn just stalked off.'

'Did Mr Sullivan tell you what happened between them?' Picone sat forward, engrossed.

'Nope, made his excuses and left soon after. I was pissed off with Baker more than him. He was the one who made this happen. But if anyone wanted to kill Martin Sullivan, it was Flynn.'

CHAPTER 71

PACER WAS STILL reeling as he hurried with Picone towards their unmarked car. Although only mid-afternoon, the sun was weakening, the shadows lengthening onto shopfronts and painted brick walls.

Pacer opened the door on the passenger side, but hesitated before getting in.

'Flynn.' He ejected the name as if it were a curse. 'Back in the frame.'

Picone stood watching, keys in hand.

'Have I missed something?' Pacer said, more to himself than his companion. 'C'mon. What else is there?'

He looked towards Picone, a glint in his eye. There was something. They could check it now, this afternoon.

'We're taking a detour on the way back to the station. There's a place in Summer Hill. Hop in, I'll give you the directions.'

Picone pulled up outside a business on a narrow street that looked like it belonged to the century before last. Pacer sprang out of the car and leaned back in.

'Wait here. I won't be long.'

Angus Monroe was at a workbench, his soldering iron poised over a panel of coloured glass delicately framed by lead. Looking up, he saw Pacer in the doorway, removed his eye protection and stood to greet him.

Pacer set in without preamble. 'You told me before that Flynn delivered the salvaged material to you. Some quite substantial pieces.'

'He did that on a number of occasions.' Monroe was up to speed, as content as Pacer was to dispense with the small talk.

'Did he have help?'

'Yes, there was a man for the unloading. The same man each time. He brought the pieces in the back of a ute. I didn't like the way he handled them. Quite rough.'

'Did you speak to the man? Get his name?'

'There were no introductions and he didn't say anything. Flynn handled the negotiations.'

Pacer took out his phone and scrolled through to a grainy photo. Arko.

'I'd recognise him even without that scar across the eyebrow,' Monroe said thoughtfully, nodding his head. No doubt, it was Arko.

Pacer sat mute on the trip with Picone back to the city. Flynn, it was Flynn. He had always felt it but had almost lost faith in his own judgement. It was happening again, Flynn lying and covering the errors while Pacer missed the vital signs. One step ahead, just like Davidson. It had to be Flynn who'd done away with Sullivan, then Arko to prevent him from talking. Who was next? The image of a young woman stumbling from bushes filled his mind. Was there still time?

CHAPTER 72

FLYNN HAD NODDED off. The morning session of hydrotherapy had worn him out and his leg ached from the resistance of the water. He'd never again think of swimming pools as places of relaxation and indulgence. He opened his eyes as Craig Thomas dropped into the bedside chair, upbeat and eager to talk.

'That information you gave me yesterday was good. Sofia and Eyland were married at the local soccer club around the time you said. I contacted the photographer and he filled in the blanks. Got Eyland's phone number. Easy.'

'You called Brett Eyland?' Flynn pushed himself upright.

'Yep, this morning, early. He was suspicious at first. Thought I was from the police. Reckoned a detective had called around, asking about his wife. I said I heard from someone at his soccer club that she'd cleared out and offered to tell him where she is staying.'

'He didn't question why a stranger would call him out of the blue?' Flynn would have if he were in the same position.

'Blokes like him do favours for one another all the time, no questions asked. He said the cops warned him off going after her. I stirred him up a bit. Said I'd heard she was bad-mouthing him and thinking of laying charges. He put two and two together, figured that's why the copper came around.'

'As long as you didn't lay it on too thick.' Thomas was sounding cocky. He annoyed people when he got like that.

'Nope, he was already planning his move. He wanted to know where to find her, practical things like that. There's a catch. It won't happen for few days. He's going pig shooting with his dog. Was getting his stuff ready when I called. "The bitch can wait," he said. "First a pig, then her."'

'And that was it?'

Thomas laughed. 'Except he invited me to go pig shooting with him.'

'You know it's urgent. You didn't apply pressure?' Flynn didn't like having to rely on Thomas, but what choice did he have?

'I wasn't going to argue with a bloke like that. Anyway, it's only a few more days.' Thomas looked unconcerned.

Flynn didn't like it. Anything could happen in a few days. Now they'd found Arko, the cops would be looking harder. Thomas was acting as if it didn't matter. He'd been more concerned yesterday. Had he spoken to someone in the business since then? Could Flynn trust him? What was Thomas passing on? That Flynn was keeping things back from them? That he couldn't take care of the loose ends? And that Thomas had to clean up after him?

Flynn shifted his position and tried to look relaxed. 'Any more said about Arko?' Edgar would have told Malcolm. How would he have reacted? He would be planning a lesson and biding his time in that cold, calculating way of his. Who would Malcolm blame? He remembered that other man who had fallen foul of Malcolm and what Edgar did on his orders. He clenched his fist reflexively.

'Nothing that I've heard.' Thomas was scrolling through Instagram, partly distracted. 'We have to stay cool and do only what's necessary.' With no more to add, he gave Flynn a cheerful farewell.

Flynn broke out in a sweat. The odds were stacking up against him. He was the only remaining link with the hit in Hawthorne Park and the rest of the mess. The police had no case against Malcolm and the business unless he spilled everything. Flynn no longer knew where he stood. Could he trust them? Did they trust him? Hold on, he wasn't just anyone. He and Malcolm went back a long way. Malcolm depended on him. He took out the burner and dialled Malcolm's private line. A woman's voice answered. Flynn recognised the haughty tone – Nerrida Kingston, Malcolm's PA.

'I'm sorry, Mr Flynn. Mr Hendry does not wish to receive calls from you at this time. He will be in touch if and when necessary.'

Flynn froze. Kingston hung up before he'd had a chance to leave a message. This wasn't looking good. Was it him on the end of the hook? He heard the familiar shuffle of the man in the room next door as he made his way towards the staircase. If old corpse could make it down, Flynn could too.

If the cops got to Sofia, he would be dead meat, one way or the other. He needed her gone. As things stood, there was a good chance the cops would get to her before Brett Eyland, the husband. Damn him and his pig shooting. He needed to pivot, take a different approach. The plan wasn't perfect, but there was no alternative. He fished the burner out of the drawer and dialled Justine Rawlings.

CHAPTER 73

PACER ARRIVED EARLY and went straight to the incident room. Picone was already there, radiating energy.

'You did great work following the Mill Street lead. Well done.' It felt good for Pacer to say it. He wasn't used to receiving compliments, let alone giving them.

'Er, thanks, Pacer.' Picone stood awkwardly and turned to the whiteboard, talking through the additions he'd made. Martin Sullivan was at the centre of the diagram and he'd included business associates and an unknown assassin. With quick hands he added lines, solid and dotted.

'Assassins, plural,' Pacer said.

'How do you figure that?'

'One to pick him up at his apartment – they don't send two drivers – and another waiting along the way. Not enough blood at the crime scene. They coaxed Sullivan out of the car, drugged and confused, stuck the knife in and tipped him into the boot.'

Picone adjusted the diagram and jabbed at Flynn's name. 'Where does he fit?'

'Flynn was involved, almost certainly. We have every reason to think he orchestrated the burial at Hawthorne Park. He had Arko in place for that.'

'Don't you think Hawthorne Park is a bit public? Why not just dump Sullivan at sea, like they did to Arko.'

'The foundations of the amenities block would have appealed to Flynn. Murderers often choose dump sites they know well. Flynn probably discovered the park on one of his runs, then found the junkyard next door and his perch on top of those containers. We know Flynn and Sullivan had

202

crossed paths and were anything but on friendly terms. So here's the big question. Was the murder personal for Flynn or was he acting on someone else's orders? What do you think, Stuart?'

Picone turned to face Pacer. 'That argument with Sullivan sounded pretty personal.'

'You think he was settling a score?' Pacer sat back, arms crossed.

'No, not really. When that happened, he was acting for Platinum Living. Besides, if it was personal, would he have waited so long? A lot of planning went into Sullivan's murder. If it was Flynn, he'd started setting it up weeks before, maybe longer.'

Pacer nodded. Picone was logical, made sense. 'We'll assume, for the moment, that Flynn was taking orders from someone higher up the food chain.'

'Platinum Living?'

'They're in our sights, but Sullivan could have had other rivals who knew Flynn and contracted him for the hit. Yes, it appears to be Flynn but we need to keep an open mind about Platinum Living. Fill in the details around what we do know.' Don't close in on one line of inquiry too soon, Pacer told himself. Picone needed to avoid that trap.

'Flynn is in pretty deep with Platinum Living, isn't he. Why wouldn't it be them?'

'Well, it might be. But listen to what I'm telling you and keep an open mind.' Pacer knew his voice sounded harsh. He was irritated and it was starting to show. Picone's expression had changed. Dial it down, he told himself. 'Sure, Flynn's on that retainer. Then he gets to do the asset stripping, which is lucrative. Anyone else would have to pay. Whatever he does for Platinum Living, they don't want it on the books.'

'Something illegal?' asked Picone.

'Not necessarily. Scoping out building sites? Checking out the neighbourhood? Keeping tabs on competitors? Property development gets grubby around the edges.'

Pacer needed a tea break, time out to settle himself. He slipped into the tea room down the corridor, relieved there was no training today. He made two mugs with ordinary tea bags. Not the best, but quick and easy. Back in the incident room, Picone accepted a mug and blew steam from the rim.

'I was thinking while you were out of the room. About Flynn at Hawthorne Park. Maybe on a job for Platinum Living, checking out building sites. After the houses in Mrs Creed's street, perhaps?' Picone thumped his mug on the table. 'They'd never sell, not in a million years. And there's some vacant land on the other side of that street. Covered with scrub and bits of railway track.'

'People succumb to pressure – you'd be surprised. They get worn down. But let's not get ahead of ourselves. This may have nothing to do with Mrs Creed and her neighbours. But I think you're onto something.' Pacer scanned the files on the table. 'You made copies of the maps and development plans for the Inner West Council, didn't you? They were here the other day.'

Picone indicated a stack of papers. 'What would you like to know?'

'What the zoning looks like around the Hawthorne Park area.' Pacer's mind returned to his trip on the light rail network, and his surprise that, despite all the development along its route, that area was still untouched. How could that be? Why had it been spared? So far, at least.

Picone flipped through the pile and pulled out pages with coloured diagrams and pored over them. 'There's a mix. Close to the bay end there's an oval. It's zoned "public recreational". It's the same zoning for the dog park. The film centre section, smack in the middle of those areas, is different. It's zoned "public purpose".'

'In other words it's up for grabs. Any interest, I wonder? Find out who owns it, will you?' Well, well, well. It made sense that developers would be after that site. At the very least it would be on their radar, going on what he'd learned about development along the light rail line.

'What are you thinking, Pacer? Platinum Living sent Flynn there to scope it out?'

'Platinum Living might have had the film centre in their sights. So might plenty of others.' An area at the back of Pacer's skull had begun to throb. Platinum Living. Platinum Living. Give it a rest. 'It's all conjecture until we know more. If it turns out that developers were interested, we need to find out if Martin Sullivan was among them. He was competitive and not the type to back down. Did he clash with a rival in the race to acquire it?' He stopped and thought for a moment. What else? 'Did he threaten a council official on the take?' An image of Baker swam into his mind, a man hovering between self-importance and guardedness.

Picone's forehead creased. 'There's a lot more to figure out, right?'

'Correct. Find out who owns that film centre.'

'I'm onto it.' Picone pulled back his chair and stood by the whiteboard. 'You said before that we should begin with what we know for sure.'

'That's right, Stuart. Follow leads, fill in the gaps and build your case around the evidence.'

'There are gaps. Like, how did Arko get that job at Hawthorne Park?

Was it just coincidence or did Flynn know someone at the council? We know that Arko was doing jobs for Flynn, maybe trusted him enough to want him in place at Hawthorne Park.'

Pacer brightened. 'And if Flynn has a plant at the council, was that the same person who paid off the certifier?' He had a strong hunch. 'I'll give Miranda De Veen a call.'

CHAPTER 74

'I'M SORRY, PACER,' De Veen said. 'Got caught up in another case. Your results came in late yesterday.' There were taps from a keyboard as she retrieved the information. 'That page you sent me – a copy of the certifier's document. You didn't say who the prints could belong to. We've drawn another blank though. No match with the banknotes.'

Pacer slumped in his chair. He couldn't believe it. Wrong again. He needed to sharpen up. What had he just told Picone? Don't get caught up in pet theories or go down blind alleys. 'That certificate was handed to me by Mark Baker.' Pacer could hear the weariness in his own voice. 'He's been on my radar for a while.' Baker was a logical suspect. He knew Flynn, minimised the relationship and was in bed with at least one property developer. Maybe not crooked but close to the edge. It pointed to Baker but it wasn't him.

'There is good news though.'

Pacer straightened in his chair.

'We ran the prints on the money against the docs found by Stuart Picone in Arko's recycling bin. They matched. A complete set on the signature page of the original contract for the building. A Craig Thomas, Manager Community Projects, signed it off. Good chance the prints are his. Mean anything to you?'

Pacer was floored. Craig Thomas, whom he had met in Baker's office, described by Marco Zanetti as Baker's sidekick. Insipid and obsequious, he was the last person Pacer would have suspected. But why not Thomas? He managed the project. He would have dealings with all of them.

He put De Veen on hold, spoke to Picone, then returned to the original call.

'I met Craig Thomas in Baker's office' said Pacer. 'He handled some documents. The plans of the amenities block. They're here somewhere.' He hesitated while Picone rummaged in a batch of files, retrieved one and flipped it open, then grinned.

'We've got it,' Pacer said.

'Third time lucky, eh?' said Miranda, before ending the call.

Thomas or Flynn? Thomas *and* Flynn? It could be both. This murder plot had a broad base.

Picone tapped his laptop, then stopped, his smile broadening. 'I've checked him out. Craig Thomas. It's all here in his LinkedIn profile.'

Pacer was aware of the platform as a social media site for professionals. Police officers were barred from using it.

'Lists his current job with the Cooks River Council. You won't believe where he worked before that.' The gleam in Picone's eye said it all.

'Platinum Living?'

'Yep, in a project management role. Goes on about his prowess in property acquisition and development. Will we pay him a visit?'

'We can do better. We'll bring him into the station. Put the wind up him.'

'Now?'

'Nice day outside. Why not?' Pacer leaped up. This felt good. The puzzle pieces were starting to fit.

Pacer's phone buzzed as he reached the door. The woman spoke quickly. Pacer's heart sank. He finished the call and looked at Picone.

'Craig Thomas can wait. This is more important.'

CHAPTER 75

PACER ENTERED THE school gates, a sickening sense of déjà vu clawing at his stomach. Nothing had changed. The spreading pepper tree at the front of the schoolyard, the same bench seats along the wall, the row of demountables. Outside the principal's office he knocked gently.

He had spoken to Mariam Ahmed about Davidson's return. Was that just last week or the week before? Things had moved quickly.

Ahmed introduced him to the family of four in a tight group on the settee. The mother, her eyes frightened and watchful, held her son in a close embrace. The boy, Joe, with tousled dark hair and brown eyes, was seven years old. A girl, several years older, sat between her parents, her expression serious. The responsible older sister, the burden of a younger sibling weighing heavily. The father's face was dark with anger but he held his counsel.

The mother spoke first, struggling to relay the facts and not the emotion. Her children were here. She needed to keep her anxieties in check. Pacer understood. His questions were bland, straightforward. Where did this happen? When did they see the man? Did he say anything, try to give the child sweets? Could they describe the dog? The conversation began to flow. The children broke in to correct their mother. No, he was further away to start with. He threw a ball and the little dog came closer. Joe could pat it, he said. He reached around the boy, lifted his hand to show him how. He liked his curly hair, touched it.

'There was something stuck in my shoe,' said the sister, Maria. 'A stone. I stopped to take it off. Joe ran ahead through the tunnel. I couldn't see him.'

'The children often go there after school. They like seeing the dogs,' the mother said. 'The park is close to our place and Maria is a responsible girl.' She smiled at her daughter. 'It's all right, darling. You did the right thing.'

'What did you see when you came through the tunnel, Maria?' Pacer asked.

'That man was close to Joe, leaning over. He had Joe's hand and was pulling him away.' The girl's eyes shone as she spoke, on the brink of tears.

'Is that what happened, Joe?'

'I don't know. I just wanted to play with the dog.' The boy looked at his father uncertainly.

'That's okay, Joe, just tell the sergeant what you remember.'

Pacer looked at Maria, speaking softly. 'Can you describe the man?'

Maria wrinkled her forehead. 'He was kind of creepy. Tall and skinny with lines on his face. He was smiling at Joe. One of his front teeth was broken off. I didn't like him. I yelled out and he dropped Joe's hand. Then he picked up his dog and walked into the trees.'

'Maria told her parents when they got home,' Mrs Ahmed said. 'They thought it best to let me know and came here this morning. Both children attend this school.'

The father spoke. 'That man didn't harm Joe. But we thought we should tell someone.' He kept his voice light but Pacer knew he felt differently.

Pacer reassured the parents. They would search for this man, keep a watch over the school. He had a quiet word with Mrs Ahmed before leaving. The police would do their best. He couldn't make promises. She of all people knew that.

Wainwright was waiting outside the school gate, concern etched across his face.

'Is the child okay? Was it Davidson?'

'The little boy will be fine. They realise the gravity of what happened, fortunately. Handling it well with the kids.'

Pacer and Wainwright talked urgently, piecing the details together. It was almost certainly Davidson from the description. Nowhere near a school this time. Or a playground. There was one on the other side of the canal, opposite Hawthorne Park but he had kept his distance.

'He's changed his MO,' Pacer said.

His blood boiled. He knew the exact place where it had happened. At the far end of Hawthorne Park near the short tunnel under the tram tracks. The part before the off-leash area, where few people lingered. The area backed by a thick stand of trees and shrubbery marking the park's boundary.

'We'll up the search, track him down and bring him in,' Pacer said. 'Before he tries again.' No more risks, no cutting Davidson any slack.

'Hold on,' said Wainwright. 'Think this through. Let's stay with the plan. We both agreed, remember? He kept the evidence. They always do. We have to get a sighting, keep him under surveillance. Let him lead us to it. Take him down for the murder.'

'I can't take any more chances. I want him inside,' Pacer said, jaw clenched.

'What could we get him for?'

'I'll charge him for what he did yesterday. A serious offence.' Put Davidson inside for a few years. Maybe more with his record.

'You want to put that family through the courts? You know Davidson will deny it.'

'I thought you were on my side.' Pacer jammed his hands in his pockets and stared into the distance. He turned back to Wainwright, about to say something, but checked himself. He'd had Davidson within his grasp before. It should have been easy, but he'd underestimated him. Cunning and devious. Smokescreens and clever lies. The charges dismissed at committal. Not even close.

'Yep. I'm sorry,' Wainwright said. 'But it's all or nothing. We put him inside for life or spend the rest of ours sweating over it.'

'Okay, I get it.' Pacer looked at his feet. It was agonising. 'I'll call the Assistant Commissioner. I need to clear it with her.'

CHAPTER 76

SOFIA LEFT MANNA House on her own, feeling confused and upset after what Justine had said. Alice and Garry had stayed behind to talk to someone about the place they were hoping to get. Sofia could have waited but didn't feel safe. They'd meet later in the little park at Summer Hill.

She chose a bench close to the community centre with a clear view of the entrances. She'd been here plenty of times. People wandered in with dogs or children and did a round on the circular path. Others emerged from the side of the supermarket laden with shopping, then up to the road where their cars were parked. The only sounds to break the pattern were the clatter of trains as they rushed by. She would know if anyone was out of place.

Alice and Garry didn't come. Sofia wondered what kept them. Alice wasn't her usual self. She was supposed to take medicine but Sofia suspected she'd stopped. Alice would get agitated or take offence. Sofia hoped she hadn't caused a scene and spoiled their chances of getting that house. That would be the worst. Maybe they had simply forgotten about meeting her here. They could be in a world of their own, those two.

The light began to fade. Sofia was too afraid to go back to her tent on her own. Besides, her husband would know about that now. Instead, she boarded the train at Summer Hill. People were getting off and crowding onto the footpath outside the station. On their way home from work, she supposed. Hardly anyone was going in her direction, towards the city. She stepped off at Newtown and slipped through the ticket barrier close behind a commuter who didn't notice. It was a short walk to the charity food place.

Sofia was glad when she saw Peta. Standing back, she searched the faces of people going by. She looked into doorways for anyone watching. Some people accepting plates of food also went to Manna House. At last Peta was alone. Sofia moved forward.

Peta remembered who she was. Sofia was overcome with relief and began to sob. It was too much. She blurted out what her friend Justine at Manna House had told her.

'My husband knows where I am. He's going to kill me. The police told him everything.'

'It's okay, Sofia,' Peta said. 'I'll see what I can do.' She made several calls. Sofia saw the tension drain from Peta's shoulders when she found a place. 'It's just a few days, but you'll be safe. Wait for a while and I'll drop you there myself. I did that before, remember?'

CHAPTER 77

WAINWRIGHT TOOK HIS time surveying the park as he did most mornings. Always alert for anything unusual, he walked the service road behind the campsite. He'd notice if someone didn't fit or was showing too much interest. All he saw was the usual assortment of visitors, dogs and their people, enjoying the warm autumn weather. The little staffy, two tennis balls between its teeth, stopped for a pat. A black labrador ambled by, sniffing his pockets for treats. Then Wedge bounded over.

Wedge was alone. Where was Garry? He was always close behind with a ball, while Alice and Sofia would stand back and watch. They weren't there either. Wainwright came in closer. Clancy was moving about, busying himself over a gas stove. Wainwright looked across to Sofia's tent. The zipper was closed. He had the sense she wasn't there.

Wainwright accepted a brew and dragged a milk crate close to Clancy's. Neither said much until their mugs were half empty.

'I know what you're wondering,' Clancy said in his slow drawl. 'Where have they gone?'

'I'm worried about Sofia. She seemed settled. I was hoping she'd stay put.' Wainwright put his mug on the gravel by his feet.

'I stopped wondering about things like that a long time ago. People drift in and out, no rhyme or reason. Just looking for the next place to eat and sleep. Sofia isn't here anymore, and Garry and Alice have cleared out as well. Those two took their tent though. Sofia's is still over there.' Clancy glanced at the blue tent with red trim.

Wainwright felt a stab of regret. He wasn't here yesterday – he'd been with Kurt on the hunt for Davidson. The one day he was elsewhere, Sofia went missing. 'Any idea where they went? I suppose they left together.'

'No to both,' Clancy replied. 'Garry and Alice left yesterday. Just packed up and went. Didn't say where they were going, might not even know themselves. They were getting restless, especially Alice.'

'Without Sofia?'

'That's right. Sofia's been gone longer. I asked Garry about it. He said she was talking about her husband again, reckoned he was after her. She was scared. Wanted to get away.'

'That can't be right. I told her the police had warned him off.' It was a shock. Wainwright spoke more loudly.

'No accounting for what gets into people's heads. It's too bad. I keep telling the young ones to stick near Centrelink, keep checking in. That way the payments don't get stopped. But they don't think that far ahead.'

'Did Garry say where Sofia had gone?' Wainwright searched Clancy's face, hoping for answers.

'He wouldn't know. That woman from the homeless charity came by yesterday to collect her things. You talked to her that day the dog-wash van was here. She might know.'

'You mean Peta? She was here?'

'She spoke to May.' May was slowly emerging from a tent nearby. Clancy caught her eye and called her over.

'John here wants to know what happened when that woman from the charity dropped by,' Clancy said to May.

'Oh, yes, Peta.' May spoke in well-modulated tones. 'She said Sofia was moving in to a shelter and would need her things. I helped her pack. Sofia stayed in the car. Peta said she was too frightened to come over.'

'Can you tell me where they went?' asked Wainwright.

'Certainly not. Even if I knew,' May said with a smile. 'She doesn't trust men. I don't blame her. You're the second one to be looking for her.'

'What do you mean?'

'Another man turned up just as Peta was leaving.'

'Did he approach Sofia?'

May hesitated, as if deciding how much she should say. 'I don't think so. But he saw her peering through the car window as Peta drove away. Came over to me, asked if Sofia was coming back.'

'What did you tell him?'

'I didn't give him the time of day. He didn't like it, either.'

Wainwright flicked through his collection of mug shots.

'Yes, that's him,' said May. 'Rough, ill-mannered.'

Brett Eyland. Wainwright shuddered. How could the man know where to find Sofia? Who'd tipped him off?

CHAPTER 78

'I DON'T THINK WE'RE allowed to have dogs in here.' Peta looked down at the black and tan kelpie sitting quietly by Wainwright's legs. 'But no one else is in today so what's the harm.'

Peta led Wainwright to the kitchen at the back of the converted bungalow used by the homeless charity. She sat in front of a plate of Vegemite toast and a mug of coffee.

'We hold our meetings here. It's comfortable and close to the coffee. Would you like one?' Wedge shuffled closer, her eyes on the toast. Peta tore off a corner and offered it. Loud crunching filled the small room.

Wainwright laughed, giving the dog another pat. 'Yes, and thanks for taking the time.'

'Obviously I can't tell you where Sofia is, not without her explicit consent. But she's safe and has a bed for a week. Hopefully they will extend if necessary, but places are scarce.' Peta made a coffee and placed it before Wainwright.

'She was afraid the husband was after her. Did she tell you about that?' Wainwright took a sip and put the mug back down. Too hot.

'Sofia came to me several nights ago in considerable distress. It was genuine – she wasn't hamming it up to get sympathy. A friend at Manna House had approached and said something about the husband. Sofia was terribly frightened and left immediately. The people she was with were to meet up later but they didn't show. Fortunately she remembered me.'

'Do you know who gave Sofia that message?'

'Someone who works in the kitchen. Sofia didn't give a name. Said she was a friend.'

'Did she repeat what the friend said?'

'I can't remember exactly; the words just tumbled out. Her husband was coming and he would kill her. The police had told him where to find her.'

'That's simply not true. About the police. Campbelltown command sent someone to warn him off.' Wainwright, flustered, shifted in his chair. Wedge pawed his knee.

'True or not, it doesn't matter. It's what she thinks.'

'I am concerned about Sofia. I have reason to believe the husband, Brett Eyland, is intending to harm her. He was at Jubilee Park yesterday, just after you left with Sofia.' Wainwright picked up his coffee again. Just right this time.

Peta sighed. 'It goes with the territory. A good many of the women I help are in a similar situation. We don't advertise their whereabouts. The husbands treat them like property. Think they are entitled to do what they want.'

'I know you do your best to keep the women safe. All the same, I'd like to be near Sofia, keeping watch. I would recognise Eyland.'

'I understand what you're saying, but it's not up to me.' There was a finality in Peta's voice.

Wainwright changed tack. 'She's close to the dog. Wedge calms her. Do you think—'

'Look, I know where this is heading. Sofia is in a shared space. They can't have dogs. Not possible, I'm afraid.'

'I need to talk to Sofia. The matter is urgent. Is there a neutral space where we could meet? She will want to see Wedge. Here, maybe?'

'First of all, she's turned off the police. It will take time to convince her. But there's something else. It's not a good idea for Sofia to get attached to Wedge. It wouldn't be the first time a homeless person has turned down permanent accommodation because they couldn't take their dog.'

Wainwright handed Peta his card. Peta would see what she could do but made no promises. Wainwright stood outside the bungalow, reporting the conversation to Pacer.

'Good work,' said Pacer. 'I'll send Stuart Picone over to Manna House for a chat. He's spoken to Justine Rawlings before. Any word on Davidson?'

'No, nothing yet. Kurt has put two more men on the search, so it's just a matter of time. Not too much, I hope. I'll join him soon. Have to take Wedge back to Jubilee Park first.'

The call over, Wainwright turned to Wedge. 'C'mon, I better get you back.'

It was another nice day, unusual for the time of year. Wainwright parked outside the Tram Sheds and took the long way round to the camp-site, Wedge trotting alongside. There was no rush without Sofia to protect. A few people were strolling through the park, but the after-work crowds out for brisk exercise were hours away.

They had reached the path by the harbour when Wainwright noticed a man in the distance, walking diagonally across the park in the same direc-tion as him. He hadn't seen this man before, or his dog. It was straining on the leash, a large, powerful breed with mottled brown fur and a thick collar. As their paths merged, Wainwright, a little way behind, got a better look. The adrenalin pumped. He knew that face. Stopping briefly to scroll the photos on his phone, he quickened his pace in an effort to catch up.

Eyland sensed the presence of someone closing in. He half-turned to face Wainwright, the dog moving with him. Yellow eyes stared out of a powerful body, all muscle and bone. With lightning speed it jumped at Wedge, clamping its jaws around the side of her head.

CHAPTER 79

PICONE ENTERED MANNA House through the front door and spoke briefly to Chris Neville, who motioned him through. Lunch service in the main cafeteria was over and volunteers were clearing the last of the tables. Picone found Justine Rawlings in the kitchen, emptying an industrial-sized dishwasher.

Justine looked up, alarmed. In deft movements that surprised Picone, she tore off her apron and disappeared through a doorway. He crossed the room in quick strides, passed through a dark corridor and exited into a lane lined with bins. Moments later he was in a narrow street, pulling up to avoid a passing car. Justine was further along, moving fast. The shabby facade of a shopping mall came into view. She entered via the fire exit. Picone sped up and reached the same spot. A concrete staircase smelling of urine led upwards. Taking three steps at a time, he climbed to a rooftop car park. Justine was halfway across, next to a battered sedan, fumbling with keys. He reached out and held the door closed, cornering her.

'I thought we had an arrangement, Justine. You do remember what I said about obstructing a police investigation?'

Justine's eyes moved this way and that, looking for a way out. 'I don't know what you think I've done.'

'You've been talking to Flynn. And you're going to tell me about it.' A couple pushing a shopping trolley walked over and stopped. Picone relaxed his position. 'Would you like to come to the station or are you going to tell me now?'

'I owe him. I told you before. He wanted information about Sofia. Any personal stuff she'd tell me. I didn't see the harm. Me and Sofia are friends anyway.' Justine gave Picone a hard look. 'Just gossip. Nothing wrong in passing it on.'

'Did you give him her husband's name?' Picone leaned in.

'Maybe. Look, he said he could help Sofia.'

'You're joking.' Picone's look was scornful.

'He's not that bad, Flynn. He helped me once, found a place for me to live. Said he could do the same for Sofia.'

'Give me your phone,' Picone demanded. Justine reached into her back pocket and handed it over. Picone showed her the list of recent calls. 'Which one is Flynn's?'

'This one. Hey, you going to give back my phone?'

'When I'm ready. Flynn called you a few times, the last was a few days ago. What was that about?'

'He found out that Sofia's husband was looking for her. Said I had to warn her.'

Picone held the phone in his hand, out of Justine's reach. 'Details, Justine.'

'All right. He said I had to use his exact words. He made me repeat them.'

Minutes later, Picone stood in the street behind the mall and called Pacer. 'You were right. Flynn has changed tack. He wanted Sofia to run.'

CHAPTER 80

PACER WAITED AT an outside table. He went there regularly on the way to his office, but had never ordered in. It was Wainwright's idea but he hadn't said why. Wainwright emerged from a small door in the side of the building a short way along. The car park exit. Ah, that was it. Wedge was with him. But she didn't look right. A thick bandage covered her left ear and cheek.

'What happened to Wedge? Was she hit by a car? Will she be okay?' Pacer spoke quickly, with concern in his voice.

'She will recover, but it wasn't an accident. Eyland's dog went for her.'

'Unprovoked?' Wainwright had told Pacer about sighting Eyland, but not this.

'Of course. The brute could have gone for either of us, but Wedge jumped in front of me. Spent the afternoon at the vet. They put her under to stitch the ear. She needed a few hours to recover.' A waiter appeared and put a coffee down. Wainwright took a long sip.

Pacer held Wedge's head between his hands. 'Brave girl.' She sat placidly, whining softly when he touched the bandage. The side of her head and neck was shaved. 'How bad is it?'

'She'll be right in a few days. Eyland's dog has pit bull in it. Luckily it let Wedge go after that first lunge.'

Pacer thought of the incident years earlier, surprised at how fresh it was. Their little dog hadn't stood a chance. Pacer had been so useless, unable to stop the attack. He gave Wedge another pat. She would recover, thankfully. But Eyland was still out there, doubly dangerous with that vicious dog. 'There's a good chance he'll go after Sofia again.' Of course he would. No doubt. Why would he stop?

'I've contacted Campbelltown police. They'll pay him another visit. Might remove the dog this time. I hope so.'

'They can take the dog, but not the man.' Eyland had come for Sofia despite being warned off. It was a close call. If Sofia hadn't been with Peta he might have succeeded.

'I'm sorry I couldn't stop him,' said Wainwright. 'He took off quickly with his dog. Wedge was in bad shape, so I didn't pursue him.'

'Just as well you didn't. Dangerous, going after him. I was wrong about Eyland, that he'd back off.' For men like him, a wife running away is an affront, an insult to his masculinity. He'd want her back. Pacer should have known that.

'Well, he had encouragement from Flynn. How did Picone's interview go?'

'Sofia's friend at Manna House did pass on Eyland's details, just as we suspected. He's a real manipulator, Flynn. Couldn't get to Sofia himself, so he put Eyland up to doing the job for him. But then he warned Sofia so she would take off. It doesn't make sense.'

'He's stuck in that rehab unit with too much time to think,' Wainwright said. 'Maybe the wait is getting to him and he's starting to panic. Or worried we'll get to Sofia before he does.'

'Perhaps both.'

'How much longer has he got in there?'

'Maybe a week, probably less. I went there yesterday, scouted around. Spotted him in the treatment unit, still on crutches but getting around okay. A useful visit for a number of reasons.' Pacer picked up the small cookie beside his cup and watched while Wedge munched it.

'You going to tell me?' Wainwright gave Pacer a questioning look.

'Bumped into an old friend while I was there. In for a hip replacement. He's in the room next to Flynn's,' Pacer said. Wainwright's smile widened as Pacer filled in the blanks.

Drinks finished, they pushed their cups aside. Wainwright reached into his jacket and placed a white cylinder in front of Pacer.

'Wedge is on a course of antibiotics. She needs a pill twice daily.'

Pacer was knocked for six. 'Whoa, I'm no good with dogs. You take her.'

'I live in an apartment. Dogs aren't allowed.'

'I haven't got time to look after a dog. Not with Davidson out there planning his next move.'

'We've got dozens of officers on the lookout. There is nothing else you can do right now.'

'I don't like waiting. It's the worst.'

'Wedge is good at waiting too. And she's the best company. My car's in the basement. Give you a lift home.' Wainwright reached over and handed the lead to Pacer. Pacer paused for a moment, before realising his hand had closed around it.

CHAPTER 81

PACER'S SUNDAY PAPER was snagged in the branches of a calliste-mon. He retrieved it and returned to the kitchen where Wedge was scooping up the last of her kibble. She trotted over and inspected Pacer's dewy shoes.

'I was only gone a minute.' Pacer gave the dog a pat. After filling the teapot, he took it to the back deck. Wedge flopped down beside him as he spread the paper. 'First the sports pages, eh, Wedge? Then the park.'

Pacer was flipping through the business section when a headline caught his eye: '*Cracks form in Platinum Living's apartment empire.*'

He put his cup aside. The first paragraphs weren't about Platinum Living at all. Rather, it was a story that had scandalised the city for months. New apartment owners forced out of their homes due to dangerous faults in construction. Cracks appearing in walls and ceilings. Vents and elevator shafts not fireproofed. Residents barred from returning. The repairs would cost millions.

The apartments in question were nowhere near Platinum Living's. Pacer read on, eager to find the connection.

Ah, there were flow-on effects for the rest of the building industry. People who had bought apartments off the plan were spooked. Many were reluctant to close the deal and some were pulling out entirely.

'I'd rather lose my deposit than get saddled with a place that could fall down any time,' one buyer reportedly said.

That wasn't the half of it. The article went on to say that any buyer who pulled out could also be forced to compensate the builder if the eventual selling price was lower. And it probably would be. People stuck between a rock and a hard place. What a dilemma.

Platinum Living was seriously exposed. It had geared up production in recent years and many of its apartment blocks were nearing completion. They raked the money in early by selling most units off the plan. That's how they raised finance for each project. The new owners ought to be paying the balance and moving in during the next weeks and months. Platinum Living was expecting a revenue bonanza. Or had been before this swell of unease. The way things were going, many buyers would pull out before settlement and Platinum Living would be caught millions of dollars short. And with a whole lot of apartments they couldn't sell.

The first of Platinum Living's buyers to default had already announced themselves. And they hadn't done it quietly. The press was onto the unfolding saga. Potentially, this was financial disaster for Platinum Living if they couldn't put a lid on it. They would need an injection of capital to complete the building work and pay creditors. And that was just for the short term.

The CEO of Platinum Living, Malcolm Hendry, had been asked to comment. 'Our apartments are sound. There is no reason for buyers to be concerned. Those faults are in the large apartment complexes with substandard construction. Platinum Living builds quality, always has.'

The article ended on a philosophical note. Emotion over reason, the danger of disruptions from left field, the chance element in any business enterprise.

Pacer had already booked a meeting with Malcolm Hendry. He was looking forward to it, more so now. The photo covering two column widths showed a man in his fifties, handsome with a full head of greying hair, oozing confidence. A self-made man, untroubled by adversity or misfortune. Or quick to head it off should it dare come his way. This was the man who had employed Flynn. What for? To do just that, to make sure he didn't lose any of that fine head of hair?

CHAPTER 82

PACER CLIPPED WEDGE'S lead onto the new collar. The vet had removed the bandage, exposing the shaved area and a row of thick stitches. Pacer bathed the ear and gave Wedge her medication.

'That's the last one. You'll be right now. We'll get over to Hawthorne Park and find you a permanent home. Plenty of people there will be wanting a dog.' Wedge searched Pacer's face and whimpered. She sat back on her haunches, unwilling to move. Did she know? Impossible. 'Come on, Wedge. We've got things to do before that.'

Pacer had spent the previous day at Jubilee Park. Most of the tents had gone. Clancy and a few others remained but were talking about moving north. The mornings were frosty and cold, a harsh winter predicted. Pacer was there because of Davidson. The man was prowling and had changed strategy. That last time, he'd chosen a quiet place, waiting for a child alone. Maybe he would try that again. Or switch to where crowds gathered, like this park. Blend in with a little dog. Another one.

Pacer parked near the tunnel under the light rail at Hawthorne and lifted Wedge down from the back seat. The area after the tunnel was heavily shaded by oaks, with open grassland closer to the canal. Back a few paces, the park ended in the scrubby bush into which Davidson had disappeared. A chain-link fence was there, just as Kurt Otway had described it. Pacer found the section marked with police tape. The wires were cut through from top to bottom, and recently too, judging by the clean edges where the cutters had worked. He peered through to an unused depot with a tin shed, a few piles of blue metal and a small car park. Somewhere in there, Otway had found the lifeless body of a cavoodle. Pacer turned away.

Pacer and Wedge walked briskly towards the other end of the park. The class for dogs in the advanced group was almost over. A dozen or more sat in a long row to the left of their owners. Pacer recognised several from the agility class. The white poodle started to fidget and stretched across to the schnauzers. Unrest rippled along the line.

Anna stood at the front of the class, Hugo by her side. He saw Pacer and barked loudly. Jess, the schnauzer, raced across, greeting Pacer, then turned her attention to Wedge. Jess's upright tail quivered in excitement.

'Of course they remember you,' Anna said, after the class. 'Who's this?' She bobbed down and stroked Wedge's back. 'What happened to her?'

'Attacked by a brute of a dog. She was with my colleague when it happened. Wedge got between them, otherwise he would have borne the brunt. She's a gutsy little thing.'

'You've had some bad luck with dogs, haven't you. Things are looking up now. Wedge is a beautiful dog, and good-natured. Except when she's defending you. And she's still a pup.'

'Actually, I was hoping someone here would take her, give her a home.' Pacer reached down and ruffled Wedge's good ear.

'You can't be serious! This time of year? Too many dogs turned in or abandoned already. Happens every year after the thrill of getting a dog for Christmas wears off. No can do.' Anna stabbed out each word.

'I can't look after her. I work, she'd be home alone a lot of the time.'

'There are ways around that. You'll have to take her on regular walks, runs.' Anna gave Pacer an appraising look. 'Won't do you any harm, either.'

'Fact is, I'm not a dog person.' Pacer felt deflated. This wasn't going well.

'No such thing. It's not about you, it's the relationship. Look at Hugo here. My best friend. You take care of each other. Or have you forgotten?' Anna had been patting Hugo when she stopped abruptly. 'I'm so sorry, I'm way out of line.'

'It's okay, you've got me pegged.'

It was true. He hadn't let anybody in since Janet. He looked down. Wedge had dropped forward and stretched out her front legs, head bowed. Jess did the same as Hugo joined in. Pacer had learned this was the signal for play. All the dogs knew it. In a sudden movement they raced away, tumbling after one another.

'Wedge wants to get moving, play with her new friends,' he said.

'Well, it's settled then?' Anna smiled in triumph.

'Looks that way.' Pacer sighed and patted the bulge around his middle. Anna was right. A bit of exercise would do him good.

Pacer called Wedge back. The small group of dogs and people walked towards Café Bones, where the dog-training club had set up a table.

'First class is starting soon. We'll get you checked in,' Anna said.

'Wedge has had some training; she doesn't need to attend a class.'

'The class is not for the dog. It's for the owner.'

Pacer walked Wedge to the edge of the canal and looked in. Sometimes you went where the current took you. He crouched down next to the dog. 'Looks like you're stuck with me, Wedge. My name's George, but you can call me Pacer – everybody does.'

CHAPTER 83

PACER ARRIVED IN good time for his meeting with Malcolm Hendry. The generous-sized reception area in steel and glass gleamed. A smiling young woman emerged from behind the desk and directed him to a beige sofa. Pacer's eyes followed her and he noticed, for the first time, an expressionless man sitting against the back wall, watching the entrance. The face was familiar, but Pacer couldn't place it.

He picked up a glossy publication. Stylish apartments and contented occupants were Platinum Living's signature. No cracks in those facades. Pacer glanced at his watch, dropped the magazine onto the coffee table and looked around. In the centre of the wall opposite were framed photos of people formally dressed. Pacer had stood for a closer look when a woman stepped out of the lift and bustled towards him. Malcolm Hendry's PA, in tailored emerald suit and pearls, wearing a serious expression, introduced herself as Nerrida Kingston.

Kingston apologised for the delay. It was a difficult time for the business. The executives were fully occupied with their communications consultants, countering some bad press and false rumours. Perhaps Pacer had seen the news reports? Mr Hendry was busy but able to keep his appointment, fortunately. She would take him upstairs and sit in on the meeting. Mr Hendry insisted she take notes.

Pacer was ushered into a room with a polished oval table and high-backed leather chairs. Light streamed in, touching down on the man standing at the far end. Hendry, tall and impeccably dressed, cut an imposing figure. His deep blue eyes were set in a large, well-formed face that complemented his athletic frame. Nerrida Kingston introduced Pacer. Hendry extended his hand.

'Malcolm Hendry.'

Pacer's grey eyes locked on Hendry's. Pacer saw a successful man, sure of himself, in control of his fate. If his business empire was in trouble, he gave no sign.

They sat opposite one another and took the time to settle. Kingston sat to one side, also relaxed, but watchful.

'I expected a visit from you earlier than this,' Hendry said. 'Martin Sullivan was a valued member of our corporate family.'

'I understand that Mr Sullivan worked in your business-development unit,' Pacer said. Lillian Zhang had told him so. Sullivan learned to size up the competition and plan deals while he was there.

'Martin was with us for a relatively short period, about eighteen months. He moved on three years ago. I think my memory is accurate, isn't it, Nerrida?' Hendry looked at Kingston, who returned a professional smile.

'Was there a reason for Mr Sullivan's early departure?' Pacer asked. 'Was his performance unsatisfactory?'

'Not at all. I employed Martin myself after a chance meeting. He impressed me immediately. Martin was looking for an opportunity and I was happy to provide it. He was a quick study, took very easily to our line of work. A good eye for function and design, with an excellent head for business.'

'I understand that Mr Sullivan was competitive, unafraid of conflict. Did this contribute to his departure from your firm?'

Hendry laughed. 'Yes and no. Martin was competitive, certainly. You have to be. This is a tough business, Sergeant. He might have upset one or two people, but I do that myself on occasion.' Hendry laughed again. 'Some thought he was too big for his boots. Not me, I liked his style. But we had a chat. We both agreed he'd do well on his own, with my mentoring.'

'And did you ever see Mr Sullivan after he left your firm?'

'Of course, at the golf club where we first met. He was doing well. I encouraged him.'

'And the people in your firm with whom he conflicted? Or other business associates? Can you assist me with their names?'

Hendry's forehead creased. 'I can't really remember. It wasn't important. Can you help on this one, Nerrida?' The question was met with a shake of the head. 'I'm sorry, Sergeant.'

'I understand you clashed with Mr Sullivan over a business arrangement shortly after he left Platinum Living. A development site in Mill Street, Leichhardt.'

Hendry laughed more heartily than before. 'You're well informed, Sergeant. Yes, he got the better of me on that one. As I mentioned, Martin had a competitive streak. I admired him for it, outmanoeuvring an old dog like me.'

'Can you explain what happened?'

'As I remember, he offered my client a better deal than I was prepared to match. Not in a financial sense, of course. It was something about accommodating the current tenants. Not wise of him, actually – that sort of thing can backfire.'

'And did it?'

'I believe there was some fallout. Nothing serious, but perhaps reputational damage.' Hendry looked down. Not a topic he wanted to pursue.

'Did he learn from that experience?'

'I did counsel Martin about crossing his business mentor. An awkward conversation, but necessary.' Hendry's look was stern.

'Was he about to do it again?'

Hendry gave Pacer a blank stare. His pupils tightened to pinpricks. Pacer found it impossible to read the thoughts behind those sharp eyes. Was he aware of some new transgression? Had he revealed too much? Was he simply confused?

A rap on the door echoed through the silence. A young man entered and moved to Kingston's side, whispered in her ear and left quickly. Kingston looked at Hendry, an urgent signal passing between them. Hendry turned to Pacer, his demeanour transformed.

'I'm sorry, Sergeant, I need to take a call. Thank you very much for your time.'

Kingston walked with Pacer to the lift. 'Please understand, Mr Hendry was shocked and devastated by Martin's death. Malcolm had hoped he'd return to the firm in time.'

They walked across the foyer together towards the entrance. The expressionless man was still there. Where had Pacer seen him before? He turned to the framed photos and stopped. 'Are these the executive?'

'The boards of directors, actually. In the middle here, we have the current board.'

Pacer peered at the faces. Hendry was near the centre, a distinguished presence.

'It's quite a small group,' Kingston said. 'That's Mr Hendry's wife, Eleanor, beside him. From inside the firm, we have the design and construction manager, and our finance executive.' She indicated the portraits of a man and a woman.

'And the gentleman standing next to Mr Hendry?' Pacer was looking at a slim man much shorter than the CEO, a man of Asian appearance, in his late forties.

'That's the chair of the board, Mr Bidanau. He's Platinum Living's major investor, a long-time supporter of the firm.'

'Musa Bidanau?'

'No, this is Mr Osman Bidanau from the distinguished Malaysian family. I believe he has a younger brother. Perhaps that's the person you're thinking of.'

Two Mr Bidanaus. Pacer knew Musa Bidanau as the investor who lost out from financing Martin Sullivan's gourmet food venture. The one he'd started with Jordan Alexander. The Musa Bidanau who was looking to break the family bonds and go into business for himself. A very disappointed Musa Bidanau, according to Lillian Zhang. And here was his big brother, Osman, the head of Platinum Living. Nothing more than a coincidence? Maybe, maybe not. But Pacer didn't believe in coincidences, he reminded himself.

CHAPTER 84

PACER WAS NOT long back from his morning walk with Wedge when the phone rang. It was John Wainwright at Jubilee Park.

'There's nothing from Kurt's team, no sightings of Davidson since the incident in Hawthorne Park. But Benny the Toe was here, hoping to find you. He couldn't wait around, had a job in Glebe. He said he'd come back.'

'What does he want?'

'Wouldn't say. Insisted on talking to you.'

'No problem. I'm at home. I'll be right over.'

Pacer and Wainwright met at the spot where Benny had parked his dog-wash van.

'Benny probably wants to show me how useful he is,' Pacer said. 'Once told me about a trainer having a fling with the committee chair's missus. Not information I wanted to know, let alone act on. But that's Benny. Takes pride in his little nuggets.'

Their heads turned at the approach of Benny's van. He jumped out, pulled Toby from the cab and hurried across. Benny's eyes were on Pacer. Important information was not for everyone. Wainwright picked up a tennis ball and walked away with Toby.

'Got something for you, Sergeant.' Benny paused for effect. 'That bloke I told you about before. You know, from my time in the slammer.'

'Have you seen him again?' Pacer was interested but tried to look relaxed.

'I was doing a job at this house in Annandale. Parked in the driveway. He was walking in my direction. Maybe he saw the van – it's got my name on it. Said he'd know my face anywhere. Real friendly. Like I said before, I don't like his sort, but what can you do? Maybe he thinks I'm his friend.' Benny paused, gauging Pacer's reaction.

'That's good to know, Benny. Did he say anything that might help the police?'

'No, nothing. Just thought you'd like to know.' Benny studied the ground, gathering his thoughts. 'I don't know if I should say this, might give you the wrong idea. Don't want you to think he's me mate or any-thing.'

'It's pretty clear he's not. So what do you have for me?' This would be good. Pacer just knew it.

'He asked for a lift. It was hot and he still had a way to go. So I said yes. Toby was between us on the bench so I didn't have to sit that close. I dropped him off in Parramatta Road.'

'Where, exactly?'

'Not far down from where Crystal Street comes in. There's this little church, on a corner. The traffic was heavy and I was stuck on the kerb long enough to see him cross over and start walking down the next street.'

Pacer called Wainwright over. Benny repeated his news. 'Gave me something for the ride. It's in the cab. I was going to throw it away. Don't know why he thought I'd be interested in that sort of thing. After he left, I wondered if he'd got me mixed up with someone else he knew inside.'

Wainwright and Pacer peered into the van. A dog-eared magazine was on the floor of the passenger's side, the exaggerated form of a naked man and a smiling child on the cover.

They stood together in silence after Benny drove away.

Pacer cleared his throat. 'Let's get over to where Benny dropped Da-vidson off, take a look.'

They entered Parramatta Road from the city end and soon spotted the church on their left.

'That looks like it,' Wainwright said from the passenger's side. 'That road is one-way. We'll have to park here and walk.'

The street was little more than a lane, flanked by high backyard fences and narrow terrace facades. A hundred or so metres in, the road forked into a smaller single lane on the left and a wider, tree-lined street on the right.

'Your guess is as good as mine,' Pacer said. 'Let's go right.'

Further along, the entrance to a laneway was concealed by trees until they were almost upon it. Pacer looked at the street sign, chipped and bent.

'Mercury Lane. This is it. This is where he went.' He felt the adrenalin.

Moments later, Pacer and Wainwright stood outside a row of four shuttered garages, neat and unremarkable.

'This is it?' Wainwright asked. 'Where he keeps his stash?'

'That's what my gut tells me.' The stash. Precious objects. Things taken. Is that why Davidson had come back? To take another look? Touch his trophies? Freshen the memories?

Pacer walked along the row and stepped closer to a garage on the far end.

'Take a look at this.' Pacer pointed to a metal plaque riveted to the shutter. '*Property of Cooks River Council*. Or more to the point, Mark Baker.' Baker, a delegator, spurning the minutiae of council business. A mind engaged with matters loftier than the keys to a repository at the edge of council's boundaries. Or so he made out.

Wainwright's expression betrayed a mix of admiration and incredulity. 'But how?'

'I was in Baker's office over the Sullivan case. I glimpsed a memo on his desk – a list of delegations for small stuff, like this row of garages in Mercury Lane. Not relevant to Sullivan but the name was unusual. Caught my eye. Baker had delegation for it, the only place on the list under his direct personal control. It struck me as odd.'

'Very much so. Why would he want the keys to something like this?'

'I think I can guess. He wanted to prevent others from having access.' Something clicked in Pacer's mind. 'Your photos you scrolled through that day with Benny at the car wash. I caught just a glimpse. I'd like to take another look.'

Wainwright handed over his phone. Pacer flicked through to an unprepossessing face, the kind to fade into the background. There was a moustache and the man was younger. Even so, he was recognisable. 'That's him, Baker.'

Wainwright studied the photo. 'Don't know him. On Vice's radar for some transgression – way back, most likely. These blokes learn quickly to keep a low profile, the smarter ones.'

'Benny claimed that Davidson had help. Baker, would be my guess.'

'We need to be sure Davidson's stash is here,' Wainwright said. 'Take a look inside the units. If we're right, we can set up the surveillance.'

'We'll do it carefully, by the book. Go in, but disturb nothing. Knowing Davidson, he'll claim we planted the evidence, presuming we find any.'

'I'll call Kurt.' Wainwright spoke briefly on his phone, then nodded to Pacer. 'He's just up the road.'

The first unit in the row was empty. Otway stood outside the second, working two delicate picks with gloved hands. Within minutes the button housing the keyhole popped out. Pacer pushed his fingers under the base of the shutter and pulled it up to shoulder height. He and Wainwright bent over as they stepped inside a space the size of a standard garage.

Touching nothing, Pacer ran his eyes over the contents. This was it, Davidson's stash. A pushbike, the tyres deflated, stood against one wall. Next to it, boxes overflowed with clothing, soiled and faded. Metal shelving held tools and household items, untidily stacked. Several pairs of well-worn trainers were scattered about the floor. Magazines, videos and cassettes were piled next to a wooden desk, testament to decades of collecting. A magazine lay open. Pacer was sickened. He wanted to leave, but a plastic box caught his eye. It was a milky colour and semi-opaque but he could make out the contents: a small red cardigan and a pair of children's shoes, with silver buckles and a flowered pattern at the toes.

It was dizzying. Things Pacer had never found. The missing evidence. Davidson throwing out hints, diverting them to the attic in his sister's house. Pacer turning the place upside down. Nothing. And all the while, Davidson taking measures, calling on his lowlife friends. Mark Baker. Perhaps others. To shift his stash here.

The detectives stepped outside and breathed fresh air. Pacer and Wainwright stared into the distance, silent, knowing it was almost over but unable to feel relief or satisfaction.

CHAPTER 85

PACER HAD INTENDED interviewing Craig Thomas days ago but was glad he'd put it off. He knew more now, could turn up the heat. He and Picone stood outside the offices of Cooks River Council, noting the entrances and talking strategy.

'I'm almost certain Thomas will leave via the back entrance. I want you to wait there and follow him. He'll be on foot. It's not far to the rehab place where Flynn is. When you get there, wait downstairs until I call you up.'

'You reckon Thomas and Flynn are in this together? But what's the connection?' Picone asked.

'Thomas handled the bribe money. That call from De Veen this morning confirmed it. Flynn prepared the dump site. Something brought them together over this. I don't know what that is but I intend to find out. Ready?' Pacer felt pumped, like a coiled spring, a sense of the end game in sight.

Pacer took the stairs two at a time. He rapped on the door then walked straight into an open plan office. Craig Thomas's desk was beside a window at the side of the room. His look of surprise morphed into anxiety. Recovering quickly, Thomas shook hands and tried to make small talk. Pacer ignored the attempt. He would call the shots from here. Thomas led them to a small meeting room at the far end of a corridor and fussed over the arrangement of the chairs.

Pacer allowed the silence to fill the room, then opened with a soft but firm voice. 'We are aware of irregularities in the construction of the amenities block where Martin Sullivan's body was found. We are hoping you can help with some details around that.'

Thomas's eyes bulged, his mouth opening and then closing. He looked at his hands then raised his head to meet Pacer's stare.

'Irregularities? I'm not sure what you're referring to.'

Thomas was stalling, vying for time to settle. Pacer knew the signs, had seen it plenty of times. He got straight to the point. 'The foundations, Mr Thomas. The steel mesh was not pinned down correctly. It was removed to allow the killers to conceal the victim.'

'Mark Baker told me about the mesh. I was appalled. Council property used like that. As project manager it weighs heavily on me.'

'Surely you are aware, Mr Thomas, that one of your certifiers signed off on those foundations days before the incident?'

'I have thought about it, wondered.' A vein in Thomas's temple had begun to throb. 'I think we used Phillip Downes for that build. A good inspector, usually very reliable.'

'Is there any reason why Downes might have certified work that had not been completed?'

'What are you suggesting?'

Pacer regarded him coolly. Thomas was on the defensive. The first crack. 'I believe that Downes was bribed.'

Thomas tensed. He seemed unsure of what would come next. 'This is dreadful, shocking.' The reedy voice hesitated before going on. 'Who would do that?

'We were hoping you could help with that,' Pacer said.

'There must be a simpler explanation. Do the police always take the most sinister view?' Thomas sat back, aware he was being appraised.

Pacer changed tack. 'I understand you knew the victim, Martin Sullivan.'

'I meet a lot of people through my work at the council.' Thomas's mouth twitched. 'Sullivan was in residential development, not my area but I met him once or twice when assisting Mark Baker.'

'You'd met him before that, hadn't you, Mr Thomas?' Pacer made it sound like a statement, not a question.

'A long time ago, before I started here. We worked at the same place, but not for long. We had nothing to do with each other.'

'At Platinum Living?'

'Yes, true,' Thomas replied.

'Martin Sullivan was a rival; you were in the same division. You were jealous of his success. Is that correct, Mr Thomas?'

Thomas sat bolt upright. Neither man moved or spoke. Finally Thomas leaned forward.

'Where is this going? Are you accusing me of something?' The words reverberated around the room.

'I have spoken to several of Mr Sullivan's colleagues. He was favoured over you for a promotion at Platinum Living. They remember your snide comments when Sullivan wasn't in the room. You resented him and couldn't hide it.'

'So what? Jobs are competitive. I had other opportunities.' Thomas sank in his chair, his chin trembling. 'People like Martin Sullivan care for nothing but the money. I'm driven to help the community, that's why I took this job.'

'You didn't stay long after that. But you kept your contacts in Platinum Living, hoping to hear that Martin Sullivan was finally out of favour.'

'Not true. I kept up with old colleagues. It's what normal people do.'

'What do you do here at the council? Supervise the installation of toilet blocks and picnic tables? Hardly comparable to the job you left.'

Pacer watched Thomas's pale skin turn a shade lighter. He seemed to shrink. His eyes flicked towards the door and back to Pacer.

'Would you like a glass of water, Mr Thomas?'

'I want to know what you are accusing me of.' Thomas placed his hands flat on the table. 'I'm not saying anything else without legal representation.'

'I am seeking the truth, nothing more. All part of my investigation. Thank you, I appreciate your cooperation.'

Thomas followed Pacer to the exit, looking around to see if others had noticed his visitor. Pacer walked past the cafe and into sunshine, a smile creasing his lips. He looked at his watch. 'In nice time for my next visit,' he said aloud.

CHAPTER 86

PACER ENTERED THE rehab unit via the front entrance and took the lift to the first floor. Checking that no one was in the corridor, he walked quietly along its length and slipped through a half-open doorway. The occupant of the room greeted him silently. A chair had been placed next to the wall separating this room and the one on the end. Pacer closed the door, sat and waited.

It wasn't long before footsteps echoed faintly along the corridor and came closer. Pacer and the room's occupant grinned at each other. Someone passed by and entered next door. Craig Thomas, arriving on cue.

They heard Flynn asking his visitor what he was doing there. There was a gruff reply. Flynn raised his voice, angry. 'I don't know what you're talking about!'

'Keep your voice down,' Craig Thomas hissed. They spoke in urgent tones, but more softly. Pacer pinned his ear to the wall.

'You've been talking to the police. What did you tell them?' Thomas asked.

'Nothing. Why would I do that?'

'They've been here. You lied about it. Edgar's kept an eye on you.' Thomas's voice pitched higher.

'I didn't tell them anything.' Flynn was angry. He adjusted his volume and spoke more quietly again. 'They're running up blind alleys, just like we figured. They'll never work it out. We're safe.'

'As long as we keep our mouths shut. And you haven't.' Thomas was losing control. 'You got them thinking I fixed up the certifier for that mesh. That I had something against Sullivan. Is that it?'

'They were on about Sullivan, reckoned I knew him too. Just fishing. You didn't come into it.'

'What about that witness, Sofia? Maybe she's talked?'

'Don't think so. She'd be too scared.'

'Well, it's either her or you. It's your fault if it's her. You should have got rid of her when you had the chance.'

There was a momentary silence. Pacer stepped into the corridor and knocked on Flynn's door. Without waiting for an invitation he entered and feigned surprise on seeing Thomas. 'Oh, Mr Flynn, I see you have a visitor.'

The two faces registered surprise and confusion. No one spoke. Pacer texted Picone, who arrived seconds later.

'Mr Thomas, I'd like you to go with Detective Picone. I need a quiet word with Mr Flynn. To the station if you don't mind. We'd like you to make a statement.'

'What's this about, you barging in here?' Flynn demanded after Picone and a silent, compliant Thomas had left. Pacer remained standing, while Flynn sat next to the bed, his legs outstretched. The heavy plaster had been replaced by a lighter plastic frame that encased the lower part of his injured leg. A single crutch leaned against the wall.

'I've come with news for you. Bad news, I'm afraid.' Pacer waited for that to register. 'A friend of yours has been found dead. Arko. We are treating the death as suspicious.'

Conflicting emotions showed on Flynn's face. Arko, who was his workmate in happier times. Arko, who poured concrete over a murder victim. Arko, whom Flynn already knew was dead.

Flynn made no reply.

'Perhaps you knew already, Mr Flynn?'

'How would I know that?'

'Perhaps your friend Mr Thomas mentioned it?'

'You're not making sense. Craig Thomas is a mate, just visiting.'

'The news of Arko's death hasn't surprised you.'

'Why don't you just get out of here,' Flynn spat. 'Stop harassing me.'

'There is another possibility. You knew Arko was dead because you were there.'

Flynn tried to speak but had no words. Finally he croaked, 'If you had a shred of evidence for that, you'd be placing me under arrest. Now get out before I have you thrown out.'

Pacer regarded him coldly, then turned and left the room.

CHAPTER 87

PACER STEPPED INTO Inspector Connors's office. No heads-up from Edith as to why he'd been summoned. It was her day off. Connors sat back in his chair, relaxed. He invited Pacer to sit. A different man from last time.

Connors nodded several times as he read through Pacer's latest notes on the Sullivan case. 'I can see progress, of sorts.' The Inspector was pleased, not that he'd get carried away with praise. That was no way to motivate an officer. 'Still nothing from that witness?'

'She is in a women's refuge. I'm hopeful she'll speak to us in due course.' What chance was there of that? Wainwright still didn't know where they'd taken her. How safe was she, really?

'A women's refuge is not under our protection. I hope you know what you're doing.'

Pacer judged it time to deflect. 'We have another suspect, a Craig Thomas.'

Connors looked into the file. 'Oh, yes, Craig Thomas, in league with Flynn. Still, it's all rather circumstantial. You'll have to get some proof. Are you going to bring him in?'

'Not yet. He made a statement, denied the bribery. We have evidence he handled the money, but with a smart lawyer, he could claim the payment was for something else.'

'And likely get away with it,' Connors replied in a superior tone. 'He didn't like Sullivan – I suppose that's a motive of sorts. Not particularly strong though. And Flynn, what would he get out of going in with Thomas? Are you sure Hendry isn't behind this? He employed Flynn, after all.'

'Hendry admired Sullivan, mentored him.' It was true. Pacer had checked at the golf club. They were seen together, on good terms, several times. He had long believed that someone high up the food chain had ordered the hit. It would make sense if Malcolm Hendry was the one. Pacer wasn't ready to let him go. He'd keep digging.

'Hendry and Sullivan might have had a falling-out, something more recent,' Connors said, as if Pacer couldn't see what was staring him in the face.

'Yes, sir, that is possible.' Pacer hesitated, judging it the right time to raise another issue.

'Hendry has a driver, name of Edgar Bailey. For protection, I think.' Pacer wondered why a respectable businessman would employ that tough nugget of a man with a record for aggravated assault. It was Edgar Bailey at Platinum Living, eyes trained on the entrance. It had nagged at Pacer. He knew that face and finally it clicked. And Bailey was also monitoring Flynn. What was that about?

'Try to make sense of it, will you? Bring me something more coherent,' Connors said, after some discussion. He snapped the file shut.

Pacer waited to be dismissed. Connors looked at him, remembering something.

'Oh, the Assistant Commissioner commended you on your progress with the Davidson case. She wants him off the streets ASAP but supports your decision to wait. A risky approach in my view. Don't botch it.'

Pacer felt the anxiety in the pit of his stomach. Sometimes the brass had your back. Other times you were on your own. Like today. Pacer tried to shake off the feeling. He didn't need Connors. The Assistant Commissioner was on side and that was much better. And there were others. Even young Picone, with his dedication and promise. Picone was waiting in the incident room with another of his 'scoops'. Pacer's jaw firmed as he headed back.

CHAPTER 88

'YOUR LIBRARIAN HAS come good again. Anything more and we'll have to put her on the payroll.' Now back in the incident room, Pacer felt better. He pushed Connors and his petty comments aside, determined the prick wouldn't get to him again.

Picone was looking pleased with himself. He'd managed to deliver the goods.

'She said it was easy, once she figured the block of land next to Hawthorne Park belonged to the State Government. It covers the film centre and the junkyard. The government has pockets of land all over the place. They keep tabs on all of them. There's a property database where proposals for the sale of government assets are documented. She looked and there it was. Someone is interested in buying it.'

'No indication of the potential buyer?' That would be too easy, Pacer said to himself.

'The state planning department keeps that kind of detail. It's confidential.'

'So we know the Canal Road Film Centre is sitting on government land,' Pacer said. 'It's zoned public purpose. That makes it attractive to developers and a target for them. The fact it currently has a tenant wouldn't put them off. Let's assume Flynn was sniffing about, perhaps scoping it out for Platinum Living. Others might be interested. Sullivan Constructions, for one. I'd like to know.'

'Having more than one developer after the same block of land could get interesting. Was Sullivan going to cross Platinum Living over that, do you think? Try beating them to it?' Picone looked and sounded excited.

'Too early to say, but that would have soured the relationship.' Malcolm Hendry would not have tolerated a second transgression. Not from anyone, even Sullivan.

Pacer spent a frustrating morning on the phone to the state planning department, most of the time on hold. Finally he spoke to a director who said he was responsible for purchase applications.

'I do the small ones,' Garth Powell told Pacer. 'Under fifteen million in unimproved value. The government is divesting itself of these parcels of land. You'd be surprised how many there are. Much better to put them in private hands where they will be developed. For the benefit of the wider community, of course.'

Powell was happy to meet with Pacer to discuss the details, but he was busy. Would next week be soon enough? Pacer was insistent. Powell agreed to fit him in the following morning.

Pacer arrived at the nondescript city tower, collected his security pass and made his way to the meeting rooms on the twelfth floor. Garth Powell, clean-shaven with an open face and pleasant smile, was waiting by the lifts. He held a laptop and opened the door to a plainly furnished room. He was bubbling with curiosity. Pacer sighed and followed him in.

'This is in regard to a murder inquiry. I need to document the victim's business dealings, recent activities and associates.' Pacer spoke in a matter-of-fact tone.

'To find a motive, that sort of thing.' Powell appeared to be enjoying himself.

'Just routine,' Pacer deadpanned. 'You mentioned on the phone that the application to buy the land was unsolicited. I'd like the details.'

Powell explained that developers often acquired government land this way. A private interest scoped out the site, drew up a concept plan and invited the state planning department to negotiate. Pacer took in the main points and let the rest slide by.

'Saves my division a lot of work,' Powell said at last. 'If the proposal conforms to our guidelines, we can usually play ball.'

Powell was warming to his subject. Yesterday he'd been too busy to see Pacer, now he had all the time in the world.

'And the parcel of land where the Canal Road Film Centre is located. Do you have the details?'

Powell opened his laptop and scrolled through several pages before looking up at Pacer. 'This property transaction will be more complicated than most. The parcel of land is not vacant. There is a tenant, a management committee. We need to consult with them. It's in the guidelines.

244

Their lease has rolled over to a short-term arrangement but the government would not terminate it for that reason. We try to be accommodating.'

It wasn't relevant, but Pacer's interest was sparked. 'So legally, you could turn them out?' He thought of Jane and the others, blissfully unaware, he guessed, that their work premises were up for grabs.

'Strictly speaking, yes, but that's not going to happen. Both proposals have made provision for retaining a footprint around the film centre and continuing the lease with the management committee.'

'Both proposals?' This was a turn-up but not a complete surprise. It fitted Pacer's theory. Had Sullivan and Hendry both thrown a hat in the ring?

'Yes. After your call yesterday I looked this property up. Unusual to get more than one firm after the same site, but it does happen. More often these days because available land is in short supply. There was a kerfuffle when we tried to offload the old hospital site in Rozelle. The community got up in arms, objected strenuously. Made it hard for the developers. When things get that difficult, developers usually look elsewhere if there are options. The Canal Road Film Centre is close to Rozelle, a good alternative, but not anything like the size of the hospital. Still, an attractive site.'

'Those two proposals, Mr Powell. You have the details?' Pacer was feeling impatient, willing Powell to get to the point.

'Both are recent – they came in a few weeks apart. Not a surprise really. The site is next to parklands with the potential for views across to Rozelle Bay. Close to public transport too. Both developers want to build apartments.'

'I'd like to see the details,' Pacer said, feeling the need to repeat his request. A frown creased Powell's forehead. Pacer reacted quickly. 'This is a murder inquiry. It could be important.'

'Proposals are treated as business-in-confidence but we can make an exception. I'll go through them with you, but I can't make copies of the paperwork, I'm afraid.'

Pacer was annoyed but didn't object. He could get a warrant later. He sat with notebook open.

The concept plan for the first proposal included apartments in several blocks. Those at the back rose to six floors while others were lower, about the height of the film centre, which sat in the middle like a beached whale. The smaller buildings were gone, either built over or replaced by gardens and a screened utility area. Pacer was no film producer, but he couldn't imagine how that would work for the film people.

Pacer pointed to an area on the computer screen. 'Those small build-ings are used by people associated with filmmaking. They will go?' This didn't make sense. The film centre needed those people close by. It was Jane's livelihood and myriad others on that site.

'According to this plan, yes. But there are compensations. The propos-er agrees to work with the State Government to upgrade the access road – Canal Road, I think it's called. A good thing from our point of view. In poor shape, not even sealed. Oh, and they are putting a cafe on the ground floor of the block closest to the water.'

'There is already a cafe further down, in Hawthorne Park,' Pacer re-torted. Steady on. Don't get involved.

'There is now, but the local council wants to pull it down. They won't get away with that unless there is something to replace it.'

'The local council, this is nothing to do with them, is it?' Pacer was puzzled.

'I said this was complicated. To sell the land for residential develop-ment, the state planning department has to work with local government, in this case, the Cooks River Council. We need them to change the zoning from public purpose to residential. We do it all the time. Just a formality, really.'

'Would that be Mark Baker?'

'Most of the time, yes. Sometimes it's his deputy, Craig Thomas. I mention Craig because he has given his support to the second proposal. Quite clever of the developer to get the council onside this early in the process. Makes things simpler.'

'Can we look through the second proposal?'

'Certainly. It's not unlike Platinum Living's, but it does include some interesting features. They want to put an exercise circuit up near the sports oval at the end. And see here, they are putting in a walkway to the light rail.'

'And the company behind this proposal?'

'A new outfit,' said Powell as he scrolled down to the final page. 'Their proposal looks professional but I still need to make some enquiries. We are careful with due diligence.'

Pacer wrote as Powell gave him the company's details. With a frown and a nod of his head, Pacer snapped his notebook closed.

CHAPTER 89

PACER TOOK THE call in the evening at home. Davidson had tried for another dog, a different rescue service this time.

'The manager called Kurt Otway immediately,' Wainwright said. 'He sent someone quickly but Davidson was gone by the time he got there.'

'What, he got away?' Not again, surely.

'Not as it turned out. Davidson was on foot so that narrowed the search area. He turned up a while ago at a convenience store. One of Kurt's people followed him home. A boarding house in Clemton Park.'

'And someone is outside keeping watch?' Pacer asked. Another stupid question. Of course Kurt had someone there.

'As long as necessary. But it might not be much longer. Vice told Kurt that the grubs have a swap meet planned for tomorrow night. Davidson might decide to visit his stash, pick a few choice items for the show and tell.'

'Tomorrow could be the day, then. How about you join me in my office tomorrow morning? We'll assemble a team and wait for Kurt to call.' It would be tense. Every minute an eternity.

'This has to be it,' Wainwright said.

Otway phoned at around one in the afternoon. Davidson was on the move. He had just left McDonald's in Canterbury Road and was walking in the direction of the city. Now he was standing at a bus stop. Five minutes later he was on board.

Pacer called Picone, who was waiting with a uniformed constable in an unmarked car near the far end of Mercury Lane.

'Davidson is on his way. Start your approach to Mercury Lane but stay well back around that corner. This bloke is super cautious, he can smell a cop a mile off.' Pacer had lectured Picone half the morning. He needed it to sink in. 'We have to get him with the key in the lock and the door open.'

Pacer hopped behind the wheel and set the radio frequency to Otway's. He and Wainwright listened wordlessly as they drove towards the church on Parramatta Road.

Wainwright checked his transport app. 'That bus route will take him towards us. There's a stop opposite the church.'

Pacer and Wainwright pulled into a spot fifty metres back from the church. They didn't dare come closer. The risk Davidson would recognise them was too great. Pacer bit his lip and stared ahead.

Wainwright glanced at him then turned his eyes back to the road. 'Kurt's watching the cameras. He'll tell us when Davidson enters Mercury Lane. Then we can go.'

That was the plan. They'd worked on it. No false moves. Pacer felt the tension in his back. Wainwright was handling it better, sitting back, almost relaxed.

Pacer spotted the 413 bus as it rumbled towards them and stopped on the opposite side of Parramatta Road. Two people stepped onto the pavement. One was a tall man in jeans and a blue hoodie. Pacer's phone buzzed. Otway had identified Davidson. Otway's van pulled in to the kerb behind the bus. A woman in gym gear got out and walked in the same direction as the man in the hoodie. They both stopped at the intersection, the pedestrian lights on red.

Davidson turned and looked directly at the woman standing behind him. The lights turned green. He hesitated. The woman stepped onto the crossing and continued at a brisk pace. The pedestrian lights flashed orange. Davidson lunged forward and made it to the other side just as the traffic began to flow.

Pacer breathed again. He looked at Wainwright in triumph when Davidson chose the road by the church. A minute passed. Another text. Davidson was in Mercury Lane. It was time.

Davidson had the shutter partway up and was standing inside the lock-up, hands on hips. He half-turned at the sound of footsteps and ducked outside. He saw Pacer coming up, pivoted to the left and ran down Mercury Lane as Picone rounded the corner. Pacer lunged forward and grabbed Davidson by the back of his collar. Davidson pitched off balance and fell backwards onto the pavement. Pacer towered over Davidson, who was nursing a damaged elbow and snivelling in pain. Pacer resisted the urge to lay in a boot. He stood back as Picone snapped the cuffs.

Pacer turned to the door of the unit, keys dangling from the lock. Wainwright stood by as Kurt filmed, waiting for a signal to go in. 'Don't touch anything yet. Melanie De Veen will be here shortly with her team.'

The objects inside had not been disturbed since Pacer's last visit. Picone bobbed under the shutter and stared wide-eyed as Pacer pointed out items they would need to make their case. Magazines, videos, clothing, and the semi-opaque box filled with a child's clothing and shoes. Pacer and Wainwright stared at it for a minute in silence.

'Seen enough?' Pacer asked Wainwright, not expecting a reply. There was just a nod.

Curious, Picone went further in, shining a torch into darker spaces. He called Pacer, his voice animated. 'I've found something at the back.' It was a blanket, creased and dirtied with grey fibres. Shards of asbestos poked out from underneath. 'Just like the stuff at Arko's depot.'

'Arko, an untidy workman, anybody's for a quid.' Pacer stood silent, deliberating. 'I had wondered why Baker made that call to Flynn. Davidson was back in town. Things were heating up and that had Baker worried. He needed Arko to shift the stash somewhere safer, off his patch, so he called Flynn, the go-between.'

'I reckon Arko brought it here in the first place. Probably used that dirty blanket to cover the load. Too bad we can't bring Arko in, get it from the horse's mouth,' Picone said.

'No, but there will be a trail. Baker was uncomfortable around me. I thought it was Sullivan's murder, that he had something to do with it. As it turns out it was just him getting nervous. No wonder he was jumpy, with Flynn out of action and Arko disappearing.'

'What's next?' asked Wainwright.

'The Assistant Commissioner needs to be told. We have Davidson, but there will be other arrests. We go after those who helped him.' Baker for one. Pacer felt a strange mix of exhaustion and elation. Almost over.

Wainwright stood beside him, the fatigue etched in his face. Pacer would have spent more time, a cup of tea together, talking things over, but Wainwright was ahead of him.

'I'm cooked,' Wainwright said. 'I just want to sleep. Make your calls and go home, Pacer. Let's start to feel whole again.'

CHAPTER 90

PACER ROSE EARLY. Wedge raced from him to the front door and back, before settling at Pacer's feet, her message clear. A fine day, crisp and inviting. Pacer used to enjoy autumn mornings, often went for a run. That was years ago.

'We'll be off soon, Wedge.'

There was time for a walk. Wedge had come to expect it. But it would be different today. No need for eyes raking across trees and the frayed edges of parks and playgrounds. Pacer felt the lightness.

His last call yesterday was to Assistant Commissioner Maxine Poulos, who choked back tears as he gave her the news. She wanted details of the surveillance, the team, the takedown. And the discovery of what was missing before: her daughter's clothing and shoes. The proof.

The conversation was long. Pacer was unaccustomed to the detailing, the back and forth, the praise. He protested. John Wainwright's part was crucial and there were others.

'You bring something more. To the families. To us. You care deeply.'

Pacer thought about that later. It was true. Janet said it too. It did matter.

'As for Baker,' the Assistant Commissioner had said in a cooler tone, 'he assisted Davidson, concealed evidence and obstructed police investigations. I expect the public prosecutor will accept a charge of accessory to murder. Will there be sufficient forensics at the lock-up, do you think, to make it watertight?'

'I'm confident the evidence will be there. We will prepare a strong case.'

'And Davidson's lawyer?' she asked before ending the call. 'His advice?'

'He said to plead guilty.'

'Thank you, George.'

Pacer touched the crystal rose bowl that Janet had so loved. The roses he put there the week before were starting to wilt but the perfume still lingered. He rearranged them and added water. Pacer finished his tea and broke off a corner of Vegemite toast. Wedge chomped it down and headed for the door. 'Steady on. Be with you in a minute.' Pacer rinsed his cup and set it aside, then reached for his coat.

CHAPTER 91

PACER WAS ABOUT to leave for work when John Wainwright phoned with the news. Sofia was ready to talk. Peta had called and set up a meeting at her office.

'And bring Wedge,' Peta said. 'Sofia is doing well, she's a strong person, but seeing that dog will give her a boost. Wedge has found a permanent home, hasn't she? I don't want any misunderstanding.'

Pacer wasted no time, out the door in minutes and on his way. Wedge bounded to Wainwright the moment Pacer lifted her from the car. She crouched while he gave her back a good scratch. Wainwright pulled a treat from his pocket. The dog followed every move and gulped it down. She was rewarded with another.

Wainwright examined the dog's head. 'The ear's healing up nicely. How's it going with her? Bet you're glad she's yours now. Lovely nature. Smart too.'

Pacer smiled. 'We're getting along fine.' Was this really him? Was he turning into a dog person? 'Okay, let's go in, see what Sofia has to say.'

It was a meeting of old friends. Wedge barked and Sofia cried. They danced about and settled together on a lounge along one wall of the kitchen. Pacer, Wainwright and Peta arranged chairs at the table. Coffees and a tea were prepared.

The room quietened. Wainwright got the conversation rolling, as he and Pacer had planned. Sofia trusted him again. She looked calmer, no longer flighty. Wainwright asked after her welfare. She was happy where she was staying, the people nice. She'd had time to think, work things out.

'That night in the park, you were there in your place behind the cafe,' Wainwright said in a soft voice. 'What you saw frightened you away.'

Sofia looked to Peta for reassurance, who said, 'You're not in trouble.'

Sofia spoke slowly in a strongly accented voice, her words carefully chosen and the meaning perfectly clear. She held Wedge tightly at first, then loosened her grip as her confidence built.

'I was asleep, then a noise woke me, it was always so quiet at night. A truck came and a man got out. I knew him, he worked on that new building.' Sofia stopped to gauge their reaction.

Pacer scrolled his phone and stopped at a photo of Arko. Sofia fixed on the image. 'Yes, that man. He went to the building; it was just foundations. He had a shovel. I heard scraping noises but didn't see what he did. I just stayed quiet. I was scared he'd see me.' Sofia looked at Peta, who nodded encouragement. 'Suddenly another man was there. I think he was in charge.'

'Did he come in a car?' Pacer asked.

'No, he came out of nowhere. He went to the truck. It was for mixing cement. He climbed up the back and looked in. Then he went to the man with the shovel and said the mix was too dry. I could hear everything. The man, the one in charge, he pulled a hose out of the truck. He took it around the front of the cafe and put it on the tap. He was so close.'

Pacer found a photo and showed Sofia. Flynn was younger than Arko, with short blond hair and even features. He wore a cocky grin. 'Is this the man?'

'Yes. I'm sure. He is like that man hiding in the park, behind the trees. I didn't see him so well. But not him, it can't be. That man was sent by my husband.'

Pacer knew otherwise but didn't contradict her. He wanted more on that night in Hawthorne Park. 'What happened next, Sofia? Back at that other park.'

'After a while that man said, "You can stop digging." He said something else. I can't remember the words. It was something like, "They'll be here soon. Stay in the truck, like I told you before. Finish the job when they go." Then he just disappeared.'

Pacer and Wainwright looked at each other. It was Flynn. Had to be. He had exited through the fence. They had him.

'You're doing well, Sofia,' Wainwright said. 'Did you see anything else?'

'The other man went to the truck and sat inside. A car came up, a nice one, expensive. It turned around and backed in but not so close. Two people got out, dressed in black. They opened the boot and started to drag something out. I couldn't see at first. Then …'

Sofia's face twisted in a grimace, her eyes wide. She clutched Wedge more tightly and slowly turned back to Wainwright.

'I wanted to scream.'

'You saw them pull out the body of a man, is that right?'

Sofia nodded. Her pupils dilated. 'I could see. There were lights on the truck.'

'You can have a break if you want to,' Pacer said.

'No, I can do this. They tried to lift the man, but he was heavy. There were things on the ground. They stumbled. The man in the truck came over with a wheelbarrow. He grabbed the body by the leg. Those people in black, they pushed him away, had angry words.'

'Can you tell us about the people in black?' Pacer could hear the hope in his voice.

'Thin people, one was taller. The small one was a woman. Their clothes fitted tight.'

'Would you recognise them again?'

'I am sorry, no. They had covers on their heads. But I can tell you about the car.'

'The car?' Pacer and Wainwright looked at each other again.

'The number of the car. There was a pencil on the ground, one that builders use. I wrote the number on the wall. Near the bottom.'

Pacer fought the urge to go, right then. A number plate. See it for himself, be reassured it was still there. If it was.

Sofia finished her story. Pacer fought back his impatience, forced himself to listen to every word. The sounds of a body dropping into a cavity, the gasps of the people in black, the crunch of gravel as they drove away. Then the truck coming in, concrete pouring through a funnel. The man from the cement truck coming close, removing the hose, then driving off.

'You'll feel better, Sofia, now you've got that off your chest,' Peta said. Sofia had visibly relaxed and was now fussing over Wedge, sharing a private joke.

'I remember one thing more,' Sofia said, looking up at the detectives, who were on their feet, readying to leave. 'The man in the cement truck said something. To the people in black. I think, maybe, he was angry with them, too.'

What she said next changed everything for Pacer. It was like a bolt of lightning, slicing the air. When the evidence doesn't fit, you question your theory. You question everything you thought was a certainty.

CHAPTER 92

JOEL FRAZER WAS waiting impatiently, hands on hips, when Pacer drove up to Café Bones. Picone had arrived earlier with the crime scene officers and closed the cafe. It was now festooned with crime scene tape.

'I'm sorry, sir,' Pacer said. 'It's short notice but necessary.'

'I've sent Genie home, told her to come back tomorrow. I hope we can open as usual.'

'I'll let you know.' Pacer walked over to Miranda De Veen, who had emerged from behind the building.

'We found it, Pacer,' she announced. 'Easy when you know where to look. My lot are over at the van right now, checking the databases. Should have something for you in quick time.'

'Wouldn't be the first time the vehicle from a crime ends up a burnt-out wreck in a ditch.'

'And I thought you were having a good day. C'mon, Pacer, look on the bright side. Hey, I hear you've got a dog now.'

'Yes, a young kelpie. She was a stray, more or less, needed a home.' And she'd found one all right, not out on the back deck where he had put her bed. She scratched at the door that first night until he let her in.

'She's made herself comfortable at my place.' At least he didn't allow her on the bed. She'd only got as far as the living room. So far. 'Dogs expect different treatment these days.'

'And they get it, by the sounds. Anyway, do you good, Pacer. I'll get over to the van, see what's come up.'

There was nothing for Pacer to do but wait. He walked further into the park. Small groups stood around, watching the police operation. The man and the border collie were back. It would take more than this to distract them from their game. A couple coming towards him stopped short, realising the cafe was closed. Not many people today and school was still in. Pacer gazed towards the trees at the far end. So many places to hide, close by but secluded, most people unaware.

Back at Café Bones, Miranda was ready with a result. 'You're in luck. The plates are current for a late-model luxury car. No report that it's been stolen or written off. The address is for a hire place on the Lower North Shore. How would you like to proceed?'

'How soon can you get over there and impound the car? Hired out or in their depot, no difference. I'll come over to your van and sign the paperwork now.'

'No point wasting time. We're almost finished here. We can go straight over to that hire place. No tip-offs, no chance for the car to go missing. Take it back to my depot and arrange for a cadaver dog. We'll give it the full forensics.'

'Can you fit Stuart into a vehicle? I'd like him to see how these things are done.' Pacer looked over at Picone, who was deep in conversation with a photographer, curious about everything.

'He's doing well, don't you think? You're doing a great job with him. You don't want to hear it, but everyone else can see.' Miranda stood with hands on hips, looking pleased.

Pacer turned, a bit embarrassed. Taking a compliment was a lot harder than giving one, not that he had much experience either way. He'd have to work on that. 'Yeah, he's doing well for a bloke new to the job. Very keen.'

De Veen gave one of her lopsided smiles. 'Yeah, sure, nothing to do with you.'

Nothing more for Pacer to do at Café Bones. He walked slowly back to his car, needing to think, assimilate the new information and arrange the puzzle pieces over a pot of tea in his office. The drive was quick, the traffic light. With no one else around, he had the incident room to himself.

De Veen's call came late in the day. 'We've got the car. On hire to a rich bloke on holiday in Avalon. Didn't take kindly to the news that his wheels were going on the back of a truck.' She laughed. 'You wouldn't believe the steep driveways and curves in the roads. Why live up there?'

'And the hire records? You have the details of who had the car at the time of the murder?'

'Certainly do.'

Pacer whistled when he heard the name. What did they say? *No honour among thieves.*

CHAPTER 93

PACER AND PICONE waited with De Veen while two crime scene officers peeled plastic wrap from the chassis of the limo. It had been placed over a lift in the centre of the depot's main examination room, like the workshop of a motor mechanic, but impeccably clean. Cameras were set up above and around. Recording equipment would capture every moment.

De Veen stepped forward, unlocked the car and opened the boot with the remote. It was large, empty and lined in dark velour. A police officer, German shepherd at his side, stepped forward. With a command from his handler the dog leaped silently into the cavity. He moved from side to side, nose pressed into the surface. On a second command he jumped out and sat, barking twice.

'That's an affirmative,' the handler said with a broad smile. 'A strong response.' He patted the dog and rewarded him with a toy. 'Good boy.'

Two crime scene officers donned protective clothing and moved towards the doors.

'It's painstaking work,' De Veen told Picone. 'They'll go over every inch, pick up stray hairs, prints, everything.'

'And blood in the boot?' Picone peered forward, looking expectant.

'I reckon,' De Veen replied. 'Even if they wrapped the body, traces would probably seep through. We won't need much to prove a match.'

'You want to spend the day here?' Pacer asked Picone, who looked pleased. 'Okay, just don't get in the way. I've got to get back to the office.'

Pacer's landline rang as he returned from the hallway kitchen. Reaching around the desk, he grabbed it in time, spilling a few drops of tea. He wiped the liquid from his sleeve as he answered. It was Garth Powell from the state planning department.

'Thought you'd want to know,' Powell said in an animated voice. 'Given this is a murder inquiry.'

Pacer had met many Powells during his time in the force. People with boring jobs and vivid imaginations who relished the chance to be part of the action.

'It's the proposal from Platinum Living. For the site around the Canal Road Film Centre. They've withdrawn it. We received an email this morning.'

'Did they give a reason?'

'No, they don't have to. But I did some checking around. Wanted to help – you know, assist the police.'

'We always appreciate that. What did you discover?'

'Platinum Living is in financial difficulties. A cashflow problem. They have a swag of properties ready for occupancy they can't sell. People are backing out of their contracts, scared about substandard construction. The problem for Platinum Living started with a trickle a few weeks ago, now it's a flood. It's been in the press. Perhaps you've seen something?'

'I was aware of the issue.' Pacer hoped Powell had more than this.

'Normally companies in this situation go to their financial backers to tide them over. Not this time. Apparently Platinum Living's usual source can't help.'

'And why not?'

'Trouble in the kitchen. Platinum Living is run by a man by the name of Bidanau. He used his family's money to set up the company some years ago and has been sitting pretty since. Has the ear of his mother, who has the controlling interest. I should have said "had". She died recently, I'm told. There's another brother, younger. With the old lady out of the way this bloke has stepped in and gained control over the family finances. Left his big brother high and dry.'

Powell had Pacer's full attention. 'I'm interested. Keep going.'

'Look, I've got this from a colleague not in a position to talk openly. But if you have the gist of it you can check through your own channels. Federal Police, Border Force. There's suspect activity coming from Malaysia, so they keep an eye out. The family company in question is Malaysian, that's how my colleague knows what's going on.'

'Are you saying that Platinum Living's boss is the brother who lost out?'

'Osman Bidanau. Conflict in the family, happens a lot when money's involved. It's been brewing for a while and came to a head a week or so ago. I'm told Osman didn't see it coming.'

'That means only one company is in the race for the Canal Road property. The one that the younger brother is behind. Musa Bidanau.' Pacer's mind raced. Craig Thomas had given Cooks River Council's support for that proposal. Looking good for him. Thomas would be expecting a substantial kickback.

'Right,' said Powell. 'Fairview Holdings. Owned by Musa Bidanau. Crazy, isn't it? But maybe his big brother will get the last laugh.'

'How do you figure that?'

'Well, property development is a lucrative business. People from Asia are falling over one another to set up shop here. Musa Bidanau looks to be of that ilk. He's grabbed his chance and gone for it. But there's a caveat hanging over his business ventures in Australia. I checked that too, before I called you.'

'What kind of caveat?' Pacer was impressed. Garth Powell could move quickly with the whiff of something beyond the mundane.

'An objection with the Foreign Investors Review Board. Musa Bidanau has been flagged for investigation on character and probity grounds.' Powell spoke with an air of authority. This information was good and he knew it.

'How did that happen? Did someone put in an objection?' If so, Pacer would like to know who.

'I don't know, but that's usually how it works. A common tactic. Wouldn't be the first time a rival tried to stymie the competition by throwing in some dirt. Anyway, I can't process Fairview Holding's application for Canal Road, or any other property, until it is cleared.'

'When is that likely?' Pacer could guess.

'He'll be waiting a long time. These things drag on,' Powell said with a sigh.

Pacer's tea had gone cold. He barely noticed as he finished the cup. He now had two rival outfits, Platinum Living and Fairview Holdings. He knew for a certainty that things between them had got nasty.

Nothing remarkable about that, swindles, double-crosses and duplicity being common features of business, and not just among the criminal classes. This time it had gone further – two men had been murdered – but exactly how and why Pacer could not fathom.

It all came back to that central question: what circumstances had led to Martin Sullivan's lifeless body being dumped under a concrete slab in Hawthorne Park?

CHAPTER 94

PACER CHECKED THE time, not wanting to be late. He had arranged to meet Karla Burns, Sullivan's girlfriend, in the city after she finished work.

He found the place, a cafe and meeting area on the ground floor of a sandstone building close to the light rail stop he had used before. The seating was well spaced, affording privacy. Pacer chose a comfortable arrangement with a good view to the side entrance. Karla spotted Pacer and walked across smiling, hand outstretched. He rose to greet her.

The first weeks after losing Martin were hard, she said, but she was getting there, her friends supportive. Switching over to full-time work was a big help and she was enjoying the job. Her living situation? Fortunately there were six months to run on the lease, which gave her time to make some choices.

'His parents contacted me. They were upset but very nice. His mother invited me to their place in Western Australia. I should go. Perhaps in a few months. They will want to know about these last years, how Martin lived, his likes and successes. I have so many photos to show them.'

Karla's eyes welled. She dabbed at the tears before turning her attention back to Pacer.

Pacer talked about the investigation, the general points, and answered her questions as well as he could. There were confidences to keep, leads still to be investigated. In his mind, arrests were imminent, but it would be unwise to say so. You never gave false hope or raised expectations.

'Are you aware of a Malcolm Hendry, CEO of Platinum Living? Mr Sullivan worked for him for a time.'

'Oh, yes,' Karla replied brightly. 'I have never met Malcolm but Martin spoke well of him. He helped Martin in his business.'

'I believe they had grown closer in recent times?' Pacer wasn't sure and needed confirmation.

'I don't know about Martin's business except in the broadest sense. But he and Malcolm had talked more often of late. I think they were working on something, exactly what I don't know. I had the feeling something was brewing.' Burns hesitated and looked at Pacer. 'Oh! Martin wasn't going back to work at Platinum Living if that's what you're thinking. He would not have contemplated that, I'm quite sure. He was so talented.' Burns dabbed her eyes again and stared into the distance.

'From what I know, Mr Sullivan was doing well on his own.' Burns was drifting to other topics, needing to be brought back. Pacer chose his next words carefully. 'He was in a competitive business. Are you aware of any rivalries or conflicts he might have had?'

'He didn't talk about things like that. But he found it hard to hide his feelings. It was after the last time he went to the golf club and met up with Malcolm. He came home rather pleased with himself, said something about him and Malcolm having a win over another business. I was a little concerned, urged him not to do anything unwise. He didn't like to be told. But no, there was no one he mentioned.'

'When we spoke last time you gave me a list of Martin's friends and associates. I wonder if there are others you may have missed, people who might have known about that trip to Malaysia?'

'There were so many. Most people liked Martin. He was open, didn't keep things secret. There were one or two he didn't like so much, but he was good at mending broken friendships.'

'I have a few names you might recognise. Can I run them past you?'

CHAPTER 95

FLYNN HADN'T SLEPT properly for days. He didn't dare. He was isolated, cut off. Edgar was out there, watching. Had been the whole time. That's what Craig Thomas had said, if he could be believed. Thomas was like a broken record. Keep your mouth shut, he kept saying.

Flynn had turned it over in his mind a thousand times. The mistakes, the treachery. Those assassins were well away. He was the only remaining link between the killings and the business. Only him. Without him the cops had nothing. With him, they had little more than a story that would be denied by those more powerful. He thought of Malcolm, a man untroubled by self-doubt. He would ride this out, this twisted joke.

Was that their plan all along? That he would take the fall if it came to that? Thomas was up to something. Flynn had never trusted him. A friend when it suited him but devious by nature. A man who did little but knew too much. What would the cops get him for? Some minor charge at best. And that witness, Sofia. Was she still on the run or had the husband found her? Flynn still needed her silenced.

Another call to Malcolm, rebuffed like the first. Nerrida Kingston should understand the need. What was wrong with her? Did Malcolm even know he'd called? Flynn had never liked Kingston and she'd made her feelings perfectly plain in her high-handed way. She was freezing him out. It couldn't be Malcolm. No, not Malcom. Malcolm needed him. They went back a long way, had weathered rough times. No, it wasn't Malcolm, it was Kingston. He'd talk to Malcolm about it one day, have a laugh over a single malt.

He was getting out of here. He didn't like to involve Sandra, but there was no other option. They both needed a holiday, a long one. She'd always wanted to see South America, enjoy the beaches and the culture. He'd mix in a little business, connect with old friends. Since his accident he'd had time to think. He wanted a new start. He raised it with Sandra. The plan appealed but she didn't understand the rush. Couldn't this wait a few weeks? No? It was settled. They would leave in a few days. He would like to go sooner.

Flynn dressed for his morning physio session in knee-length chinos, sweat-shirt and light jacket. He flopped into the chair and glanced at his watch. He was beginning to enjoy the exercise, feeling the strength returning to his limbs. His progress was excellent, the physio had said. One more day of this and he'd be gone.

The burner vibrated from inside his jacket. Flynn retrieved it and spoke his name. He recognised the voice on the other end and almost dropped the phone. Why wouldn't they leave him alone? He braced himself.

CHAPTER 96

MINUTES LATER, PACER and Picone walked into Flynn's room. They didn't knock. The arrogance.

'You have some interesting friends,' Pacer said without preamble. 'Let's start with someone who hasn't been able to call lately. Martin Sullivan.'

'I told you before, I didn't know Sullivan.' Flynn didn't try to hide his disdain.

'You were seen arguing with him. He'd made a fool of you over a property deal in Leichhardt.' Pacer spoke in a matter-of-fact tone.

'So long ago I can hardly remember. I'd forgotten, in fact, until I saw a story on TV about his murder. I was in hospital, after intensive care. It was a shock.'

'I bet it was. A shock, I mean,' Pacer said.

'I hadn't seen Sullivan since that other time. He meant nothing to me.'

'It was a shock because you thought the police would have found a different man.'

Flynn was thunderstruck.

Pacer continued. 'They brought the wrong body. If you'd waited around you would have realised.'

'You sound crazy. Who concocted this story?' Flynn said. What was going on? How could they know?

'Let me fill you in. You were at Hawthorne Park that night. You expected a smaller man, not Martin Sullivan. So did Arko. You remember Arko, your offsider? Poor Arko. He did what he was told and what did he get for it?'

'You know what you are? Incompetent. You're putting this on me because you have no clue.' Flynn tried to stand, but the Detective Sergeant was pressing in.

'Let me tell you something I do know,' Pacer said. 'Several people were in on this. It was carefully planned but something went awry in the final stages. The killers brought the wrong man. Arko was there, saw everything and he paid with his life.'

'It wasn't me. I wasn't there.' Flynn felt a wave of relief. They knew about Arko but had no proof of his own involvement. They were guessing. Maybe Sofia hadn't talked, or maybe she hadn't seen enough to identify him.

'Can you offer any information relevant to our inquiries?' Pacer asked.

'About what?' Flynn almost spat the words. What was this? Were they about to offer a deal? Probably a trap.

'Perhaps you are close to someone involved in the murder. Or you heard something we should know,' Picone said in a conciliatory tone.

'You mean Craig Thomas, don't you.' So this was the game. The green detective playing good cop. They wanted him to snitch. Well, well.

'Go on,' said Picone.

'Thomas is a trumped-up jerk. A bit player always wanting more of the action than he's ever going to get at Cooks River Council. Shoots his mouth off, says more than he should.'

'And what was that?' continued Picone.

'Look, anything I know is second-hand. Craig Thomas was always hanging around that build in Hawthorne Park. Arko mentioned it. He said Thomas hired him to do something but didn't say what.'

'Did Thomas talk about what happened that night?' Picone asked.

'No, but he was rattled. I'm not surprised he messed it up, whatever it was he was up to. He's hopeless.' Flynn looked at the older detective. Was he trying to suppress a laugh?

'Let's not play games, Mr Flynn,' Pacer said, cutting in. 'There's something you're not telling me. Who was behind this? Who ordered the hit?'

'How should I know? Ask Craig Thomas.' Flynn looked away.

'I'm asking you first,' Pacer replied. 'Think of this as an opportunity.'

'For what? Do you always talk in riddles?' Flynn looked down. A precipice opened before him. The wrong step would pitch him off the edge.

Pacer stepped to the window and looked towards the car park, eyes fixing on something out there. 'I'll leave that with you. Time may be of consequence.'

With that, the two detectives turned and left.

CHAPTER 97

FLYNN WAS IN no mood for physio. They could sit there waiting but he wasn't going today. He needed to plan. He stood and moved across to the window, looking in the same direction as had the Detective Sergeant. The car park was half-full. The dark sedan was there again this morning, tucked in between an early model Toyota and a VW hatchback. There was someone in the driver's seat, but from this angle the head wasn't visible.

Why was Edgar there? If he believed Craig Thomas, it was because the business no longer trusted him and Edgar was to report on the comings and goings of the police. But what if it was the other way around? What if the business had seen through Thomas, and Edgar's job was to get him away or provide some kind of backup? That scenario made more sense. Flynn was way above Thomas in Malcolm's estimation. No one, not Thomas or Nerrida Kingston, could change that. Flynn had spent hours thinking it through. If Kingston hadn't stood in the way, he and Malcolm would have sorted it out long ago.

Flynn felt sanguine. He had options. He would go to Malcolm and they would come to an agreement, work out a strategy that suited them both. Flynn knew the underbelly of Malcolm's business and had never let him down. He would get past the gatekeepers and they would talk.

Outside, the clouds were rolling in. Flynn zipped his jacket against the autumn wind. He pushed on the fire door and grasped the metal handrail with his free hand. Aluminium crutch clanged on hard metal as he manoeuvred his way down. At the bottom he stopped to catch his breath, then headed towards the dark sedan. A face, expressionless and cold, watched his approach. Flynn stopped short, a ripple of anxiety passing through. Did he have this right? He chided himself. He would go on. It was now or never. The window slid down as Flynn took the remaining steps and drew level with the driver.

'I have to see Malcolm. There are things he needs to know.'

'Tell me – I'll pass it on.' Edgar's voice was deep and flat.

'No, in person. It's important; tell him that.'

'I'll make a call. Go back to your room.' The voice had taken on a harder edge.

Flynn was tired from the exertion. He leaned the crutch against the chair and flopped back on his bed. He would have gone with Edgar there and then but there were protocols. Calls to make, a meeting place to be arranged. Still, he felt good. The way would be smoothed and Edgar would come back for him.

He reached in his pocket for the burner and called Sandra. He caught her in time. She was about to leave, intending to visit. She did that most days, came after his morning physio session. She had that tone in her voice, a slight whine that women use when not so happy. He had missed physio. He was going out without clearing it with the staff.

'It's business. It can't wait any longer.' He was relieved she didn't ask for details. He had always discouraged that kind of talk.

'I'll see you this evening, then, will I?' Sandra asked, concern in her voice.

'Of course. Look forward to it.' Flynn kept it light.

Flynn stood and looked out the window again. The car hadn't moved. A light drizzle had started to fall. He thought it through, what he would say to Malcolm. There were rats in the ranks. He would tell him that too, like that other time.

There was one more loose end, that witness, Sofia. No point pretending she didn't exist, with Thomas shooting his mouth off. Flynn would talk to Edgar. Edgar would do anything to protect Malcolm. He was a better bet than Brett Eyland. Edgar would find Sofia and finish the job.

Flynn lay down again and dozed off. His eyes shot open. Edgar was standing at the foot of the bed. How could a heavy-set man move without making a sound? Flynn rose and followed Edgar silently down the stairs and into the back seat of the sedan. He heard the door locks falling into place. The wipers slashed against rain sheeting in.

Flynn wondered where he would meet Malcolm. Not at head office, never there. It would be somewhere private, no unwanted ears or eyes to mute the conversation.

The traffic was light as the car glided slowly through suburban streets. They didn't go far, their destination not ten minutes away.

Flynn peered through the gloom as the car turned into a driveway of compressed clay. A corrugated iron building was just ahead. Edgar pressed a remote and large doors swung outwards. He drove through.

'Wait over there,' Edgar said, pointing, as Flynn dragged his leg across the seat and pushed himself up with the crutch. The single globe protruding from the wall illuminated a small part of what appeared to be a large warehouse. Flynn peered into the gloom. No chair, no furniture at all. Edgar stood facing him, poker-faced. Flynn was unsettled. Where was Malcolm? The minutes were ticking by.

Finally Flynn heard footsteps echoing on the cement floor as a man entered the building and walked towards him. It was Malcolm, but something was wrong. The face was set hard and the eyes bored into his. Malcolm stood silent, regarding him. Flynn felt the colour draining from his face.

'Whatever they've told you, it's wrong.' The words tumbled out. 'I've given the cops nothing. I'd never cross you. Never.'

CHAPTER 98

STUART PICONE STEPPED onto the second floor, pushing a trolley piled high with files and boxes of exhibits. The desk sergeant handed him a pass and indicated a room on the left. Picone manoeuvred the trolley inside and grabbed at files tumbling forward as Pacer came over to help. Wainwright went to a machine and made Picone a coffee.

'This is everything on your list, sir.' Picone spread the files across the conference table.

'More space here than in our incident room upstairs.' Pacer looked around. Detectives didn't get to the second floor too often. You had to be sure, the evidence tight, the interview responses of suspects calculated. A fitting place for your end game.

'Let's start with Musa Bidanau,' Pacer said. 'What do we have, Stuart?'

'Nothing new on the car he hired.'

'I know that, but we all need to hear it, be on the same page.' No assumptions, no misunderstandings.

'Bidanau has an apartment in Lane Cove, bought just over a year ago. The limo examined by forensics was hired by him and garaged there at the time of Sullivan's murder. Sullivan's blood and other traces were found in the boot. Its tyre tracks were picked up at the crime scene.'

'So we have the car.' Wainwright said. 'But Bidanau didn't drive it that night, did he.'

'He flew out of the country a few days earlier,' Pacer replied. 'But it was kept in Bidanau's locked garage. He supplied the keys to the killers. Must have. After the murder, he came back for a brief visit before returning the car to the hire place. Very neat. He arranged for Sullivan to be murdered and made sure he was out of the country when it happened.'

'He let the killers use his car? Brazen, don't you think?' Wainwright asked.

'Yes and no,' Pacer replied. 'He thought the body wouldn't be found. But Sullivan was a much bigger man. The cavity Arko prepared was too small to conceal Sullivan's body. Bidanau had overlooked that. Probably never crossed his mind.' They always miss something, no matter how clever they think they are. Pacer smiled at the thought. Arko had argued with the killers that night. He'd been expecting a different man. Sofia had heard enough to make that clear. Pacer's rethink of the facts had pivoted on that revelation. When the evidence doesn't fit ...

Pacer continued. 'Probably enjoyed the whole thing, the victor, riding in a car that had held the body of an adversary.'

'So Musa Bidanau's motive checks out?' Wainwright asked.

'Sullivan raised objections to Musa Bidanau's Australian business interests on probity and character grounds. Successfully. Probably at Hendry's behest. They were after the same development property at Hawthorne Park, so Hendry would have wanted him out of the picture. Clever, really.'

'Wasn't there a falling-out between Sullivan and Musa Bidanau a few years ago, when Sullivan lost his money over that gourmet food venture?' asked Picone.

'That's right, Stuart. Another reason for Musa Bidanau to go after Sullivan.' Pacer was pleased. Picone was joining the dots.

'What's happening with the surveillance?' Pacer asked.

'Bidanau flew in late last night and moved in to his Lane Cove apartment. Alone. He seems unaware that we are watching,' Picone replied.

'Good,' Pacer said. 'All to plan then. We'll bring him in this afternoon.'

'That worked out well,' Wainwright said. 'Musa Bidanau flying in at the right time.'

'No accident,' Pacer said. 'He has a hearing with the Foreign Investors Review Board. A second chance. Or so he thinks.'

'You fixed that?' Wainwright said.

'No, it was Connors's idea. He made the arrangements.'

Wainwright's eyebrows rose. 'You're kidding.'

'Connors comes up with the goods when it suits him.' Like this time, with the sniff of a prosecution and a notch on his belt to impress his seniors. Pacer wouldn't say as much in front of Picone. Too soon to let him in on how things really worked.

The conversation stopped at raised voices and scuffling outside. Picone stuck his head out and turned back to the others. 'Our man has arrived.'

Pacer listened at the door. 'Good. They're taking him to the interview room. We'll let him stew for a while.'

Wainwright was still puzzling over Bidanau's role. 'Lots of things don't gel for me. Musa Bidanau was the intended victim but there was a switch. How did that work?'

'Osman Bidanau hired assassins to kill his little brother because he'd swindled him. Couldn't let that go. Wanted revenge, obviously. Osman knew who to call. You don't just pull out the phone book and call up killers of their calibre. It takes reach of a certain kind. There is a long-standing arrangement with the Bidanau family, according to the feds.'

'They killed Arko,' Picone said, 'because he saw them on the night they killed Sullivan.'

'So it would seem,' Pacer said. 'Their privacy has more value than a human life.'

'Any chance of bringing the killers in?' asked Wainwright.

'Little to none. They keep their heads down, work for selective clients. There is not even a description. There are some who don't want them caught. Too useful.'

'Yeah, I see what you're getting at. But you still haven't explained how Musa Bidanau did the switch and had Sullivan killed instead.' Wainwright looked puzzled.

'Well, in short, Musa Bidanau found out what was in store for him. He knew the killers, guessed who his big brother had hired – it was a family business after all – and put in a higher bid.' Pacer waited for that to sink in.

'How did Musa Bidanau find out?' asked Wainwright.

'Someone clued him in. I'm not sure who, but I can guess. There is one person playing both sides.' Pacer hesitated. 'Who would that be, Stuart?'

'It would have to be Craig Thomas. He knows Flynn and used to work at Platinum Living. We know he's also in with Musa Bidanau. Thomas backed his bid for the Hawthorne Park site. Thomas heard something about the murder plot from Flynn or one of the others and told Bidanau. Maybe Thomas even told him who put that objection to the Foreign Investors Review Board.'

'Good theory, Stuart.' Pacer looked pleased. He thought the same. Thomas, a low-life, would collaborate with anyone willing to pay him a kickback for useful information. A white-collar version of Arko.

'What about the original murder conspiracy?' said Wainwright. 'The plot to kill Musa Bidanau. Hendry's scheme, wasn't it? With Flynn and Arko at the dump site?'

Pacer turned to Picone. 'What do you think, Stuart?' An interesting puzzle.

'It points to Hendry but there is no hard evidence for his involvement in the plot,' Picone said. 'It's circumstantial. He has a motive, but Osman Bidanau's is stronger. We should consider all possibilities.'

Pacer nodded. 'It's important to keep an open mind. Well done, Stuart.' Consider all possibilities. Cheeky devil.

Pacer's phone buzzed on the table in front. He picked it up and listened before exclaiming, 'Bloody idiot! What's he playing at?'

The others were looking at him. Pacer tried to sound calm but didn't feel anything like it. 'That was the rehab unit. Flynn's gone. Took off down the fire escape. Followed a bloke into a dark sedan.'

CHAPTER 99

THE RAIN ON the iron roof was beating harder now. Malcolm stood immobile. Flynn was afraid he hadn't heard over the din. Then Malcolm spoke. His tone was quiet and controlled. Flynn strained to hear the words.

'You were nothing before me, just a pathetic drug pusher preying on the weak.'

Malcolm's restraint masked a deep fury. Flynn had witnessed Malcolm's moods. He struggled to find the words to soothe him but could not. What had he done to set Malcolm off like this?

'A simple favour for a friend, that's all I asked. Make someone disappear.'

'It wasn't my fault. There must have been someone else who knew, someone from the business. I don't know who.' Flynn had racked his brains but still had no idea.

'How much did Musa Bidanau pay you? Don't I compensate you enough for your loyalty?' Malcolm's voice was strengthening, his tone rising.

'No, it wasn't me. Everything was arranged just as you wanted. The pick-up, the delivery, the dump site. Okay, I wasn't there when they brought him in. Arko stuffed up, bad choice, I admit that.'

'You want me to think you are just plain stupid? What you did is pure treachery. Worse, you and Bidanau turned on Martin.'

'Why would I do that?' It was true. Flynn hadn't a clue why they hit Sullivan.

'I told you to lay off him after that Mill Street fiasco.' Malcolm's voice shook with fury.

'I never saw him after that. You have to believe me.' Flynn knew Malcolm wouldn't. It was too late.

'A good fit, you and Bidanau. Both of you after Martin, wanting him out of the way. Bidanau's a wrecking ball. Maybe you didn't know. Martin fixed it so Bidanau can't do business in this country. But that wasn't enough to stop him ripping off his family, tearing holes in my business.'

Malcolm turned towards Edgar, waiting at the edge of the light.

'Look, wait. I can help you.' Flynn held his hand forward, as if to stop the advance. 'The cops want to know who was behind the hit. I'll take the fall. They're onto me already. They'll believe me when I say I wanted revenge on Sullivan, that I acted alone with Arko's help. They won't look further. I'll make sure.'

'You think I need anything from you? You're an even bigger fool than I thought.'

Malcolm gave a final piercing stare and walked away. Edgar's expression changed to a saw-toothed grin. He clenched and unclenched his fists. Taking Flynn by one shoulder he spun him around, Flynn almost losing balance.

'There's a door over there.'

Flynn hadn't seen it, an ordinary door to a small office. A narrow shaft of light showed at the bottom. Flynn grasped the handle, turned it slowly and limped in.

The room was brightly lit. Flynn glanced around. Each wall, up to the ceiling, was covered in plastic that swayed with the inflow of air. Heavier plastic lined the floor, covering the lighter material tucked in beneath. Flynn's feet felt glued to the spot.

Hot breath on his neck. Flynn turned, his eyes drawn to the object in Edgar's hand. Edgar swung the mallet towards Flynn's injured leg. Flynn pivoted away but wasn't quick enough. He fell to the floor, screaming in pain as the blow glanced off the plaster. Edgar stood over him, holding the mallet high. The next blow was aimed at Flynn's knee but he scrambled out of the way, the mallet swinging through empty air.

It occurred to Flynn that Edgar was drawing this out, enjoying himself. There was no contest. Flynn was helpless and that rock of a man knew it. Now Edgar was coming at him again. Flynn grasped his crutch with both hands and swung at the side of Edgar's knee. It connected. Not a heavy blow, but enough to throw Edgar off balance. Edgar roared in anger, spit flying. He turned and swung the mallet towards Flynn's head. Flynn saw it coming and ducked. With Edgar again off balance he rose to his knees and, gasping in pain, jabbed the end of the crutch under Edgar's chin. Not quite an uppercut but good enough. Edgar's head jerked back and the mallet flew from his hand.

Flynn dropped the crutch and rolled over. He had the mallet. He flipped back and smashed it into Edgar's ankle. There was a satisfying crunch and a cry of pain. Edgar dropped to the floor, temporarily immobilised. Flynn stretched closer and delivered a blow to the side of the head. Edgar stopped moving.

With pain ripping down his leg, Flynn scrabbled on all fours to the entrance of the building. The crawl seemed endless. Flynn felt lightheaded, like that other time, fighting to remain conscious. A hand grabbed at his good ankle but he kicked it away. Summoning all his energy, Flynn scrambled faster, making it to the doors and onto the rain-soaked drive. Muddy water flowed into his sleeves and up to his elbows as he clawed his way forward. He chanced a look. Edgar, on all fours, had reached the doors and was almost in reach.

Looking up through the downpour, Flynn glimpsed a face. He thought he recognised the owner, knew he did, but it just couldn't be. He stopped dead as Sandra walked past him towards Edgar. Flynn heard a scream and looked back. A stilettoed heel was twisting into the bones of an outstretched hand.

'Come on, the car is over here. Quick.' Sandra half-dragged Flynn the short distance.

'How did you know?' Flynn choked back tears.

'I followed you from rehab. I could see it ending badly. Pity you couldn't.' Sandra belted them in and started the engine.

'But ...' Flynn was shocked. She knew? All along?

'Shut up. We're going. Now.' Sandra drove out of the clay driveway and into light traffic. The rain was easing.

'Where to?' Flynn felt numb, could barely register what was going on.

'Somewhere to get you cleaned up.' Sandra looked straight ahead.

'I'll call the police, make a deal. It's the only way to stop Hendry.' Flynn retrieved his burner from an inside pocket, found Pacer's number and hit redial.

'Don't be a fool,' Sandra said. 'Toss that thing out the window.'

Flynn obeyed. He felt free momentarily. 'We can't go home.'

'Of course we can't. Get my bag, it's on the seat behind me.'

Flynn opened the bag and gasped. Passports, travel documents, money. 'You mean ...?'

'Yes, today. We'll talk later.'

CHAPTER 100

PACER'S PHONE VIBRATED but the call cut out abruptly.

'That was Flynn,' said Pacer, pressing last caller dial and waiting until the tone rang out. 'John, get a bearing on that phone.' He wrote down the number and handed it to Wainwright.

'If we get a ping, I'll take a squad car.' With a nod to Pacer, Wainwright was gone.

Pacer said, 'We need Malcolm Hendry in here before he tries anything else. I'm issuing an arrest warrant in case he won't come willingly. Conspiracy to murder should do it.' Hendry, up to his neck in it.

Pacer spoke to the desk sergeant. He would send a car for Hendry immediately. 'A busy day,' Pacer said, on his return to the room. He had a spring in his step.

'They're ready next door,' Picone said.

'Let's get in there and nail him.' Pacer's voice was as hard as his words.

The interview room was prepared with recording equipment at one end of a wooden table and a camera operator in the far corner, adjusting the focus on the man sitting sullenly in a metal chair. Craig Thomas looked up, defiant. His lawyer sat next to him.

'How dare you send uniformed police to my office, treating me like a criminal. I answered your questions.' The detectives ignored him, taking their time removing their jackets and getting themselves comfortable. Picone turned on the recorder and signalled the camera operator to start.

'We'll pick up where we left off last time, shall we?' Pacer asked, not expecting an answer. 'You hated Martin Sullivan because he was the success you were never going to be. When the opportunity presented itself, you conspired to kill him. Isn't that correct?'

'So we're back to your supposition that I bribed a building inspector. That's pathetic.' Thomas sat back, looking smug.

'You weren't good enough for Platinum Living and your career at Cooks River Council was going nowhere. You wanted money and influence. You looked around for a partner, someone you could offer the advantages of your position, someone looking for a foothold in property development. You found that person, didn't you, Mr Thomas? Would you like to tell me about it?'

'Sullivan? You've got to be joking,' said Thomas with a smirk.

'You met with Mr Sullivan several times over the weeks before his death. Talked business, discussed his plans, listened to him sing the praises of Malcolm Hendry. It must have rankled. But you are good at that, aren't you – hiding your feelings, your dislikes and resentments.'

'Sure, I met up with Sullivan. What's wrong with that? We had a lot of colleagues in common, talked shop. You think I resented him, but I'm bigger than that.'

'But your new partner wasn't Martin Sullivan, was it. It was Musa Bidanau. You backed him on a proposal to acquire a site near Hawthorne Park, a plum development opportunity. Your big chance to ingratiate yourself came when you learned of a plot to kill him. Am I right, Mr Thomas? I'm giving you a chance here.' Would Thomas admit this crucial point? Would he risk it, hoping their interest in him would end there?

Thomas whispered to his lawyer, who nodded. 'Okay, I knew Bidanau. I wrote a memo backing his proposal. Nothing wrong with that. It was in the public interest. And you're right. I heard on the grapevine that he was on someone's hit list and I told him. Nothing wrong with that, either.'

'Do you know who wanted him dead?' Pacer didn't expect the truth.

'How should I know? Maybe he had more than one enemy. Why don't you ask Flynn?'

'Something puzzles me,' Pacer said. 'Bidanau learned of the plot and was safe enough. Why did he strike out at Mr Sullivan? Was Sullivan the one who wanted him dead?' Pacer knew it wasn't.

'Sullivan wouldn't have had the guts.' Thomas spat the words.

Pacer moderated his tone. 'Was killing Mr Sullivan your idea?'

Thomas examined his hands, avoiding Pacer's gaze. 'I just warned a friend. I had nothing to do with what happened after.'

Picone gave Thomas a enquiring look. 'Why miss an opportunity? I think substituting Martin Sullivan was your idea. Clever, in a way. The groundwork was done.'

'Clever maybe, but it wasn't me.' Thomas had rearranged his features and was looking smug again. 'Bidanau didn't like Sullivan either.'

'Really? You shared some laughs as you put the finishing touches on your plan.' Picone checked through his set of notes. 'You were together at a club near the Spit, a few days before the murder.'

'You should have been more careful,' Pacer said. 'The barman has excellent hearing.'

Thomas looked shocked.

'Bidanau had lined up the killers, but only you knew enough about Mr Sullivan's plans to arrange the pick-up from his home that evening. You had that information, Mr Thomas, and you passed it on to Bidanau.' A few snatches of conversation overheard by the barman. That's all he'd needed to piece it together.

'All bullshit.'

'Someone cancelled Mr Sullivan's regular limousine service. Was that you?' Pacer was guessing, but it made sense. Sullivan would have told him which service he used. Easy to get it out of him.

'I don't know what you're talking about.' The colour was draining from Thomas's face. Pacer had seen it before as the man started to lose his composure.

'Where were you on the night Mr Sullivan was murdered?' he asked.

'What was it, a Sunday? Probably at home watching Netflix.'

'Nowhere near Martin Sullivan's apartment in Russell Lea? That's strange, because we have you on traffic cameras near there. Couldn't help yourself, could you? Just wanted to make sure things went as planned.'

Thomas demanded a break. Picone snapped his notebook closed. The detectives stepped outside.

'What happens next?' Picone asked.

'Thomas gets his big chance. He can get in first and implicate Bidanau or expect Bidanau to shift the blame to him.' Pacer knew how it would go. Thomas, a self-serving man with no loyalties, would jump at it. Already scheming to sway the judge, no doubt.

Wainwright walked in, looking troubled.

'You got a trace on that phone?' Pacer asked.

'We found it lying by the side of a road in the back streets of Leichhardt. No sign of Flynn, but a man was lying injured nearby, semi-conscious. Edgar Bailey. Looked like he'd been in a fight. Needed an ambulance.'

'I wonder who ended up worse off?' Pacer said. 'Hendry sent Bailey after Flynn. He must blame him for the whole mess. With help from Thomas, no doubt.'

Pacer spoke to the desk sergeant.

'A message came in a few minutes ago,' the officer said. 'The squad car we sent for Malcolm Hendry came back without him.'

'Not at his office? Did they go to his home?'

'No, they spoke to the PA, a Nerrida Kingston. Hendry is on his way to Malaysia for a business meeting with the chair of the board.'

Hendry was reporting to Osman Bidanau, the chain complete.

'Coming back when?' asked Pacer.

'She didn't say.'

CHAPTER 101

MALCOLM HENDRY EXITED the airport terminal into hot, perfumed air. He followed the chauffeur to a sedan parked awkwardly nearby and dropped into the plush upholstery. The sounds of shouting and car horns receded as the door was closed by a gloved hand and the car eased into traffic. He texted his wife, Eleanor, assuring her he'd arrived safely. He would have time to rest before the meeting.

He opened his laptop and examined the figures again. The latest report had come in overnight. Hendry frowned as he compared the new figures with yesterday's. Marginally worse. He snapped his laptop shut and thought about the meeting later that day. Osman Bidanau was an unforgiving man, not interested in excuses. He would be agitated, angry, just as he was when he phoned days before. That police officer had been asking about Martin Sullivan when the call came in. He had implied some sort of double-cross. When he'd thought about it later, Hendry had dismissed the idea, but not before having a long, hard think. He was not the type to take anything, or anyone, for granted.

The car pulled in to the covered entrance of a five-star hotel. Hendry walked into the lobby and was met warmly by the concierge. At reception he was greeted by name, as if an invisible message had been passed along. The entrance to the lifts for the executive floors was to one side of the lobby. Hendry stepped in, followed by a woman he hadn't previously noticed. His skin tingled, not because she was attractive, although she was, dressed in form-fitting black, but because of a vague unease, as if he knew her, or felt as if he should have known her.

The doors opened and he followed the woman out, curious about who she might be. Distracted and in muted light, Hendry did not realise immediately that he had come out on the wrong floor, a basement. In front of him was a van, its rear doors open. The woman turned to him and smiled. He sensed another person behind and began to turn his head. He heard a swish as something passed over and settled around his neck. There was a tightening and a sharp pull.

EPILOGUE

'LEAVE IT, HUGO.' Anna's voice rang out as her little pugalier raced over to an English bulldog slowly lapping a doggychino near the side door of the cafe. 'Come back. Now,' she added, hands hanging helplessly by her sides. Too late. Hugo had slid in under the bulldog's heavy jowls and was slurping its milk. In one deft movement, he grabbed the bowl in his teeth and darted away, frothy liquid splashing behind.

'I'm sorry, I'll get you another,' an embarrassed Anna said to the amused owner of the bulldog.

'Crafty little fellow, isn't he,' said Pacer, a smile in his voice. He stood next to Anna as Wedge ran over to the pugalier and the two dogs licked the last drops from the bowl together. 'What a pair.'

'I bought a doggychino for Hugo, just the once, but that was enough. He was hooked. I think it's the sprinkle of liver treats on top.' Anna retrieved what was left of the bowl and dropped it into a bin by the cafe. 'Time for class. I'd better get going.'

Pacer watched as Anna and Hugo led a motley group of dogs onto the green, owners by their sides. That was fourth class, the pinnacle of achievement at Hawthorne Park dog school. The group eased into a circle, marching clockwise in formation, then pivoting in the other direction. They looked like good, well-behaved dogs, strutting their stuff with their proud owners. Pacer knew it wouldn't last. The park was crowded on Sunday mornings and sooner or later someone who couldn't care less would walk through and upset the group. Or one of the dogs, likely Jess the miniature schnauzer, would get bored and run amok.

There was an hour to wait before Wedge's turn in third class. In just a few months she'd already got that far. Pacer was proud but not surprised.

The little kelpie was smart and curious. And the best friend he'd had in years, or maybe forever. Fully grown now, her injury nicely healed. He owed Anna a thing or two. Just think, he could have given her away. Pacer reached down and gave Wedge a good pat.

John Wainwright was waiting at a table by the canal, two mugs in front of him. He pushed one forward as Pacer sat opposite and nodded in thanks.

'Nice you could come by this morning. As good as any place to meet.' Pacer thought of their beers together at the Tram Sheds, intent on finding ways to protect Sofia, or to track down Davidson. It was better here. A grunt from Wainwright told Pacer he felt the same.

'I dropped in at the hospital yesterday afternoon. Thought you'd like to know. Clancy's in there with a nasty bout of pneumonia,' said Wainwright.

'Too bad. Reckoned he was the one to get others into hospital when they got sick. His turn now. Do you think they'll get him a decent place to live when he recovers?'

'His mob from up country want him home,' replied Wainwright, 'but Clancy insists he's going back to the railway arches. He's worried about May and the others. Feels responsible somehow. I think he's a bit sweet on May, known each other a long time. I asked him about Alice and Garry. Clancy hasn't heard, but figures they'll turn up again one day. Another reason he wants to stay there.' Wainwright sipped his coffee and leaned over to ruffle Wedge's ears. 'Miss them, do you, Wedge?'

'Alice and Garry deserve a chance. I hope they find a life up north, get settled somewhere and never come back.' An image of a whimsical young woman and a softly spoken man flashed through Pacer's mind. To thrive, they needed a simpler life in a kinder place, far away from Sydney streets. It occurred to Pacer that he, too, was choosing to escape the city for the next chapter in his life. Did Wainwright know? Had he heard on the grapevine?

Pacer found Wainwright looking at him expectantly. Yes, he knew. 'I suppose you've heard I have a new posting, just a secondment to start with. Senior Detective with the squad in a regional centre. Out west, a good few hours away. Janet, my late wife, was from out there. A country girl. I only visited the area a few times and that was years ago. I'm going to give life in the country a try. Who knows? I might stay on.'

'Well, quite a change for you, and a good one, if you ask me. A different kind of policing, relationships matter more out there. You've got to take the time, get to know them. People trust you.' Wainwright looked thoughtful, then his eyes creased in a smile. 'Different crime profile too, more sheep stealing than house breaks. Or homicides.'

Pacer laughed. 'I don't mind mixing it up a bit.' Enough talk about him. 'What about you?' he asked Wainwright. 'Anything come up?'

'Just this week, in fact. The Super called me in, reckons they've identified a cluster of assaults and homicides on homeless people around city parks. She thought I'd be interested in investigating. No one has paid much attention till now. I get a small squad and minimal interference from the brass – as long as I get results, of course.'

'Couldn't be a better fit. You know the territory like the back of your hand. And the people too. They'll talk to you.' Mention of the Super reminded Pacer of the Poulos case, the Super's little girl. He couldn't imagine where she found the strength to go on. Pacer looked at his hands, not sure what to say next.

'A bit of a change for both of us,' said Pacer. And talking of new starts, Stuart Picone has scored a place on the next course that Kurt Otway is running. Can hardly wait. In the meantime, he's working with Miranda De Veen, engrossed in the world of forensics. Even likes the fingerprinting. Miranda marvels at his youthful enthusiasm.'

'This one will floor you. Good thing you're sitting,' said Wainwright, not to be outdone. 'Connors is getting promoted to Chief Inspector.' He waited for a reaction, but Pacer sat impassive. 'You're not surprised?' he added.

'Nope, that's how it works. Connors solves several serious crimes – he tracks down a dangerous paedophile, plus his accomplice and gets to the bottom of two murders ordered by a criminal syndicate. That's leadership for you.' Pacer felt the injustice of it, the long hours of dedication put in by so many others. It made a difference that the Super knew.

'Too bad he missed the bloke who ordered the killings. Any word on Malcolm Hendry? He was just one step ahead of us, wasn't he,' said Wainwright.

'No sign of him after he stepped off that plane,' replied Pacer. 'Osman Bidanau spoke to the Malaysian police, says Hendry never turned up. Fishy, given what I think we know about Bidanau's part in all this. We'll never get to the bottom of it, if you ask me. Flynn is another matter. He'll come back eventually. Trouble is, what can we nail him for? The case looks weak, can't see the prosecutors going for it.'

'Me neither. Flynn conspired to kill a bloke who is alive and well and most of the witnesses are either dead or missing. That bloke has nine lives. Must be running out though.'

Pacer's attention was drawn to a whippet and its even thinner owner, a young bloke in a hoodie, walking towards the training area. Was he really going to toss a ball through the middle of Anna's group? Pacer sighed as the dogs in the class howled and yapped at the intruder. A cacophony, the noise echoing around the park. Anna gave the owner a serve, but the damage was done.

Wainwright had noticed too. 'Don't trust any bloke who uses his dog to make trouble.' He finished his coffee and returned both empty cups to the cafe. 'Gotta go. See you again before you leave town?'

'Yep, for sure,' said Pacer, offering his hand. He watched as the training class broke up, people wandering back towards the cafe, Anna and Alison Cassidy among them. Wedge joined Hugo and Jess at the cafe's side door, hoping for a treat, but Charlie, the older schnauzer, sidled up to Pacer, expecting a back rub. Pacer obliged. 'Looked pretty good out there until that whippet tore through.'

'Happens all the time,' said Anna. 'But we don't let it spoil our fun. Ready for your class?' she asked Pacer, who nodded and called to Wedge.

Alison Cassidy bobbed down beside Wedge and rubbed her neck and ears. 'Sofia misses Wedge but understands why she can't take her home.'

'You've seen Sofia?' asked Pacer, his pulse quickening. 'Is she okay?'

'I know the people in the charity who took her in. I got to know her a bit when she was here … before … and wanted to know how she was doing. Been to see her a few times now.' Alison stood and looked at Pacer thoughtfully.

'I just want to know if she is okay. I won't ask where she's staying.'

'Actually, she's doing great. Has a job she likes and a nice place to live. Sofia is smart and makes friends easily. Her sister is coming to visit soon, all the way from Palermo. That will make a real difference.'

Pacer smiled his thanks. The relief. Sofia happy and safe. It made his day. With Wedge by his side, Pacer trotted over to join the class.

Acknowledgements

This book is set in the Inner West of Sydney, Australia, the treasured home of the people and dogs depicted in its pages. The main action centres on Café Bones in Hawthorne Park and the Leichhardt Dog Training School, frequented by the author over several years. Many of the dogs in this book were inspired by my observations during these visits, including my own miniature schnauzers, Charlie and Jess, and the antics of their companions at agility training. Hugo, the cheeky pugalier, and his human, Anna Brennan, were part of the park's, and the cafe's, earlier history. My sincere thanks to Michael, manager of Café Bones, who has given his encouragement for this book project.

I would like to acknowledge the support I have received from Malcolm Knox and his patient mentoring as I learned to write crime fiction. My sincere thanks also to those who commented on earlier drafts of the book: Sharon Bower, Heather Cobban, Alison Crogan and Linda Dewey. The Writing Circle of The Women's Club, Sydney, has given cheerful advice over the years, as has Ann Beaumont, with her considerable experience in writing and publishing. Tully Rosen, co-founder of Ruff Sleepers, spoke to me about the lives and hardships of homeless people and the value they place on their canine companions.

The high quality presentation of this book was made possible by Susan McCreery (copy editing), Maggie Cooper (layout and design) and GetCovers.com (cover design).

www.ingramcontent.com/pod-product-compliance
Lightning Source LLC
Chambersburg PA
CBHW030651260626
47157CB00007B/2587